Praise for Excess Baggage

"I couldn't put down this immensely readable first novel ... Karen Ma takes the reader on a wild romp from China of the 1960s to the sex clubs and fashionable art galleries of the 1990s Tokyo. The book is great fun and at the same time packed with wisdom about the struggle between traditional Asian families and the imperative to get rich."

—Barbara Demick, author of *Nothing to Envy: Ordinary Lives in North Korea*

"A moving account of alienation and displacement in a Chinese family split by modern China's political and social upheaval. With vivid prose, Karen Ma takes us on a momentous journey with a Chinese family as it tries to grow new roots in a foreign land."

—Yan Geling, author of *Banquet Bug, White Snake* and *The Flowers of War.*

"Effortlessly captures the suspicions and dependencies of a dysfunctional family transplanted in stages from China to Japan, unwrapping its members' flaws, feuds and life-giving fascinations. Buoyed by brushstrokes of gentle humor and not an ounce of pretension, the author conjures up characters with an unexpected emotional charge."

—-Oliver August, author of *Inside the Red Mansion: On the Trail of China's Most Wanted Man*

"An intensely intimate portrait of a Chinese family's turmoil as it struggles to endure in the battered and impoverished Chinese diaspora in Japan. Karen Ma brings her deep experience in Asia to bear in penetrating into the souls of Chinese and Japanese alike, exposing the fragility of hope and the depths of cruelty, the clash of cultures and the search for identity. In prose that is alternatively gripping and wrenching, *Excess Baggage* asks the questions that haunt all exiles from their homeland: who, after all, are we?"

—Edward Gargan, author of *China's Fate*

"I am particularly impressed with the subtle way Ma describes the relationship between mother and daughters and that of the complex feelings of rivalry and affection between the two sisters. Well done for a first novel!"

—Liu Hong, author of *Starling Moon*, *Magpie Bridge* and *Wives of East Wind*.

Excess
Baggage

Excess Baggage

A Novel

Karen Ma

China Books, Inc.
San Francisco

Published in the United States of America by

Sinomedia International Group
China Books
360 Swift Ave., Suite 48
South San Francisco, CA 94080

Library of Congress Cataloging-in-Publication Data

Ma, Karen.
  Excess baggage : a novel / Karen Ma.
      pages cm
  ISBN 978-0-8351-0046-5 (pbk. : alk. paper) 1. Sisters—Fiction. 2.
Chinese—Japan—Fiction. 3. Families—China—Fiction. 4. Domestic fiction.
I. Title.
  PR9450.9.M3E93 2013
  823'.92—dc23

                                                      2013005891

Cover design: Tiffany Cha
Text design: Rick Soldin

Printed in the USA

Contents

Prologue

It was a mid-July afternoon in 1962. At the foyer area near a communal staircase inside an old Beijing house, Yan was hard at work scrubbing a piece of clothing on a wash board, a bucket of water next to her. The weather was nice, and Yan wanted to finish the laundry in time to take advantage of the sunny afternoon. The building wasn't big, and housed only two families: she and her family—two young girls and a baby boy—resided on the ground floor's two-room unit; and the Li family, two girls and their parents, lived upstairs.

"Mama, I'm going to Shanshan's upstairs. Won't be long ..." a young girl in a bright red Chinese jacket, her two jet-black pigtails dancing in the air, announced to Yan at the foot of the staircase, a sweet smile on her face. Peiyin, Yan's first born, was only a week shy of her 8th birthday. She had just returned from her school, and as always, she liked the idea of doing homework with Shanshan, her best friend and upstairs neighbor.

"Just a second, Pei. Ma has something to tell you," Yan said, stopping her daughter before the girl could move beyond the first step. She paused briefly, as if pondering how she might break the news to her daughter.

"I just got a telegram from your father," Yan said finally, a hand searching for her pants' pocket. "There has been a change in our travel plans—your father said we can't bring all three of you children with us to Hong Kong, not all at once."

"But why?" Pei said, her dark round eyes shining with alarm.

"I-" Yan swallowed hard. She clearly had difficulty proceeding with the conversation.

It wasn't the first time that Yan saw the anguish and disappointment in Pei's eyes. It broke her heart to see Chinese history had to repeatedly inflict such pain and cruelty on her people, and in the Zhang family's case, it was her first child, her most beloved of her three children, who was made to pay the dearest of prices.

Two years earlier, in 1960, China had experienced the worst ever famines on the back of the disastrous Great Leap Forward campaign, a large-scale drought and a devastating flood.

Almost overnight, food items—rice, corn flour, wheat, oil, salt, and meat—had to be rationed. In the beginning, the people of the city were still given some rice, meat, and vegetables, but as the months wore on, these quickly became rare commodities that could only be bought from time to time on the black market. Eventually, even corn flour and wheat were in short supply; they were only given half a gram of corn flour per person per day, and this was granted mostly in the absence of meat. For a family of five, they barely received half a kilo of meat per month, including the fat they had to use to cook their food with.

Meiyin and Da Wei, being three and four years younger than Pei, were blurry about the hardship for the most part. But Pei suffered. At age six, she was constantly crying for food because she was only fed cornmeal soup and a steam bun to last for the entire day. "Mama, my tummy hurts. When can we eat again?" she would moan with tears in her eyes. At times she would beg for a morsel of pork, complaining that her intestines were "rusting" from lack of the taste of meat. Yan remembered swallowing her tears and hugging the child, telling her to go stay in bed until the hunger wore off.

As the shortage of food became more desperate in 1961, Beijing was turned overnight into a city of beggars. Everywhere Yan and the children went they could feel and smell death and hunger. Schools were closed and work hours cut, pushing children and "non-essential" workers to roam the wasteland in search of food.

Yan and the children stayed mostly at home, afraid of the sight of corpses on the streets. Those who perished first were mostly migrant workers from the poverty-stricken north. In China's far north, worst hit by famines, Yan heard many people resorted to eating snakes, rats, and even grasshoppers. The weak, the old, and the very young were the first to fall prey to the Death God. Healthier people were plagued with edema, their legs so swollen they could not stand.

In those days, Yiwen, Yan's husband, was the only one in the family who continued working at his work unit as a municipal official in the best way he knew how. But when Yiwen was finally let go from work, he became seriously worried for his family. He took to the streets and joined long queues of people in front of the police station to apply for an exit permit to leave China. He wasn't immediately successful. But in time, through a friend's introduction, he was given a contact in Hong Kong. A few months later, Yiwen left with a couple of friends for the south, from where they snuck out on a night boat by bribing the guards, eventually reaching the cash-rich and freewheeling Pearl of the Orient. With his friends' help, Yiwen was able to quickly find a job and set himself up in a small apartment in Hong Kong. He was lucky, because a year later, when many more Chinese immigrants made the trip to Hong Kong, known as the "Great Exodus of 1962," over half were arrested and deported back to China.

When Yiwen returned briefly in the summer of 1962, after the immigration at the borders finally relaxed a bit, he asked the family to join him in Hong Kong. Yan was elated. The wait was over! The family could finally be reunited and leave all the misery behind. But she was wrong. A week later an unexpected telegram arrived from Guangzhou, throwing her completely off balance. Yiwen had gone down south to work out the travel documents with the local immigration department. The telegram carried a simple message: "I cannot obtain exit permits for all three children. Can one of them stay with Laolao?" The local authorities in charge of controlling the floodgates to Hong Kong evidently insisted that only two children be allowed to leave China with Yan and Yiwen.

Yan remembered feeling crushed by the news. How was she to choose among her own children? There was no question that she would take Da Wei, him being the baby, but which daughter should stay behind? Unable to choose, she took the matter to her mother and younger brother Feng.

After a long talk with her mother and brother during an overnight trip to Dalian, Yan decided, just as Feng had suggested, that it would be best to leave Pei behind. Pei was the older of the two girls and had already started school. She would be the least bothersome to her brother and elderly mother—perhaps even useful. Yan promised her mother the arrangement would only be for a year or two, and the matter was settled.

Back in Beijing, Yan agonized for days over how she might break the news to Pei, her heart shredded to pieces over the thought of leaving behind her first-born—her precious daughter whom Yan believed had single-handedly saved her troubled marriage with Yiwen. Yan and Yiwen had had a tumultuous relationship, in part because theirs was an arranged marriage. Yiwen, being a forward-thinking college student at the time in Dalian, had been adamantly against their marriage from the start and almost immediately ran away from home just days after their wedding as a protest to his parents.

Yan found him seven years later in Beijing, well after the Sino-Japanese war was over and only when she had properly buried his parents, who had died in succession of tuberculosis. The year must have been 1953, because she vividly remembered it being one year before they had their first National People's Congress, China's national legislature. She'd found him skinnier but well, and in a way, manlier than before. She was surprised he didn't turn her away. Maybe he was overcome with guilt, not having written a single word to her in seven years. He looked particularly ashamed when she told him both of his parents had passed away. Perhaps out of gratitude he had let her stay in

Beijing, and together, they started a new life. A year later, Pei was born. It was the sweetest moment of her life because Yiwen had taken to Pei like a bear to honey, thus reviving a relationship that would otherwise have died.

But despite her partiality for Pei, Yan found she was now in the impossible position of having to leave Pei behind in her mother and brother's care. Under Yiwen's instructions, she was to leave Beijing with her two younger children for Hong Kong on a Friday in just three days. Worried that Pei might put up a huge struggle at the train station before their departure, Yan decided she would keep vague about her departure time and date with Pei. She also decided she would leave early for the train station with the younger children on the Friday, and have Feng pick up Pei from school later that day. It would all be for the best, she told herself. Seeing the hurt in her beloved child's face would simply be too much for her to bear. She was afraid she might not be able to stick with the original plan and break down at the last minute by either not making the trip or by taking Pei with her. Then what would she do? She would have ruined the original plan, Yiwen's plan, of getting the biggest break for the family.

She knew it was not at all fair to Pei, but she had no other choice. And in the deepest of her heart, she was also hopeful. *Yes, it would be hard for Pei, but it would only be for a year or two,* she told herself. *She was doing this for the common good of the Zhang family. It was their ticket out of China. It was an opportunity to make a better future for the children, all of the three children.*

"Ma, why can't we all go together to Hong Kong?" at the foot of the staircase back in Beijing, Pei was tugging at Yan's coat again, waking her from her guilt and wandering thought. "You promised Ma, you promised that we would all go!"

"Dear, it's not that Ma didn't want us to all go, but there was a new law in Hong Kong that said each family going to Hong Kong can only bring two children. So what do you think we should do, dear?" Yan had tried her best to deflate the impact.

"What? What are you talking about?"

Yan tried again to explain to Pei, when she knew very well it was all too much for an eight-year-old to digest the message. "Do you think you can stay with Grandma and Uncle Feng like a good girl while waiting for us to come pick you up? It would only be a year."

"No! Why me? Why can't Meiyin stay? It's unfair! So unfair!" Predictably, Pei put up a huge fight. She screamed, her feet stumping. As her mother's favorite child, Pei was used to getting her way, and she didn't like the idea of being the second best or playing second fiddle to anyone.

Yan didn't argue with Pei, but only hugged her daughter deeply. "How about if we settle this matter by drawing lots?" she caught Pei quite off guard after luring her back into their flat, where Meiyin was playing a game of marbles alone on the floor. "I'll have two slips of paper in my hands, one written with the word 'go,' the other written with the word 'stay.' And whoever of you girls gets the slip that says 'stay' must stay. Is that clear?"

Unbeknownst to Pei, Yan had written the character 'stay' on both pieces of paper. She knew if Pei were made to open her slip first, she would not have time to discover what was written on her sister's slip.

The idea worked, and though Pei continued to protest about being made to stay, she was soon distracted by Yan's promise of buying her a new pair of shoes on display at Dalian's Number One Department Store. Then again, Pei was far too young to fully understand what destiny was to befall on her. Even Yan, at the age of thirty-four, did not fully grasp the implications of this simple game of lot-drawing, that by her own manipulation of her daughter's fate, she had essentially sentenced her first-born to a lifetime in exile—a decision she was to regret for the rest of her life.

Part One

Tokyo

One

In the beginning, it was just a hum, barely audible, quietly gnawing its way into her consciousness. She tried to fight it off, holding desperately onto that space halfway between dreaming and awareness, until the scream of the runaway siren got too loud for her to ignore. Pei woke up with a start, and for a moment she wasn't sure where she was. It came back to her in a rush as she saw the tatami floor and felt the thick futon quilt that encased her.

She sat in the dark, slowly taking in the small Japanese room enclosed on three sides by doors, two of them *fusuma* screens and the third a heavy glass door that opened onto a tiny balcony. The ceiling was so low she could make out its wood grain in the reflected light off the street. She'd been in Tokyo ten days now, but she still found it hard to fully believe she'd finally made it out of China.

In the adjacent room, she could hear her mother breathing. The two were now flat mates in a tiny apartment swamped with boxes and cheap furniture. The room where Pei was sleeping was the apartment's only bedroom. Since her arrival, her mother had slept in the living room.

Life with her mother hadn't been exactly peachy. She was easily irritated by her, she found. It seemed that her mother understood so little about her. The night before, they had had a heated argument when Yan served her, of all things, a bowl of noodles with sea bream and chives.

"I don't like noodles, especially with *fish*!" Pei had pushed the bowl aside after barely taking a look. She went rummaging through the fridge and took out a store-purchased *onigiri*. "I much prefer rice," she'd said. She casually peeled the wrapping off the rice ball and began munching on it. She hated the fact that her mother still thought of her as the little girl whom she had left sitting on the doorsteps back in China. Her mother didn't know the first thing about her as a grown woman. Yet she never bothered to ask her what she'd like to eat or do around the house. Why couldn't her mother try to invest some time to get to know her again, instead of making all these stupid assumptions?

"What? Since when did you prefer rice to noodles?" Yan, who'd been washing dishes in the sink, abruptly turned to face Pei. "You used to love fish, and noodles were your *favorite*."

"That's ancient history, Mother." Pei had turned to Yan with a snort. "Just how much time have you spent with me in the last thirty years? How would *you* know my likes and dislikes?"

Her mother was stunned by her reaction. "I cooked you noodles thinking you might be hungry after school," she said after some time, her brows knitted. "The least you can do is to show a little appreciation."

Pei had looked away without saying a word. She continued to munch on her rice ball, her face hardened.

"Pei?" Yan edged closer to her, an aggravated look on her face. "I'm talking to you. Look, if you're angry you should speak up. What is it?"

Pei got up to fetch some cold buckwheat tea from the fridge. "Don't you think I have a right to be angry at you about something?" she said pointedly.

"Is it about China? Is that it? Child, you know darn well that I couldn't possibly have taken you out. Everyone in China then had to stay in and that's that."

"P-l-e-a-s-e! Not the Cultural Revolution mantra again," Pei had blurted out in frustration. "The Revolution ended in '76, and we're in the middle of the 90s now."

"Look, I went back in 1980 with every intention of bringing you out of China. But you were already a married woman and a mother of two when I saw you then. What was I to do? I couldn't possibly invite you all to come, now could I?" Her mother raised her voice. "How was I to feed an extra four mouths when I was barely scraping by as a janitor?"

Pei let out a sigh after a long silence. "It's never convenient with you, Mother, is it? You said you couldn't bring all three of us children to Hong Kong because of some immigration restrictions. But that was a lie, wasn't it? Wasn't it really about the money?" Pei's voice grew shrill. " Shanshan's mom said you chose to leave me behind like some leftover sack of potatoes because you and father were afraid you couldn't raise all three of us children in expensive Hong Kong. Wasn't that the *real* reason?"

Yan had opened her mouth and was going to say something, but nothing came out. "That decision of yours robbed me years of opportunities," Pei continued. "Look at me. In two years I'll turn forty. I don't have a husband, my children are not with me, and I'm starting out in a foreign country from the bottom up!"

"Pei, be fair. I never told you to leave your family. It was *your* idea to leave them."

"That's for sure. And if it weren't for my persistence, I'd still be stuck in Dalian. I'd die a woman haunted forever by thoughts of 'what ifs'."

"Pei, that's quite enough," her mother had snapped. "Although I don't agree with the way you perceive things, I can't stop you from feeling what you feel. But for now, let's just drop it."

It was so easy for her mother to forgive and forget, pretending that things were all fine and dandy now that she was reunited with the family. But not for her! How could Pei ever forget the frustration and loneliness of waiting at her maternal uncle's cold, cold house for her mother's return all these years, every night crying herself to sleep? On so many frosty winter nights, she remembered witnessing her cousins snuggled closely to her uncle and aunt on a warm bed, and she alone was banished to sleep on a cot in a freezing shed in the back of her uncle's house. She was a mere eight-year old child when her mother had left her. She'd believed her mother when she said she would come back for her after one or two years. By the time she saw her mother in late 1980 after China finally opened up, she was already in her late twenties and a mother of two boys. Yan essentially had missed the most important years of her life.

You promised to come back in one or two years. But why didn't you? Pei remembered vividly how she had asked Yan pointedly during that first visit of hers in 1980.

Yan had hemmed and hawed, an embarrassed look on her face. In the end, the only thing her mother could utter was that she'd tried to come back in 1964, two years after their departure, but somehow she wasn't able to because Da Wei had fallen desperately ill with a viral infection, and that they were further delayed while waiting for the issuance of their permanent Hong Kong residents' cards without which, they were told, they could not leave the island. But Pei wasn't convinced. It sounded more like an excuse. A very lame excuse.

What about the year before that? Pei were persistent for some real answers, but again, Yan was tongue-tied. In the end, Pei realized what she *really* wanted from her mother wasn't even the "reasons why", but for Yan to hear her out about all her bottled-up anger and frustrations over the long years, that what really incensed and bothered her all these years was the fact that she had been made the only sacrifice in the family to stay behind in China while the rest of the family lived in cash-rich, freewheeling Hong Kong and later, Tokyo.

She also wanted Yan to know how disappointed she had been with her as a mother because she had failed the only promise she had ever made to Pei—that she would come and retrieve her from China within two years. Sure, the outbreak of the decade-long Cultural Revolution in 1965 had complicated things, really complicated things. But Yan and her siblings left in 1963. And if Yan had tried harder to work things out, really tried, she would have had enough time to come and get her before China's iron gate came tumbling down in 1965. Yan clearly didn't try very hard, and as a result, Pei was made to pay the ultimate price of being left in China during one of the worst times in its recent history. She was like a fettered beast locked up in a cage. She lost out on everything, the worst of which was the opportunity to a full life! And for that, she would never forgive her mother.

Tick, tick, tick ... Pei sat up and reached for the alarm clock sitting on the tatami floor: 4:30 a.m. She rearranged her pillow and tried to go back to sleep, but was increasingly conscious of the weighty *kakebuton* over her. Why were these Japanese quilts so heavy? She preferred the lighter ones in China. She peeled away the towel coverlet tucked under the quilt, hoping it would lighten the load, but it didn't. She tried extending her legs onto the floor to feel its coolness, but that didn't help either. So she sat up again, staring at the quilt cover, tracing her fingers along the river of silver clouds that made up the curved pattern, before letting out a yawn.

She turned on a reading light and looked around, reminded in the dim light how dowdy the furnishings were. In one corner, a small plywood desk was piled high with books and newspapers. Sandwiched between the desk and the only real wall in the room were a couple of folding chairs that were stowed away in the evenings to make room for Pei's bedding. On the other side of the desk stood a chest of drawers that supported a bright red fifteen-inch Toshiba television. Leaning a few inches away, against the glass door, was an upended black *kotatsu,* its four legs now sticking out as if to greet Pei.

The opposite end of the room held a plastic closet on wheels, Japan's solution to tiny apartments, its metal frame covered with cheap brown vinyl that zipped open on one side. Her mother had emptied it to make room for Pei's clothes, but its limited size meant that half of Pei's belongings remained in her two suitcases, which were now stacked in a corner. Pei moaned every time she had to dig for her clothes.

Her mother's pad was a sore reminder of Pei's own disappointment in life, the cluttered furniture a mirror to her disquieting mind. How had the Zhang family come to this? She could count several Chinese families that she knew of who had made something of themselves after just five, ten years of living in Australia or Canada. She felt ashamed that she was even part of this family, this pathetic tribe that had been out of China for three decades and yet had nothing to show for it. If she had the Cultural Revolution to blame for all her misery in life, what excuse would her *fancy*, overseas family have for being such an utter failure in life?

Pei would never forget her surprise upon first entering this dump. As soon as she took her shoes off, she saw the supposed kitchen—little more than a narrow corridor shoddily fitted with a sink and stovetops at one end. From the corridor she was led to the "two-room apartment," an elongated tatami room divided in halves by a thin paper screen.

The biggest shock came when she went to the bathroom and realized it was a tiny closet with nothing more than a hole in the ground. No tub, no shower. Bathing involved walking ten minutes through some chaotic shopping streets to the nearest *sento,* or public bath. And they called this a wealthy and civilized nation? Her house in Dalian, which she'd considered small and shabby, now seemed positively spacious.

"Congratulations, Pei. Looks like you're finally going to be able to leave China to earn some *waihui* and get rich," her coworker Dongmei had said jealously at Pei's farewell party at the Number One Department Store. "Don't forget us, your less fortunate friends back home when you've struck gold like our old buddy, Xiao Yu," she added, referring to their mutual friend and colleague who'd left five years earlier to Vancouver, Canada, and began to gather a small fortune there by selling dubious herbal Chinese hair growth products to unsuspecting overseas Chinese and local Canadians. Rumors had it that Xiao Yu had accumulated at least half a million Canadian dollars in personal wealth, and everyone at the department store had been extremely green with envy about Xiao Yu's lucky star.

Earn foreign currency and get rich? But how could Pei possibly do that living with her mother a couple centimeters above the poverty line? Three decades out of China and her mother could not even save enough to buy an apartment. What self-respecting human being would put up with such an existence? Xiao Yu would put her mother to shame! And more to the point, how could she let her daughter down after making her suffer so much in China? Didn't she ever think of her daughter's future? As far as she was concerned, she was a victim of history as much as a victim of her parents' bad planning, especially that of her mother's.

Through all those years of waiting, Pei never imagined her mother could be worse off than she was. Only two days earlier, she had learned that her mother worked as a janitor, cleaning Tokyo offices at daybreak. What would her friends back home think if they knew that? How duplicitous of her mother to hide this from her during her visit to Beijing a couple of years ago. How did she end up with such a depressing family when so many others were swimming in money? What a nasty end to the years of misery she'd endured trying to flee China for Tokyo: a mother who cleaned up after others, dusting cigarette ash and scraping gum from carpets!

Reading the disappointment on Pei's face about the small flat, her mother had explained that Pei's father wasn't providing much financial support since he left Tokyo for Osaka some fifteen years ago, most likely because he'd met someone new. Her mother claimed she had no choice but to find whatever odd jobs she could as an older woman with broken Japanese. But how could she allow this to happen to herself, letting Father trample on her like that? Where was the beautiful woman she remembered? Over the years, her mother had soured, her face looking sad and beaten. She probably drove Father away.

"What rotten luck!" Pei blurted out in her bed, surprising even herself. She covered her mouth and listened for any stirring from the adjacent room, but was relieved to hear her mother's steady breathing.

Pei shifted her gaze to the two gray suitcases in the corner—wedding gifts from her best friend, Shanshan. They looked a bit worn, but they were the only valuables she'd brought with her.

Thirteen years ago, against Shanshan's advice, she had married a man she barely knew after a blind date. Guomin was ten years older than her, a long-distance truck driver whose work took him to Inner Mongolia half the year. But Pei had been desperate, willing to do just about anything to form a "home" of her own. She couldn't stand the loneliness and the gaping hole in her heart— this feeling that she didn't belong anywhere or to anyone. Shanshan had been right, of course. Guomin had remained a stranger throughout their marriage. Still, Pei was elated when she became pregnant with Da Shan and Da Hai.

Those suitcases were the first things she thought of on that fateful afternoon a month and a half earlier, when she heard from the Japanese consulate that her visa had finally been approved. Cradling her brown passport with that exquisite green rectangular stamp bearing a chrysanthemum seal inside, she became so emotional she nearly choked up. An agonizing three-month wait and mad scrounging around for documents she hadn't known existed had finally produced a ticket to the outside world.

She knew for a fact the crucial reason behind her beating the odds of getting the visa was because Da Wei, who worked for a large Japanese trading firm, had agreed on paper to act as her guarantor, which meant he'd be responsible for all her living expenses, housing, or any cost-bearing activities she might incur, all of which were big considerations for the Japanese immigration officers. For once, her lucky stars were aligned, and for that, she was grateful.

Getting the go-ahead though meant she must choose either to go to Japan *alone,* or stay behind with Guomin and their two sons. It was the most difficult decision she had to make in her life. But in the end, the idea of saying no to her ticket out was simply unimaginable.

Pei knew she would be rupturing the family, but everyone seemed to be leaving China. Besides, she'd waited thirty years for the right moment to join her family outside, and she wasn't about to let go of this opportunity. This might be her last chance, the very last. Freedom to travel overseas from China was not a guaranteed privilege. Who knew what tomorrow might bring? Besides, she wanted to secure a better future for her boys outside of China. What better way to do this than to get out first and pave the way?

When Guomin came home that night, she'd tried her best to soften the blow. "It will only be a year or two," she said. Then it hit her that she was sounding just like her mother thirty years ago. It was an alarming thought. Yet she refused to believe that she was following in her mother's footsteps. Surely she would not abandon her boys the way her own mother had abandoned her! Surely she'd do a much better job at getting her boys out of China. She was determined that she'd be a much better mother than Yan.

"I know you, you're never happy!" Guomin had yelled at her. "All you think about is improving your lot. Why not join the rank of those heartless ones, selling your soul while you're at it?" This was a reference to their upstairs neighbor, Ren Ling. Two years after Ren Ling departed for Australia on a nine-month music scholarship, she still hadn't bothered to write or call her husband of three years. Rumor had it that she'd gone on to marry another man in Sydney.

"I'm doing this for all of us," Pei had countered. "Once I'm settled, the boys will be able to come abroad and study. They can sail into the best universities, have a better life."

"Don't flatter yourself. This isn't about us. It's all about *you*, and you know it!" he screamed at the top of his lungs. "The fourteen years we've been together, there has never been a day when you don't bring up leaving China some day to join your fancy family overseas. And once you're out, you won't remember your last name, let alone me and the boys." Guomin had slammed the bedroom door shut that night, leaving Pei to sleep on the couch. Two days later, Guomin's tone changed. "Fine. If you want to leave that badly, then leave. I won't stand in your way," he had said. "But once you are out the door, you won't be welcome back."

After this proclamation, Pei started eating most of her meals out. Guomin pressed for a divorce a week later and said he would take the boys to his mother's. He kept the boys from her and told them she was "abandoning" them. He drank heavily and verbally abused her, banging on things and picking fights.

She could understand Guomin's anger but remained adamant that she was doing this as much for the boys' future as for her own. Becoming wary that Guomin might block her exit with a court order as her departure date edged closer, Pei signed the divorce papers he had left on the table and slipped out early one morning to head for Shanshan's. She could no longer bear his cursing and mental torture.

Before leaving, she had paced back and forth for a long time in front of the boys' room with hesitation. At the last minute, she decided not to wake them to say goodbye, not wanting to see the hurt and confused looks on their faces. She left a note, asking the boys to behave themselves and promising to retrieve them when she could.

Shanshan had helped her weather her last few days in China as the whole town seemed to jeer at her and whisper behind her back, calling her a gold-digger with a heart of stone.

"Cheer up, Pei! Make something of yourself and come get the boys when you're rich and famous," Shanshan had told her at the airport.

Yes, she'd come back when she was rich like Xiao Yu, she told herself. In fact, she'd talk to Xiao Yu and get her to impart a few tips on how to set up a similar business selling hair growth products in Japan, she'd decided. Xiao Yu had had her chance at striking it rich. Now it was her turn. And once she'd made her fortune, she'd then fetch Da Shan and Da Hai and put them on the path to glory in America, although how exactly she was to do this she still hadn't a very clear idea. Then she would find Guomin and tell him to his face how wrong he'd been about her. Dead wrong!

Something hit the fusuma door from the adjacent room. Her mother must have gotten up! Pei looked up at her alarm clock: 5:30 a.m.

The thin paper screen door suddenly slid opened. "I saw light coming from your room. You up already? So early?" her mother said, looking at her. There wasn't a hint of residual anger on her face from their row the night before, at least as far as Pei could tell.

"Yes. I couldn't sleep—there's so much on my mind," Pei said dryly.

"Child, it's time to look forward, not backward. And the sooner you get on with it, the better," her mother said.

Here we go again. Her mother was so afraid of any mention of their past. It must be her guilty conscience speaking. "I wasn't thinking about China, if that's what you're referring to. I was more wondering about ways to get started with a small business here."

"What's your big idea?" her mother said, a surprised look on her face.

"Importing hair-growth products from China! It's a business with proven success."

"Wait, how do you suppose you can do business here without any Japanese language skills? You need to focus on studying Japanese first."

"Sure, I'll study Japanese, but that doesn't mean I can't start preparing for a business on the side. A friend of mine in Canada has been doing a darn good business selling 101 Hair Growth Solutions, and I want to do the same thing here."

"Like shipping the products from China and start selling them here?"

"That's the plan. But to start up, I'll need a bit of capital."

"How much are you talking about?"

Pei shrugged. "Perhaps four thousand dollars to start? I need to buy a few thousand bottles of them and store them somewhere—some place hopefully that won't cost too much money. Then I'll sell them at temple fairs, or at bazaars."

Her mother shook her head. "I don't know about that. I wouldn't underestimate how difficult it might be to import Chinese cosmetic products into Japan. The Ministry of Health and Welfare has very tough guidelines, and you must obtain prior approval before you can start selling beauty products here. Besides, I really don't have that kind of money to loan you, and I doubt that your father would be of much help to you either. It's hard enough to get him to pay for your tuition at the language school, you know. Why not wait a bit? As soon as you acquire enough Japanese speaking skills, I'll help you find a job, and you can slowly build your savings up. Here in Japan, every immigrant starts out this way."

"No, I *won't* wait," Pei cried out, her eyes narrowed. "I've waited enough years all my life and I'm *done* waiting."

"Well then, if you have a way to raise funds, certainly don't let me stop you," her mother said rather dismissively before leaving for the kitchen.

"And I *will* find a way, I swear!"

A moment later, her mother hollered from across the kitchen. "Want me to cook you something for breakfast? It's almost time for you to go to school now."

"No, thank you. I'll cook something myself!" Pei shouted back. She really couldn't deal with her mother's suffocating gestures of kindness. After all these years, it was a bit too little, too late.

Two

Vivian had promised her mother she'd be on time. Yes. Eleven o'clock sharp at Shimbashi Station. But at 10:15 she was still standing in front of her dresser in her underwear, fiddling with her clothes. The red wool dress would be too hot. The navy-blue pantsuit would be too formal. Vivian paced in front of the full-length mirror, intent on finding the perfect outfit for the reunion. She looked vacantly at the pile of clothes she'd scattered on the *tatami* floor and reached for her coffee mug on the bookshelf. This meeting was like no other, and she knew she had to get it right.

Finally, at 10:30, she slipped into a purple chiffon blouse, a pair of black wool-blend slacks, and a charcoal-gray Italian suede leather jacket—a pricey item she'd acquired the previous month with half of her monthly wages as a freelance translator. She dug around her drawers for her black beret and carefully tucked her short, wavy hair beneath it. She pushed her eyeglasses into place, studied her reflection, and smiled.

On her way to the subway, she bought a copy of the *Japan Times,* and she began flipping through the pages as soon as she got on the train. *Looks like 1992 may go down as the end of the party everyone has enjoyed for decades,* she thought as she scanned through headlines on Japan's sluggish economy, the softening of land prices, and the fall of stocks. There wasn't a single news story that was remotely uplifting! Vivian let out a grunt and shoved the papers into her leather handbag.

Vivian knew she should care about the financial crisis and what it might mean to her own job, knowing translations of PR materials were often among the first expenses companies would cut during a downturn, but at the moment, she just couldn't focus on anything else but the thought of seeing Pei again. It wasn't her first meeting with her older sister, but after discouraging Pei from coming to Japan all these months, what would she say to her now?

She wasn't sure how she really felt about her sister coming to the family after so long, except for this gnawing sense that Pei's arrival would certainly upset whatever tenuous equilibrium they had managed as a dysfunctional family barely scraping by in high-cost Tokyo. Pei, her older sister and the most-cherished child in the family, had always been on the lips of her mother. According to her mother, Pei was not only the smartest of the three children; she was also a perfect child who could do no wrong. Vivian, the boring second daughter, didn't mind hearing all those stories about her sister as long as she was far away. But now that Pei was here, what would it all mean to the Zhang family? More precisely, what would it mean to her now?

Vivian also found it particularly hard to understand why her older sister had chosen to leave China, leaving behind not only a husband but her two young sons. All her life, Vivian never tasted the life of being on her own turf and amongst her own kin. In Hong Kong, she was called a Mainlander, which carried the connotation of being a country bumpkin. In Japan, she was always this "other" who never fit in any category. She always had to work doubly hard to prove her worth wherever she went. She dreamed of one day going "home" and experiencing the luxury of being just herself. And yet here was Pei, her older sister, who deliberately threw away everything she had to leave "home." Did her sister not understand the importance of being on her own soil; the privilege of never having to apologize to anyone for who she was?

Vivian studied and worked in New York for six years. And since her return three years ago, following a break up with a boyfriend, she'd been thinking of going back to *laojia* in Dalian and visit all her extended family with her older sister. After all, Pei was her only connection to their mother country—a place so close to her heart and yet seemed so out of her reach, because not having been home for three decades, it was practically a foreign country to her. So intent was she with this idea she'd initiated a reunion trip to see her sister two years ago in Beijing with her mother. The trip only whetted her appetite of wanting to see more of her ancestral home in Dalian. But now, with Pei having left China, Vivian's sole link to their hometown was all but gone. Why had her sister given up everything she had in their home country to come to a foreign country was something Vivian could not fathom. Just what did her sister expect to find here? Gold? Her sister had landed in Tokyo two weeks ago from their ancestral home of Dalian, and Vivian chose not to meet her at the airport. She just couldn't deal with it. No, not yet.

As she emerged from the depths of the Tokyo subway, Vivian instinctively rubbed her cold hands together. She could see her breath in the chilled air. She picked up her pace toward the open square right in front of the station.

The square was strangely quiet and lonely this morning. Only a handful of people loitered around the fountain, now filled with caked mud and dead leaves. A lone vendor was selling pink roses and bright yellow chrysanthemums. Except for the familiar, slightly burnt aroma of coffee brewing at the nearby Doutor Café, the place was worlds away from its usual weekday bustle.

Vivian immediately spotted Yan, their mother, standing with Pei in front of the shiny black locomotive on permanent display in the square. She waved to her mother with a broad smile, concealing a nervous peek at Pei.

Vivian was reminded, once again, that her sister was taller than her by about half a head. Even at age 38, Pei came off as a good-looking woman—she had their mother's slim, oval-shaped face, long slender eyes, and high cheekbones, setting her apart from Vivian and Da Wei, both of whom unfortunately were carbon copies of their father's flat nose and round face. But Pei looked paler than Vivian had remembered her from their Beijing visit two years ago, and Pei's badly permed hair made her look cheap. Her mustard-yellow trench coat, short floral dress, ankle-high nylons, and white sandals didn't help either. She looked like a Chinese Shirley MacLaine.

Vivian acknowledged Pei with a nod and an uneasy smile.

Their mother tapped her on the shoulder. "There you are. What took you so long?"

"The stupid train was delayed in Tamachi Station. Sorry."

"Meiyin, you look nice," Pei said.

Vivian blushed, even though she was secretly happy that Pei had noticed her meticulously put-together attire. She didn't know why she had this need to feel sophisticated around her sister. Perhaps she needed to advertise the fact that there was a clear distinction between the two of them. That she most definitely had the upper hand when it came to the family because she was the more cultivated one of the two.

"She doesn't like to use 'Meiyin' much these days," her mother said. "She mostly goes by 'Vivian' now." Vivian thought it odd that their mother should choose to tell Pei this tidbit now. During their Beijing reunion, their mother was perfectly fine with Pei calling her by her Chinese name. Then again, now that Pei was here, perhaps this was as good a time as any to tell her everything because the truth would come out sooner or later.

"Why Vivian?" Pei asked with piercing eyes.

"Because that's what the American nuns called me at my international high school in Yokohama." Vivian shrugged. "My Chinese name was too difficult for them to pronounce, so they decided to give me an English nickname, that's all."

"Oh," Pei lowered her gaze. "So you went to international schools too, huh? Lucky you!"

Vivian didn't quite know how to react to this remark, knowing very well that Pei, like many other Chinese her age, had been forcibly taken out of school in China during the Cultural Revolution. For ten years, no school children had attended a single class. She and Pei may only be three years apart in age. Yet the life courses they ended up taking were as different as night and day. Now Vivian really wished her mom hadn't brought up this trivia about her English name and the international school. Why remind Pei how much she'd missed out on in life by being stuck in China? Vivian peered at her mom, as if asking to be rescued.

"Hey, Vivian, come. Don't just stand there," their mother said, almost right on cue. "Your sister has come all this way. Aren't you even going to greet her with a proper hello?"

Vivian hesitated. She opened her arms slowly to give her sister a stiff hug, her chin touching the rough, scratchy collar of Pei's polyester dress. "Welcome to Japan," she said with a grimace.

Her sister did not hug her back. "What was *that*, Meiyin?" she said sharply, shrugging off Vivian's arms. "Mind you, we don't hug each other like that back home—gives me the goose pimples. You ought to save those for your fancy *laowai* friends from your international school."

Vivian's face colored as an awkward silence settled over them. Having told Pei that Japan wasn't exactly paradise and that she'd be better off in China, Vivian couldn't very well expect her sister to be cheery with her. In fact, the two hadn't spoken since Vivian last wrote Pei in the spring.

"Mom, where's Da Wei?" Vivian said, quickly turning to Yan.

"Hi!" Just then, Da Wei emerged from behind the locomotive. Although he'd gained a few pounds, he was as cheerful as ever. At thirty-three, he was the youngest of the three, but his receding hairline made him look older.

"How did you sleep the last couple of nights, Big Sister?" Da Wei asked, turning to Pei. "I hope the Japanese futons didn't keep you up all night."

"No, the futons were just fine," Pei said, patting Da Wei's shoulder.

"Well then, shall we?" Da Wei gestured and started walking.

Shimbashi Hotel was only a short walk from the station. Vivian caught up with Da Wei as he led the way to the hotel. They briefly chatted about Da Wei's work, and as they walked, he showed her his recently purchased Sony Walkman. As a sales manager at a large Japanese trading firm, Da Wei's payoff for the long and arduous hours he put in for work was buying up the latest gadgets. And Vivian, being eighteen months older, was always curious about what her kid brother was up to even if she didn't share his love of gizmos.

Once inside the hotel, Vivian immediately saw her father, Yiwen, who was waiting in the lobby. Shorter than Da Wei by at least three inches, her father, as usual, had on his tweed hat, which made him look like any other middle-aged Japanese businessman. He smelled clean in his Old Spice aftershave.

"Morning, Father," Vivian said with a wave.

Her father nodded. "And where're your mother and sister?" he asked, his eyes blinking incessantly. *Was it nerves?* Vivian wondered.

"They're right behind," Vivian answered politely.

Pei gave a little cry as she entered the hotel lobby with their mother. "Baba, Baba!" she blurted, rushing over to her father. When Pei reached out with both hands to grab him, Vivian could see she was near tears. But their father just stood there like a *kakashi* scarecrow, his mouth tight, his hands barely extended. Even a long-lost friend from childhood deserved a better welcome than this, Vivian thought. She looked away with a frown.

By the time the family reached the Golden Phoenix on the second floor, it was already eleven-thirty. A queue of eager patrons jostled each other near the entrance. Shimbashi, after all, was a mini Chinatown, and Dim sum was as popular among brunch-goers here as it was in Hong Kong, particularly on a Sunday morning.

"*I-ra-sha-i-ma-se.*" A Japanese waiter offered the traditional welcome greeting. "How many are you, sir?"

"Four ... er, I mean five," Da Wei said, casting a sidelong glance at Pei.

Vivian followed his gaze. Yes, they were not used to including a fifth wheel. How strange to have another family member suddenly emerged from the distant past, unabashedly claiming territory like some vengeful ghost.

As they stood and waited for the waiter to return, Vivian tried to recall when their father had last set foot in their Tokyo home since his unannounced escape to Osaka. Their mother had always complained about his long absences, saying that asking to see him felt harder than flattening mountains. He always had so many excuses.

Their father hadn't wanted to come up to Tokyo this time either, except he'd run out of excuses. "What do you mean you're not coming?" her mother had yelled at maximum decibels over the phone. "Your oldest daughter has traveled all the way from China to see you, waited for this moment all her life, and it's not convenient for you?"

Later, Vivian's mom had recounted to her that their father had wanted to use his impending overseas business trip as a reason to wriggle out of coming to Tokyo this time. To his credit though, the old man did come in the end. Perhaps behind his indifferent exterior, there was still a shred of conscience buried deep down in there somewhere.

The waiter reappeared at the reception desk. He looked apologetically at Da Wei. "I'm sorry, sir. All of our tables in the dining hall are filled. But if you are willing to pay an extra 2,500 yen[1], we would be happy to seat you in one of our private rooms."

Da Wei and Vivian both turned to look at their father, who was standing a few steps behind them near a wall. He hesitated, stretching out his arm to peek at his Rolex before giving a nod. He shifted his weight from one leg to the other, unwittingly highlighting a new pair of expensive brown Italian shoes, which caught the sunlight from across the hallway. Vivian frowned. *Who's buying his shoes these days?* She wondered.

Long ago, before Vivian had celebrated her fifteenth birthday, she remembered her parents shopping together on weekends

---

[1] In 1991, the exchange rate was about 130 yen to a dollar. 2,500 yen was roughly twenty US dollars. Throughout the book, the yen-dollar rates were calculated at this rate.

for groceries and daily necessities, until her father suddenly came up with the excuse one day that business was better in Osaka and it would make more sense for him to stay there. He hadn't exactly moved out of their Meguro home. It was more like he'd *snuck* out of the house, making off with a piece of luggage every time he stopped by. Before long, his closets were empty, and his home visits dwindled to once every six months, generally overlapping with a business trip to Tokyo. Even then, he'd rush off after a few hours.

"Why don't you come home anymore? Entertaining clients shouldn't stop you from seeing your wife and children." Their mother's complaints had become a ritual whenever their father showed up at the door. She didn't care if Vivian and Da Wei were sitting right in front of them. The arguments had grown so intense that he eventually stopped coming to the house altogether. For the past twenty years, on the few occasions when he couldn't avoid a family meeting, he would insist on going to a restaurant. And so to restaurants they went, now only once a year, usually during the Lunar Chinese New Year.

Vivian sighed with relief when the waiter reappeared a moment later and led the five into a room at the end of a hallway. The sooner the meal got started, the sooner they could go home. The private room looked spacious, at least for Tokyo, but Vivian decided the baby blue wallpaper was a disaster. It made the room look pale and uninviting. The round dining table was also too big—large enough for ten people.

Her father was the first to sit down. Vivian noticed that Pei didn't need any prompting, sliding down effortlessly into the chair right next to their father. She sure knew how to grab an opportunity! Vivian pulled out the chair on the other side of their father and gestured for her mother to sit there. Her mother declined, having moved herself several seats away from everyone so she now faced her children's father directly across a vast span of table.

"I want to sit as far as possible from your father so I don't have to talk to him," she said pointedly, making sure he heard her.

She patted a chair, motioning for Vivian to sit next to her instead. Vivian gave her mother a give-me-a-break look, but obediently complied.

Vivian pretended to be studying the ceiling, her gaze fixed on a wood-framed lamp in the shape of a dragon's head. *These family meetings!* Only Da Wei seemed oblivious to the gathering storm at the table. Returning from a brief visit to the men's room, he casually took the empty seat next to their mother and started cracking noisily on the black watermelon seeds brought in by the waiter in a lacquer bowl.

"Excuse me, what kind of tea would you like today?" a waiter asked Da Wei. "We have oolong, jasmine, and pu-erh."

"How about oolong?" Vivian blurted out before Da Wei had a chance to respond. Oolong, or black dragon, was her favorite. Like most Japanese, she had grown quite fond of the mellow flavor of the Fujian tea over the years.

Da Wei turned to Pei. "Is that all right with you, Big Sister?"

"I prefer jasmine," Pei said.

Da Wei nodded, turning to the waiter. "Jasmine it is, then."

Vivian sucked on her teeth and looked down at her chopsticks. She brought them out of their paper wrapper and folded the wrapping neatly into a dainty paper accordion. She hated jasmine tea! How could anyone like a tea that smelled like cheap perfume? Oolong was so much more subtle and aromatic. She particularly liked the brand of oolong called Dongding, or "frozen summit," because it had such an exquisite, clean aftertaste. Only a country bumpkin who knew nothing about tea would settle for something as lowly as jasmine. Then again, in China, for most of the 60s and 70s, people like her sister were grateful just to have enough to fill their bellies.

The waiter brought the tea and handed Da Wei a menu, which he promptly passed on to his father with the help of the Lazy Susan. Everyone seemed to hold their breath as the old man studied the menu quietly. After several minutes, he looked up, firing off orders in impeccable Japanese to the waiter without bothering to consult with anyone else. He probably felt justified in doing so, Vivian thought, since he'd be picking up the check at the end—the only family tradition that had remained unchanged over the years.

No one spoke as they waited for the food. The room was quiet, and the only noise they could hear was the intermittent whines of a baby from the room next door. Da Wei and Vivian tried to keep busy by cracking on seeds. After a while, Da Wei, who had developed the habit of telling jokes when he was uneasy, started recounting a funny TV show he had watched the night before. He grew more and more animated with his tale, switching between Mandarin Chinese and Japanese in *chanpon* speak, until he succumbed to a sudden fit of coughing. A seed had gone down the wrong way.

"You all right? Want some tea?" their mother asked, searching for the teapot.

"No, Ma, I'm fine," Da Wei said, shaking his head as he extended a hand to cover his cup.

Pei, sitting near the teapot, sprang to her feet. She poured tea into their father's cup until it was about to spill. He raised a hand to signal her to stop.

"So, how are the little ones?" their father finally said, looking at Pei. His Chinese sounded stiff to Vivian's ear. It occurred to her that during the few times when the family did get together in the past, they mostly ate in silence. Or else their speech would be peppered with Japanese. Their father must have gotten out of practice using Mandarin Chinese only to chitchat.

"They are fine, very well-adjusted. Very bright and getting good grades at school. I'm quite pleased with them really," Pei answered. There was a deliberate non-mention of Pei's divorce on the part of their father, Vivian noted. *Typical of their father,* she thought. Then he wouldn't have to address the issue that he'd ducked out on his responsibilities of helping Pei's entire family coming out of China.

"How tall are they now?"

"I'm not sure. Last time they had a checkup, they both measured about 135 centimeters."

"That's tall for eight-year-old boys, no?"

Pei winced. "Actually, they just turned ten in August. But yes, they are considered quite tall for their age."

"Good! Very good. It's best when boys are tall."

Vivian leaned back against her seat, leaving a wide gap between herself and the table. Stupid small talk! She stood up and walked abruptly to a nearby wall, where a pair of Chinese calligraphy paintings hung in heavy wood frames. One of them said, "Three generations under one roof," the other, "In perfect harmony with one another." Vivian smiled.

"What're you looking at?" Vivian's mom said

"Nothing, just admiring the calligraphy. Isn't it exquisite, Mom?" Vivian pointed to the one on harmony.

"Yeah, indeed! What style is it?"

"I think it's in the *kaishu*, block script style. I wish I could write like that."

"You could have, if only you'd listened to me and practiced your brushstrokes more diligently when you were in elementary school," Vivian's mother said. She was talking about their days in Hong Kong, when the family was, well, like a family, and their father always showed up for dinner after work.

Luckily for Vivian, her mother was able to tune out the familiar sermon when the waiter returned with a fresh pot of jasmine tea. But there was no sign of food. From the corner of her eye, Vivian saw Pei get up and pour hot tea into their father's cup. It must have been the third cup of tea she'd poured for him. Their conversation hadn't advanced much beyond the twins, with the focus now on universities and the boys' possible majors. *Pei had better not be thinking about asking Father's help for the boys' tuition,* Vivian thought. *If so, she'll be sorely disappointed.*

Vivian's stomach growled. She was about to complain when a waitress arrived with their first dish—five varieties of cold cuts and jellyfish salad. Da Wei, who had not said a word after his coughing fit, gently maneuvered the Lazy Susan so the large serving plate rested in front of their father. Once again, all eyes turned to him.

"Okay, let's eat," he said, raising his chopsticks to gesture everyone to join in. He gingerly placed a golden slice of roast duck on his plate, before passing the serving chopsticks to Pei.

Pei stood up and piled their father's small plate with heaps of roast pork, jellyfish salad, and "white-sliced" chicken. "Here, Father," she said. Then she filled her own plate with cold cuts and walked it over to Da Wei. "Here you go, Little Brother!" she chirped, replacing Da Wei's empty plate with the full one.

"You really don't need to bother with that, Big Sister. Just let everyone help themselves—"

"It's really no bother," Pei interrupted. "I'll—"

"Wait, I've got it," Vivian said with lightning speed as she grabbed an empty saucer from the table, filled it with a small mountain of meat, and placed it in front of their mother.

"Here, Mom. Jellyfish salad. Your favorite," she said with a smile.

"Thank you, dear. I know I can always count on you to remember me," their mother said, smiling back.

Vivian continued serving herself. Before sitting down, she stole a glance at Pei, but her sister didn't notice. Pei was totally absorbed in her food, chewing her meat with poise and enthusiasm. The room fell silent again, save for the occasional noises of chopstick-clicking and tea-pouring.

A moment later, Pei broke the silence with a question: "Father, um, I was wondering . . . how long do you think it would take to master Japanese?"

"That depends," their father answered, looking up as if surprised to find the family all still there.

"I mean, how long did it take you to learn the language?"

"Can't recall, really. It was such a long time ago. But I suppose if you were diligent, you could do quite well after two years."

"Two years! Heavens! How does a newcomer afford two years of tuition?"

"As far as tuition for Japanese language school goes, you needn't worry about a thing. The first year's tuition is already taken care of, and if need be, we'll take care of the second year too," their father said, meeting Pei's eager eyes.

"You mean it?" Pei broke into a smile.

"Of course. And if your father can't afford it, I'm sure everyone at the table will help out," their father said, referring to himself in the third person. "We all recognize how important it is that you have what it takes to be happy in Japan. Right, Da Wei and Vivian?"

"Yes, definitely." Da Wei nodded.

Vivian also nodded, although with much less resolve. "It's important, that's for sure," she uttered under her breath. Their mother, who seemed lost throughout much of the conversation, remained silent. She was fingering a green handkerchief in her hands, deep in some distant memory.

"Thank you, Father, and everybody, for your support. It means so much to me." Pei paused briefly, as if to collect her thoughts. "Really, I feel very fortunate that you're here, Father. I wouldn't be in Japan if it weren't for your help."

It was misplaced gratitude, and Pei should have known better, Vivian thought. The truth was that their father hadn't lifted a finger to help Pei's visa. Had it not been for Da Wei, who had agreed to pay for all of Pei's food and housing during her stay in Japan as a guarantor, as well as running around to different bureaus to collect the right papers for her, and, most importantly, stamped his impressive company seal on all the documents that he would be responsible for any expenses incurred by Pei, all of which were extremely important in the eyes of the Japanese government, she'd still be sitting somewhere in Dalian. What a blatant bid to ingratiate herself with the old man!

Perhaps Pei had read Vivian's mind. Without missing a beat, she turned to Da Wei and said, "I also want to thank Da Wei for helping me. Brother, I'm forever grateful." She raised her teacup in tribute.

Da Wei nodded and raised his cup in return.

Pei didn't mention a word about Vivian or their mother, and the slight hung awkwardly in the air. Vivian played with the edge of the tablecloth until the barbecued pork buns, shrimp dumplings, and spare ribs in black bean sauce finally arrived. She kept busy with her chopsticks and was delighted when more dishes followed: large servings of seafood chow mein, ginger and black pepper beef, sweet and sour soup, and sautéed mustard greens.

"Vivian and Da Wei, I want you two to listen," their father said as the waiter brought in the dessert. He cleared his throat, demanding everyone's attention. "Your sister has come all this way to be with us. She's penniless and has yet to master Japanese. She will need a great deal of help from both of you. I want you to do your utmost to help her in whatever way you can. It's your duty, being the younger brother and sister."

"Of course, of course." Da Wei nodded agreeably. "That's the least we can do."

Vivian found it difficult to nod. She only managed to squeeze out a half smile. That was Father for you! It was so like him to talk like that. What a master at evading his own responsibilities by delegating them all to others. *But what about you, Father?* She wanted to blurt out. *What do you pledge to do for Pei now?*

Then, out of the corner of her eye, Vivian caught their father motioning for the waiter to bring the check. He rose even before he'd finished his dessert. "I've got to go now. It's getting late," he said, wiping his mouth with a napkin, ending the reunion abruptly.

Vivian couldn't remember how she got on the train after leaving her family at the restaurant. Or how she got home from the station. She was deeply preoccupied with the recurring image of a faded photo with ruffled edges. In the center of the photo was the round face of a pretty, little girl with two pigtails. The girl couldn't have been more than eight years old. Snuggling next to her was another round-faced child a couple of inches shorter. The younger girl, with short, wavy hair, wore a delighted smile, revealing a missing front tooth. Sitting on the lap of the bigger girl was a plump baby boy, his hands waving in the air.

Vivian had memorized this snapshot of the past—a picture of the three children in happier times. But that was thirty years ago. The family would splinter a few weeks after the picture was taken, with Pei left behind in China while the rest of the family moved on to Hong Kong and eventually to Japan. Given the rift that followed, they might as well have gone to Mars.

Three

"*Sayonara. Mata ashita.*" In the elongated schoolyard of Yoneda Language Institute, Pei practiced her Japanese farewells on Su Jun and Ah Dong, two of her Chinese classmates whom she'd only just met three days ago. She waved at them enthusiastically with one hand, only to retract it quickly in mid-action. Realizing her mistake, she bent her body to affect a forty-five-degree bow with a lowered head. The Japanese language was never just a verbal expression—it should always be accompanied by gestures and culturally specific bodily movements if the meaning of the words were to be rendered fully. This had been taught to Pei just that morning by Mrs. Ohashi, Pei's gray-haired homeroom teacher at class B-1.

Mrs. Ohashi always had so much to say, and sometimes, she would keep the students in the classroom for an extra fifteen minutes after the bell just so she could finish her point. That day though, Mrs. Ohashi had dismissed the class early because of a domestic emergency.

Once on the street, Pei instinctively began walking in the direction of Toranomon, where she would normally catch a bus home. She thought she would wait on the *obento* lunch she'd brought with her. She wasn't that hungry anyway. Then she remembered she had agreed to meet with her sister and ought to be taking the Chiyoda Line for the Shin-Ochanomizu Station.

The night before, Meiyin, or was it Vivian? had rang to invite her out for tea in the school district of Ochanomizu. Pei hated her sister's English name because it sounded so bogus and pretentious. Besides, she refused to be reminded in any way of her sister's western education.

On the phone her sister had mentioned something about wanting to show her a couple of interesting Japanese bookstores in the neighborhood. Pei suspected that there was more to the meeting than just the bookstores. The idea of Meiyin wanting to be nice to her just didn't sit well. Why would she do such a thing? She'd tried so hard to dissuade Pei from coming to Japan. Or rather, to stay put and rot in China. Was this a truce her conniving sister was offering after ignoring her repeated pleas for help in getting a visa?

Pei took her watch out from the pouch of her large handbag. It was thirty minutes past noon. She had never been to Kasumigaseki Station before. But judging from her map, the stop should only be a few minutes away from her school. Looking for the right entrance to the station, however, was more nightmarish than Pei had anticipated because she soon found out Kasumigaseki was so big it actually encompassed three different subway lines: the Chiyoda Line, the Marunouchi Line, and the Hibiya Line. That meant there would be at least six street-level entrances to the mammoth, subterranean underground system if not more, and not all of them would necessarily lead her to the right train.

After some struggle and a lot of asking around, Pei finally located an entrance to the Chiyoda Line and bought her ticket. The silver train was one of the slickest Pei had ever seen. She hopped into a car toward the front of the train and took a seat near the door. She was immediately greeted by fluttering flyers of magazine ads suspended from the car ceiling. The flashy, ecliptic colors looked a bit out of sync with the muted and predictably beige and blue interiors of the train. The coexistence of contradictions!

It was midday and the train wasn't crowded. There were only about twenty-odd passengers in the entire car. Sitting across from Pei were three ladies in their late forties or maybe early fifties. They were all immaculately dressed in their expensive leather jackets and fall coats, with their hair primed, noses powdered, and lips painted. They were happily chattering away like high school girls, very much looking forward to whatever outing it was they were heading for. Pei wondered which offices their husbands were slaving at right at that moment.

Elsewhere in the train car, Pei noticed most passengers without companions were reading some sort of newspaper or *manga* magazine. Those who weren't reading had their eyes closed. Pei leaned back, legs crossed, and let her mind wander a bit before recalling a reading assignment she had to complete for the following day. She brought out her textbook, *Japanese for Beginners*, and opened to Chapter Five. It was a chapter about a foreigner named Lisa visiting a Japanese friend in Mejiro. Pei became totally immersed in her book, only looking up when a fellow traveler jabbed her with his elbow.

"Bakayaro!"

Pei did not know much Japanese vocabulary yet, but she recognized it to be a nasty swearword, something to the effect that she was a dumb ass. Startled, she looked up, amazed to see an older Japanese man with a deep, receding hairline and thinning, gray hair glaring at her. "Don't you have any manners?" the man growled as he dusted his wool pants off with a hand. He was dressed in a grayish, expensive-looking suit, quite new.

Pei then realized the man was upset with her crossed legs—her propped-up shoe must have brushed against the grumpy old man's pants. She straightened up a little, bringing her leg down to the floor. For a split-second, Pei considered apologizing. But the rudeness of the man made it impossible for her to swallow the insult. She looked away, pretending nothing had happened.

"You're foreigner, aren't you?" the man barked, peeking at the cover of Pei's textbook. *"Yappari*—I thought so. Which one are you, Korean or Chinese?"

The man reeked of *sake*. Pei ignored him, turning her body all the way around so her back faced him. But the incident had so upset her that she couldn't focus on her reading now. She sensed the eyes of other passengers falling on her, making her extremely uncomfortable. She looked down hard at her book, thumbing the pages as if she were looking for something specific. She was very thankful when the conductor announced the train's arrival at Shin-Ochanomizu Station over the intercom.

Pei walked out of the station with a dampened spirit. She had never been insulted like that before. Even if she had soiled the man's pants, it had been an honest mistake. She found it incredible that a well-dressed, seemingly well-educated man could have been so mean to her, humiliating her in front of the whole world with such xenophobic remarks.

The noise and hubbub of the street outside the station restored her mood a bit. It was filled with mom-and-pop-style grocery stores, restaurants, and cheap eateries. The sight of the restaurants reminded her she hadn't eaten lunch yet. Down the street, a homey Chinese restaurant caught her eye.

Walking inside she raised the short, red-and-white store curtain. "*I-ra-sha-i-ma-sei.*" A waitress in her thirties greeted her. Her accent was so strong, Pei knew immediately she wasn't Japanese. The small-framed woman was wearing a baggy sweatshirt a couple of sizes too large for her. The woman had combed her shoulder-length hair into a ponytail and wore a pair of faded blue jeans and dirty, white sneakers. Pei quickly read the menu and ordered a *gyoza* set lunch: ten skinny fried dumplings with a side dish of rice and a bowl of egg-flower soup.

"Are you Chinese?" Pei blurted out when the waitress brought over her food.

"Yes," the woman nodded with a smile.

"Which part of China?" Pei continued her question, switching to Mandarin.

"Fuxin," the woman said.

Pei bit into one of the dumplings and nodded. "That's a neighboring city of Shenyang, near where I'm from. How long have you been in Japan?"

"About six months. And you?" The woman smiled in encouragement.

Pei ignored the waitress's question. She thought that since she was the customer, she ought to be in control of the conversation. "You like it here?"

"Ai, there's no such a thing as a like or dislike for us newcomers. I am only trying to survive," the woman said with a sigh. "I am going to a language school, and I work here whenever I can," she said as she brushed away a strand of stray hair from her face.

"Do they pay you well here?" Pei looked at the kitchen counter to see if anyone was eavesdropping. Luckily, the cook had gone to the toilet. There was only another customer sitting in a far corner.

"No. Not really. I'm only paid 550 yen an hour. But I do get two free meals and a bunk bed in the storage room. The chef is my boss. He's a second cousin, been here twenty years. He said he couldn't pay me more because my Japanese isn't good enough yet. He said he's doing me a huge favor by hiring me because no one else would have given me a chance with my bad Japanese."

"He's taking advantage of you!" Pei raised her eyebrows. She'd heard and read enough to know that the standard minimum wage was 750 yen.

"I know," the woman nodded in agreement. "But when you are at the mercy of others, what can you do? You only wish to get beyond the apprentice stage quickly and hope for a better job later. If only I had a rich relative." The woman went on to say how one of her more fortunate friends had gone to California and received 8,000 dollars from her Chinese family and relatives to start her life over in the US. "I really envy her—she's so lucky," the woman said with a hand over her chin. "When you're with your family, you have such a head start . . ."

The slamming of a door suddenly alerted the waitress. The woman dashed back to the counter.

When you're with your family, you have such a head start. Pei took a sip of her egg-flower soup. She was also with family. But did she really have a head start? Were her parents and siblings fully embracing her now that she was in Japan? Were they ready to do what was best for her?

She had no reasons to doubt her brother and her father, both of whom seemed eager to help her cope with her new environment. What she wasn't sure about was her sister and mother, especially her mother. She remembered a conversation they had while walking out of the Shimbashi Hotel on the day of their reunion, which had left her feeling very unsettled.

"So, what do you think of your father?"

Her mother's question had caught Pei off guard. She shrugged. "He seemed perfectly fine to me. But then again, I've only seen him for a total of two hours—"

"Your father is no longer the caring man you remember," her mother had said, cutting Pei short. "In the last five years, he's been home three times, for a grand total of about six hours. If I were you, I wouldn't pin too much hope on him. If he helps you, fine. If he doesn't, you'll just have to understand. We've been carrying on like this for years, and you won't be an exception either."

Pei said nothing.

"Well?"

"Mother, why are you doing this to me? Just because you and Father don't get along doesn't mean he won't be nice to me. I know he wants to help me. I can feel it in my heart. Like it or not, Mother, I'm his daughter! Why can't you accept that?"

Her mother shook her head. "I am only trying to protect you, Daughter. But if you don't want to hear it, then suit yourself."

Neither daughter nor mother spoke again that evening. Pei wasn't bothered, because she had found silence oddly comforting. Silence had always been her most effective coping mechanism while growing up. In fact, she'd perfected the art form with her mean-spirited uncle, whom she despised with a vengeance even long after his death. But she hadn't expected she'd be using it on her mother. She had turned the thought in her mind over and over again that night, wondering why her mother wouldn't want what was best for her.

Then again, her mother had never been an optimist. Since China opened its doors in 1978, her mother had made three trips to China to visit her, yet she never once encouraged Pei to come join her in Japan. Her excuses had always been the same—that things in Tokyo were extremely expensive and life there was a struggle.

It was as if her mother had never had confidence in her. trusting that her daughter could make a new life for herself outside China. Did it ever occur to her mother that she also deserved a chance? Or that as a mother she had an obligation to make it up to her daughter, to compensate for all those years of unfulfilled responsibilities as a parent and caregiver?

Even at the most recent visit her mother had made just two years ago, she had stuck with her original line: good jobs were hard to come by in Japan because the Japanese wouldn't give away their best jobs to some foreigner, especially if the foreigner was another Asian who looked just like them.

What a bunch of excuses and lies! The problem as far as Pei could see was that the years of living overseas had turned her mother into a pessimist and a pathetic old lady. She was so negative and bitter about everything. Pei swore to herself that she wasn't going to be like her mother. She was going to show her family that she was far better and more capable than them, and that she had what it took to come out ahead, way ahead of them. She'd been through so much in life already in the absence of her parents, and had weathered through the notorious Cultural Revolution. Now that she was out of China, this land of frenzy and unpredictability which in the course of a decade, had wrecked the futures of tens of millions of people her age, then anything was possible! Anything!

When Pei found her way back to the central exit of Shin-Ochanomizu Station, Meiyin was already waiting in front of the ticket machine. She stood out in her red leather jacket and new denim jeans. Too bad her over-sized glasses and unmanageable wavy hair made her look like a goldfish with enormous eyes.

"It's turning out to be a fine day, isn't it?" Meiyin said with a wave.

Pei nodded. "Finally it's letting up a bit after days of dark clouds."

"Come, I want to show you a couple of interesting bookstores down the road." Meiyin gestured for Pei to follow.

They passed by many sports supplies shops, stationery stores, and a university campus until they reached a quaint shopping street called Suzurandoori. The short street was lined with bookstores. Meiyin stopped in front of one of them and motioned for Pei to enter. "This is the famous Uchiyama Bookstore," Meiyin said. "Surely you've heard of Uchiyama Kanzo before." Pei shook her head. "He was a book dealer in Shanghai in the '30s and became good friends with many Chinese writers, including Lu Xun," Meiyin said with authority. "But his claim to fame was when he used his Shanghai bookstore to hide Lu Xun from Japanese soldiers."

Pei looked at the front of the store and saw four Chinese characters: *Nei-Shan-Shu-Dian* or Neishan Bookstore. She had heard of a Mr. Neishan before, but not Uchiyama. But that was because Neishan was the Chinese reading of the name Uchiyama[2]. Small wonder she didn't recognize the name when Meiyin mentioned it.

"I always come here when I need to catch up on my Chinese reading. Chinese books are not easy to come by here in this city."

Pei nodded. "That's good to know," she said mildly, following Meiyin into the store. She looked around the shelves and saw some titles that amused her, *A Beijinger in New York,* and *The Ugly Chinese.* Meiyin pointed out to Pei the many Chinese language textbooks on display in a far corner. She went on to say she once

---

[2] The Chinese ideographs as a writing system was first introduced to Japan in the fifth century. These scripts were not only given Chinese readings, but the corresponding Japanese readings as well. "Neishan" essentially is the Chinese reading of the name "Uchiyama," which are written exactly the same in the Chinese scripts. So unless written, the two different readings can sometimes lead to confusion.

met a second-generation Chinese in Yokohama who didn't speak a word of Chinese. "I felt really sorry for the woman. I should have told her about this bookstore."

That was when Pei remembered the half-Chinese, half-Japanese *chanpon* speak Meiyin was using with Da Wei over the reunion lunch at the Golden Phoenix. She was tempted to tell her sister that it wouldn't be long before she too would forget her mother tongue.

When the two came out of the bookstore, Meiyin took Pei to a traditional teahouse just a few doors down. Over Japanese green tea and sticky rice cakes, Meiyin asked Pei about her language school. Pei tried to be polite, but deep down inside she was getting bored with the whole afternoon. Where is this leading to? She wondered. It occurred to her this was really the first time the two of them had sat down alone. In 1990, when Meiyin had visited her in Beijing, their outings had always been a family thing—there was never a time when the two sisters had actually went out alone. She didn't know what to make of Meiyin. Was she friend or foe? Just when Pei was about to announce her departure, Meiyin surprised her with a white envelope.

"What's this?"

"A gift from me!" said Meiyin. "Inside, there's one hundred thousand yen, which should last you a while, even in expensive Tokyo. I hope the money will provide you with a soft cushion."

Pei held her breath. One hundred thousand yen! She did a quick math in her head: that was roughly eight hundred American dollars. "That's very thoughtful of you," Pei said without betraying any emotion. She folded the envelope and tucked it neatly into her purse. Meiyin then settled the bill and the two walked out silently toward the subway station.

At the station, Pei gave a feeble wave to Meiyin before her sister left for the opposite side of the platform. She knew her younger sister was fishing for a heartfelt thank you from her. But how could she be so naïve? Thirty years of her youth! Did Meiyin really think those long, suffering years were only worth eight hundred dollars? She thought of the day when she was eight again. She thought of the game her mother made her play with Meiyin. She thought of how she lost the game to her younger sister. And after that, everything had changed.

As far as she was concerned, Meiyin had stolen her life.

Four

Vivian squinted at the sunlight seeping through the half-drawn blinds of her studio apartment. The clock radio next to her bed read 11:30. She stretched her arms and slowly crawled out from under her *kakebuton* quilt, then climbed down the loft ladder in search of her cordless phone. Eventually locating it by the leg of her desk, she pushed the speed-dial button and waited.

"*Wei?*"

"*Wei!* Good morning, Mom! How're you this morning?" She yawned into the phone.

"Not bad. Did you just wake up? It's almost noon, and I've already put in four hours of work this morning."

"I went to bed late. Was up all night finishing this awful translation." Vivian rubbed her eyes. "I've got to send the darn thing in by one o'clock." She walked into the living room, where she'd left a small mountain of paper and notes on the dining room table. She found a pile of freshly printed pages among the scattered mess and tapped the stack gently against the tabletop.

"What kind of translation is it this time?" her mother asked.

"The usual. An instruction manual from a camera company that wants to export to China. It's incredibly boring. I have translated forty pages or so, and half the time I don't even know what they're talking about."

Vivian worked as a part-time technical translator over the weekend. Eighty percent of her work involved some kind of electronic appliance. She couldn't remember how many washing machine and fax machine manuals she had translated. Although it was her livelihood, she despised every word she rendered. She would rather do something more interesting, like translating for an arts journal, the kind of work she did when she lived in Manhattan as an art history student in the late 80s. She graduated with a M.A. degree in Asian Art History from NYU, so she was able to pick up a few part-time gigs from some of the New York galleries through introductions. But demand for that sort of translations in Tokyo was rare, and it often didn't pay that well.

Because Vivian also received a B.A. degree from a Tokyo university majoring in Japanese, she was able to get steady work as a freelance translator on contract with a translation agency, easily earning $1,000 a month working over the weekend. During the week, she worked three days as a glorified secretary for a Japanese boss filing papers and pretending to be a Chinese-Japanese interpreter. Her work there not only helped her secure a work visa, but earned her another $2,000 a month. Not bad considering most Japanese men her age were pulling a similar salary but working crazy hours.

With the combined income, she was able to rent a small apartment in the quiet but posh residential area of Gakugei Dagaku in western Tokyo.

"Boring or not, it's a lot better than cleaning toilets or washing dishes. You know, Vivian, you're *very* lucky," her mother said.

"Yes, I am," Vivian said, acknowledging her mother's reference to Pei, who had yet to learn survival Japanese.

She was indeed thankful that her grasp of English and Japanese had afforded her such relative comfort in Japan. If there was one thing she was grateful to her father for, it was the decision to enroll her in an American high school in Yokohama. She'd learned there that if you wanted to prosper in Japan as a foreigner from Asia, knowing Japanese was not enough. You also needed to know English, and know it better than most Japanese. Knowing English could earn respect, open doors, and help you pocket some extra cash. The Japanese believed English was tough for them to master and that other Asians were somehow better at the game, and so she was all too happy to exploit their feelings of inadequacy.

Before Pei arrived, her mother had suggested that she share her apartment with her sister. Vivian had pretended not to hear. Sure, her apartment was bigger than her mother's, and yes, it came with a bathroom of its own, but so what? She wasn't about to share her living space with someone who seemed so selfish, willfully leaving behind her children in her obsessive quest for money.

In all of the letters Pei had written, Vivian saw that the single biggest concern her sister had was how she could get out of China. Vivian was very irritated by this, as it seemed that Pei had everything already: an ideal husband, two adorable sons, the stability of a state job, and her mother's full approval. Why would she want to throw everything away just to become a second-class citizen in Japan?

Her sister had no clues about what it was really like to live on someone else's turf—she seemed to have a rose-tinged view that living in Japan would mean she would have the same rights and privileges as any other Japanese. How wrong could she be! Had she any idea that as an outsider, or more precisely, an *alien*, as the Japanese like to call anyone non-Japanese, you must constantly justify your existence to the authorities. One false move and you would be driven out. Vivian was fed up with her sister and many other Mainlanders like her who readily bought into the myth that Japan was a land paved with gold and ready for the plucking. All the while, Pei knew not the first thing about the country, or cared to spend some time to study about it. Greed. It seemed her sister was motivated by nothing but pure greed, like so many other Mainlanders rushing to get out of China, and Vivian was sickened and disgusted by this.

On the other end, her mother was going on and on about some friend at work. "Because her husband has died so suddenly, he didn't leave a will. Now Sagami-san is not talking to her daughter because her daughter wants her own name listed as the rightful homeowner instead of the mother's. Imagine not talking to your only daughter! The poor woman is going to spend the New Year's holidays all by herself—"

Vivian put the receiver down on the desk and went about her business. At times like this, Vivian had learned it was best just to let her mother blabber. Her mom was trapped between four walls all day. She needed to air some of her frustration. Vivian fed a stack of paper into her fax machine, whisking her translation away with the push of a button.

She picked up the phone again. Her mother was still not quite done with telling her story. "Mom," Vivian lowered her voice into a whisper, "is *she* around?"

A momentary silence. "You mean Pei?" her mother finally said.

"Who else?" Ever since Pei's arrival, Vivian found herself using pronouns when referring to her sister. She couldn't help it; she had a strong urge to create a shared confidence with her mother. She needed to have her mom on her side.

Vivian could still recall how proud her mother had been of Pei during their Beijing reunion trip two summers ago. Compared with Vivian, Pei seemed a success in every way. She had produced not one, but two sons, and she was working as an assistant manager at the largest department store in Dalian. Vivian, still single, was a freelance translator, which by Chinese standards was synonymous with being unemployed. Even now Vivian could still see the broad smile on her mother's face, her hands forever patting the heads of her twin grandsons.

"Why can't you be more like your sister?" Her mother had nagged on the first night of their reunion after Pei, Guomin, and the two boys had retired to their hotel room. "Look at her—she has a stable job and a happy family, a portrait of what a successful woman ought to be. But you! The more books you read, the more muddle-headed you seem to have become. I don't know when you will make up your mind to find a real job and settle down with a family."

Her mother's overt endorsement of Pei's life made it all the more difficult for Vivian to comprehend her sister's resolve to leave China. Even if Japan was indeed a lot richer than China, how could Pei have the heart to leave her boys behind, given what she had been through as a child?

But on a deeper level, Vivian was also deeply worried that by Pei coming to Tokyo, that her hard won relationship with her mother would be seriously threatened. In the long absence of Pei, Vivian had been the de facto "favorite" daughter of their mother's. But now that Pei was suddenly here, would her older sister, the original favorite daughter of their mother's, dethrone Vivian again? Vivian had long resigned to the fact that her relationship with her absentee dad would not amount to anything. But her mother was the one parent whose love she could not afford to lose.

Disturbed about Pei's decision to come live in Japan, Vivian had tried everything to stop her. In several letters she'd written, she had deliberately downplayed the appeal of Tokyo by pointing out how difficult it was for foreigners to get jobs in Japan. Then suddenly Pei's letters had stopped coming. Only weeks later did Vivian realize Pei had sidestepped her by writing directly to their mother and Da Wei. Pei begged and pleaded with them, even threatening suicide at one point until their mother gave in. Taking advantage of Da Wei's job at a large Japanese trading firm, which qualified him to be Pei's guarantor and sponsor, their mother made sure Pei was able to get a visa. Before Vivian could get her head around all this, Pei was on her way to Tokyo.

For the first two weeks after Pei's arrival, Vivian had tried to bury their differences by making overtures to show her sister around. After giving her an envelope containing a stack of ten-thousand-yen bills, she'd half-expected her sister to give her at least a hug. But instead, Pei merely nodded with a half-smile. Pei's blatant insensitivity to her good-will gesture made Vivian all the more exasperated with her sister. She was becoming more and more convinced that the real motive behind Pei's move to Japan was not to be *with* the family, but to suck money *out* of them. All those years of waiting must have clouded her sister's mind, turning her into a bitchy, hateful woman, and she was sure Pei was bent on payback. Why else would she be so ungrateful?

Her mother cleared her voice. "Of course she's not home! She's at school," she said, sounding a little irritated by Vivian's question.

"So, how is she doing lately?"

"Fine, I suppose, given the circumstances. But she only speaks when she has to. Sometimes I feel like I'm living with a stone Buddha. I have no idea what she's thinking half the time. I wash her clothes, feed her, and I don't ever hear her say 'thank you.' Instead, she tells me my food is all wrong."

"Mom, you should know better. Some people are incapable of expressing gratitude. And the more you try to cater to them, the more they will come to expect from you."

"But what am I supposed to do? She's helpless and has no money, which I'm sure is partly my fault. After all these years, I never dreamt—"

"Mom, don't let her guilt you into thinking that way. It wasn't your fault; well, not entirely. They don't call the Cultural Revolution a human catastrophe for nothing!"

"It's not that simple. She's all alone and has nothing to fall back on. She's really at our mercy here." Her mother let out a long sigh. "Old debts! That's what this is really about."

"I warned her about how hard things would be in Japan, but she wouldn't listen."

"Vivian, your sister may have some unrealistic expectations, but she's still your sister. The least we can do is to help her until she can stand on her own feet. Don't you agree?" Her mother's voice had grown pleading.

"Help her?" Vivian snorted. "I'm not sure I know how. She wants everything, and she wants it now. And then she never says 'thank you'. " Vivian told her mother about Pei's reaction after she'd presented her sister with the gift money.

"How about finding her a job? Putting her in touch with reality might help her adjust. Besides, I can't possibly support her without her chipping in at least a little bit."

"Ma, she doesn't speak any Japanese. Who would hire her? Unless, of course, Da Wei is willing to help hire her at his company. Have you asked Da Wei? Maybe he can help by hiring her as a messenger girl."

"Vivian, you know that's not going to work. Da Wei's company is a large corporation, and everything there is done by the book. Besides, Da Wei already did Pei a huge favor by serving as her guarantor. I can't keep asking him to do the heavy lifting on behalf of Pei. We are her kin too, so it's really our turn to do something now.

"I suppose you have a point," Vivian said finally. "But how am I going to find an employer willing to hire her?"

"There're always jobs out there. How do you know if you don't try?" Her mother paused, then softened her tone a bit. "Vivian, I wouldn't bother you if I didn't need to. Last week I got her a cleaning job at my company, but she quit after two days. She said it was too degrading to wear a janitor's uniform. Maybe she would be more willing to work if she were at a restaurant. At least she would be with other people, and she could practice using her Japanese. Vivian, please! Help her find some work as a kitchen helper, a dishwasher—whatever she can do in the late afternoon after school. I really don't know what else to do with her."

Vivian sighed. "Okay, Mom, I'll try."

"Thank you." Her mother's voice perked up a bit. "I know I can count on you. You're my good daughter, after all. Let me know if you hear of anything—"

The fax machine let out an agonizing screech. A page had jammed midway in its underbelly. The paper feeder was acting up again. Vivian pulled the machine from the wall and was just about to open up its lid when she knocked over a dusty cardboard box that was tucked behind the machine among a stack of notebooks. The box spewed its colorful contents onto the floor: a set of Chinese paper cuts, a couple of decorative zodiac animals made with clay—now reduced to broken pieces—as well as a box of Chinese herbal tea and a lime green silk scarf. These were all gifts Pei had sent her months before while she was lobbying to come to Japan.

Chinese paper cuts and clay figurines? Pei thought Vivian could be bought with some cheap folk crafts? How absurd! And a green scarf! Vivian hated green. Vivian swept the broken pieces and all the useless little items into a dustpan, and swiftly threw the lot into the bin. Done! She needn't be reminded of them again.

What was it about Pei that aggravated her so much? Sure, her sister was an opportunist, but who wouldn't be under the circumstances? And why couldn't she be a little more charitable toward her? After all, hadn't she fared much better than Pei?

Then it came to her.

Your sister, Pei, always did very well at school, unlike you and Da Wei. I never had to say anything to her, and she would always come home with the best grades. Why can't you and Da Wei be more like your sister?

It was one of their mom's favorite lines, one Vivian had heard over and over again through most of her teenage years. There were many similar tales their mother liked to tell. To her mother, Pei was the saint-like child who could do no wrong. Little by little, Pei became a synonym for the perfect child that Vivian could never measure up to. In time, she'd grown sick of hearing her sister's name.

Her mother had told Vivian more than once that Pei was not only the smartest child in the family, she was also the reason their father had returned after initially running off from their arranged marriage. It was no wonder that Pei should occupy such a special place in their mother's heart, a place Vivian could only regard with envy. To Vivian, Pei's presence in Tokyo was a threat, one that she couldn't bear.

Five

The classroom was quiet. So quiet that the only thing Pei could hear were the tiny scratches of pens on notepads and the occasional crackling of papers. Whenever Mrs. Ohashi wrote a vocabulary list on the whiteboard, the class would immediately fall silent. Nine pairs of eyes, in nine Asian variations, stared so intently at the whiteboard Pei worried they might burn a hole in it. Everyone there knew that whatever *kanji* their formidable teacher wrote on the board would invariably end up in a quiz a day or two later. Mrs. Ohashi was infamous for giving tests on a moment's whim, and everyone hated her for that. A slip in school marks could mean a cancelled student visa—something no one in the class could afford.

"Uh . . . *sensei?*" Sitting at the front row of the classroom, Pei suddenly spoke up, startling everyone in the classroom.

"*Ohashi sensei,*" Pei raised her voice. "The *kanji* you've just written . . . it's missing a dot."

Pei's heart was beating fast. Her Japanese might not be perfect, but she knew she was right about this particular script. When it came to languages, she had enormous confidence. She pointed at the whiteboard, drawing an imaginary dot in the air.

"A dot?" Mrs. Ohashi turned sideways to face the class, her eyes drawing a blank. She stepped back a little from the whiteboard and looked in the direction of Pei's finger. "Where?"

"Here! Why don't I just show you?" Pei sprang from her seat and charged to the whiteboard. She stopped in the middle of the board and left a rather conspicuous black circle on the right-hand side of the symbol[3].

Pei had never been noted for her tact. When she knew something was wrong, she had to tell it like it was. Back in China, she'd once insulted her department chief by pointing out at a group meeting that he had mistranslated an English term in an ad. She knew she was right, being the only one who had an English degree in her section. After the meeting, the department chief had taken Pei aside and reminded her that it was at his recommendation that she was allowed to go on to a night college, and it was he who signed the *danwei* papers to subsidize half of her tuition. "How could you be so smug and ungrateful?" he'd growled at her.

That year, Pei lost a promotion her boss had promised her. That was when she'd realized she must leave China. In China, it wasn't your personal ability that mattered, but who you knew and how important you could make those above you feel. Unfortunately, she had neither of those attributes. Her parents didn't help with connections either. They had been gone too long to leave her with any usable *guanxi*. And although her teachers all told her she was a bright student, she had been raised an ugly duckling under someone else's roof all those years, her temperament "all twisted," according to her uncle. She longed for a place where people would recognize her talent and appreciate her for who she was, where she wouldn't have to worry about having to "go through the backdoor" as was the norm in China. She became obsessed with the idea of leaving China, fueled by her younger sister's sudden visit to Beijing two summers ago.

Back in the classroom, all eyes were on Mrs. Ohashi. The small class was quietly waiting for a reaction. "I see. Now let me

---

[3] The Chinese script writing system was introduced to Japan in the fifth century, which the Japanese called "kanji," literally Han characters. In Japan, the official list of Toyo Kanji, or kanji for general use, totaled about 1,860. Although many educated Japanese have a good command of the kanji, the average educated Chinese still has a better grasp of the Chinese writing system because full literacy in Chinese language requires a knowledge of between three and four thousand characters.

check ..." Mrs. Ohashi adjusted her gold-rimmed glasses and patiently thumbed through her dictionary on her desk. "Ah, *soo ne.* You're right." The teacher looked up from her glasses, a half smile on her face. "I've made a silly mistake, haven't I?"

Someone at the back of the classroom started whistling. Pei recognized it to be Ah Dong, one of the only two male Chinese students in the class. The twenty-seven year old former chef from Jiangsu made a name for himself as a troublemaker for speaking disrespectfully to teachers. But he was well liked by the Chinese students because he'd always stick up for his compatriots in trouble. "When you are in a foreign country, you've got to stick together," he liked to say.

"I have always heard that Chinese are better at *kanji,* and I can see that now," Mrs. Ohashi said, her cheeks pink with embarrassment. She wiped the *kanji* in question off the whiteboard and replaced it with a freshly written one, this time with the dot intact. "Come to think of it, you were the ones who invented the Chinese characters in the first place, so why shouldn't you be experts, right?" She laughed lightly, turning to meet the eyes of the class for the first time.

Pei nodded readily as she returned to her seat. She caught Ah Dong sticking a thumb up at her, and she smiled back.

The school bell went off at noon. "Okay, class, it's time for lunch," Mrs. Ohashi said with another uneasy smile, her face betraying signs of great relief. "I'll see you all in the afternoon."

Six weeks! It had only been six weeks since Pei had started her Japanese lessons at Yoneda Language Institute, and already she was gaining a reputation as a cocky, bright student who would not hesitate to chip at her teachers' dignity by openly pointing out their errors. Her unrelenting corrections of Mrs. Ohashi's *kanji* writing had brought her a certain respect with some fellow Chinese students, but at the potential expense of her teacher's goodwill, the value of which she had underestimated.

As soon as Mrs. Ohashi left the room, half of the students scampered out to the small courtyard, some driven by their need for a nicotine fix. Others rushed to a nearby 7-Eleven for its *obento* lunch specials.

Pei decided to stay in the classroom. The weather had turned quite cold in the last couple of days. It wouldn't make for a very pleasant break eating in the chilly air. Toward the back of the classroom, two Korean students quietly discussed a grammar problem. Another stay-behind, Su Jun, was making instant noodles with hot tea. Su Jun had a young child back in Fujian somewhere, Pei had heard. She had a reputation as someone who was very frugal. It was the third day in a row Pei had seen her making instant noodles. Didn't she know the chemicals in the noodles could kill her?

Pei strolled over to her with her lunchbox. "Su Jun, how about some chicken?" She took the plastic lid off her lunchbox, revealing a tub of glistening, white rice and some stewed chicken in bamboo.

"No, thank you. I can't." Su Jun waved a hand at Pei, her face flushed. She looked tired, most probably because of her late-night gig as an *obento* factory worker. Pei heard Su Jun worked as late as 2:00 a.m. sometimes in order to earn some extra cash.

"Be careful about eating too many cup-noodles. There isn't much nutrition in them, and there're all kinds of preservatives."

"I know," Su Jun said. "But I really don't have a choice. I want to save as much money as possible so I can buy a house back home." She smiled, showing her not-so-even teeth. "A lot of my *tongxiang* in Fujian have done just that, returned home with heaps of money to build houses and business empires. That's my dream."

"Where around Fujian are you from?"

"You've heard of Yongding?"

Just when Pei was going to ask Su Jun more about her village, she saw Chen Hong coming toward her from the back of the classroom, swaying unstably in her purple high-heels. "Hey, Zhang Peiyin," she said, waving at Pei. Pei thought she had seen Hong leaving the classroom with the other students. When did she sneak back in? Su Jun took the opportunity to scurry back to her desk.

"You sure showed her, didn't you?" Hong said, shaking her head. She had a new hairdo, her freshly cut bangs accentuating her flowing, black hair. She wore an eye-catching turquoise blue business suit that brought out her curves and the black of her pupils.

Pei turned to Hong with a self-conscious smile. "You mean Ohashi *sensei*? Well, she's been making quite a few mistakes lately. I thought someone ought to give her a jolt. She should know better than to come in unprepared. She seems to have forgotten that she's teaching a group of *kanji* experts here."

"You're the expert, not me." Hong waved her meticulously painted purple nails as she sat down next to Pei. "You know, I'm a zero when it comes to the written Chinese language. I was yanked out of middle school when I was fourteen. But then again, I was never into the Chinese language anyway. How about you? Let me guess: you must have gone to *Beida* and majored in literature."

"It wasn't *Beida*, but I did go to a pretty good university," Pei said without looking up. She picked a morsel of meat from her lunchbox, sending it gracefully into her mouth with the help of her chopsticks. "Dalian University of Foreign Languages is the name. But my university has nothing to do with my knowledge of Chinese. You see, I majored in English," she said with her mouth full.

"English? You speak English too?"

Pei nodded. "I learned of the fine details of Chinese characters during my brief time working as an editor at a literary magazine."

"My, I didn't know we have a scholar among us." Hong rolled her perfectly made-up eyes. "I hate people like you. I can't even put together a Chinese sentence properly. Now my boss is pressuring me to learn some English. She said it would be good for my work. Would you teach me English?"

Work? Pei couldn't help but redirect her gaze at the tight, turquoise business suit Hong was wearing. The young woman looked stunning. Pei suddenly felt ugly in her loose slacks and dowdy green sweater.

Hong had always been a puzzle to Pei. She seemed very different from the rest of the students. A rumor was going around that back in China she was a Shanghai street hawker. By some miracle, she'd managed to crawl her way up from the bottom of society and somehow make it to Tokyo.

Pei would never have guessed Hong's humble start, judging from the way she looked. Tall, confident, and endowed with a perfect figure and pearl-like skin, she would always arrive at the classroom half an hour late in her spiky heels and super-mini black leather skirt. Once in a while she would wear a red, body-hugging dress and black tights. Every time she walked in she would be oozing expensive perfume—money never seemed an issue to her. Her entrances were usually greeted by Ah Dong's wolf whistle, his eyes following her to her seat.

"Xiao Hong, what is it that you do?" Pei asked, her hand gesturing at Hong's suit. "You're always dressed so impeccably."

"You know, the kind that requires a lot of sitting." Hong giggled. "And sometimes a little singing too."

"You mean you work at a *karaoke* bar?"

Hong shook her head. "Something even better!" She took a sweeping glance at the classroom, and seeing that no one was near, whispered, "I work at a hostess club in Shinjuku." She dug out a pack of Cabin Mild from her handbag and lit up a cigarette.

"A hostess club? I heard those jobs pay a lot," Pei said under her breath.

"Uh-huh. You can make a bundle if you're good at it. Most of the women I know in this line of work make about twelve thousand yen a night in four, five hours." Hong paused to puff out a plume of smoke. "But I make more."

"*Chotto!*" A Korean student who had been eating at her desk at the back of the classroom came charging toward them, her eyes burning with hostility. "You're not allowed to smoke in the classroom," she hollered in Japanese, her finger jabbing at a no-smoking sign on a nearby wall.

"Sorry. *Gomennasai.*" Hong quickly switched to Japanese, giving a wave as she ground her cigarette out on the floor. "Stupid busybody," she hissed in Chinese after the young woman was out of earshot.

But Pei barely heard her, lost in thought over what Hong had just said. "Did you say you make more than twelve thousand yen a night?" she asked. "How, uh, did you find a job like that?"

"Hey, if you want it bad enough you *will* find a way." Hong rose to her feet, swinging her handbag over her shoulder. "Say, want to join me for a cup of coffee outside? I am dying for a smoke."

Café La Mille was just a short walk away from their school.

"Excuse me! Two cups of Blue Mountain," Hong said, raising two fingers at the waitress the minute they sat down.

Blue Mountain! Pei remembered having heard of the brand in Dalian. She studied the menu and noticed that the coffee was eight hundred yen, the most expensive item on the menu.

"Don't worry. It's on me." Hong leaned back easily against the cafe's soft green velvet couch. She was sitting opposite Pei, her legs crossed and her dangling foot swaying gently to the soft music playing in the background. On the wall behind her hung a large painting of water lilies in an ornate gold frame. Nearby in a corner stood a cyclamen, its bright red blossoms blending perfectly with the salmon-pink of the wall. "Nice, isn't it?" Hong said, smiling.

"Sure is." Pei nodded, her eyes focused on an antique frosted-glass lamp opposite her. It was the first time Pei had stepped into a coffee shop quite this fancy. Until then, she had only been to cheaper chains like Doutor. It dawned on her that eight hundred yen was just about what Guomin—now her ex-husband, she reminded herself—was paying monthly for their heavily subsidized apartment in Dalian. Some coffee!

As if to emphasize its exclusivity, the waitress brought Pei's coffee in a delicate silver-rimmed bone china cup. The bottom of the saucer said "Noritake." Hong's cup and saucer were of a similar pattern, except they were gold-rimmed. Pei raised the cup to her mouth and took a small sip. Ugh! The dark water tasted bitterer than she'd expected, like Chinese herbal medicine.

Hong saw the scowl on Pei's face. "Not used to it? Try this." She poured some cream from a dainty silver pitcher into Pei's cup. "It's the best coffee in Tokyo."

Pei shook her head after another sip, her lips pressed.

"Don't tell me this is your first time? Oh, of course, they don't have coffee shops in the rustbelt Dalian! In Shanghai, there're dozens on Nanjing Road alone."

"Of course they do." Pei straightened her posture, bristling. "There are at least two cafés selling coffee in the city center of Dalian. In fact, I used to frequent the one at the Furama's."

"You did? And what coffee did they serve there?"

"Can't remember. I had jasmine tea, I think. I don't like coffee much."

"You what?" Hong let out a laugh, her back arching. "Look, if you want to impress people, learn to drink and eat foreign foods. That's why drinking coffee is better than drinking tea, especially at a coffee shop. Dear! Drinking Chinese tea at a coffee shop! I can't believe you did that." Hong stirred her cup of Blue Mountain with a dainty ceramic spoon, an incredulous look on her face. Pei suddenly felt like a country bumpkin invited to high tea for the first time.

"Besides, coffee shops here are not just for coffee-drinking," Hong continued. "They are places you hang out in to cultivate your style and aesthetic sense. Just look at this place! How often do you find coffee shops in China with such flair, complete with classical music and Picasso paintings?"

Picasso? These paintings? Pei craned her neck to take a good look at the pale pink water lilies in the frame behind Hong. "I've never heard of Picasso painting water lilies before. Are you sure they're not by Monet?" Pei had always admired Western paintings and had read a few books about Western art. But she couldn't say for sure which painters painted exactly what.

"Mo who? Mo Nai? Never heard of him. Oh, never mind. All I'm saying is that it's important for young women like us to cultivate an image of sophistication. That's the only way you can meet the right kind of people and get ahead."

Pei nodded, impressed. How did this ex-street-vendor become so worldly?

"You're a regular here, aren't you?"

Hong didn't respond. She leaned all the way to the back of her couch, her feet propped up on the edge of the glass table, the pointed tips of her purple high heels now sticking up. "Ah! I'm so tired." She yawned with her eyes closed. "I was up until two last night."

"Xiao Hong." Pei cleared her throat. "I heard you used to sell clothes in Shanghai. Is it true?"

"Ha!" Hong let out a small laugh, her eyes opening just a sliver. "Funny how rumors get started." She struggled to sit up, tapped a cigarette from a pack, and proceeded to light up. "Well, I don't normally like to talk about my past," she said slowly, "but I like you. You've been kind to me."

Hong was talking about the school notes, which Pei would always generously lend her whenever Hong needed them. In the past, before the two were better acquainted, whenever Hong saw Pei in the hallway, she would always smile and find some excuse to make small talk with her. It took a while for Pei to realize what Hong was really after—her notes. Every time a big test was imminent, invariably Hong would come begging for Pei's notebook. Pei didn't mind. After all, it was a backhanded compliment that she was a good student.

Hong paused as if to collect her thoughts. Then she said in a monotone, "Yes, I used to sell knickknacks and women's accessories on the street. You know, women's underwear, cosmetics, bags, those sorts of things. But it wasn't in Shanghai. I did it in Yancheng, where I grew up. It was a long time ago though. Hated every minute of it. In fact, I hated everything about Yancheng. I was so happy to leave town."

"Why?"

"Why? Can you imagine living in a smelly, rat-infested shed and sharing a bed with two other siblings, your old man always drunk and grumpy, your mother always whining about not having enough money?"

Hong looked straight at Pei and took a deep drag from her cigarette. "My old man used to be a construction worker, but he got hooked on gambling after he was injured in an accident and lost his job. Every time he lost money, he would come home drunk and smash things around. My mother wasn't home much, being a factory worker working night shifts, so I naturally became his punching bag. I was the only daughter at home and had the impossible task of waiting on him. One time he whipped me with his leather belt because the noodles I cooked for him were too salty."

Pei blinked. Hong's story reminded her of her own abuse at the hands of her uncle. When Pei was barely nine, she'd had the difficult job of keeping the coal in the kitchen stove burning after school. The idea was that when the adults returned home from work they could start cooking right away. One time she was careless and let the fire go out. When Uncle Feng came home and realized dinner was not ready, he immediately came after her with a broom. She wasn't allowed to eat that night, but had to wash all the dishes in the freezing cold kitchen by herself, while her two boy cousins sat on the toasty warm *kang*, cracking away on peanuts and drinking tea with their father.

This sort of abuse continued until she left her uncle's house. When she was sixteen, the government sent her for re-education with peasants in Harbin near the Soviet border. It was hard work, raising farm animals in the bitter cold and building roads, but she was happy to be with other young people. At least there everyone was treated equally, and she could pretend she was part of an extended family.

"My mother was forced to sell whatever she could on the streets when her factory went bankrupt," Hong started again. "I was the oldest child, so part of the responsibility was quickly shuffled to me. I had no choice but to quit school. I was only fourteen. My mother soon realized selling women's garments and knock-off bags was a better way to make a living, so that's what I sold. I did it for three years. Three *fucking* years," Hong said, stubbing her cigarette out in an ashtray.

Pei nodded. Another oldest child! *Why is it that we always end up on the wrong side of the bargain?*

"I'll never forget those years! You're out from morning to night, dining on dust and the wind all day long. Then there were days when you had to dodge the rain and the police—it's just exhausting."

"So you quit and left town one day?"

Hong shook her head, a dark shadow crossed her face. She seemed distant, lost in a faraway place.

"Hey, you okay?" Pei peered at Hong from across the table.

Hong shook her head again, her eyes tightly shut. "It was my old man," she said between her teeth. "I came home one night after work to find him waiting outside our house with a stranger, an ugly, fat, middle-aged man with a gold tooth. My old man insisted that I go have dinner with them. So I did. The rest of the evening was a blur. I became very drowsy after taking a soda from the man. It turned out he'd spiked it. I woke up later on a bed at some cheap hotel, with Gold Tooth trying to rip my underwear off. I screamed, struggling to fight him off . . ." She paused briefly, her breath uneven. "He wouldn't let me go, yelling in his alcohol breath that he'd paid one thousand *yuan* to deflower me, that my father owed him a lot of money, and that he could have his way with me anytime he wanted. I became so angry I pushed him away with all my strength, grabbed my clothes, and ran out the door." She looked away into the distance, as if she was talking about someone else.

"Hong . . ."

"I didn't go home that night, or the night after, afraid that my father would turn me over to Gold Tooth again. I hid at a friend's place. On the third morning, I borrowed some money and boarded a train for Shanghai. I couldn't bear the sight of Yancheng again. I really should have left home long before. They never loved me—my old man and my mother. I was nothing more than a slave to them." She bit her lower lip.

Pei shook her head. "I'm so sorry."

"But I have to thank them in the end." Hong looked up for the first time. "If I hadn't left home, I wouldn't be here. I wouldn't be having this fine cup of coffee with you, now would I?" She winked, a hint of smile on her face. "You know, Shanghai is a fascinating place. I just love—" She raised her hand to stop a passing waitress. "Hey, bring me a pack of Salem, would you?"

Hong turned back to Pei, her composure completely regained. She was almost like a different person now.

"For all its charm, Shanghai is a Sahara when it comes to job opportunities. I tried out a few odd jobs at three-star hotels there, cleaning rooms, waiting tables, doing whatever I could, but I was always tired and broke." Hong paused for emphasis. She went on to tell Pei how she'd run into a few Chinese working in Japan two years before, and how they all said Japan was an easy place to make a fortune. All one needed to enter the country was a visa as a language student.

"When I heard that you only needed proof of a twelve-year education for the visa, I started thinking seriously about Japan. I quickly had a fake diploma made for me. Only later did I realize I also had to pay the first six months of tuition as part of the application. You know how much the tuition costs. I didn't have that kind of money, and I was devastated."

The waitress came back with Hong's cigarettes on a silver tray. Hong left a one-thousand-yen note on the tray and deftly snagged a cigarette from the pack. She tapped it against the glass tabletop. "But I'm not the type to give up. Someone later suggested I find a sponsor in Japan—a person who could help with the tuition. I started hanging around five-star hotels, hoping to meet a tourist or businessman from Japan. I did meet a few Japanese men, but none of them were helpful. I was becoming quite desperate. Finally, I convinced the owner of a bar near a five-star hotel to let me work there as a part-time hostess."

"That's how you got started?"

"It paid off. The place turned out to be a gold mine for meeting Japanese businessmen. And a year ago, I met Mr. Ishida."

Becoming more animated as she told her story, Hong went on to say that Mr. Ishida was married with children, but frequently visited Shanghai to watch over a construction project. She and Ishida soon began an affair, and she became his steady girlfriend during his frequent trips to Shanghai. When she first suggested a move to Japan, he was reluctant. But he eventually agreed to become her sponsor. On her arrival in Tokyo six months ago, he helped her pay the first year tuition at Yoneda. He even rented her an apartment.

But Ishida's wife soon discovered their affair. She immediately threatened him with a divorce. Ishida panicked. He started making plans to end the relationship, all the while pretending nothing had changed with Hong. Then one day he stopped calling. Whenever Hong would ring his office, he would avoid her calls, pretending he was out of the office or otherwise busy with a customer.

"Men are such weasels. They promise you the moon when they want to sleep with you. But the minute they're caught, they slink back home like puppies with their tails between their legs. But I was no dummy, thank God for that. I'd stashed enough money in the bank for just such a day. And a few days after we broke up, I found a job."

"That's the hostess bar job you mentioned?"

Hong nodded. "Except we call it a club. The place is run by a Taiwanese woman—a very shrewd woman, I might add. She opened the club in Shinjuku a few years back when the economy was booming. It's a tiny space, but Mama-san has hired five hostesses: three Chinese and two Taiwanese. We alternate working three nights a week, from seven-thirty to half past midnight."

Hong said the job involved flirting with the customers, who were either lonely salary men in need of pampering or overworked executives looking for a good time. Her job was to comfort them with soothing words and happy laughs.

"You hand-feed them food, you wipe their mouths—you pretty much treat them like you would a baby, short of putting diapers on them. Ha! It's no accident that hostess clubs here are called babysitting services for overgrown boys."

Hong, who was sniffling a bit, was suddenly overcome by a coughing fit. She cleared her throat, leaned toward the table, and to Pei's great dismay, spit into her Noritake cup. Pei flinched. Although she wasn't sure what Noritake ware was worth, she could see that they were beautiful cups.

Hong carried on as if nothing had happened. "You know, you can learn so much about Japanese society working as a hostess. I just love it. I mean, where else can you get paid two thousand yen an hour to chat with guys?"

Pei frowned. "I thought you said you could make more than twelve thousand yen in five hours. But at two thousand yen an hour, that only adds up to about ten thousand yen a night."

"Well, most of us start out at that rate. But you earn more after six months. And if you can bring extra business to the club or have the customers order a bottle of whiskey, you make another twenty percent in commission. Not bad, huh?" Hong raised her eyebrows at Pei.

"So that's why you see women dragging customers into their clubs from the streets."

"It's a big incentive. Plus, I get tips from customers. I'm one of the best girls there. In a good month, I could pull in three, four hundred thousand yen. That's two, three thousand dollars right there, all cash!" Hong rubbed her thumb and forefinger together.

"Three thousand dollars!" Pei swallowed hard. That was almost an entire year's of her salary at Number One Department Store.

"That's not all. You get lots of perks too, like free dinners and gifts from customers." Hong flashed a ruby ring at Pei. "See? This is from Mr. Tanaka, who comes to see me almost every night. Okay, he's a bit greasy, and he's got awful bad breath, but he's loyal and always brings in a friend or two to help me 'generate business.' He's a money god, and thanks to him, I'm the best-paid girl at the club." Hong gave a self-satisfied grin.

"Hong ... how did you find this job?"

"Why? You interested?"

Pei nodded shyly. "Although, I'm already in my thirties. You don't suppose—"

"How old are you exactly?"

"Thirty-four." Pei could hear the lie in her voice.

Hong grimaced. "If I were you, I'd stretch the truth a bit. In this line of business, everyone lies. And Japanese men like their women young and naïve, you know what I mean?"

Hong reached for her lighter, but Pei grabbed it and quickly lit the cigarette for her. Hong took a deep puff and slowly exhaled. Even in the early afternoon, the whole café was fogged up with smoke. It seemed everyone was smoking but Pei.

"I bet they'd believe you if you say you're twenty-eight."

"Would they really?" Flattered, Pei held up her chin with the back of her hand.

"Of course they would. But you should buy some nice clothes, visit a beauty salon, and fix yourself up a bit." Hong gave Pei's unkempt, shoulder-length hair a disapproving look. "The good news is, Mama's always looking for fresh faces. If I put in a good word, I think we can get you in."

Back in the classroom, Mrs. Ohashi wrote a whole new series of expressions on the whiteboard. But Pei had trouble focusing on what she was saying. Her mind was racing with images of her potential new life, sitting at a fancy Japanese club, pouring whiskey for men in suits. The wall of liquor bottles, the dim lights. She remembered reading somewhere in a local newspaper that there were three kinds of jobs open to new Chinese immigrants in Japan: the standing kind, the sitting kind, and the lying down kind. The least-paying jobs were also the toughest, requiring the worker to stand all day. Ironically, the best-paying jobs were also the easiest—jobs that required you to lie down. Jobs that could turn a couple of hours into a pile of hard cash!

She remembered that her mother suggested she take a job working as a kitchen helper near her school. But those jobs only paid 750 yen an hour, which was Japan's minimum wage.

Minimum wage! Pei couldn't imagine putting herself through the humiliation of working all night in a grimy kitchen for minimum wage now that she knew she could be making three times as much just sitting down. *TO GET RICH IS GLORIOUS!* She remembered the paramount leader Deng Xiaoping's golden words. The hostess job was sounding more and more appealing. For two thousand yen an hour, she saw nothing wrong with pouring whiskey for businessmen. There was no rule that said she had to have sex with them. She was not a child; she should be able to fend off drunken men speaking dirty to her. But what should she say to her sister if she came to her with a job offer? Then there was her mother. How was she to mention the word "club" to her mother?

That night, Pei lay wide awake in her bed, her head spinning. One minute she imagined going shopping with Hong to buy work clothes in Ginza; another minute she saw the angry face of her mother, her mouth spitting out some incoherent words. She didn't fall asleep until the small hours of the morning.

Six

Vivian had been sitting comatose at her desk at Amano Enterprises, staring at a blank notepad in front of her. She was thinking about Peter, wondering how he was doing. She could still see him reading *Orientations* in his leather chair at his Central Park West apartment with his gold-rimmed glasses lowered to the tip of his nose.

Three years had passed since Vivian broke up with Peter. Twelve years older, Peter was an art history professor at New York University, where Vivian had majored in Asian Art History. Peter was one of her teachers, and he almost immediately took an interest in Vivian. Peter said he liked her spunk and artistic temperament, but Vivian knew better—he was really a Rice King at heart, much preferring Asian women to Western ones. He kept telling her how going out with her reminded him of his college days as an exchange student in Taiwan. The courtship lasted four years, but since their breakup she hadn't heard a peep from him. Coming back to Tokyo was partly an attempt to forget Peter, but so far it hadn't worked. Often she still had to resist an urge to call him or write him a short note.

Vivian felt something crawling on the back of her neck. Startled, she shrugged her shoulders and shook her head violently. She turned and saw it was only a small fly, which eventually landed on a windowsill.

Vivian pushed her glasses back into place and refocused her attention on her notepad. From a couple of desks away came Becky's chatty voice, "And yes, do check out the health resort

Kamalaya when you go. It's sooo divine . . ." There she went again! Becky Sampson, the copywriter, was supposed to be verifying some finer points with a freelance translator about an article but ended up having a long, windy chat with him about a trip she'd taken to Bali. Typical!

Vivian slouched back into her chair with a groan. Having no work could be a lot worse than having too much work. She put her notepad away and cleaned the clutter on her desk. She needed to look busy, that much she knew. She gazed out the window; the fly was buzzing and battering itself against the pane. *You can see where you want to go, but you can't get there. That makes the two of us.* She closed her eyes.

Vivian, I beg of you, can't you find your sister a job? It was her mother's voice. She wished her dad were still around in Tokyo. She wished her dad were more like a real father who'd assume some of his rightful responsibilities as a parent.

Growing up, Vivian had benefited very little from her father's guidance or support. He had been an absentee dad since she graduated from middle school. While her friends from high school looked to their fathers for advice on college and career choices, Vivian had to find every single job on her own; her mother wasn't much help because she didn't understand much Japanese or about the way of the world.

Vivian considered running to a newsstand for a copy of the *Arubeito News*, the best employment magazine in Tokyo. Then again, she'd better not. Not with Noriko Wada, the executive secretary, lurking around.

Noriko had been Yuji Amano's personal secretary for ten years. At thirty-three, she was at least twenty-four years younger than the boss, but she acted more like his mother than his assistant. In part because Amano was frail, divorced, and living alone, Noriko followed him everywhere, carrying his briefcase for him, picking lint off his jacket, arranging his doctors' appointments for him. She'd even do flower arrangements at his house when he had an occasional guest. He couldn't do anything without her. And because he seldom made it to his luxurious office more than once a week, Noriko had become the de facto boss of the staff.

Noriko was fiercely protective of Amano. Convinced the foreign employees were somehow out to get her boss, she wanted to make darn sure no one got away with anything that wasn't work. To make certain nothing escaped her eagle eye she'd even arranged the desks so she faced all three of the foreign staff members across the spacious hallway. Vivian, Becky, and Patricia were also forced to punch a time card whenever they came in or out, so leaving the office without a good excuse was unthinkable. The only time they were spared this requirement was during their lunch breaks, and even then, they had to watch the clock carefully.

Vivian looked at her watch: 11:30—another half-hour to go. She peered up from her desk. Becky was still on the phone; it would be another two hours before Patricia was to arrive.

"Hey, what's with that long face?" Becky asked five minutes later, ambling over to Vivian's desk, her pink coffee mug in one hand.

Vivian shook her head. "These stupid rules! Why do the folks here insist on treating us like preschoolers? What's it to them if we go out just a couple of minutes early?"

"Shhhh!" Becky cocked her head, suggesting that Noriko and her assistant, Teruko, were within earshot.

Becky was a forty-something former magazine editor from New York. Soft, round, and vivacious, she had a full head of wild blonde locks that reminded Vivian of Bette Midler. From the first day, she had liked Becky, not only because she was fun and witty, but also because she was the only person in Japan with whom she could talk about New York. Vivian had fond memories of her days in Manhattan, when she was a graduate student at NYU. Seven years ago she went to New York on a trip and fell in love with the city and the art scene. She ended up staying, after deciding to pursue a master's degree at the university. Only Becky could fully appreciate it when she said she missed eating in Little Italy or the strip of Indian restaurants on East 6th Street, shopping at Zabar's, and hanging out in Washington Square. Within a few weeks of joining the company, Vivian had adopted Becky as her confidante and life consultant. From Vivian's messy breakup with Peter, to her sister coming to Japan, to any work-related gossip, whatever was on Vivian's mind would land in Becky's ear sooner or later.

After making sure Noriko and Teruko had walked off to the copy room, Becky gave Vivian's shoulder a light pat. "Hey, we're paid to sit here; so there. Try to look on the bright side. We're paid twenty bucks an hour to read the paper. It can't be that bad!" She chuckled, handing Vivian a copy of the *Mainichi Daily*.

Vivian took the paper half-heartedly. "Want to have lunch today? I need your advice."

"Okay. How about Mugen? Haven't been there in a while."

"Deal!"

Becky had been with Amano Enterprises for almost three years. The official copywriter and "communications manager," she was also responsible for teaching English twice a week to the thirty-plus Japanese employees working at half a dozen Amano subsidiaries dotted on the west end of Shibuya. Not only was she the only foreigner who had stayed with the company longer than two years, she was also the only foreigner who had ever worked there full-time.

Before Vivian joined the company there had been a string of part-time foreign staff that came and went like pollinating bees. There was Kiki from Ghana, Alain from France, Mamba from Nairobi, and Sami from Finland. A month after Vivian had her interview with Amano, a tall German blonde named Patricia Seibert came to the office unannounced. She'd met Amano briefly at a party and decided to surprise him by making a quick visit. He gave her a job on the spot.

Vivian knew why these *gaijin* workers came to Amano— she'd been in their shoes herself. He not only gave them a decent salary with little real work required, but he also offered them a much-coveted work visa. In those days, few companies would offer a foreigner a work visa for less than a full-time commitment. Working for Amano essentially meant they were free to do whatever they wanted on the side while enjoying legal immigration status.

Most of the foreigners who came knocking on Amano's door were wannabe artists or former English teachers looking for a break. Patricia, who fancied herself a jazz singer, was no exception. By night, she worked at a piano bar in Akasaka Mitsuke, and by day, for three afternoons a week, she hung around Amano's office pretending to be a Japanese-German interpreter. Her work didn't go much beyond the occasional teaching and translation for Amano's many dubious side businesses. Most of the time she just sat at her desk painting her nails or setting up her nightclub gigs.

"So, what do you think is wrong with Amano? Why does he hire all these foreign staff when he doesn't have any real work for them?" Vivian had asked Becky one day.

"You know, I really think we're meant to be Amano's poodles, his show dogs," Becky had said with a laugh. "Whether we do any real work or not is unimportant. We're something exotic and meant for display, period."

"Show dogs! That sounds about right, except for one thing—I'm not one of the dogs. I'm not *exotic* enough for Amano." Vivian pulled her eyes to make them look more slanted. "You know why he hired me? Because he felt guilty about the Chinese."

"Guilty? How's that?"

"When I came in for the interview, he let slip that he believes he owes it to the Chinese to be nice to them. He was a soldier during the Sino-Japanese War. Evidently, when he was fleeing from the People's Liberation Army soldiers at the end of the war in 1945, a Chinese family in a village near Xi'an saved his life by hiding him in a potato cellar."

"He told you that?"

Vivian had nodded. "That said, I think he really prefers Westerners in his heart." She reminded Becky of a promotional photo shoot he'd arranged a couple of months earlier. On that day, Amano had come in all dressed up in his silver Italian suit and politely asked Becky and Patricia to accompany him to a nearby studio. But he hadn't said a word to Vivian. Vivian later found out that even Brian from the travel section had been invited to the photo shoot. She was the only foreign employee deliberately left out.

"You see, Amano wanted the 'international image,' which in his mind means being with people with blond hair and blue eyes. I guess I look too much like any other Japanese."

"Okay, you're not a poodle, but you're still a dog. Perhaps a garden mutt?" Becky had said mischievously with a laugh.

Vivian had shrugged.

At 11:59, Vivian and Becky finally slipped out of the office together. Mugen, tucked down a back street near their office in Shibuya, was a macrobiotic Japanese health food restaurant popular with local expatriates. Decorated with simple wooden designs and blue-dyed fabrics, Mugen exuded a tranquility that was reminiscent of a Zen teahouse. Burning incense, low-hanging ink painting scrolls, and the soft background music of the *shakuhachi* flute added to the ambiance. They each ordered a 1,200-yen lunch special that came with a tofu entrée, steamed seasonal vegetables, brown rice, and miso soup.

"So, Viv, what's on your mind?" Becky asked as they drank hot buckwheat tea.

"It's my sister . . ." Vivian slowly recounted the many trials and tribulations of her mother's efforts to get Pei adjusted to life in Tokyo.

"Get this: my sister has only been here ten weeks. She barely speaks Japanese, and I was given the formidable task of finding her a job."

Becky raised an eyebrow. "Not that it's impossible."

"Perhaps not. But you're not the one trying to find that one percent of employers willing to take on a non-Japanese speaker." Vivian paused to let the waitress warm up their tea, then snorted, "She would be darn lucky if someone wanted her for a kitchen helper."

"Why? You don't think she can handle a job like that?"

"No, I don't. You don't know my sister. She has this attitude that she deserves to be handed a lucrative, white-collar job on a silver platter."

Vivian went on to recount how Pei had walked out on her janitor's job. "You know, most Chinese students start out doing these kinds of menial jobs. I can't understand why she thinks it's beneath her."

"Probably because she knows she can count on you and your family to support her financially for a while," Becky said flatly. "Who wouldn't want to take the easy way out if they could?"

Vivian waved a hand in exasperation. "She's unrealistic. Sure, our parents are here, but Mom's broke and she never learned to save a dime when she could. As for Dad, he's such a cheap ass. I'd be really surprised if he ended up paying the full-year tuition for her Japanese language school. If she got all her schooling paid for, she would be way ahead of most other newcomers here. Even so, she'll still need to earn some money on her own. There's no free lunch in the real world, and the sooner she learns that, the better off she'd be." Vivian wagged her hand excitedly, accidentally knocking her teacup across the table.

"Hey, calm down!" Becky spoke soothingly as she wiped up the spilled tea with a napkin. "Look at how worked up you are!" she laughed.

"I just don't understand why she's so demanding with everyone. She expects us to cater to her every whim. It's not like she's twelve. She's thirty-eight!"

Becky frowned. "Vivian, I think you need to be more patient with her. Sure, your sister can't expect you and your family to help her forever, but you have to allow her some time to find her feet."

Vivian thought for a moment. "You know what her problem is? She has been in China too long. In China, under the socialist system, everything is, and has been, about connections and who you know. You don't apply or compete for jobs, you wait for your parents to retire and save their jobs for you, or for them to pull strings to secure a job for you under the table. But it doesn't work that way here in Japan or in the U.S. for that matter. Ultimately you have to go out and hustle yourself for a job. I certainly had to do that all by myself to get where I'm, as my good-for-nothing dad didn't lift a finger to help me with anything. Yet my sister has all these unrealistic expectations on me and my mom to "fast forward" her to a better life without her paying her dues. Well, it doesn't work that way outside of China. And it's particularly aggravating when she doesn't even acknowledge that we're doing all these things for her. It's as if she's saying 'we owe it to her'. It's just so incredibly annoying."

"So how's that you and your family managed to leave China, but not your older sister?" Becky asked.

That was when Vivian told her friend about the strict Hong Kong immigration law banning all Chinese immigrating families from bringing more than two children per household in the early 1960s, and how her mother's final effort at retrieving Pei in 1965 failed because of the outbreak of the Cultural Revolution. "I know it could have been me staying back in China, but sometimes, it pays to be the younger sibling. It was pure luck on my part, I guess," Vivian added.

"Then I can see how your sister is so upset with your mother and you, being the only one in the family made to stay behind. Not to mention she has yet to make some monumental adjustments to a new way of living here. Just think how lucky you and your younger brother are. Compared to her, you two had it made. Now how about trying to be more patient with her instead of complaining?"

Vivian felt her annoyance growing. Why would Becky take her sister's side instead of hers? She used to be so much more understanding and supportive. Hadn't she been listening?

A Japanese waitress dressed in a blue cotton kimono arrived with their food. "*Omatasei shimashita,*" she said, putting their trays down.

On a dark lacquer tray laid an ornate basket filled with delicately prepared tofu and salmon tempura. Next to the basket, a splatter of small, dainty plates held sweet pickled plums, marinated mushrooms, and steamed carrots and yam. In addition to the miso soup and rice, their trays also included a potato salad served in an aqua-colored, lotus-shaped dish.

A love of Japanese food was something Vivian and Becky both shared. Their conversation instantly shifted to the food and Becky's recent trip to Southeast Asia, crowding out the subject of Pei.

The afternoon flew by. Luckily for Vivian, she was kept busy by the company's latest project—a brand new art gallery that her boss had decided to open in a bid to make Amano Enterprises appear more sophisticated as a business. The new art director of the gallery wanted Vivian to help out with the translation of an exhibition catalog for the gallery opening. For the first show, featuring five contemporary Chinese artists and a total of thirty paintings, there was a rush to finish all the background information. This left Vivian with over thirty pages of translation to wade through. Finally, this was a subject she could relate to. She wished Peter could have seen her there—he would have been proud of her.

☙—☙

Two days later, Vivian found herself waiting near Ueno Station for her sister. Caught in an unexpected rainstorm, she stood drenched under the narrow awning of a fruit stand, her hands struggling to balance the two heavy shopping bags she was carrying.

A cold drop of water hit her forehead from the canopy. Vivian put down her bags and dug deep into her handbag for a handkerchief, but the best she could come up with was a wrinkled piece of tissue paper. She decided the tissue could best be used to wipe off the water drops on her eyeglasses, which were now clouding her vision. She put her glasses back on and searched for her sister in the direction of the station. The station exit was a splatter of colorful umbrellas, but there was no sign of Pei anywhere. Vivian stretched her dampened sleeve to bare her wristwatch: 4:45. Pei should have been here fifteen minutes ago.

From her handbag, Vivian took out the *Arubeito News* to confirm the address. Yes, the restaurant should be in that alley-way. She tore a page from the magazine to mop the rain from her hair. Another five minutes dragged by. *Damn it! Where is she? She's always late!*

Vivian was just about to cross the street to make a phone call to her sister when she spotted Pei rushing over from the station. "Why are you so late?" she snapped. *Mainland folks never have any respect for time,* she thought.

"Oh, I got delayed in the traffic," Pei said unhurriedly. "You should have seen it. The station was packed with people seeking shelter from the rain. It was hard to pass by them."

Vivian clicked her tongue. "The least you could do is to apologize for being late. I've been waiting for twenty minutes in the rain, you know," Vivian said, her eyes burning with anger. One thing she couldn't stand about her sister was her perpetual inability to say "thank you" or "I'm sorry," a trademark of the Mainland Chinese folks.

"I was only a little late. What's the big deal?" Pei asked, frowning.

"It's so like you Mainland folks—you're never punctual. Not only that, it never even occurred to you that you have inconvenienced other people!" Vivian glared at her sister. It never occurred to Vivian that her remarks could be hurtful to her sister. Pei opened her mouth to say something, but nothing came out.

"Forget it. Let's go sit down somewhere and get your resume done properly." Vivian turned down Pei's offer to share her umbrella and went on ahead in the rain in search of the nearest café. Pei followed awkwardly, her umbrella bumping repeatedly into the awnings of stores along the way.

At the café table, Pei handed Vivian two resume forms: one blank and clean, the other wrinkled and scribbled with ink. The scribbled one was a draft written in Chinese. Using Pei's draft as a guideline, Vivian filled out the blank form in Japanese. When she handed the form back to Pei, she pointed out that the age box had been left blank in the original.

"How old should I say I am?" Pei asked, looking at the form.

Vivian thought for a minute. "Say you're thirty-three. Otherwise they might worry you're not tough enough for the job."

Pei nodded and penned "33" in the box, then folded the form neatly in a white envelope and carefully tucked it away in her handbag.

"You know what to say at the interview, right?" Vivian asked.

"Of course," Pei looked at Vivian in a way that said, "What do you take me for?"

"Don't forget to say you'll do whatever they ask, that you will give it your best."

Pei nodded, a frown on her face.

"And don't forget to bow and smile a lot."

"Please, can you stop treating me like a child? I'm not an idiot!"

Vivian gave her sister a dubious look. "It's late. Let's go."

A few doors away, the two stopped at a Japanese bar-restaurant. Hoisted in front of its entrance was a large white lantern with the word *Tombo* written on it in bold brush work—the Dragonfly. The door had been left ajar. Vivian peeked in. This early in the evening, the dimly lit restaurant looked barely open. The two walked inside.

The place was rather small, with just eight seats by the counter and three narrow tables, each barely big enough for four people. A bald, fifty-something Japanese man who called himself Ogawa came from the back to greet them. Dangling a cigarette in his mouth, he motioned the two to sit by the counter.

Mr. Ogawa took a quick glance at Pei's resume. "Which one of you is applying for the job?" He squinted from behind the counter, taking the cigarette briefly out of his mouth.

"She is," Vivian said, pointing to Pei.

Mr. Ogawa eyed Pei skeptically. "You speak Japanese?"

"Yes, a little," Pei said, smiling self-consciously.

"How long have you been in Japan?"

"Uh, six months," Pei said meekly.

There was an awkward silence. Vivian kicked Pei's leg lightly below the counter, urging her to speak some more Japanese. But Pei would not move her lips.

"This could be a problem," Mr. Ogawa said slowly, his hand rubbing his chin. "It's like this: I need a waitress badly, but you are not it. Your Japanese is just not there yet. And you don't have any experience waiting tables." He dropped the resume on the counter. "Tell you what. I could use a part-time kitchen helper for a while, until our busboy comes back from the hospital. He had a motorcycle accident, you see. You interested?"

Pei nodded.

Mr. Ogawa laid out the work conditions, which involved working five hours, from six to eleven, four nights a week, for 750 yen an hour. The job would involve helping the main chef prepare food, washing dishes, and cleaning up the kitchen. When the phone rang, Ogawa went to answer it behind the counter.

"Seven hundred fifty yen is not bad, wouldn't you say?" Vivian asked, seizing the opportunity to sound Pei out.

"I guess so."

"Look, you will make some money and practice your Japanese. It's a good deal."

"I suppose."

"Then it's decided," Vivian said.

When Ogawa returned from his phone call, Vivian helped make arrangements to have Pei begin working the following day.

On the way back to the station, Vivian kept hoping Pei would thank her for all she'd done. But other than offering Vivian part of her umbrella against the drizzle, Pei remained quiet. Vivian wanted to say something, but gritted her teeth.

"Oh, I almost forgot," Vivian said at the station, grabbing hold of Pei's shirtsleeve just before the two were to part for their respective train platforms,. "These are for you." She handed Pei the two large shopping bags she'd been carrying. "If I'd known it was going to rain so hard, I'd have waited."

"What's in them?"

"Some clothes I don't wear anymore. Thought you might be able to use them."

"Oh!" her sister uttered coldly.

"Of course you're not obliged to wear them if you don't like them." Despite her gripe with her sister, Vivian did take to heart Becky's advice on becoming more understanding of Pei. She thought her used clothes might help her sister save some money. When she was a student at NYU, she was used to taking hand-me-downs from school friends and their parents. She always welcomed them as gifts because they helped her a lot as a struggling student paying her own dues and tuition. Little did she know that hand-me-downs were considered inappropriate gifts by many Mainlanders, particularly because the idea of recycling hadn't caught on with the Chinese in the 90s.

"I know," Pei said, taking the bags and turning to leave.

Vivian looked at the back of her sister and shook her head. *What did the woman want?* Whatever she did, there was just no pleasing of her sister. She was a lost cause.

Seven

Pei barely said hello to her mother when she got home.

"You hungry? Dinner's on top of the fridge," her mother said.

"Umm."

"What's wrong? Didn't you like Ogawa-san?" her mother asked causally, as Pei hung her coat up by the door.

Pei spun around, a surprised look on her face. "How do *you* know we talked to someone by that name?"

"Your sister told me."

"She called you just now? Does she report *everything* to you?"

"Pretty much so, and I expect her to. You don't think that's right?"

"No, I don't!"

"Why not?"

"*Why*? You should know why."

"What're you talking about?" Her mother was clearly struggling to remain calm. "Are you trying to pick a fight with me?"

"I'm sick and tired of you two sticking your noses into everything I do. I'm not a child, I can take care of myself," Pei said, stomping off to her room and sliding the screen door shut. She wished the room had a real door instead of the flimsy paper screen. She couldn't even have the satisfaction of banging it shut to make a point.

"Sticking our noses into your business? I think not. We did it because we *care* about you," her mother shot back.

"Care about me? That's laughable!"

Her mother ignored the barb, and the room fell silent. Pei could hear the sound of their next-door neighbors' TV seeping through the thin wall.

"Hey, your bags! Don't leave them by the door!" her mother called from the living room a few minutes later. "They look bulky. What's in them?"

"Just some *garbage* from Meiyin. I thought she tells you everything."

She heard a loud rustling of plastic bags. "Say, these look nice. Have you seen them yet?"

"Mother, what do you think you're doing? Just leave them alone!" Pei said, poking her head out of her room.

"Look at this wool jacket—it still has a price tag on it," her mother carried on.

Despite herself, Pei came out of her room. She saw her mother holding a charcoal gray jacket with a thin lapel and gasped. "Good heavens!"

"No? Don't like it? How about this one?" Her mother held up a navy-blue wool dress in her other hand.

Pei frowned. She squatted down next to her mother to pick over the clothes, which were now scattered all over the floor. She saw a lot of navy and black in the pile. "Ugh. They're clothes you'd wear to a funeral." Pei threw the clothes on the floor and sulked back to her room, but this time left the screen door open.

"It's not that you don't approve of the colors. It's more because they're used clothes, right, Pei?"

Pei did not answer. In China, when Pei and her sister were still little girls, Pei always got new clothes. Vivian, as the younger daughter, was always the one who got the hand-me-downs. Pei found it strange that she should be on the receiving end of this cycle now.

"They say, 'When you're hungry, you are not picky about your food.' You can't afford to buy new clothes yet. You haven't even started working." Her mother folded the clothes neatly and put them back in the bags. "If I were you, I would take them graciously."

"But I'm not you, Mother. I have my own clothes. Besides, I didn't come all the way from China just to take some old, crappy clothes from Meiyin. I'd much rather wait and buy new clothes in the latest fashion with my *own* money now that I have a job." Pei sat at the desk in her room and spoke with her back to her mother. "My philosophy is: If it's not new, I'd rather not have it at all. I've worn enough old clothes during my childhood at your mean brother's house.

"Besides, Meiyin was extremely rude to me today—she yelled to my face, saying 'you Mainland folks are never on time' when I arrived a little late at the train station this afternoon. To her, I'm not her sister, but some Mainlander person she can't stand. And in her eyes, all Mainlanders are some country bumpkins with no culture. It never occurred to her that it was downright rude to address me as such. So like hell I'll wear Meiyin's hand-me-downs just so she can feel good about herself. I won't give her that satisfaction!"

"Where did you get this stinky pride?" her mother snapped. "Here your sister is trying to help you save money and you take it as an insult! And yes, you may have a job now, but I tell you, I had to plead with your sister to help you find this job, so you'd better do your best to keep it this time."

"You *what*?" Pei twisted her body to face her mother, her eyes narrowed in fury. "You're such a busybody, I swear. If you had so much time on your hands, you should have learned how to keep your husband happier so he wouldn't run away," she blurted. She hadn't meant to say it like that, but it was too late to take it back now. And although she didn't think her mother was entirely to blame for her parents' break up, she did loath Yan for not having tried harder to keep the family together. If only her parents were still together, she and her mother certainly wouldn't be stuck together in this rat hole. Her mother! She was so useless! She never tried hard enough for anything.

"You shut your mouth, you ungrateful brat!" her mother shouted with a raised arm, as if ready to smack Pei across her face. She was now red all the way down to her neck. "You don't know anything, so don't you dare make judgments about me." She stood by the *fusuma* door, glaring hatefully at Pei for what seemed like an eon. Finally, she took a deep breath and walked away.

The house fell silent again. Pei could hear the neighbor's bathwater running. She took her notebooks out of her school bag, scattering them on her desk. At times like this she was grateful she had homework to turn to—a much-appreciated distraction from this "home" which she found increasingly suffocating. A couple of minutes later, Pei heard her mother sigh. Then the light in her room went out, followed by the closing of the *fusuma* door. After that, all was quiet.

In her tiny bedroom, Pei felt free again. Nighttime had become her favorite time. These were the only hours she could claim as her own, away from the watchful eyes and constant nagging of her mother. She pulled her chair up closer to her desk and began rummaging through her school bag for her pocket-sized dictionary. She touched something small and soft. She opened her bag and saw that it was a small blue felt box. Ah, the present!

In the heated argument with her mother, Pei had forgotten all about this little surprise. She opened the box and carefully drew out an exquisite moonstone set on a gold ring—a gift from Hong. Pei slipped the ring onto her middle finger, stretched her hand against the light, pleased with its pale blue shimmer.

"Here, Pei, would you like to have this ring?" Hong had asked her during their lunch break earlier that day.

"Don't you want to keep it?"

"No, I have too many of these darn rings lying around. I can't keep up with all the presents from my club patrons. What can you do? They all like to buy gifts to please me."

Pei had mentioned Hong to her mother a week earlier. She purposely focused on her friend's materialistic acquisitions, pointing out that her comfortable life was afforded by this night job of hers, which "only involved some singing and pouring drinks for customers."

"Sounds to me like a dancing girl's job," her mother had said in surprise. "You're not thinking of joining your friend at some sleazy bar, are you?"

"It's not what you think, Mother. Besides, it pays three times what you make as a waitress," Pei had countered.

"Pei, you have only been in Japan for three months, and already you are getting these funny ideas. Don't forget: you are a mother of two, and no child would be proud of a mother who sells smiles and flesh for a living."

"Who said anything about selling flesh?" Pei had been jarred by her mother's choice of words. Did her mother think she would really sink so low as to consider prostitution? Hong had said no one could force her to do anything that she didn't want to do. All she had to do was pour liquor and crack jokes with clients. What could be so wrong with that?

Still, the mention of her two sons left her feeling uneasy. She thought of Da Shan and Da Hai, and was reminded of the many letters she'd sent them. Guomin must have intercepted them because she never heard from the boys. Her repeated calls to Guomin's house didn't help. He always hung up on her the minute he heard her voice. Pei had wanted to tell them everything about what she was going through, but she also wondered what they would say if they knew she was contemplating taking a hostess job. Would they understand that she was doing this mostly because of them, that she had so many plans for them, but all of them required money?

Well, if they didn't know now, they would someday, Pei decided. In fact, they might even appreciate the fact that her leaving China would open doors for them. How else could she find better opportunities for the two of them? Someday they would see that by her leaving, she was essentially ensuring their chances of entering Western universities and eventually seeing the world. They wouldn't have to be stuck in China like she was. They would see.

When Pei arrived at Tombo late in the afternoon the following day, Mr. Ogawa was already waiting. He was eager to show her to the kitchen hidden behind the high counter. Although small, the kitchen was neat and well organized. At one end there was a stove. Nearby, on a low end table, a dozen pots and pans were stacked up in three piles. In the middle and right behind the counter laid a long chopping board for cutting vegetables and meat.

Directly behind the counter against a wall was a cupboard filled with dishes and plates in every shape and size imaginable—square dishes, round dishes, rectangular ones, and even fan-shaped ones, in hues of blue, white, brown, and light green. In the rear of the kitchen, a small washroom held two sinks and a couple of towel racks. This, Pei soon discovered, was where she'd be spending most of her time, washing and cleaning dishes.

After showing Pei the kitchen, Mr. Ogawa handed her a Japanese-style wrap-around apron and set her to work. Her first assignment was to help Mr. Hayashi, the chef, cut up two large bowls of white radishes. Mr. Hayashi, who looked to be in his mid-fifties, told Pei that the white daikon radish was an essential garnish for a variety of Japanese dishes.

Plump and light-hearted, the round-faced chef appeared to approach his work with a sense of joy. While cooking, he was always humming old Japanese love songs and making jokes, even though Pei couldn't understand most of the lyrics. He was kind to her, taking time to show her how to do her job properly. "Wait, Cho-san," he said, addressing Pei as Miss Cho—Cho being the Japanese reading of her surname, Zhang—"you cut the radish like this to make the slices thinner," he told her. "There, don't they look much better that way, like the waves of the sea?"

After the radishes, Mr. Hayashi gave Pei some cucumber and carrots to cut. With the help of a vegetable cutter, which looked very much like a cookie cutter, Pei was instructed to turn the carrots into shapes of maple leaves and plum blossoms. She'd never seen vegetables cut in such delicate, dainty shapes. In China, carrots were usually sculpted into shapes of exotic birds or trees. *Small, think small. Japanese have a love for things miniature*; Pei suddenly remembered this tidbit she'd read somewhere about the Japanese culture. So that's what they were talking about!

Things got more hectic toward evening, and Pei was kept so busy washing dishes in the back that she didn't even have time to go to the toilet. By the end of the night, she felt as though she'd learned a great deal about the Japanese food culture. Mr. Hayashi even taught her that there was a front view for every type of container served. For a half-moon plate, for example, the straight side was the front. All in all, it wasn't a bad start for a first day. Or so she thought.

"One second, Cho-san!"

Just as Pei was about to leave Tombo, having already changed into her street clothes and punched her time card, Mr. Ogawa came rushing from behind the cash register where he'd been sitting.

"I saw you signing out after you'd changed into your street clothes. That's company time, even if it's just a couple of minutes." Mr. Ogawa blocked her way with his folded arms, an irritated look on his face. "I don't know what you do in your country, but here in Japan you always change clothes on your own time. Is that clear?"

"It's her first day, Ogawa-san. I'm sure she didn't mean any harm," Mr. Hayashi said from the back kitchen, popping his head out.

"This doesn't concern you, Hayashi-kun. Go back to work." Mr. Ogawa waved the chef back into the kitchen, then turned back to Pei. "Another thing: I noticed you came in ten minutes late today. In Japan, when you work for someone, you must arrive at least five minutes before work is to begin. Otherwise, you'll inconvenience others and make a nuisance of yourself. This is something you must avoid at all costs. Do you understand?"

"Uh ... *hai*." Pei nodded. She felt her cheeks burning. She wanted to defend herself, but her imperfect Japanese failed her. She stood frozen by the restaurant door, as if waiting for permission to be dismissed.

"Take these rules to heart. Now that you're in Japan, you must do what the Japanese do. Otherwise, it would be meaningless for you to have come here."

"*Hai*, I understand!" Pei made a quick half bow and dashed out of the restaurant, her heart still pounding when she was out on the street. A few steps later, Pei realized she had left her train pass on top of the timer. Back at the entrance of the restaurant, now only distinguishable by the dim light coming from within, she hesitated. She gently slid opened the wooden sliding door, then froze. From inside the restaurant she could hear Ogawa raising his voice toward the back kitchen.

"Did you see? She didn't say a word when I pointed out all her faults. Bah! Someone once told me the Chinese never apologize for their mistakes. It turns out to be true."

"Give her some time. She's quite new to this country, didn't you say yourself?" Mr. Hayashi replied.

"And what if she doesn't change?" Mr. Ogawa grumbled. "Did you notice she was using the company phone to call home during the break? I couldn't believe my eyes. She's so clueless."

Pei gently slid the door shut again. She felt butterflies in her stomach. She had stood on her feet all evening washing dishes, her fingers swollen and her legs now sore, and this was her reward for a day of hard work? She decided to retrieve her train pass the following day.

On the train home, the restaurant scene replayed itself in her head over and over again. She wasn't used to being chided at work, especially over something that seemed so trivial. The more Pei thought about it, the angrier she became. In China, if she were ten, fifteen minutes late to work, nobody would bat an eye. And what was the fuss about changing into the uniform before punching in the time card? Why begrudge the two minutes it took to change one's clothes? How petty and small-minded! Pei had never liked her prickly former boss, Lao Wang, at the Number One Department Store. But compared to Mr. Ogawa, he seemed positively noble and generous.

Pei didn't mention the incident to her mother when she arrived home. She spent another night tossing and turning, pondering what to do about her new job.

The following day, Pei waited eagerly for Hong to come to class, but her seat was empty again. Her attendance had been erratic lately. During recess, she picked up a public phone in the hallway and dialed Hong's number.

"Hey, is that you, Zhang Peiyin? What're you doing calling me at this hour? Don't you have class?"

"Xiao Hong, I haven't seen you in two days. You okay?"

"Can't be better. Been really busy at the club, though. You know, I'm thinking seriously of quitting school—I can't get up so early in the morning anymore."

"Quit school? What about your visa? Don't you need the attendance record for your visa?"

"Not anymore! One of my regular clients has just offered me a job at his firm, complete with a work visa. The best part about the deal is that I don't have to go in every day."

"So that's it? I won't see you at school anymore?"

"Guess not. Why? Does it matter?"

"I—well, actually, I'd really like to see you."

"You mean now? I can't. I'm still in my nightgown."

"I could wait."

There was a brief silence. "You know what, why don't you come by my apartment? It'd be easier that way."

Half an hour later, Pei, having decided to cut the afternoon classes, arrived at Hong's posh apartment in Ebisu. Hong greeted her in a fancy pink nightdress. She gestured to Pei to sit on her white leather sofa and went to the kitchen to get some coffee.

Pei studied the apartment. The living room wasn't that large, but it had a hardwood floor. In the middle of the room stood a slick, round, glass-top dining table and four black leather chairs. There was a bay window and a quaint balcony, which let in the sunshine.

On the coffee table, Pei noticed an ashtray littered with cigarette butts. Scattered by the ashtray were five empty beer cans, some of them smeared with lipstick. It appeared Hong had had company the night before.

Hong came out of the kitchen with a coffeepot and two cups. She placed the cups on the glass table and poured Pei some coffee.

"So, what's going on?" she asked, sitting next to Pei.

"Xiao Hong, I desperately want to change jobs."

"Change jobs? Are you working now?"

Pei nodded. "I just started work as a helper at a restaurant yesterday," Pei said, avoiding Hong's gaze.

"A kitchen helper? You mean you're not even a waitress?" Hong snorted with contempt. "Why would you take a job like that?"

"My mother and sister kept pushing me, and I just couldn't say no."

"But the work is just too filthy, too demanding, right? See, I told you so."

"It's not even the work that upsets me. It's the boss." Pei told her friend about her first day at work. "I got the feeling that Mr. Ogawa doesn't like Chinese much."

"I've heard it all before."

"I don't understand the Japanese. Why are they so obsessed with time? My boss was watching me so closely I felt I couldn't even go to the toilet when I needed to go."

"At least your boss let you know early on that there's a problem," Hong said. "I know a young Kunming girl who worked as a janitor. After slaving away for a month, she went to collect her paycheck, only to find it was half of what she'd expected. Her employer told her it was because she had been late almost every morning, and all those five- or ten-minute periods had to be deducted from her paycheck under company rules. So each time she was late, she got a thirty-minute pay deduction from her wage. The fact was, she was pretty much close to being on time, but that was not good enough for the boss, who insisted that she should have been there ten minutes before her work began."

"That's it, Xiao Hong. I'm quitting today. I can't work like that."

"And then what?" Hong asked, lighting up a cigarette.

"I was hoping you might help me find a job at your club."

"At Club Asia?" Hong took a deep drag of her cigarette. "That's not a problem, except Mama-san would expect you to come in a little early too, just like the rest of the bosses here," she said, slowly blowing out the smoke.

Pei nodded. "At least the money would be a lot better."

"And your mother? Wouldn't she be upset about you quitting your restaurant job?"

"She doesn't have to know everything."

"Okay. I'll have a talk with Mama-san tonight," Hong said as she got up. She disappeared into her room and came out a few minutes later in a T-shirt and jeans. "You know, I don't understand. If your mother and sister are both here, why do they need you to work so urgently? Why can't they help you get by until you have finished language school?"

"Yeah, you would think that, except they're unreasonable people," Pei said, shaking her head. "Sometimes I feel like I don't really belong to that family."

Hong looked up. "What do you mean?"

"I'm just too embarrassed to say."

"Come on, you can tell me. Aren't we good friends?"

Pei looked down at the floor, her hands cradled in her lap. "Remember I told you once that my family got out and left me behind in China when I was eight?"

"Yes," Hong nodded.

"Sometimes I feel my mother and sister think of me as a poor cousin who has come to their door begging for food. They're so afraid of me asking for money. They tell me they want to help me save money because things are expensive here. But the truth is, what they really want to save are their own pockets."

Pei then told Hong about the used clothes Vivian had given her two days ago. "Now, if my sister was really interested in helping me, why couldn't she have just taken me to a department store and bought me new clothes, instead of treating me like a pan-handler?" She deliberately left out the part about Meiyin having given her one hundred thousand yen in gift money so she could make a stronger case for herself.

Hong nodded. "This sister of yours, what is it she does for a living?"

"She's an interpreter, or something close."

"An interpreter! Then she must make very good money, no?"

"I don't think she works full-time. She has several part-time jobs."

"Still, she's been out of China for a while, right?"

"Yes, since she was five."

"Five? How did she get out of China so much earlier than you?"

"Bad luck, I suppose," Pei said, heaving a long sigh. Then she told Hong about her parents' decision to leave her behind because of Hong Kong's immigration restrictions.

"So your mother forced you to stay?"

"Not exactly," Pei said, looking away. "She made my sister and I play a game of lot-drawing, and I lost."

"Did your mother try to come back for you?"

"She came back two years later, in 1965, after she had become a resident of Hong Kong. But by then immigration control in China began to tighten because of the Cultural Revolution, and no one was allowed to either leave or enter the border in Luohu. So in the end, she never came. "

Pei got up from the sofa and walked slowly toward the bay window. "I think I have a cursed fate," she said, pulling the curtains to one side, keeping her back to Hong so she could hide the tears that had been welling in her eyes. Swiftly, she wiped her cheeks dry with the back of one hand. "There's a popular proverb from the south that goes something like this: *This umbrella may look identical to the next one, but it has a completely different handle.* You know, that really sums up the story of my life."

"I know that one." Hong nodded sympathetically. "But let's see if we can't get that luck of yours to change."

Eight

I was Monday, Noriko's day off, and Teruko and Vivian always made a habit of going out to have lunch at a chic western-style deli near their office. In a matter of weeks after Vivian joined Amano Enterprises, she quickly found a kindred spirit in Teruko, and the two became steady lunch pals.

"Guess who I saw having dinner last night at the Golden Elephant?" Teruko said mysteriously to Vivian.

"Who?" Vivian asked, her eyes peering above her glasses.

"Patricia and Matsunaga," Teruko said, her brows raised for emphasis.

"Our Matsunaga? The rotund art director?"

"Yup!"

"Hey, let's not jump to conclusions. Maybe they'd run into each other on the street and decided to have a meal together. What's the big deal?"

"Yes, possible," Teruko said, then leaned closer and whispered, "but if that's the case, why would the two sit next to each other, with Matsunaga holding Patricia's hand?"

"They held hands?" Vivian paused, "Hmm, interesting. Wait, how old is Matsunaga—isn't he close to sixty?"

"Not quite. I think he's in his mid-fifties."

"But he's married, right?"

"Yup, with two beautiful grown daughters and a wife," Teruko said, wiping her mouth gently with a napkin. "Although I heard he doesn't go home to his wife anymore. They'd been living separately for some time now."

"Okay, I can see why he would find Patricia attractive, but what's in it for her? I mean, why a married man, and at his age? He could pass for her father. It's not like there aren't enough young, single guys out there."

"Who knows? Maybe she's bored. One thing I do know is that Matsunaga sometimes goes to Bar Blue, where she sings. Perhaps one thing led to another, and before you know it, things spin out of control."

"Geez, you sound like you're an old hand at this. Tell me, have you gone out with married men before?" Vivian always thought Teruko was a cute woman. With her baby face, large sparkly eyes and long eyelashes, Vivian was sure she would have no trouble attracting attention from the opposite sex.

"I wish." Teruko made a face. "My mother keeps such a tight leash on me I'd be lucky to get a date, any date. Get this: my curfew is midnight, and if I were even one minute late, I'd be grounded for a week." Teruko pursed her lips.

"Okay, so you have a tough mother. But that shouldn't stop you. Surely you've heard of love hotels, haven't you?" Vivian said meaningfully.

"Well, I wouldn't know the difference. You see, I'd never had a boyfriend," Teruko said sheepishly, her face a little red.

"What? You mean you're still . . .?" Vivian had to stop in mid-sentence. She didn't have the heart to spell it out, especially because she knew Teruko was twenty-seven.

Teruko went on to say that she was the only daughter and her parents were very protective of her. "Sometimes I wonder if I'd end up a spinster."

"Well, we have to do something about that," Vivian offered.

"Like what?"

"How about a blind date? Have you tried those before?"

"Blind dates? No, I don't do those. I've already been to many *omiai* meetings. My mom and my aunt are always trying to set me up with someone, but I never like any of the guys they introduce to me. I find the whole idea very forced, unnatural, and unromantic!"

"If that's how you feel, you ought to go to more parties and pubs. Say, a friend of mine is having a Salsa bar party this weekend. You want to go with me?"

"Actually," Teruko paused, "there's one guy that I'd really like to get to know. I was hoping you might be able to help me . . ."

"Oh? Who is it?"

"Do you know Watsu-san—the tall, handsome, blonde guy who works at Amano's travel company?"

"Ah, you mean Brian Watts?"

"Yes, that's him," Teruko nodded with a smile. She produced a card from her handbag. "You see, next Tuesday is Valentine's Day. I know that in America you exchange cards, so I went and bought this card thinking I will write something clever and leave it on his desk. But the problem is, I really don't know where to begin. Can you help me?"

"Sure." Vivian took the card and studied it closely. The card was pale pink with a big red heart in the center. "Hey, this is a brilliant idea, Teru-chan. I heard Brian has been in Japan for a while. So I'm sure he's used to getting chocolates from young ladies. But by sending him a card, you will no doubt separate yourself from the rest of the potential contenders. How smart of you! Now, what would you like to say to him?"

"I don't know. What does one say to a guy in a situation like this?"

"How about simply 'I'd like to take you out for lunch sometime. Would you be interested in coming'?"

"Isn't that a bit forward?"

"Teru-chan, the whole idea of sending someone a card is very forward. So why not get right to the point and say it like it is?"

"You don't suppose I would scare him away?"

"*No.* Not at all! In fact, I think he will be flattered, especially because it's an invitation from a charming girl like you."

"Think so?" Teruko asked with a shy smile.

"Absolutely!"

After lunch, Teruko had to run some errands, so Vivian went back to the office by herself. Once inside, Vivian noticed a giant bouquet of red roses sitting on Patricia's desk. Patricia was facing away from the office entrance. She didn't even see Vivian coming through the door.

"Wow, that's some bouquet. Who's that from, Patricia? A new admirer?"

"Oh that? Yup, from a *new* friend," Patricia said without looking up at Vivian. She was sitting on her desk, painstakingly coating her nails.

"So, who's this new *friend* of yours?"

"A guy called Shinji, the manager at Bar Blue. Guess where he's taking me next Tuesday night?" Patricia looked up briefly at Vivian, her nailbrush in one hand, "Chez Matsuo in Shoto. How's that for a Valentine date?"

"Whoa, he's out to make a point, isn't he? Sounds like he's *in love*. And you? Do you like him?"

Patricia thought for a moment. "Hmm, he's kinda cute, I guess. He's been asking me out since last December. I finally said yes. Sure hope this one won't turn out to be another loser!" Patricia put her nail polish down, her ten fingers stretched out to separate her newly painted pearl-silver nails.

"Why? You've been unlucky lately?"

"You might say so." Patricia gently blew on her nails. "I dated this divorced executive for about a year. At first he was great, attentive and everything. Then he started working later and later . . ."

"This executive guy, does he have two daughters?" Vivian was referring to Matsunaga. She was sure Patricia's ex-boyfriend was Matusnaga.

"Huh? What're you talking about?"

"Oh, nothing."

"Anyway, our dates would get pushed back later and later into the night. Often, when we finally got around to finishing dinner, it would already be near midnight. Of course by then there was no time left to do anything except sleep. It got really boring after a while."

"No time left? To do what?"

"Oh, stop being such a prude. Of course I'm talking about *sex*. I wouldn't expect him to help fix my toilet at that hour, now would I?" Patricia gave Vivian an annoyed look. "Sometimes I wonder if it's an age thing. He was fifty-five when I met him." She straightened her back, and put her hands in her lap. "When a man gets to be that age, sex just doesn't seem to come as natural."

"What's that again? What doesn't come natural?" Just at that moment, Becky walked into the office with a stack of textbooks in her arms. She'd just finished her lessons at a nearby company. "What're you guys talking about?"

"Sex with older men," Vivian blurted out. She was tempted to say "sex with scumbag Matsunaga, the old fart who cheats on his wife."

"And?" Becky unloaded the books onto her desk.

"That sex with older men is a bore," Patricia laughed.

"Well, then, why not give younger men a try? My Daisuke is only twenty-eight—satisfaction guaranteed," Becky said rather proudly.

"Daisuke? Your boyfriend? And he's only twenty-eight? You're *kidding*!" Patricia looked at Becky with a dropped jaw.

"She's not kidding!" Vivian interjected. "And let me tell ya, this guy's really cute too."

"Beeeecky, turns out you're a cradle snatcher! He's what, at least fifteen years younger than you, right? Tell me, how did you meet him?"

"He was one of my students."

"Ah, the good old English school connection! Does he work for a *shosha*?"

"Nope, he's a textile designer. Used to live in Kyoto and works for a firm designing *kimonos*. His work took him to California on a business trip and he fell in love with the idea of living there. So he came up to Tokyo to take an intense English course at my school."

"And that's when you moved in for the kill. So, what's he like in bed?" Patricia said unflinchingly.

"Oh, like a firecracker. But why are you asking me, Patricia? You're the social butterfly—you ought to know. Oh, I get it: you only specialize in older men."

"Heck no. It's just that my last couple of boyfriends happened to be slightly older. I do admit, though, that I like my men slightly more advanced on the social ladder, someone who's got enough money to shower on me. This automatically leaves out many younger Japanese men."

"Japanese men? You mean you only date Japanese men?" Vivian turned to Patricia, her brow raised.

"No, it's not like I have radar for Japanese men. But I work at a piano bar, and many of my patrons happen to be middle-aged Japanese men. You know how it is; it's in Akasaka Mitsuke, not your white-boy Roppongi kinda place," Patricia said a bit defensively. Then she smiled to herself. "But you know what, I do prefer going out with Japanese men, now that I've been in Japan a while."

"Oh? What about all those stereotypes about Japanese men not being good boyfriend material? That they're unromantic and rather chauvinistic?" Vivian was intrigued.

Patricia pursed her lips, shaking her head. "I don't find that at all."

"I agree. Chauvinistic is not the first word that comes to mind," Becky chimed in. "Most Japanese men I have come across are quite the opposite of the established stereotypes. Well, at least the men from southern Japan. Daisuke, for one, is very soft-spoken. Even his dad is very agreeable and lets his mother decide on everything around the house. His dad is from Kyushu."

"Yeah, that's my observation too. Besides, this romantic thing, it really depends on your definition of the word." Patricia switched her crossed legs so one of her black pumps now rested across her right thigh. "Give you an example. A year ago I went on a disastrous date with an American guy I met at a party. He suggested that we meet up in Roppongi at a famous Italian restaurant he knew of. He said they had the best homemade seafood pastas and Tiramisu there. Well, guess what, the darn place was closed that night, so what did we do? We wandered around the street for a long time and ended up at Denny's. Talk about romantic!

"The thing that really bothered me was that he didn't have anything interesting to say. He didn't know the first thing about Europe, but kept asking me stupid questions like do I eat a lot of sauerkraut and sausages, or do I feel guilty about what the Nazis did to the Jews, blah, blah, blah. Then when it came time to pay, he said, 'Oh, the total came to 4,328 yen—that's 2,164 yen each.' Huh? Can you believe that?"

Vivian sucked her teeth. "Boy, that's pretty bad!"

"A Japanese guy who wants to woo you, on the other hand, would send a cab to your door," Patricia continued. "And he'll be sure to pay for your dinner, and send you back home in a paid cab. Now that's class," Patricia sighed.

"Yeah, I'm with Patricia," Becky said. "I think a lot of the *gaijin* men here are either clueless or really spoilt. They don't know how to treat women right, and yet sex is always the first thing on their minds. You know how long it took me to convince Daisuke to go to bed with me? Two months!" she raised two fingers. "What a change that was from the guys I used to meet back home."

"You two make it sound like Japanese men are the catches of the century out there. Either you two happened to be *very* lucky, or you have stayed in Japan too long."

"You don't have to take our word for it. Try dating Japanese men yourself and you'll know what we mean," Patricia said.

"I don't think that's going to happen. Once I went out with a youngish Japanese guy whom I thought was rather cute. The problem was, he wouldn't stop talking about his British ex-girlfriend. I mean, he clearly liked me, but he told me he's only interested in dating Western women. So there," Vivian shrugged.

"That's too bad. You know, most of the white guys out there are just pigs. They have no appreciation for women. Even the ugliest Joe without a college degree could find a job here teaching

English or pretend to be a PR expert and get laid. So they let it go to their heads. I wouldn't touch any of those guys with a ten-foot pole." With that, Patricia hopped down from her desk and grabbed her handbag. "Okay, enough talk about the ugly white men. Got to go down to buy some CDs—I need *inspiration* for my gig tonight. You gals need anything?" Patricia always played hooky on Monday afternoons, taking full advantage of Noriko's day off.

"Nay, Madam, you go ahead." Vivian waved her goodbye.

That was Patricia for you—she always had an opinion about everything. Vivian wasn't sure she liked Patricia. She was pompous and self-righteous. Yet like many of the white males she'd attacked, she too was living a fabricated life. She too had managed to reinvent herself by taking advantage of the Japanese weakness for the white skin, carving out a niche along the way.

Then again, Vivian was also painfully aware of her own hypocrisy in this reinvention game. If Patricia had used her whiteness to advance herself in this Disneyland, then she'd used Amano's war guilt toward the Chinese to hitch a free ride. Strictly speaking, they were beasts of the same color. They were both keenly aware of the fact that as foreigners, self-reinvention was the only way to beat the game if they were to make it on someone else's turf.

c/3 — c/3

Seven days later, on a Monday evening just a day before Valentine's Day, Vivian found herself lingering late at work—she found it difficult to make herself dash home the way she normally did. Earlier that day Becky and Teruko had discussed ways to celebrate Valentine's Day, which was only a day away now, and all that talk had made Vivian depressed. Everyone seemed to have a boyfriend, or something close to it. The thought of spending another St. Valentine's Day alone made her feel ill. *You're getting to be an old spinster with no marriage prospects whatsoever!* She could hear her mother's voice in her head. It wasn't her idea to stay single. In an ideal world, she'd have loved the idea of getting married and starting a family. But things didn't work out that way for her. Now she wondered if she'd have to spend the rest of her life by herself.

Finally, at half past six, she found herself jumping on a train at Shibuya Station, not knowing exactly where she was headed. She got off at Ginza and wandered aimlessly until she reached Mitsukoshi Department Store. It might be nice to mingle among busy shoppers. Anything was better than going home to her dark, cold apartment.

Since she'd come back to Japan she'd dated a couple of guys, but neither relationship worked out. She was beginning to wonder if she'd lost her womanly charm. At thirty-five, she didn't consider herself that old. Still, when someone ditched you for a woman ten years younger, you would begin to wonder.

Vivian thought of how she and Peter used to frequent the Asian art exhibits at the Metropolitan. Or they would try to catch an old Chinese movie at one of the archives. At the end of their dates they would always eat at a Chinese restaurant, followed by a rendezvous at his apartment. But that was three years ago. Since their breakup, Vivian had hardly visited an art gallery, much less a movie theater.

At 6:45, Mitsukoshi was still bustling with people. Vivian wandered through the first floor's precious-stone-and-jewelry section. The necklaces, earrings, and bracelets glinted at her alluringly. Vivian lifted up a pair of earrings, held them close to her ears, and peered into a mirror. No! What was the point when nobody would even look at you? In Japan, a woman in her mid to late thirties was practically over the hill. She sighed and gently put them down. She ought to go home.

Before leaving, Vivian decided to go down to the basement deli section to buy a bite to eat. At the stairwell, she accidentally bumped into a tall foreigner going the opposite way. "Excuse me," Vivian said, adjusting her glasses as she looked up.

"Vivian, is that you?" The smiling man spoke with an English accent. He had thin blond hair and a square jaw, his teeth white and neat. He looked vaguely familiar, but she couldn't place him.

"I'm Jack, friend of Peter Pearson's. Remember? Lucky Cheng's in the East Village?"

"Yes, now I remember—you and Natalie had a party there!" Vivian said, nodding in recognition. Jack was one of the artist friends Peter loved to party with in New York. As an art history professor, Peter got invited to dozens of gallery shows every week. "By the way, Peter and I loved that party! So, what're you doing in Tokyo?"

"I'm on a six-month artist exchange program. Am hard at work on a series of paintings now. I'm looking to do a solo show, hopefully at a Ginza gallery."

"Wow, in Ginza? That would be quite an accomplishment! You must invite me to your opening when that happens," Vivian said, smiling. "How's Natalie? Is she here with you?"

"Actually, we're not together anymore," Jack said, lowering his gaze. "We were divorced eight months ago."

"Oh, I'm sorry. I didn't mean to—"

"It's all right. There were problems. To be honest, she met someone else. Well, it's all for the best, I suppose."

"That must be hard. Listen, Jack, if you want some company, or someone to talk to, just give me a call." Vivian fished a business card from her purse and handed it to him.

"Sure," he said, glancing at the card. "Actually, have you eaten yet? Perhaps we can have supper together."

"You mean now?" Vivian hesitated. But there wasn't anything waiting for her at home, and it sounded like a good plan. "Okay, why not?"

"Super. I know of a small Italian restaurant nearby. It's only a few minutes away."

The windows of the restaurant in a Ginza back alley were decorated with pink and red hearts in anticipation of Valentine's Day—a big business night for most restaurants there. Jack led her to a quiet corner table. An awkward silence ensued, but after a glass of wine they both began to relax a bit.

"So, what did you do all day?" Vivian asked, a hand scratching her neck.

"I visited art supply stores. I found this incredible store in Kyobashi, called something Ito. Really big, with all kinds of Japanese rice papers and office supplies. You been there before?"

"Sure, dozens of times. They have a great selection of Christmas cards there too."

"You mean they celebrate Christmas here?"

Vivian nodded. "Big time. Except instead of it being a family thing, it's more of an excuse for couples to go out. By the way, how was your Christmas?"

"I was mostly by myself," Jack said, pressing his lips together. "But Peter very nicely invited me to his house on Christmas Day. It was good to see him."

"So—how was *he*?" Vivian found herself asking, even though she knew she didn't want to know the answer.

"You know Peter. He's very laid back, as usual."

"He's still with that Feifei woman?" Feifei, a twenty-four-year-old art student from Taipei, was the reason Vivian had broken up with Peter. At first Vivian had bought his line that he was busy with his new courses, until she ran into the two dining at the Dragon Pearl Café in Chinatown. Vivian was devastated that her four-year relationship could be so readily replaced by a woman who could barely put an English sentence together. She never saw Peter again after that.

"Yes." Jack let out a wry laugh. "They're very tight. She moved in with him recently."

Moved in? The news poured down on Vivian like a bucket of ice water. During their four year courtship, Peter had always resisted upon the idea of living with her, even though she'd been keen to move in with him.

"You know, I just don't understand what Peter sees in that woman. She's not his intellectual equal by any stretch of the imagination," she said, trying to keep her tone light.

"But she's very bubbly and keen about many things, and she has a great sense of humor."

"What you didn't mention is that she's also very young— young enough to be Peter's daughter." Vivian could still see her mother's tear-streaked face and shriveled body in bed after her chance discovery of her father's betrayal. She was almost certain that her father's mistress was a younger woman. Men! They are all alike.

"I'd give Peter more credit than that," Jack said mildly. "It's not just youth that he sees in her. Besides, not all men fall for younger women. Look at Natalie and me—Natalie is two years older than I am. But I went for her because I thought she was very independent, very ambitious. I guess, in retrospect, maybe she was too independent-minded for me."

Slowly, over their meals of salad and pasta, Jack told Vivian about how he and Natalie had broken up, and how she had fallen in love with her new boss at the bank she worked at. Before she left she'd taken all her belongings, leaving just a note behind. Jack said he had applied for the artist exchange program as a way to run away from their apartment, which was filled with the memories of her.

"We were married for three years. Three years, and I thought we were really happy together!"

"Jack, I know it hurts. But trust me, it does get better. That's how I survived my breakup with Peter."

"That's different. You two weren't married. In fact, you'd never even lived together."

"Yeah, you're right," Vivian said, despite the stab in her heart. She hated the fact that Jack had brought up the part of her history that hurt her the most. She took a sip of white wine from her glass and quickly changed the subject. She told Jack how he shouldn't miss the opportunity to see Kyoto and Nara before he left Japan. She was very pleased when the desserts arrived.

After dinner, Jack suggested that Vivian come to his apartment to see some of his paintings, adding that he was staying only a short walk away from Ginza. Again Vivian hesitated. Two lonely hearts on the eve of Valentine's Day! Was Jack coming on to her? An image flashed across her eyes: she was sleeping naked with Jack next to her. She had always found Jack vaguely attractive. Could this proposition lead to something promising?

"Sounds like a good plan," she heard herself saying.

Jack's apartment was smaller than she'd expected. Other than a coffee table, the six-mat-size room held only a bed. Jack gestured for Vivian to sit on the bed and quickly disappeared into the kitchen. He re-emerged a few minutes later with two cups of Earl Grey Tea and a small plate of cookies. He handed Vivian a cup.

"You can start out with the smaller paintings," Jack said, retrieving half a dozen canvases from behind a closet door. They were mostly unframed oils the size of a coffee table book. Some of them were still lives; others were landscapes and flowers.

Vivian examined each piece with delicate hands, handing them back one by one to Jack. "They're beautiful, Jack. I really like the soft colors."

After returning the paintings to the closet, Jack handed Vivian a couple of photo albums. "Here are some photos of my work, taken at a recent exhibition in Florence."

Vivian flipped through the albums. They were filled with photographs of framed large and medium-sized paintings, many of old-style tin toys like bicycles and mobiles against light orange and purple backgrounds.

"These are wonderfully whimsical. When was the exhibit?" In truth, Vivian thought them garish and silly.

"About a year and a half ago," Jack said, a hint of pride in his smile.

"Such bright colors! Florence must have been a blast," Vivian said. "How long were you there?"

"Three months—long enough to have Natalie become unfaithful to me," he said, handing her another album. "Here, I have some more, done in the last four months."

Vivian opened the book to find images of Natalie, page after page, done from different angles in charcoal, pastels, oil, and watercolors against somber backgrounds.

"A book of Natalie?" Vivian looked up at Jack.

"Yup! She was the only thing I wanted to paint for months. Crazy, isn't it?"

"Did you do these from photos?"

"I did them mostly from my memories of her. Sometimes I looked at old pictures of us together. I just had this compulsive need to keep drawing her. I don't know why. But I felt better afterwards. I guess I needed to get her out of my system."

"Obviously you still care about her very much. You can tell from these drawings." Vivian pointed to a water-colored Natalie in a sheer floral gown, her long blonde hair loosely coiled on the top of her head. She looked like a goddess.

Jack shrugged.

"Can I use your bathroom?" Vivian felt the urge to get away from the mountains of Jack's albums. She couldn't look at another portrait of Natalie, or anything painted by Jack.

"Sure. It's across from the kitchen."

The bathroom was tiny, one of those unit baths. Vivian sat on the toilet bowl and covered her face with both hands. This was a disaster. What was she thinking, coming to Jack's at this hour? She looked at her watch—10:15. Should she leave?

"It's getting late. I should go home," Vivian said when she came out of the bathroom.

"So soon? Why don't you stay a little longer? I can warm up your tea."

"Um, I should go. I have a big meeting tomorrow morning."

"Really? That's too bad."

Jack brought her long coat out from his closet and helped her put it on. "Well, Vivian, thank you so much for coming. I had a wonderful time." He gave her a kiss on the forehead.

"I did too, Jack. Good night!"

Vivian walked out of the apartment with a deep sigh. She felt used, having served as a 'borrowed ear' for Jack all night. Then again, she knew she would have gone to his apartment anyway because she'd wanted to find out more about Peter, whether she liked to admit this to herself or not.

She gazed up at the sprinkle of bright stars shimmering against the dark purple sky. Peter and her: they were two stars set on different courses, much like Jack and Natalie. But what forces had brought her and Jack together that night?

She had wanted so much to be close to someone again. It had been almost a year since she'd last spent the night with a man, and she missed the feeling of intimacy. But Jack's repeated mentions of Natalie had been a huge turnoff. The last thing she needed was to be someone's substitute lover. She had enough heartaches of her own to take on more problems.

The streets were quiet, the silence broken only by the occasional rumblings of a distant train. The night wind felt cold on her face, the chill pricking like a thousand tiny needles on her skin. She tightened her scarf around her neck as she headed for the station.

The sound of an approaching train set her feet in motion. She quickly bought a ticket from a machine, flew down the stairs, and hopped onto the train just as the doors were closing.

Nine

Behind Ueno Station, Pei scoured the racks of pantsuits in a shop, pulling the clothes off the hangers to try and get a better look. She was in a rush to find the perfect outfit for her interview at Club Asia. It was the third shop she'd visited, and she was still out of luck. Hong had only called her about the interview the night before, and she had been at class all day so she hadn't had time to go shopping. Hong had told Pei to arrive at her house by 5:30 sharp, and time was running out.

Most of the suits looked okay, but none of them were cheap. They started at ten thousand yen. Toward the back of the shop, Pei found a bargain rack. "Excuse me. Is this six thousand yen after the discount?" Pei held up a purple pantsuit with green leaf patterns.

The young store assistant looked up briefly from her book. "Yes, it is. It's such a bargain now," she said, before going back to her reading.

"Can I try it on?"

"No. We don't allow fittings for clothes on sale."

"But why? How else can I tell if it fits me?"

"Sorry, but it's a company rule."

Rules, rules. There are so damn many rules in this country! Why can't these Japanese learn to relax? Pei took the suit and walked toward a full-length mirror near the glass counter. She held the jacket against her shoulders, twisting this way and that, imaging how it might look on her. The rich purple contrasted nicely with her pale skin; it might just be perfect for the interview. But what about the pants?

"Look, I really need to try the pants on," she said, heading toward the fitting room out the back. "There's no one else in the shop. Who's to know if I broke a rule or two?"

Just as she was about to open the fitting room door, the store assistant rushed over to strong-arm the room door closed. "No, a rule is a rule."

Pei felt her temper rising. "Who came up with all these ridiculous rules?" she muttered more loudly than she'd intended.

The clock's hands were inching closer to 5:00. She knew she must buy an outfit before she left the store, or she would end up in her jeans at the interview. She checked the waist of the pants in her hands and decided they would fit her. Pei grabbed the suit, hanger and all, and dropped it on the glass counter with a bang. "Now wrap it up, will you?" she demanded.

The woman hastily folded the clothes and put them in an orange shopping bag. "That will be six thousand yen. And by the way, all sales are final, according to our company rules."

Pei felt something explode inside her. She couldn't hold it in. "Screw your stupid company rules," she hissed, slapping the money on the counter. She'd had enough with people ordering her around and telling her what she could and couldn't do.

"Excuse me, but you can't be screaming and yelling like that here, disrupting the peace and causing a scene," the woman said haughtily. "I don't care if you are a customer. Now please take your money and leave the shop." She swept the bag of clothes under the counter.

"Who the hell are you to tell me what I can and can't do?" Pei yelled back. "I already paid, so the clothes are mine now." She yanked the bag from the woman's hands.

The woman took a sharp breath. "Just leave this shop," she said firmly. "You're not welcome back here ever again. We don't like barbaric foreigners!"

"Don't make me laugh. I wouldn't come back even if you begged me to," Pei said as she stomped out of the store. She was still fuming two blocks away. But she felt strangely triumphant, as if she had finally managed to vent some of her frustration toward a people she couldn't understand.

Hong was painting her toenails when Pei arrived at her door.

"What you got there?" Hong said, pointing at Pei's bag.

Hong took one look at the suit and gasped. "Wrong color, wrong style! You'd look like a rice-pudding wrapped in lotus leaves. Don't you get it? The bar business is all about flirtation. You need to show a little bit of flesh to tantalize the opposite sex." She sized Pei up and down. "Come here," she said, leading Pei to her bedroom. She brought out a low-cut salmon-pink suit from the lineup of clothes in her closet. "We're almost the same size, and this might just fit you." She handed Pei the suit.

Pei brought the outfit close to her chest and peered into the mirror on Hong's dresser. "It's very nice, but I think it's a bit too sexy for me. I don't have the body for it," she said sheepishly, handing the suit back to Hong.

"How about this one?" Hong dragged out another outfit, this one a little subtler: a maroon one-piece dress embroidered with delicate, golden beads around the bust.

"You don't think it's too short for me? I feel very self-conscious in short dresses." Pei stretched the dress out with both hands, her brow knitted.

"You have nice legs. You should show them more often. Come, try it on in the bathroom," Hong urged.

When Pei emerged, Hong gave her the thumbs up. "You look very elegant in it. Mama will absolutely love you."

Pei studied herself in the mirror, twisting her hips left and right, then bit her lip and nodded.

"Now we've got to do something with that hair of yours," Hong said, pointing to the seat in front of her dresser.

Pei obediently sat. She waited as Hong applied a thin layer of gel on her hair and slowly combed it into a bun. As she watched Hong work on her hair, tears began to well in her eyes.

"What's the matter?"

Pei shook her head. "All my life, no one was ever as kind to me as you've been," she said, swallowing hard. After a brief moment, she looked up, her eyes still glistening.

Hong handed Pei a tissue, which she took to wipe her nose.

"The last time someone combed my hair like that was my aunt. I was about eight living at my uncle and aunt's house in Dalian," Pei said, as if to herself.

"My aunt was the only one who was kind to me. If I were banned from eating with the household, she would sneak me a morsel or a steam bun saved from the dining table. But she died too soon; she was killed in a car accident. After that, my uncle became ill tempered and mean-spirited. He was never pleased with anything I did for his family. I did the cooking and the kitchen chores while his own sons would linger with him at the table eating snacks and drinking tea.

"He often told my grandma how stubborn and disrespectful I was. If he was upset with me, he would come after me with a broom. As punishment, I often had to sleep in an outside shed that was freezing cold in the winter. But that only made me more stubborn. I really *hated* him."

"Why didn't you write your mother and tell her about all this?" Hong asked, meeting Pei's eyes in the mirror.

"I didn't know how. Besides, my mother never wrote. Well, I got a letter from her once, perhaps fourteen months after her departure. I was so excited, thinking she was finally coming to get me. I couldn't wait for my aunt to read the letter. But it was only a note to say that my little brother had fallen very ill that summer and she couldn't come for me just yet.

"I was so devastated I skipped school and spent an entire day wandering in the streets that day. *Liar,* I kept calling my mother. I didn't go home until dark. Naturally, Uncle gave me a severe beating for my bad behavior. I thought of running away many times, but I held on because my mother had promised in the letter that she would come back the following year. From then on, I checked the mailbox every day after school. That was the only thing that kept me going. But you know what? The letter never came."

"Your mother never bothered to try to take you out of China? Not even once?"

"Yes, she did once, in the mid-60s, two years after she first left me in Dalian. But by then it was too late—the Cultural Revolution had begun, and no Chinese residents were allowed to leave China. By that time, my mother already owned a Hong Kong residency card and was warned by friends that she mustn't go back to China, or she might risk not being able to get out again.

"After my mother left, all I could do was to hang on to a shred of hope—the hope that what everyone was saying was true. In those days, everyone seemed to be saying that the movement couldn't go on for more than two or three years, like so many other political campaigns before it. Who would have thought the Revolution would boil over and drag on for as long as a decade? For an eight-year-old child, a decade is an eternity! And it wasn't until 1978, after China reopened to the world, that I found out my family had already moved from Hong Kong to Japan."

Pei used the soiled tissue to wipe her eyes, which were wet with tears again. "When I found out they'd moved to another country I felt so very lonely, not sure if there was a soul left on this earth that really cared about me. I might as well be a forgotten sack of potatoes left on the shelf of a train. I think I rushed to marry because I couldn't stand the loneliness any more. I wanted so much to have a home of my own—a home where I felt I really belonged."

Pei looked at Hong's reflection and noted her surprise. She realized this was the first time she had ever mentioned a husband.

"Did you love your husband?" Hong asked.

Pei shrugged. "We're very different people, with a large age gap. He's ten years older than me. Then again, I might have stayed married to him for the sake of our two boys had I not seen my younger sister in Beijing during a family reunion.

Pei could still remembered vividly her initial meeting with Meiyin. It was at the Beijing Hotel when Pei first saw her little sister, after a break of thirty years. She was shorter than Pei had expected, by about half a head than her. Meiyin, standing next to her mother at the hotel lobby, was in her jeans and T-shirt, her short wavy hair unkempt. She was a bit Tom-boyish, yet at the same time, a bit bookish in her large spectacles, not particularly impressive really. She also came off as a bit stiff when she said hello to Pei, as if she'd forgotten how to speak Mandarin properly.

Just as they were heading for the exit, a foreign tourist stopped them to ask for directions to go the Forbidden City. Without missing a beat, Meiyin started explaining to the man in very fluent and impeccable English on how to get there. Her accent was very American, like that of a native speaker. It was then and there that Pei found out Meiyin had not only lived in Hong Kong and Tokyo, but New York as well. All those experiences could had been Pei's had she been given the same opportunities to see the world. How awful she had been robbed of all those opportunities!

"Seeing Meiyin rekindled all my jealousy and indignation when I thought of all the opportunities I'd missed. I constantly wondered what life would have been like for me if I'd been the one taken out of China, not her. I couldn't shake the questions out of my head: Why was I the only one in the family left behind in China? And who should have the right to condemn me to a life of exile when the rest of my family live in riches and comfort?"

"Speak no more, my friend. You're getting a little too philosophical for me," Hong said, patting Pei gently on the shoulders. "Besides, that was the past. Tonight, there's a new opportunity coming your way that will surely help change your life for the better. So cheer up! Don't let the past spoil it for you now. Hey, check it out: your hair has never looked better. See?" She swiveled Pei around and used a hand mirror to show her the elegant upsweep.

Pei looked up at Hong, wiped her nose again, and smiled. Hong was right. This was a big opportunity she had been waiting for, and she mustn't let it slip through her fingers.

Club Asia was located in the basement of a five-story building in an alleyway near Shinjuku's entertainment area, the

Kabukicho. Along the basement hallway, seductive neon signs in pink and blue glowed with promise. Pei nervously followed Hong as they passed a bar restaurant, a massage parlor, and a dubious-looking coffee shop. Hong stopped in front of a black metal door with a purple sign overhead that read, *Kurabu Ajiya*: Club Asia. She gingerly rang the bell.

"Ah, Xiao Hong! Come in." A tall, middle-aged woman who spoke in heavily accented Taiwanese Chinese beckoned them through the door. Pei quickly gathered that this was Hana. "Mama, Mama . . ." someone in the back hollered. "Coming!" In a flash, Hana disappeared before Pei could even say hello.

The so-called club looked more like a storage room the size of a closet. At one end of the dimly lit room was an L-shaped purple sofa accompanied by two round glass tables. On the opposite side of the room, five black velvet chairs encircled a wooden coffee table. Across from the velvet chairs there was a small stage with a karaoke machine. In the middle of the room was a bar. The glass shelves on the wall were filled with whiskies and hard liquors of every kind imaginable. Hidden beneath the counter were a mini fridge, a small portable burner, and a toaster so Hana could reheat a small frozen pizza or boil some noodles for the salary men. The club could hold up to fifteen people, if lucky.

Because Hana wanted to keep her girls fresh for her customers, she had them rotating in shifts so no one would be working two days in a row. Pei waited at the bar as Hana and Hong greeted the customers. Growing accustomed to the dim light, Pei watched one hostess dressed in a tight leopard-print top feeding a morsel of food into the mouth of a man sitting next to her. The woman, who looked straight out of school, had long, brown hair with bleached-white streaks. Another woman, dressed in a light green traditional Chinese *qipao* dress, was pouring liquor into the man's glass. "Mama, another Thai salad please!" the woman in *qipao* called out in perfect Mandarin. She had shoulder length hair and pretty, slender eyes that reminded Pei of a classic Chinese beauty on scrolls. Pei thought she looked vaguely familiar, but couldn't place her.

"Yes, coming," Hana called back and quickly ducked behind the counter.

When Hana and Hong both returned to Pei, Hana had in her hands a large bottle of oolong tea and two glasses. She poured the tea into the glasses, then gently pushed them to Hong and Pei. "So, who do we have here tonight, Xiao Hong?" she asked cheerfully, hopping onto the stool next to Pei.

"Ah, Mama, this is Zhang Peiyin, the one I mentioned to you the other day. She's smart and a good student at school. I think she'd do well at the club," Hong said.

"I'm not boasting, but I'm also a good singer. I won a karaoke contest in Dalian once," Pei chirped. One of the best things about being in a new country was that you could reinvent yourself in whatever way you wanted, Hong had said on the way to the club, and Pei had taken the comment to heart.

"Ah, a woman of talents!"

Now that Hana was sitting close by, Pei got a better look at her. Hana had her hair dyed a reddish-brown, which she'd pulled back into a ponytail. She had painted her lips a deep purple, forming a stark contrast to the thick layer of white powder smeared on her round face. She was dressed in a tight black see-through top, vaguely revealing a violet bra. Every time she laughed, bulges of flesh would jut out between her stomach and the bottom edge of her bra.

When Pei first saw Hana, she thought the woman might be in her early forties. But the wrinkles near the corner of her eyes and the saggy skin around her neck suggested she was closer to fifty. An older woman trying a little too hard? Maybe. Still, there was something charismatic and admirable about her.

Hana sized up Pei too, before turning to Hong with an approving smile. "You know, Xiao Hong, your instincts are spot on. Miss Zhang has a nice disposition about her. But we must do something about those awful nails." That was when Pei noticed Hana's long, meticulously manicured silver nails. Pei flashed a quick look at her own untrimmed nails and hastily hid them under the counter.

"So, Ms. Zhang, how old are you?"

"I turned thirty-two just a couple of months ago," Pei said, then blushed when she realized she'd lied very poorly.

"You look at least thirty-six to me. But that's okay. Most Japanese men won't know the difference, especially in this dim light. If you want to work here though, you will have to start telling our customers that you're twenty-eight. You got that?"

"Yes, Mama-san." Pei nodded readily.

"Also, I don't know about your marital status, or if you had children. But as far as Club Asia goes, everyone working here is single and without kids. You understand what I mean?"

"Yes, of course." Pei nodded again.

Their interview was cut short when the doorbell rang. Two more Japanese men walked in. Hana and Hong immediately went to the door to help the men out of their coats. Hana led them to the coffee table and gestured for Pei to come join them. She left Hong and Pei sitting with the men and went to fetch some hot hand towels.

Both men looked to be in their late twenties, and one was taller than the other by about half a head. Hong seemed to know the taller one quite well; she was practically throwing herself at him. "Suzuki-san, where have you been the last two weeks? I've missed you *sooo* much," she said in a coquettish voice. Pei was surprised at how fluent Hong's Japanese was. It was the first time she'd heard Hong speaking the language.

"I've been very busy with work lately," the tall guy said as he loosened his tie. "By the way, this is Sato-san, my college pal. He just arrived from Osaka today."

"Welcome, Sato-san. I'm Chen, same as the Hong Kong singer, Agnes Chen. But you can call me Momo," Hong said with a coy laugh. "Oh, and this is my friend, Cho-san. She's trying out here as a hostess tonight."

Pei bowed lightly from her seat. She could feel her face getting feverish. She wished Hong hadn't introduced her like that. She had no idea her friend was such an outstanding actress. Luckily, Sato-san, his face also a little red, bowed back deeply.

"So, Suzuki-san, you want a new bottle of Suntory or something entirely different?" Hana, who had returned with the *oshibori* towels, wasted no time in drumming up business. "You finished your bottle-keep[4] when you were here last time, remember?"

"Ah, indeed. Let's see, how about a bottle of Johnny Walker?" Suzuki suggested.

"Excellent idea! Four Johnny Walkers on the rocks coming right up—two for the ladies as well, right?" Hana pointed her chin at Hong and Pei.

"Yes, of course," Suzuki said with a nod. He was soon swaying to the music blaring from the karaoke machine, his hands waving in the air.

Pei remembered hearing one bottle-keep at a bar like Club Asia could easily cost up to ten thousand yen. And it was up to Hong and Hana to help Suzuki and his pal finish the bottle quickly so they could sell them another one. By the time the two men paid for their cover charge, food, and drinks, Pei imagined the tab for the night could easily come to thirty thousand yen, if not more. It was a good business, this thing called "snack bar."

Pei could tell Hana was a very competent manager. In just a matter of seconds Hana brought out four glasses of whiskey and two food dishes, a tofu salad and a grilled herring called *shishamo*. The fish was Suzuki's favorite, Hong explained to Pei, adding it was part of the bar hostesses's job to remember the likes and dislikes of customers.

But Suzuki's heart wasn't in the herring that night. "Oh, it's *Ai-wa-katsu*—'Love Will Conquer All,' my all-time favorite. Momo-chan, come sing with me, would you?" With that, Suzuki pulled Hong to the stage and started singing with her. Pei found herself facing Sato alone. The silence was awkward.

---

[4] Essentially a bottle of liquor that can be saved for next time. It's common practice in Japan for a bar or small restaurant to sell alcohol in a larger bottle size for a mark-up, then keep it for the customer when he returns. The customer is only charged for the glass and ice service on subsequent visits, but this helps ensure repeated business for the bar owner.

"Uh, miss, what did you say your name was again?"

"My name is Zhang. Oh, I mean Cho." Pei quickly recovered from the mistake of pronouncing her name in Chinese.

"Cho! That's a very common Chinese name, no?"

Pei nodded.

"Which part of China are you from?"

"Dalian, in the northern part of China, although I used to live in Beijing when I was a little girl."

"Dalian? You mean Dairen? Ah, I've heard of Dairen. My firm has some dealings with the city. So you been here a while?"

"Four months."

"That's all?" Sato peered into Pei's face with his small eyes, his square face now a stark red. "Your Japanese is very good, very good indeed. So Cho-san, how old are you?"

"Twenty-eight. And you?" Pei was fully aware of the presence of Hana, who had come back to the table with a bucket of ice cubes.

"Twenty-eight! Um, I couldn't tell." Sato hunched over the table to take another sip of his whiskey. "You're three years older than me! I'm twenty-five and single. You married?"

"Of course not. None of my girls are married." Hana cut in before Pei could answer, as if she didn't trust Pei to remember to give the right answer. She added a couple of ice cubes to Sato's glass and poured in some more of the apricot-colored liquid.

"Ah, wh–what about a boyfriend? You . . . must have many." Mr. Sato began to slur his words.

"No, and she's looking for one. Good opportunity, Sato-san?" Hana said, patting his shoulder meaningfully before leaving.

The bar suddenly felt very stuffy and hot. Pei looked at the stage, wishing Hong would return. Technically, she was only in for an interview. Hong and Suzuki, now in a tight embrace, were yammering something not quite coherent into the microphones. Although Pei could see the lyrics flashing across the big screen, she couldn't make out many of the words. The two were glued to the screen when their song ended, showing no signs of returning any time soon.

"Excuse me, where's the *o-te-a-rai*?" Sato got up suddenly to ask Hana.

"It's just by the front entrance on your left," Hana said with a smile. She was always smiling.

As soon as Sato stumbled off to the toilet, Hana immediately came to Pei with an empty ice bucket. "Quick! Pour out the whiskey." Her back to the other customers, she gestured for Pei to empty the amber water from her glass. "Here, a hostess's job is to make the customer drink up his bottle of alcohol as fast as she can manage. But to do this you need to rid of yours quickly too," she added, winking.

Pei nodded as she watched Hana pour out the contents from all four glasses and refill them with fresh whiskey. Before leaving, Hana added ice cubes and water to each glass.

Pei pretended not to notice when Sato came back. She had swiveled her chair to look away from him. One of the salary men was lying on the lap of the hostess in the tight leopard-print top, the rest of his body spread across the sofa. He was obviously quite drunk. Another man had an arm around her shoulder, his other hand busy feeling her breasts, to the giggly protest of the woman. But there was no sign of the third man and the hostess with the slender eyes.

Pei felt goose pimples rising on her arms and neck. Hong had told her about what men did to women at clubs. Still, she wasn't quite prepared for what she saw.

"Kiss, kiss me …" The music screamed in the background. Pei thought it was part of the lyrics that Sato was humming, until she felt something prickly near her ear. She turned around in alarm and caught sight of Sato's approaching lips. The man had his eyes half-closed, his neck a crimson red. Pei quickly dodged away. Sato lost his balance and hit his head against the wall. "*I-t-a-i!*" He let out a mournful groan, a hand covering his temple. Hana came rushing over.

"Sato-san, you okay? Listen, Cho-san is a guest tonight, so you can't be rude to her. If you want a kiss, you can kiss me all you want, okay? Here," Hana pointed at her purple lips. But Sato was too drunk to take up the offer. He straightened a bit with effort, leaning against the wall, his hand still on his temple.

Pei felt a tingle in her face. She wasn't sure if it was because she was embarrassed or because she felt humiliated. But before she could decide on her next move, she saw another red-faced Japanese man charging toward Hana.

"Mama-san, Mama ..." It was the man who had been sitting with the pretty woman in *qipao*. He had the young woman in tow by the wrist.

"Yes, Hasegawa-san, what can I do for you?" Hana said with a gracious smile on her face again.

"Mama, what sort of bitches have you hired here? This Li-san of yours, she refused to entertain me outside the club!" Hasegawa yelled, yanking the woman forward. "And when I told her she was a snob, she gave me a slap on the face. Is this how you teach your women to treat your customers?"

"Hasegawa-san, I'm so sorry if one of my girls did not meet your approval. But can you explain what happened exactly, before—"

Li-san twisted from the man's grasp. "Mama, don't listen to him," she said breathlessly in Chinese. "He tried to force me to go in a love hotel with him. And when I said no, he grabbed my breast ..."

At that moment, Pei remembered the woman was Li Juan-juan, one of the students in class B-2 at Yoneda. At school, she was always very quiet and simply dressed. No wonder Pei hadn't recognized her immediately.

"You whore, what're you saying in that funny language of yours?" Hasegawa barked at her. "Don't forget: you're nothing but a prostitute and a *shinajin* here. What right do you have to play hard-to-get?" He roughly grabbed her arm.

"Who are you calling a *shinajin*? China is no longer a colony of Japan, you pervert! You'd better watch your mouth!" Li Juan-juan shot back angrily in Japanese. She shook her arm violently and broke free from his grip.

"You whore, I'll—" Hasegawa raised a hand, as if ready to smack Li-san across the face.

"Oh please, Hasegawa-san, let's not use hostile language here. Can't we discuss the matter outside the club?" Hana spoke in a soothing voice, gesturing for the two to follow her outside the club. One of Hasegawa's companions came to Hana's rescue, half pulling Hasegawa out of the door.

"What's all the commotion about?" Suzuki said to Hong when they returned to the table.

Hong shrugged. "Nothing. Just that arrogant Li-san again. I've never liked that woman—she's always troublesome and so full of herself. Let's not worry too much about her. How about some whiskey, sweetie pie?" Hong raised her glass to clink it against Suzuki's.

"Yeah, by all means." Suzuki held up his glass and took a big gulp.

Just then, Sato groaned, and proceeded to vomit all over himself, the table, and the carpet.

Hong rolled her eyes at Pei and let out a swear word in Chinese.

"I'm sorry. That Sato, he probably had too much to drink." Suzuki got up and tried to wipe some of the vomit off Sato's pants with a soiled towel. "The poor fellow just broke up with his girlfriend and had a few beers before coming to the club."

"Don't worry about that. We'll handle it." Hong disappeared behind the counter and came out with a thick roll of paper towels and a few hot *oshibori* hand towels. She handed Suzuki the towels and instructed him to take Sato to a clean chair. Then she pulled off a large strip of paper towels and threw the rest to Pei. Without any hesitation, Hong swiftly covered the carpet and the soiled chair with her strip of paper towel, covering her mouth and nose with her other hand.

Pei, slowly waking up from her shock at being made to work, covered the table with sheet after sheet of paper towels, meticulously wiping off the vomit. She wasn't quite prepared to be a cleaning lady on the night of her big interview. Could she handle a job like this even if the pay was three times better than the restaurant job? She wondered. But where else could she make some fast cash? And lots of it! She reminded herself that her early plans of selling the 101 hair growth products from China had fallen through because Xiao Yu, her friend in Canada, wouldn't do anything to help her, even though she had promised in the beginning that she would help Pei start a similar business in Japan.

A moment later, Li Juanjuan returned to the club with a lowered head. She slipped behind the counter and into a small door. It turned out there was a small changing room behind the counter. Hana, Hasegawa, and his pal came through the club door a few minutes later and went back to the long sofa. Hong wasted no time reporting to Hana of the accident on the carpet. Hana rolled her eyes but said nothing. Instead, she went back to the counter, opened up a new bottle of Suntory, poured it into two glasses, and walked them over to Hasegawa's table. Again, she was all smiles.

"Mama-san, we've got to go," Suzuki said when Hana finally made her way back to his table. "I've got to take Sato home!" Suzuki held a hand out to Sato, who had slumped over in his clean chair.

"But the night is still young," Hana said in protest. "Come on, Suzuki-san, stay a little while longer. Don't let the little incident at the other table disturb you."

"No, Mama. We really have to go now. Besides, I have a very early meeting tomorrow." Suzuki got out his wallet.

"Very well then, I won't keep you. Promise that you and Sato-san will come back soon. Okay?"

"Sure, Mama," Suzuki said, leaving three ten-thousand-yen notes on the table. The evening had cost the men close to two hundred fifty dollars!

After sending the two men out the door, Hana quickly returned to Hasegawa's table. She'd forgotten all about Pei.

A few minutes later, Li Juanjuan emerged in jeans and a sweater, her long coat in one hand. She passed by Hana's table without saying a word, leaving the club as quietly as a ghost.

"What's going to happen to her?" Pei asked Hong.

"She's probably not coming back," Hong said, shaking her head. "Mama doesn't tolerate anyone who's disrespectful to her customers. She has always been a bit arrogant, that Li-san, as if she's above it all. I really don't think she's suited for this line of work. I wish I hadn't helped her get hired."

"You're the reason Li-san is here?"

"Well, not technically! Mama did like the fact that she's my schoolmate, but she had another friend who also knew Mama, and one thing led to another."

"But what happened just now wasn't Li-san's fault. After all, isn't the term *shinajin* very derogatory?" Pei asked. She had heard the word discussed in class just a week earlier, after a student spotted it in a local Chinese newspaper. The term was widely used by the Japanese imperialists in reference to the Chinese during the Sino-Japanese War. It was loaded with racist undertones.

"Yeah, but you can't let little things like that bother you. They're a bunch of drunkards anyway, these salary men. If you want to be in this line of work, you've got to be thick-skinned and stay focused on one thing and one thing only—making money. Otherwise, why bother? Think you can handle that?"

Pei thought for a minute. A lofty, brownstone university building flashed across her mind's eye. She never had the opportunities to go to a western university. In fact, she never went to a proper university at all, only a night university in China. She swore she'd make sure her own boys would get into a U.S. university and secure the kind of opportunities she was denied of all her life. But to do that she needed money, lots of it. "I certainly want to make a lot of money, if only Mama-san would let me. You think she would?" She looked up at Hong.

"We'll have to see about that." With that, Hong went over to Hana's table and whispered something into her ear. Hana took a fleeting glance at Pei and mumbled something in Hong's ear. Then she turned back to her customers, and it was business as usual.

"Mama said she's busy right now and can't come over to say goodbye," Hong said when she returned, then paused to grin. "She said she's interested in having you come back to work for a few weeks on a trial basis, say from next Monday. You game?"

Pei eyes brightened. "That sounds great, except she hasn't mentioned anything about the pay."

"Oh, the pay! She will start you up at 1,500 yen an hour for the first two months, with you working from seven-thirty till half-past midnight. If you work out, she'll raise your pay to 2,000 yen an hour. Not bad, I'd say."

"That sounds wonderful. Please thank Mama for me."

"I've got to do some work now. I won't see you to the door."

Pei tried to calm her nerves as she walked out onto the street. She'd seen more that night than she had in the thirty-eight years of her life put together. The idea of starting a new job at Club Asia both excited and worried her, given the incident involving Li Juanjuan.

You've got to be thick-skinned! As she hurried along the quiet alleyway home, Hong's words crept back into her ears. Did she have what it would take to do the job? Could she ward off the wandering fingers of drunken Japanese men?

Then the greenish-gray of one-thousand-yen notes flashed in her eyes. Two thousand yen an hour! That was almost three times as much as what she was making at Tombo. Where else could she make that kind of money and fast forward her boys' chances of getting into a good U.S. university? Yes, of course she could handle the job. In fact, she must. It was too good of an opportunity for her to pass up.

Ten

"What are you reading?"

Vivian was immersed in her newspaper when Becky came peeking in her cubicle.

"The 'help wanted' ads? Why? Is your sister out of a job again?" Becky asked, her handbag still on her shoulder.

Vivian put a finger to her mouth, looking around the office to make sure no one else was listening. "It's for me this time," she said in a hushed voice.

"For you? Are you planning on leaving us?" Becky whispered back.

"I can't take sitting here all day doing nothing anymore," Vivian said. "At least you can go out and teach a lesson or two. Since Rijicho put a hold on the art gallery project, I haven't had a single page of translation to do."

"But you're not going to find anything that pays you nearly as much. The economy is taking a nosedive, and no one's hiring."

"Still, I've got to do something. I'm afraid if I don't do it *now* I may never find a real job again," said Vivian. She didn't want to end up like her mother, who had never cultivated any real skills and now had to do menial jobs in her old age.

"Of course you will. You're talented," Becky said as she picked up the stack of papers from her desk. She was headed for her first class of the morning. "Catch you later," she said with a wave.

Vivian waved back to her friend before returning to her papers. She saw a lot of ads seeking Japanese males in their twenties and thirties, mostly in banking, advertising, sales, and trades.

Jobs for women, particularly those open to foreigners, in contrast, were spotty at best. "Japan's an old boys' club of the strictest kind. If you're a woman, you've got one strike against you. If you're a woman and a foreigner, you've got two strikes against you. But if you're a woman and a foreigner of Asian persuasion, then you are in trouble," Vivian remembered a perceptive young Indian woman she met at her university once telling her.

Vivian's eyes wandered from ad to ad for quite a while, until she spotted one for an in-house translator, which didn't have a specific gender requirement. The company, a small publishing firm specializing in producing PR materials, wanted someone fluent in both Japanese and English with at least a couple of years of experience in translation. The cited hourly rate was about ten percent more than what Vivian was earning at Amano Enterprises. *Not bad,* she thought.

She waited until Noriko and Teruko were both out of the office to pick up the phone.

"Hello, I'm calling about the ad you placed in the English paper. Are you looking for an English translator?" Vivian spoke English, thinking she'd have a better chance of getting the job if she emphasized her English skills.

"Yes, and what's your nationality, Miss?" asked the man who had answered the call.

"Chinese, but I lived in America for over half a decade, and with working experience too. And I have a degree from a reputable college there."

"Then we have a problem. We're looking for someone who's either Japanese or a *native.*"

Vivian had learned that the Japanese used the word "native" not to mean an aboriginal person living in Hokkaido, such as the Ainu, but someone who was a native English speaker. "Sir, I may not be a native, but I can do English and Japanese translation just fine. In fact, I've lots of experience—"

"Miss, that's not good enough. You need to be either Japanese or an American."

Vivian sighed. "Yes, you're right. Sorry for taking up your time."

Native speakers! It had been a while since Vivian last looked for a job, and she had forgotten all about the Japanese obsession with native speakers when it came to white-collar jobs. When she first came back to Tokyo three years ago, she was able to land a job as a translator at an ad agency through an introduction. The boss was nice enough not to insist that she had a white face. All she needed was to turn in a sample translation and she was hired. But when the boss retired, she found herself out of favor. That was when she decided to look for a new job.

A year ago, when Vivian went for her first interview with Amano, the man had offered her the job on the spot, with work visa and other benefits thrown in. He never made any bones about her not being a native. She'd had no idea how rare such employers were at the time. Quitting Amano Enterprises evidently would not be as easy as she had thought.

Some ads in the paper did say "any nationalities welcome," with the promise of a work visa for suitable candidates. But those usually involved telemarketing or insurance sales. A few years back Vivian had tried out at a Japanese-American venture company that sold self-improvement seminars. She'd quit after only two months because she didn't know how to sell the seminars to her friends and friends' friends.

As she was mulling over other options, the idea of teaching Chinese suddenly came to her. If she couldn't be a native speaker of Japanese or English, then perhaps she should fall back on her Chinese. She was, after all, a *native* Chinese.

Quickly she skimmed through the paper again for ads posted by language schools. She found two likely possibilities, although she soon realized one school was at least two hours away from home. She opted to focus on the second one, which had branches all over Tokyo. She discovered one of their branches was in Shin-Okubo—about a twenty-five-minute train ride from her apartment. She dialed the number.

"Are you a native Chinese?" asked the woman in Chinese. She spoke with a Japanese accent.

"Yes, and born in China," Vivian tried to sound authentic. Sometimes she wondered what exactly would qualify a person to be a real native. If a person had only spent her first five years in her mother country, would she still be qualified as a native-native?

"And how soon can you start work?"

"In a week or two."

"Can you come today or tomorrow for an interview?"

"Tomorrow would be better. And can you tell me if this is a full-time job?"

"No. We're only looking for someone who can teach three nights a week, two hours a day."

"You mean just six hours a week?"

"Precisely."

"How much is your hourly pay?"

"That depends on your qualification and experience."

"Fair enough. Then tell me this much: how much do your best qualified teachers earn?"

"Roughly 1,500 yen an hour. But everyone starts at 1,100 yen for the first three months."

"Is that all? You do know most English schools pay their teachers at least 3,500 yen an hour."

"Yes, but this *is* Chinese we're talking about. Chinese is not as popular as English. Besides, it's not a mandatory subject for college students here."

"But I have two degrees and have taught at an American university before," Vivian said, referring to her teacher's aide experience at New York University. For two years, she was an assistant to a professor teaching first and second year Chinese to her fellow students at the university. It was one of the best gigs Vivian had while going to grad school, which helped her pay her own tuition.

"Doesn't matter. Ours is the best-paying school in town. Most schools only pay 1,000 yen an hour."

"And I don't suppose you pay for prep-time either."

"Nope, just the flat rate. So are you coming for an interview?"

"Ah, let me think about it."

"Suit yourself. There are plenty of Chinese out there who're dying to get this job. We get dozens of applications every day."

"That's because they don't know any better," Vivian said, before noticing the phone had already gone dead. She slammed the phone down in exasperation. So much for her job search!

After work, Vivian went to a teahouse near Yurakucho Station. Pei had suggested they meet at a coffee shop, but Vivian wanted to go to a teahouse instead. There was something special about watching the green tea leaves slowly unravel and expand in a delicate cup, anticipating its aromatic flavor. She had no idea at the time that it was her obsession of becoming more "Chinese" that drove her to loving anything related to the Chinese culture, as if there was a gaping hole in her heart she needed to fill in order to feel whole as a being. She ordered Dongding oolong and sat down at a table.

Pei had called Vivian two nights before, saying she wanted to see her. She mumbled something about a friend desperately needing help to go study in the US. Vivian was dubious. In the six months since Pei had arrived, her sister had never once taken the initiative to call her. Every time they'd met, it had always been at Vivian's suggestion, or their mother's. Would Pei break this code of conducts simply because some friend of hers needed her help?

The story of a friend wanting to study in the US also had a familiar ring to it. Vivian knew Pei had always wanted to go to the US. Could this so-called friend be none other than Pei herself?

Vivian was prepared to tell it like it was. It wouldn't be easy for Pei to survive in a fast-paced US city like New York. In Japan, at least she could lean on her family; American society would be a lot tougher on her. Vivian felt she might have been more encouraging if Pei were in her twenties or even early thirties, whereby she could have negotiated the transition from living in a socialist system to that of a capitalist one much faster. She could learn the ropes easily enough through earning a new degree and start over again. But Pei was pushing forty, and her English was far from fluent. The best Pei could hope for in a city like Manhattan would be a low-paying job at McDonald's or a grocery store in Chinatown.

The thought of New York brought back memories of Vivian's days at NYU. When she was a graduate student there she used to wear a jade bracelet of a cool-melon green that she'd bought in Chinatown for fifty dollars. She was almost certain the bracelet was made of plastic instead of jade, but she'd felt a desperate urge to buy it at the time. She often had the feeling of not knowing who she was among so many foreign students at the university. The "jade" bracelet helped her cling to her Chinese identity, however removed she felt from it at the time.

Vivian always thought the greatest tragedy of her life was never having really lived in the land of her ancestry. She'd been a mere preschooler when she left China. Over the next three decades, she'd learned a lot more about Japan and the US than she had about her own country of origin.

This irony tormented her while she was on campus. Classmates and acquaintances, realizing she was Chinese, would routinely quiz her about anything related to China. *Do you know how to do fengshui? Can you teach me how to play mahjong? What's the essence of Laotzu's philosophy,* they would ask. And each time she would grow bright red with embarrassment, for she was as clueless about China as any Susan or Jack who happened to be walking the streets of Lower Manhattan. She began to develop a keen interest in anything Chinese—so much so that she changed her school major mid-course from Western art history to that of China. But beneath the veneer of her longing was also a feeling of shame that she was, in fact, a "fake" Chinese. She dreamed of going back home to *laojia* someday. Somehow, she felt only by living in China could her Chinese-ness be made whole again. In that sense, Pei was a lot luckier than her because there was never a question about her sister's Chinese-ness, she having been a resident of China for decades. Vivian had dreamed of going back to China ever since her return from New York. She was back in Tokyo, and China was only a hop away.

Yet, thoughts of going back to China also terrified her. She wasn't sure if she had the courage to go live among kinsmen in a country that seemed so alien to her. If Pei were still in China, Vivian would at least have a readily available "home" to go back to. Her sister could also serve as a personal guide to help her decode all the cultural landmines she knew she was bound to step on. Whatever was on her sister's mind that afternoon, Vivian decided she'd try to convince Pei to someday return to China with her.

Vivian barely had time to take two sips of her tea when she saw Pei walking into the teahouse. There was something rosy about Pei's face that Vivian hadn't noticed before. She looked younger and prettier, with a new hairdo that was highlighted with a tinged reddish brown in the middle. She also looked sexier and chic in a suede leather mini-skirt and a tight green blouse showing a bit of cleavage. Vivian couldn't remember ever seeing her sister wearing anything low-cut before. She must have taken some serious fashion lessons from a friend.

"How about some oolong tea?" Vivian offered to pour some of her tea into an empty cup that was already on the table.

Pei held up a hand. "I don't like anything that's fermented— smells like mildew to me. I'll have jasmine instead." She waved at a passing waitress to place her order. "So tell me, what's it like to be a student in the US?" She started with her questions before she even had time to warm her seat.

"Wait. I thought it was your friend who's looking to study in the US. Where is she?"

"She couldn't come, so I'm supposed to take notes for her."

Vivian snorted with a laugh, but decided not to embarrass Pei with further comments.

"Well, that would really depend on many things," she started. "If you have enough money to go to a good university in a large US city, the experience would likely be very rewarding. I had a great time studying in New York." Vivian went on to tell Pei about some of the things she did as a student at NYU: her visits to the many galleries in the Village and Soho, and her lazy afternoons reading at street cafés off Washington Square.

"Is it difficult to apply to a US college?"

"Again, it depends on things like which state you want to go to, and whether the university is famous. Of course, the mediocre universities are always easier to get into, because often they are only out to make money. But there're many unscrupulous agents out there trying to part your money from your wallet. So I'd tell your friend to be extra careful."

"If I had a way, I'd really like to try to get into a college in New York!" Pei said, finally admitting to her sister about the real reason behind her coming that day. "They say you can make so much money there if you have a US degree."

Vivian laughed. "And how would you do that? For a good university in New York, you'll need a TOFEL score of at least 580 points! And let's say you did pass the test, how then would you pay for the tuition? Twenty thousand dollars is the least you will have to fork out for a year at a private college anywhere in the US now. Then you need a US sponsor on top of everything else."

Pei pursed her lips. "Don't you have any friends in New York who can help me—I mean, my friend—out?"

"Sis, you can't be serious! Americans are not like the Chinese. They don't take lending money to friends very lightly."

"I'm not talking about the money. That I'll worry about later. I'm talking about finding a sponsor."

Vivian thought for a moment. "I did have a close American friend—he was my former boyfriend. But you know how awkward it is to go back to ask an ex for a favor."

Pei toyed with a matchbox in her hands, pushing the black matches in and out of the paper-drawer, then blurted angrily, "Why did you leave America? So many people dream of going to America their entire lives. But you! You gave it all up to come back to Japan."

Vivian wasn't about to discuss with her sister about Peter, that in part, leaving New York was her way of escaping a past, a failed romance. Instead, she decided to take this chance to reveal to her sister another reality about the U.S., a reality that few Chinese knew about from the outset. "Please don't talk to me like that, because you have no ideas what I've been through. Yes, America's great, but something was missing." Vivian paused, searching for words. "You've always lived in China, and this might be difficult for you to comprehend, but when I was in New York, I met people who wouldn't look me in the eye when they talked to me. They talked past me as though I didn't exist."

"Why?" Pei looked at Vivian, her brows raised.

"Because I'm not white! Being non-white can still pose a big disadvantage for many in the US. Sure, Americans are not supposed to discriminate against minorities, but that doesn't mean there aren't subtle prejudices. Even Chinese-Americans who were born and raised there can run into these problems.

"Another thing: in America, people don't make such fine distinctions between Chinese, Koreans, or Japanese. We're all conveniently put in this basket of 'Orientals,' which is an exotic way of saying we all have yellow skin and slanted eyes. I was so confused about who I was there I bought a plastic jade bracelet to help remind myself—and others—that I'm Chinese. I didn't take it off until I came back to Japan."

"But Japan is a foreign country too."

"Yeah, but here, at least I can pretend I'm one of them. Besides, it's a lot closer to China." Then Vivian let out a sigh. "Sometimes I'm really sick of being a foreigner who doesn't belong anywhere. For as long as I can remember, I've always been an outsider living on someone else's turf. Even when I was in Hong Kong people called me 'an immigrant from the big continent' all the time. Someday I'd really like to go home to China where I belong. I want to experience the joy of being in the land of my own ancestors without having to apologize for who I am. You know, I wish you were still living in China. Maybe someday, when you're ready to move back home, you can show me around?" Vivian said, peering at Pei.

Her sister frowned with obvious annoyance, but merely shook her head. "I don't think I'd ever want to move back. Not until I've made something of myself."

"I see," Vivian said, nodding. After an awkward silence, she changed the subject to Pei's work, asking her if she was doing well at Tombo, to which Pei made an evasive reply. Vivian nodded again. She found that other than talking about studying abroad and looking for jobs, there really wasn't a whole lot she could discuss with her sister. Everything with Pei was about how-to's or where to find the next big opportunity to make more money. She felt she and Pei might as well be on two different planets.

When the two left the teahouse it was already half past six. Vivian made a half-hearted suggestion that they go to her favorite noodle restaurant near the station, but Pei said she was headed for a party at a friend's somewhere in Shinjuku. Then she spun on her heels and disappeared down the street.

Eleven

On Tuesday afternoon, Pei arrived at Hong's door in Ebisu at 4:45—about two and a half hours before she was to start work at the club. She tingled with nerves and excitement; it was going to be a special night. After three weeks of working as a stand-in hostess at Club Asia, Hana had called to tell her that she'd been hired as a regular at the club, adding that she should take care to dress up as much as possible for her official debut.

For the last couple of weeks she had made a habit of coming to Hong's to change, usually arriving around six. Hong had an unlimited supply of makeup and clothes that she had either grown tired of or didn't mind sharing, so it seemed like a good idea to just get dressed together, especially on the nights when Hong also had to work at the club.

Pei realized she was earlier than usual today, but she thought perhaps she and Hong could go get a bite to eat first, then come back to change together. More importantly, she wanted to share the good news with her best friend. Perhaps they could raise a toast to her finally being hired.

Twenty seconds went by after she'd rung the bell, but no one came to the door. Pei tried ringing again; still no answer. Then it hit her—although Hong's work schedule overlapped with hers most weeknights, Tuesday was the one night she usually had off. *Oh dear, what if she's away for the entire evening?* Pei was specifically hoping to borrow Hong's silver gown. How was she to prepare for her first night without a dress? In a pang of panic, she began pounding on the door.

Just then, the door swung open. Hong, dressed in a pink nightgown, popped her head out, her long black hair unkempt. "What on earth do you think you're doing, woman?" Hong hissed.

"I–I was worried you might not be home. Mama-san asked me to start work tonight, and I don't have any suitable clothes. I thought—"

"What do you think this is? Your private dressing room? Don't you *fucking* realize tonight is my night off?"

Pei blushed; Hong had never cursed at her before. She was like a different woman.

"Who is it?" a man's impatient voice thundered from the back of her bedroom. He was speaking in Japanese.

"Oh, just a neighbor from next door," Hong answered in a sweet voice.

Evidently, she'd been entertaining. Pei couldn't be sure if it was Hong's Japanese boyfriend. All she knew was she had come at a very bad time.

"Sorry, Hong! I should have called first."

"*Bakayaro!* Am I going to get my service or not? I paid for an hour and I should get my full hour's service, Goddamn it," the man grumbled in a deep voice.

"Coming!"

It was sounding less and less like Hong's boyfriend. Pei had heard a rumor that Hong sometimes worked as an escort in addition to her job as a hostess. But it had never occurred to her that her friend would be entertaining a customer at this hour.

"You sure know how to pick a lousy time," Hong grumbled, her face now a deep red. "Wait here," she ordered, leaving the door ajar. A minute later, she reappeared, clutching a shopping bag full of clothes and gowns that looked vaguely familiar to Pei.

"Here, I've been meaning to give these to you for some time. Consider them a gift. But do me a favor—don't bother coming back to this apartment again. You're just too pathetic. Now get out!" She shoved the bag at Pei, giving her a forceful push.

Pei staggered backward. "Wait ... where am I going to change at this hour?"

"How should I know? I don't care if you have to change on the street," Hong said, then slammed the door shut.

Pei shuddered at the loud bang. She stood frozen in front of the door, unable to believe what had just happened. After some time she left the apartment building. Still in a daze, she wandered along the street until she found a telephone booth. She opened the door, fell to her knees, and started sobbing, letting streams of tears roll down her cheeks. In her thirty-eight plus years, she found she'd always been on the outside looking in, with no one really understanding or caring to understand her. Her uncle despised her. Her grandma was too old to comprehend her. Her mother, after thirty years, didn't want to hear her out. Her brother, being a typical salary man working fourteen hours a day and often on overseas business trips, could offer little practical help to her. She had long resigned herself to the fact that she could expect little from her younger sister, with whom she shared almost nothing in common.

For a while she'd believed that at least Hong was someone she could confide in and count on. After all, they were two lost souls in a strange land struggling to make it. Then this! Pei couldn't decide if she was more heart-broken about losing Hong's friendship or being humiliated by her like that. She'd never been called "pathetic" before. Either way, she'd lost the last person on this earth whom she thought she could call a trusted friend. Now she was back where she'd started, abandoned and utterly alone.

Then the thought of calling Minoru Mito, a club client she'd gone out with a couple of times outside of the club, came to her. For the past couple of weeks, she had been working to build her client list at the club, and one of her regulars was Mito. Although at fifty-six and with thinning hair and a bulging belly, the man wasn't attractive by any means, Pei was intrigued by him because he spoke some Chinese. As it turned out, the man had spent his first seven years as a child in Shanhaiguan—a part of the Great Wall not far from central Beijing.

A few minutes later, she stood up in the booth, her face tight from the long cry. She vaguely remembered Mito, who owned a real estate business, had said his office was near Shibuya Station, only a couple of train stops away from Hong's apartment. She began thumbing through the pages of a public phone book in search of Mito's work number. She found Mito's company and decided to call, not knowing exactly why.

"How nice of you to call!" Mito sounded pleasantly surprised, and just as she'd predicted, he invited her to come to his office. When she arrived, he was already waiting at the station for her.

"That didn't take long, Pei-*chan*," he said, greeting her with a smile. Ever since their dates outside of the club, Mito had been in the habit of calling her "chan," a more endearing term of address used between close friends and family members. "You all right? You look like you've been crying," he said, taking her by the hand. "Come. Let's sit down somewhere and you can tell me all about it."

On the street, Mito hailed a taxi and instructed the driver to take them to Nogizaka, which was a couple of stops away from Shibuya.

Pei raised her eyebrows, confused. "We're not going to your office?" she asked.

"It's a bit crowded in there tonight—not very convenient for private talks."

"Oh. Where're we going then?" Pei said, a hand still clutching onto the bag of clothes from Hong.

"To my friend's place. He has a small coffee shop not far from here," Mito said.

Once settled at a corner table, Mito took Pei's hands in his. "So tell me, what's bothering you?" Before she could speak, Pei's eyes welled with tears again. Slowly she told Mito what had happened in front of Hong's apartment door.

"That's horrible. That's no way to treat a friend!" Mito said, his hands gently rubbing Pei's. "Listen, if there's anything,

anything at all that I can do, please don't hesitate to tell me. Consider me your newest best friend."

Pei nodded, wiping her eyes dry with a tissue. "Thank you for saying that. You're very kind," she said in a small voice. Then she looked up as if something had just come to her. "Actually, I do need a favor. Do you think I can change somewhere? Tonight is my debut night at the club. I'm finally being hired as a regular there, and I need to look my best," Pei said, adding that the bathroom at Club Asia was too tight and small, and there wasn't even a mirror for her to check her makeup.

"Oh?" Mito glanced at Pei's bag of clothes. "I have an idea: why don't you come and change at my friend's hotel? It's just down the road."

A few minutes later they were in front of a nondescript, shady-looking, three-story building tucked behind a small road. Pei noticed something peculiar about the building—there were no windows on the first two floors and only a few very small ones on the top one. In the front, a tall gray wall blocked the view of the entranceway. On one side of the wall a small purple neon sign read "Murasaki Inn."

Mito went to the reception window by the entrance and spoke in a low voice to a middle-aged woman. The woman nodded and produced a set of keys from a drawer. She came out a minute later and led the two upstairs to a stuffy room at the end of the corridor. After bringing in two *oshibori* towels and some teabags, she bowed and left, closing the door behind her.

Pei scanned the room and saw that it had a twin bed in the middle, covered with a pink bedspread. Next to the bed, two red sofa chairs stood on either side of a small coffee table. On the far side of the bed was a small bathroom. "They let us use one of their rooms?" she asked.

Mito nodded with a smile. "Pei-chan, why don't you go ahead and change? It's ten past six now. If you hurry, maybe we can get a bite to eat before you leave for work." Mito sat on the side of the bed.

Pei looked at him with hesitation, her bag of clothes still in her hand.

"What's the matter? You worried?" Mito said. He got up again and gave her a pat on the shoulders. "You don't need to worry. I won't do anything that you don't want me to," he added, gently caressing her arms with his large hands. When he saw that Pei didn't object, he started kissing her on the neck.

"No ... no. I can't ..." Pei tried to push him away, but he was strong and his grip was firm.

"Pei-chan, I really like you. Let's be friends," Mito said, pressing his lips over her mouth. "We can be very special friends," he said breathlessly between kisses, a hand reaching under her blouse.

In an instant, he had lifted her up and taken her to the bed, his hands beginning to unbutton her blouse. "No, wait ..." Pei tried to stop him, but in the confusion she ended up unbuttoning herself. She didn't know why she had called Mito. Maybe she'd wanted this to happen all along. She'd felt so lonely and abandoned. All she knew was that she needed a friend, someone who would talk to her, someone she could snuggle up to very closely and not worry about being cast away.

Mito began gently kissing her shoulders, then her breasts. Pei felt a shiver in her spine all the way down to the tips of her toes. He rubbed his strong hands around her shoulders, her chest, her abdomen, and then down. She felt her underpants coming off. She shut her eyes, her mind numb.

She felt a sharp pain when Mito was finally on top of her. She let out a moan, her hands curled into fists. In the darkness behind her closed eyes, she felt she was a small starfish washed away into sea by the pounding waves. Weak and fragile, she was totally consumed by the boiling water. She couldn't place herself, until she sensed her body sinking, sinking to the very bottom of the ocean. A few moments later, she heard Mito's thunderous groans, which sounded distant and foreign to her ear.

She hadn't been with a man in almost two years, not having shared a bed with her husband for the last eighteen months of their marriage. She'd never liked being intimate with Guomin. Sex was something she merely put up with as a wifely duty and a price to pay in order to get what she felt had been missing all her life—a home of her own.

It suddenly dawned on her that she was doing it all over again. Was she offering up her body in exchange for the feeling of being *at home* with someone, even if this someone was a total stranger? Then she quickly decided that Mito wasn't a total stranger. She had known the man for two weeks now. He clearly liked her and desired her, and she desperately wanted to feel desired. So what was so wrong that they should find each other in bed like this? Pei half-opened her eyes to see a hint of a smile on Mito's face. He put an arm over her shoulder, his breath more even now. Pei snuggled close to him, her eyes closed again.

They lay there like that for what seemed like an eternity, until Pei, worried about work, got up to shower and change into her club clothes. She walked over to the bed when she was all dressed, hoping Mito might take her to work. But he didn't move; he'd fallen asleep. She saw beads of sweat gathering around his temple. Gently, she wiped them off with the edge of the bed sheet.

Her watch said it was seven. She had to leave now if she didn't want to ruin her first big night at the club. She went to the door, switched off the light, and began turning the doorknob.

"Come back when you're done with work. I'll be waiting here," Mito said in a muffled voice, his face still buried in the pillow.

Pei's heart skipped a beat. "Okay, I'll see you in a few hours," she said. Then gently, she closed the door behind her.

She knew she wasn't in love. But strangely, she felt lighter, as if a huge weight had been lifted off her shoulders. Tonight was her debut night at Club Asia. Tonight was also the night she'd accidentally started something with a new man in her life. Where they would lead her, she had no idea. Yet the mere fact that she'd started something reinvigorated her. At last she had something to look forward to. She smiled and headed happily down the street, forgetting about her earlier rift with Hong.

Twelve

Two months later, Vivian arrived at her mother's on a Sunday afternoon to help her prepare a dumpling dinner. Da Wei was turning thirty-four today, and according to the Zhang family's tradition, a feast of homemade dumplings was called for.

With the advent of modern conveniences, machine-made dumpling shells were readily available at supermarkets. But to Vivian's mother, who took great pride in her cooking skills, they were never good enough. This meant before the stuffing and wrapping could even begin, someone had to be the dedicated shell-maker, cutting up small flour dough, flattening them, and turned them into palm-size wrappers with the help of a rolling pin and old-fashioned muscle.

Dumpling making in the Zhang family had always been a collaborative effort between mother and daughter. Yan, being the head chef of the family, had always assumed the more difficult tasks of dough kneading and the preparation of the stuffing. Vivian, being slower with wrapping, had always been the designated family shell-maker, often leaving the wrapping to her mother.

For the stuffing, Yan liked to include such ingredients as chopped Chinese bok choy, minced pork, prawn bits, and a sprinkle of shallots. Except on the rare occasions when Vivian's father happened to show, she normally would only prepare about 120 dumplings—plenty for the three in the family. That afternoon, however, having an extra mouth to feed and wanting to make doubly sure that the family would not appear stingy in Pei's eyes, Yan had decided to make twice as many dumplings.

Vivian arrived a bit late that afternoon at her mother's door. Once inside, she was immediately turned off when she found Pei was already busy at work rolling out the shells on the *kotatsu*. Sitting on the tabletop of the *kotatsu* was a large pile of shells that had been set on a piece of wax paper. Not only was her sister faster than her at dough rolling, she also appeared to be far better at it.

"Sis, now that I'm here, why don't you take a break? I'll handle it from here," Vivian said, putting on an apron. She kneeled down next to Pei, waiting for her sister to hand over the rolling pin.

"I don't mind. I'm used to doing this," Pei said without looking up.

"All right! If you want to hoard the table, then I'll just go watch TV and relax," Vivian said with pursed lips. She untied the apron and went to sit in the adjacent room. With the remote in hand, she switched on the TV, turning the volume up full blast.

"*Ai-ya*, what's going on in here?" Their mother, who had been kneading a piece of fresh dough, peeked in from the kitchen. "Vivian, you'd better come back and do the stuffing! Da Wei's coming in just half an hour!"

"*O-k-a-y!*" Vivian said, clicking off the TV. She went back to the table, took up a pair of chopsticks, and dug into the stuffing bowl. She scooped out a small chunk of the meat stuffing and slapped it onto a shell. After folding the dough into a half moon, she meticulously squeezed around the edges to produce a fat, pot-bellied dumpling.

"Good heavens, what do you think you're doing? Working on a piece of embroidery?" Pei looked up with a frown. "It'll take you all night the way you do it. Here, let me show you how to do it properly." Pei lifted an empty shell, filled it with stuffing, and finished the wrapping with a couple of quick but decisive squeezes. This all happened in the blink of an eye. "See how quick this is? This way, not only does it help secure the edges, it also prevents the juices from escaping while being boiled."

"Why don't you do it all yourself then?" Vivian dropped the chopsticks and went to sit in front of the TV again. *Why is it that some people always think their way is the best way?* With one click of the remote, a Japanese dating program came on the screen.

"What's gotten into you today, Vivian? Why are you sitting down again?" Yan called, sticking her head out from the kitchen.

"Big Sister thinks she's better at doing wrapping too. So why not just let her do the whole damn thing? She's fast; she can finish everything in time," Vivian said, raising her voice across the living room.

"Meiyin, or Vivian, whatever fancy name you want to call yourself, I suggest you not use sarcasm on me," Pei replied, rubbing her nose. "You may have gone to college in New York and you may speak English, but making *jiaozi* is one thing you will never be as good at it as I am. When I was at Uncle Feng's, I used to make three to four hundred dumplings in one go during holidays, feeding as many as ten people. So I ought to be faster and better at this than you. No reason to get jealous!"

"Jealous? Don't flatter yourself! It's not like we are here for some competition. In case you've forgotten, we're only here for a family get-together!"

"Competition or not, it's good for you to know that you don't excel in everything. In fact, there are quite a few things you'll never be as good as I."

"Oh yeah? Like what?" Vivian just couldn't help herself.

"Like speaking Chinese! You should know that your Chinese is hideous. You sound like a foreigner, your tones and vocabulary all funny."

"Is that so? Well, I've got news for you too, Sis—your Chinese isn't exactly the standard *Putonghua* either. You have a thick Dongbei accent, like some country bumpkin!"

Pei narrowed her eyes. "At least I don't speak it with a Japanese accent. Only those who've grown up outside of China speak so stiffly."

Vivian felt a sudden burst of anger because Pei's remarks hit her where it really hurt. "Who're you calling stiff?"

"That's enough, both of you!" Yan said, standing in the doorway between the kitchen and the living room. "Pei, save your breath! Your sister didn't come here for a Chinese lecture today." Then she turned to Vivian. "And you, Vivian, why don't you concentrate on making the shells and let Pei do the wrapping? Now get to work!"

There she goes again. Mom is always on Pei's side! Vivian grudgingly went back to pick up the rolling pin, although she made sure there was plenty of space between her and Pei. Under Pei's watchful eye, Vivian felt self-conscious about the way she rolled out the shells. She was half expecting another snide remark from her sister. But Pei said nothing.

"Mother, I can't stay long. I have to leave around five-thirty," Pei spoke up after a while.

"What? That's only ten minutes away. Why so soon? I thought you didn't need to go to work until eight."

"I'm starting a new shift. I can't be late," Pei said, her eyes avoiding Yan's.

"What new shift? I thought Tombo was closed on Sundays," Vivian said.

"I don't work at Tombo anymore."

"What? Why not?" Vivian looked up.

"Because I quit. What's it to you?" Pei snorted.

"Don't forget I was the one who got you that job. You owe me at least an explanation."

"I didn't like Ogawa-san; he was always picking on me. That's why."

"Picking on you? Like how?"

Pei told the story about what had happened at Tombo three months earlier, when she tried to go back to pick up her train pass.

"Heavens, haven't I told you? When you report to work, you need to go there at least five to ten minutes before your shift begins. That's a basic courtesy here. The whole idea is so you don't *inconvenience* your coworkers or your boss."

"Just listen to you. You've totally gone native—so apologetic and timid, like a typical Japanese. You know, you'll make a perfect sheep among them!"

"Humph." Vivian whacked her rolling pin on the table. "Sheep or not, I've been here a lot longer than you have, and I know a thing or two. If you want to be successful here, I suggest you shut up and listen."

"Successful? Are you telling me you consider yourself a success here? Don't make me laugh, little sister. After all these years, just what have you got to show, huh?"

"Pei, be quiet! What has gotten into the both of you today?" Their mother charged into the living room again, her arms akimbo.

"I'm not done yet," Pei said, looking straight at Yan. "You're no different, Mother. Look at the two of you. You've been out of China for more than three decades, and what have you accomplished? Ma, your television is tiny, your apartment the size of a shoebox. There's not a single piece of furniture here that's worth anything. When most other people your age are enjoying the fruits of their success by relaxing at home, you have to scrape up a living by cleaning toilets and mopping floors. Honestly, I couldn't believe my eyes when I first came here. I'm actually quite embarrassed for you. My Shanghainese friend, Chen Hong, has only been here two years, and already her apartment looks *ten times* better than yours!"

Pei then turned around to face Vivian. "And you are worse! You've gone to college and beyond, stealing from me the kind of opportunities I could only dream of. But you've wasted them all. Look at you—at age thirty-five, you are still single. You don't even have a real job. You're pathetic. I'm not boasting, Meiyin, but if I had been given your chances in life, I'd have made something of myself by now!"

Vivian stared at her mother, her mouth dropped. *How dare Pei! Just who the hell did her sister think she was, calling her pathetic!* While Vivian knew Pei was not a modest woman by any means, she never would have expected Pei to be so outspoken and openly contemptuous of her and their mother. Her sister had not the faintest idea how hard it was to earn an honest living in a foreign country like Japan! Pei had the luxury of having a ready pad waiting for her when she arrived fresh off the boat, her tuition at her language school all paid for. Just how would she know how long it had taken the family to get where it was, modest as it may seem in her eye! As far as Vivian was concerned, Pei was an ungrateful brat who had turned around to bite the hand that fed her!

"So that's how you see us?" Vivian said with a mock laugh. "Fair enough, maybe Mom and I are both failures. Why don't you show us what you've got then? This is your big chance, because the Zhang family is counting on you to rectify its name."

"You just wait and see. And I won't need thirty years."

The front door suddenly swung open. "Mom, I'm here!" It was Da Wei. "Hey, what's with the sour faces?"

Seizing the moment, Pei threw off her apron and ran out the door without saying goodbye.

"What's with her? And where's she going at this hour?" Da Wei asked, taking off his shoes at the front door.

"Oh, she's upset because Mom's apartment is evidently too small for her," Vivian said, making a face. "She's also angry that I think too much like the Japanese. I guess after having been here eight months, she's beginning to think that she could do a lot better on her own."

"What's Vivian talking about, Mommy?" Da Wei put down his briefcase and went to sit in front of the TV.

"She's being sarcastic. We just had a fight with your big sister," Yan said, and went on to tell Da Wei about what had transpired.

"That's right, Da Wei," Vivian chimed in. "Big Sister said we're all an embarrassment to her. She thinks we're all total dead-beats, right, Mom?"

"Did she really say that?" Da Wei looked up in disbelief.

Their mother, now finishing up with the wrapping of dumplings at the *kotatsu,* only shook her head.

"Hmm, that's what I call being cocky and ungrateful. She was acting very strangely today. Mom, did you two have a fight before I came in?" Vivian said, looking at her mother.

"No. She came back from school just an hour before you arrived, and everything seemed fine—until you showed up, of course."

"I wonder . . . You don't suppose Big Sister is planning to move out of here? Otherwise, she wouldn't have been so rude to you," Da Wei said thoughtfully.

Vivian nodded. "You have a point, Da Wei. Although, I can't imagine how she can afford a place of her own yet, unless she's thinking of moving in with that Shanghainese friend of hers."

"Or with that Japanese man!" their mother said suddenly, as if the thought had just entered her mind.

Da Wei switched off the TV. "What Japanese man?"

"The one who has been calling your big sister every night. He usually calls the house at around one or two in the morning, which is very strange indeed. Honestly, your sister is not her usual self these days," their mother said, adding that Pei had been coming home very late, her face all done up with makeup. "She told me her friend had found her a job at a different restaurant that pays a lot better, saying that there's even a karaoke machine in it. Seriously, if you saw her walking on the street, you wouldn't recognize her."

"Come to think of it, she was dressed quite provocatively three months ago when I saw her," Vivian said. "She said she was going to a party in Shinjuku."

"There's more," their mother said. "She hasn't been sleeping at home much lately either. She says she has to work so late she sometimes misses the last train home. Evidently, she has been staying with a friend from work, or so she claims."

"That explains it. Big Sister must be thinking of moving in with this guy," Da Wei said. "Where do you suppose she met him?"

"At the new restaurant, no doubt," Vivian said.

"You don't suppose Big Sister is actually working at a karaoke bar?" Da Wei said, staring at his mother. "There are tons of such bars in Shinjuku."

"I'm not sure. But here, I found this in her coat pocket the other day," Yan said, wiping her hands on her apron as she turned to find something on the kitchen shelf. She brought back a match-box and handed it to Da Wei. On the black matchbox was a silver name printed in katakana: Kurabu Ajia.

"Club Asia? Mom, this is a Mama-san type of a snack bar," Da Wei said, his eyes still fixed on the matchbox.

"Well, looks like she has turned herself into a decadent bar hostess," Vivian snorted. "Working at a restaurant! Yeah, right. What a liar!"

"So what should I do? Forbid her to go to work?" their mother said with a frown.

"There's not much you *can* do, Mom. She isn't a child, and you can't very well ground her," Vivian said. She found it odd that their mother should be so lost about what to do with an adult child of hers who had gone astray. It was as if their mother was trying to compensate for all the years of her as an absentee mother to Pei during Pei's teenage years. How sad and tragic! Those years would never come back now.

"If I can't stop her from leaving the house, I can certainly chase her out of the house."

Da Wei shrugged. "And what would you have accomplished by doing that? It would make no difference to her either way."

"That's right, Mom. She has her Japanese boyfriend to turn to now. It'd make it that much easier for her to move in with him. But whatever her plans might be for the future, I hereby renounce my responsibilities with her. Please don't expect me to lift a finger to help her again. I mean, who does she think she is, calling us both failures? She thinks she can do better on her own? Let's just see what she can do for herself now!"

"Maybe she's good for a while, especially since I'd just wired her two hundred thousand yen," Da Wei said.

"And why would you do a thing like that?" Vivian asked with wide eyes.

"Because she said she was always broke." Da Wei went on to say that six weeks earlier, Pei had called to ask him to prepare a few documents for the extension of her student visa. In the course of their conversation, Pei mentioned she was about to take another field trip with the school, adding that the trip would cost her seventy thousand yen, which would pretty much wipe out all of her savings. So he offered to wire two hundred thousand yen into her account.

"When did you send the money?" their mother asked.

"About three weeks ago. But evidently I didn't do it fast enough for her," Da Wei said, adding that Pei had called his office repeatedly to make sure he had indeed transferred the money into her account.

"She's *so* greedy!" Vivian blurted out. "Did she even thank you for your tremendous generosity? You know, what really irks me about that woman is that she thinks everyone owes it to her. It's always 'me, me, me' with her."

"Well, maybe to Big Sister, saying 'thank you' is a sign of oppression. It would put her position way below ours, which would not sit well with her," Da Wei said. "Besides, she probably feels she's entitled to everything we own."

Vivian nodded. "You're absolutely right. I also heard that in socialist countries, people think whatever is given to you is within your rights! There's no such thing as a thank you." Now why hadn't she thought of that earlier? Perhaps she'd always been too emotional with Pei, taking everything with her a bit too personally.

Just then, the pot that was sitting on the kitchen stove boiled over. "*Ai-ya*, I forgot all about the *jiaozi*," Yan said, rushing to the kitchen. In a minute, she came out with a large plate of steaming dumplings. She left them sitting on the *kotatsu*. "Enough about your sister for now. The dumplings are ready, so let's eat."

Vivian brought over a few cushions and placed them around the *kotatsu* before sitting down. "Honestly, Mom, I really meant what I said a minute ago about Big Sister. I've never been insulted like that in my entire life," she said, shaking her head.

Da Wei bit into a dumpling and chewed thoughtfully for a while. "She probably said those mean things because she is still very naïve and overly romantic about the outside world." He said this with the confidence of a sage. "In her mind, the world is like a gold mine ready to be plucked. This is why she presumes anyone who's not rich or famous outside of China is either lazy or brain-dead. I say leave her alone for a while. She needs to go out there, experience a few setbacks before she will finally come to full grips with reality."

"Well said, Little Brother. From now on, perhaps you should help Mom keep an eye on Big Sister, because Mom is going to need a lot of help." Vivian patted her brother on the shoulder.

"I'm afraid I can't. I'll be leaving Tokyo soon."

"Leaving Tokyo? You mean on a business trip?" their mother said as she passed a bowl of vinegar to Da Wei.

Da Wei shook his head. "I'm going to Taiwan to help manage a branch office there. They're talking about an assignment for a year or two."

"What? And you didn't bother to tell me about it?"

"Mom, this was a complete surprise to me too. I didn't find out until just yesterday. It was a last-minute decision."

"Is this some kind of a promotion?" Vivian asked.

"Sort of. I'll be their very first non-Japanese employee to manage an overseas branch," Da Wei said with a proud smile.

"Really?" Yan's eyes lit up.

"Way to go, Little Brother," Vivian said, giving Da Wei a firm pat on the back. It occurred to Vivian that of the entire Zhang clan, Da Wei was the one who was truly successful, not a small feat given the exclusive society of Japan. With her head tilted, she eyed her brother, wondering if his company would have given him the opportunity had he been a woman. "So when do you leave?"

"In two weeks."

"Does this mean I won't be able to see you for an entire year?" their mother asked, sounding alarmed.

"No, Mom. The headquarters are here, remember? I'll still have to come back and forth for important meetings and to be introduced to clients. Besides, Taiwan is only a couple of hours away by plane. I'll come back often enough and whenever you need me to. Don't worry."

"That's good!"

"Come, Mom, this is a happy event. Don't ruin it with your silly worries," Vivian said, tugging at her mother's sleeve. "This turned out to be more than just a little birthday party. We should bring out some beer and celebrate."

"Great idea! This definitely calls for a toast, because it's your promotion," their mother said, running back to the kitchen. She returned with two cans of beer and three glasses. "Come, let's all have a toast!"

"To Da Wei, for a happy birthday and a successful career," Vivian said, raising her glass.

"Yes, here's to you, my proud son!"

"Thank you, both of you," Da Wei said. He barely raised his glass because the beer was almost brimming over the rim. He took a hearty drink from it and sighed with satisfaction.

Thirteen

"Say, Zhou Jing, what souvenirs would you take with you if you were going home to your *laojia*?"

At Club Asia, Pei was sitting with a fellow hostess from Sichuan. Zhou Jing was the young woman she'd seen dressed in a leopard-print top when she first came to the club for her interview. The two women were tucking advertisement cards into packets of tissues while sipping iced tea at an empty table. It was almost nine, and they hadn't had a single customer yet. Business began to slow shortly after Pei joined the club four months earlier, and it continued to get worse. Earlier in the week, sometimes they would serve only two or three customers for the entire night. That was why lately, Hana hadn't bothered to come in until well after nine. During these long, slow nights Pei had begun an unlikely friendship with the buxom, young woman—someone with whom Pei had initially thought she had very little in common.

"You're asking the wrong person. I haven't been back home in over two years. Remember?" Zhou Jing said, smacking her trademark red lips, which were enthusiastically painted a little outside the edges of her mouth.

At Club Asia, Zhou Jing had the reputation as the loudest dresser among the girls. She owned an assortment of the most eye-catching tops. Today, she had on a red form-fitting blouse with a hole cut out in the shape of a heart, revealing a deep cleavage.

"Although, when my cousin went home for Chinese New Year earlier this February," she continued, "I asked her to take two boxes of dried *shiitake* mushrooms to my mother. My mum was really tickled—she just loves the meaty Japanese mushrooms."

"What about relatives and friends? What would you give them if you were going home?"

"Relatives? I'd give them cigarettes if they were men. You know how it is with Chinese men—they're all smokestacks."

"And the women?"

Zhou Jing stopped stuffing tissue packets and gave Pei an impatient look. "Why are you asking all these questions all of a sudden? Are you going home soon?"

Pei nodded, looking past Zhou Jing. "I had a dream about my two boys a couple of nights ago. I keep dreaming about them lately." She sighed.

"*Two* boys? How did you get around that one? Did they fine you?"

Pei shook her head. "They're twins."

"Oh! That's lucky."

"It's been almost a year since I last saw them," Pei said, her mind wandering back to the morning when she'd left her apartment in Dalian without saying goodbye. She never heard from the boys since, not with Guomin's constant interference. Her letters sent to them were never answered, and Guomin would always hang up whenever he heard her voice on the phone. Now she wished with all her heart that she had made a bigger effort to see her sons before leaving China. She hated herself for not trying harder. Avoiding conflicts by sneaking out—it was such a Chinese trait, and she was sorely reminded that she had done no better than her mother in the way she said goodbye to her boys.

"How old are they?"

"They'll be eleven in just two weeks. I want to see them in time to celebrate their birthday over their summer break. Last year, I was so consumed with my visa application to Japan I didn't manage to do anything special with them."

"Well, then you should go. What's stopping you?"

Zhou Jing was an illegal immigrant. The twenty-three-year-old former kindergarten teacher first came to Tokyo on a tourist visa to visit her cousin, who was married to a Japanese.

She liked Japan so much she decided to overstay her visa in order to work at Club Asia. Although Pei didn't initially take to the woman, thinking she was a bit loud and immature, over time she had found Zhou Jing's warmth and enthusiasm refreshing and endearing. She also thought she could learn a thing or two from the young woman. After all, she had worked at Mama-san clubs for more than eighteen months and knew much about the business and the clients. Most importantly, Pei appreciated her new friend's frankness and honesty. Zhou Jing said things the way she saw them—not like Hong, whom Pei realized hadn't always been straight with her.

Since the incident at Hong's apartment, Pei got the distinct feeling that Hong had been avoiding her deliberately. She went so far as to change her work schedule so she wouldn't have to come to the club on the same nights as Pei. It was this vacuum that had brought Pei closer to Zhou Jing.

Pei toyed with a tissue packet. "It's the money," she said slowly. "I keep thinking I might not have enough. This is my first trip back home. I need to think about presents for relatives and former colleagues. You know what folks are like back home. Whatever you give them, they want them by the dozens. Fountain pens, lipsticks, everything has to come in assortments of tens and twelves. But here, even the smallest gift items can cost so much."

"Forget about the quantity. Go with the quality, or at least buy something that would give the impression that you've paid a bundle for."

"Like what?"

Zhou Jing thought for a second. "How about knock-off goods—bags, watches, perfume, wallets? I suggest you go to Ueno. Sometimes they have the authentic stuff there too, apparently stolen from somewhere. They're not too expensive, around two or three thousand yen apiece."

"Hmm, that's a thought!"

"And don't forget to advertise to your relatives and friends that they're authentic name brands, very expensive."

"Still, it's not going to be cheap. I need to buy at least ten to twelve gifts, and even at two thousand yen a piece, it will easily cost me over twenty thousand yen."

"I don't think you can do any better than that. When you go home, everyone will look at you like a celebrity. And they all want some of your glory and good fortune. If you skip the gesture, they will call you names behind your back. They might even curse your mother!"

"I know. I must raise enough money within the next few days somehow. But business has been so slow. What can I do?"

"How much do you need?"

"Total? At least two hundred thousand yen."

"Surely you have saved some money."

"I do have some savings, but it's for my boys' education. I can't touch it. I need to save lots of money, lots."

Zhou Jing thought for another while. "Why don't you ask Mama for a small advance? I bet she would at least loan you fifty thousand yen."

"And the rest?"

"You can always go to your Mito-san for help."

"You think that's a good idea?"

"Why not? He's your boyfriend. Why keep a boyfriend if he can't help you? Besides, what's one or two hundred thousand yen? I know Xiao Hong used to make him spend a lot more than that."

"Xiao Hong? Are you saying that they used to date each other?"

"Oh, you didn't know?"

Pei shook her head.

"Oh, well, they were lovers until about seven months ago, when she met her current boyfriend, who evidently has quite a bit of money. You should have seen how she treated Mito—she refused to sit with him when he came in, making quite a scene."

Pei was taken aback. How was it possible that Hong had kept this from her. She felt like a fool thinking that Hong was her best friend. "No wonder she was all funny about me seeing Mito.

You know, Xiao Hong and I used to be very close friends. But now we don't even say hello."

"I know. To tell you the truth, none of us here really likes Xiao Hong."

"I noticed that too, but why?"

"You know how she is: she's like a bee after honey when it comes to men. Once she has her eyes set on a target, she won't let go until she lays claim to it."

"You mean she stole someone's boyfriend?"

Zhou Jing nodded. "This new boyfriend of Xiao Hong's . . . what's his name? Yamada, I think. Anyway, he was originally interested in Li-san. Li-san, being her usual proud self, was letting him do the slow chase. But as soon as it became obvious to Xiao Hong that Yamada had a successful business, she immediately switched targets and started coming after him. All right, I suppose any guy who comes in the club is fair game. Still, she was blatant and thought nothing of attacking Li-san behind her back, slandering her in front of Mama-san and the customers. It became really unpleasant and ugly after a while. After that, we all learned to be extra careful with our special customers around her."

"So that's why she hated Li-san so much. How ironic. I heard it was Xiao Hong who first introduced Li-san to the club."

"Do you know why she recommended Li-san, or you, to the club?"

"Because we all went to the same language school. No?"

Zhou Jing shook her head. "It's because of money. Did you know for every fresh face she brings in the club, she gets to keep fifteen percent of their hourly wage?"

"You're kidding!" Pei said, stunned. "You mean to say I could have been paid more? Wait, how much do the girls make here?"

"Mama started all of the girls' wages here at 1,700 yen an hour. I bet you get a lot less than that."

"No kidding! I was started at 1,500 yen an hour. Are you saying Xiao Hong has been keeping the rest of my hourly pay?"

Zhou Jing nodded again.

"That snake. How could she do that to me? So she has been skimming a thousand yen from me every night. No wonder she was always the one who brought me the paycheck," Pei said, her head shaking.

"She calls it the 'introduction money.' Xiao Hong takes the cut from every girl she has brought in."

"What does Mama have to say about this?"

"Ha, what does she care? All Mama worries about is how to bring more customers into her shop. Because Xiao Hong knows how to charm the men into the club, she's Mama's favorite girl. She's golden here, and no one can touch her."

Pei looked at Zhou Jing, her eyes narrowed. "I bet you could though, if you wanted to. You're younger, and you're smart! You can beat her at her own game!"

Zhou Jing rolled her large eyes. "Easier said than done. I may be younger, but Xiao Hong has this incredible talent with men. The Japanese men seem to fall all over her. Must be her snake charm! They say Japanese men like Shanghainese women because they are clever and sophisticated. But most of all, they know how to play to men's vanity. Men just adore you if you know how to make them feel important and good about themselves. Me? I'm just too honest. I can't believe I've lasted in this business for a year and a half now, and at Club Asia, for almost a year. Sometimes I really don't know what I'm doing here."

"You talk as if you're thinking of quitting."

Zhou Jing let out a weird laugh. "Funny you should say that," she said, pausing briefly. "You know, I keep thinking I should quit and start something on my own. I feel so tired having to smile and pretend to be happy all the time. Seriously, I smile so much the muscles around my mouth hurt when I get home. I'm sick of the lies too; sick of telling the men how much I miss them when their bad breath and wandering fingers make me want to puke. The longer I work here, the less I respect myself. I used to feel that I was someone special, someone deserving respect. Now I just feel cheap."

Pei thought about Zhou Jing's comments for a moment. "What would you do if you quit?"

"Start my own boutique, maybe."

"A boutique! But that takes capital."

"That's why I'm still here. I thought I should wait a few more months and think things over. I'm still young; I can hold out a little longer. But then again, maybe I should just find a rich sponsor. It's easier to have someone else help out, just like Mama."

"You have any prospects?"

"At Club Asia? You can't be serious. The men who come here only come because they fancy a certain girl. But once they get the girl to sleep with them, or find a new target, they quickly disappear."

Pei nodded. She wondered if Mito thought like that too. Ever since their first night, Mito had leased a room at Murasaki Inn. Pei had made a habit of meeting him there, turning the place into a love nest and a convenient changing room whenever she had to dress up for work at the club. But how long would she be able to hold his interest?

Pei left work early that night. Business was so slow Hana finally asked her to leave at 10:30—two hours earlier than usual.

On her way home, Pei kept thinking about her conversation with Zhou Jing. She heaved out a sigh as she slowly approached the station. How she wished she were young like Zhou Jing. No. She didn't even need to be twenty-three. If only she could shave off eight or ten years from her thirty-eight, life would be so much easier. With fifteen years difference, she could practically be Zhou Jing's mother. The thought made her feel old and unattractive. Funny in China, she was never once made to feel inferior to other women because of her age. Now, this feeling of inadequacy was paralyzing her. If Zhou Jing could take time to think her life through because she still had many choices and options, then what about her? What choices did she have at her stage in life?

Pei saw a public phone at the corner of the train station. Without thinking, she picked it up and dialed Mito's home number, a number he'd cautioned her not to use except in the event of an emergency. Mito hadn't shown up at the club or Murasaki Inn in over a week. There hadn't been any explanations or phone calls. It wasn't like him at all. Until then, he'd been a loyal patron of hers at the club, coming at least twice a week to see her. She wondered what was keeping him away.

"*Moshi, moshi.*" It was Mito's voice.

Pei was relieved. "Hi, it's me, Mito-san! Sorry to call your home, but you haven't been to the club, and I was beginning to worry." Pei continued to address Mito by his last name even after they had become lovers. Perhaps it was the age gap between them—Mito was eighteen years older than Pei and had always been like a teacher to her. Every time they got together he always taught her a thing or two about Japan, be it the Japanese society, its culture, or the language itself.

"Wait, I need a couple of minutes. Can you call me back?"

Pei called back a moment later.

"Hi! My wife was in the living room listening. I didn't want to be too obvious, so I'm taking the call in the study." Mito's tone was apologetic.

"You don't suppose your wife knows?"

"I don't think so, but I can't say for sure. We don't say much to each other these days, other than about the bills, or our children and their school problems. Honestly, I don't think she cares either way, just as long as I keep putting money into the bank account. Ha! You know, she hasn't cooked for me in the last three years. These days I sleep in the study, and we keep two separate rice cookers in the kitchen. We might as well be divorced, the way we're carrying on. Anyway, enough of that! Why did you call, my sweet?"

"I haven't seen you in a while. I really miss you."

"Ah, I was away in Kyoto on a business trip. I just got back last night."

"There's one more thing. Mito-san, I need to go to China for a quick trip in about a week, and I desperately need some help with buying the plane ticket. I was wondering ..."

There was a pause. "How much do you need?"

"About two hundred fifty thousand yen. The ticket and hotel, they all cost so much," Pei said. She exaggerated the amount, remembering what Hong had once said to her: *With men, you can never be too polite. Make them spend as much as they can on you whenever possible.*

Another pause. "Well, our coffer is a bit tight this month. But perhaps I can spare two hundred thousand yen. Why don't you come to Murasaki Inn tomorrow afternoon? It's been a while."

"Yes, indeed. It's been a long while," Pei said, her mouth broadened into a delighted smile.

Part Two

Dalian

Fourteen

Yan was standing in front of her tiny kitchen sink, a frown on her face. From the faucet the water was gushing down like a cascade, hissing noisily into a blue pail she'd bought from the market earlier that morning. Heaped on the kitchen counter, a twisted pile of half-washed laundry waited to be rinsed.

Yan normally wouldn't have bothered with hand-washing the laundry. Not after she had already worked all morning cleaning offices in Otemachi. She'd just as soon take a nap or read a newspaper, but today she had no such luck. Her ten-year-old washing machine had given out on her, and the nearest Laundromat was fifteen minutes away.

If her dirty work uniforms could wait, Pei's rain-soaked jeans from the night before couldn't. Pei had told her she was going back to Dalian for a ten-day visit to see her two boys, and in her own words, "to right a wrong she'd committed before she left China." Pei was leaving in just two days, and Yan knew she needed to have all of her daughter's more presentable clothes ready—Pei was forever griping about not having enough clothes to wear as it was.

Yan bent over the narrow kitchen sink, rubbing the new denim with her bare hands. The icy cold water dug deep into her skin, stinging every pore.

"*Ittekimasu*—be back soon."

The lilting voice came from Mika, the neighbor's daughter. From the narrow kitchen window, Yan could see the girl's long pigtails bouncing in the mid-afternoon sun. She was skipping happily away with a friend, probably to a nearby store. Mika's smiles were heartwarming, reminding Yan of the Pei she remembered from long ago in Beijing. *Mama, I'm going to Shanshan's upstairs. Won't be long....* Pei was waving to her at the foot of the staircase, a sweet smile on her face. She was two weeks shy of turning eight, perhaps a few months older than Mika. But she had the same dark, sparkly eyes. Even the pigtails were similar. They were just as long and silky, perfect as those of a doll.

The kitchen sink was almost full now. Yan stopped the water and threw in more laundry. Pei's jeans were thicker than she'd expected. She had to really wring hard to get the soapy water out. She knew all the effort would be for nothing—it was very unlikely that she would get a thank you from Pei at the end of the day. More probable would be a chilling silence. She was getting a lot of silent treatments from her daughter these days. It had been nine months since their reunion lunch at the Golden Phoenix, and Yan couldn't remember seeing Pei smile once. It was as though she'd had all the joy wrung from her, like her soggy jeans. All that was left were scowls and frowns.

These days, whenever Pei was home, she was mostly fiddling in her room in silence. There were hardly any chitchats between mother and daughter now. Pei almost never ate dinner at home now, and she was always rushing to get out of the door by about five-thirty, claiming she had to get to work at some restaurant, though Yan knew very well this so-called restaurant Pei worked at was some sleazy bar by the name of "Asia-something." About three or four times a week she wouldn't make it home until close to 1:00 am, and even then, she would talk on the phone for a while before finally going to bed at 2:00 in the morning. How she was keeping up with the school work was a mystery to Yan.

"Aren't you working at a snack bar, not at a restaurant like you said you are?" A few weeks earlier, Yan had confronted Pei about her restaurant job, looking her straight in the eye after mentioning the matchbox she had found in her daughter's coat pocket.

"But I *am* working at a restaurant," Pei had said. It looked like she wasn't going to admit to anything, even though the evidence was stacked up against her.

"Then why are you practicing singing all the time with the tape recorder the minute you get back home these days? What sort of restaurant requires you to sing?" Yan had demanded.

"Mother, you're stuck cleaning offices all day. Just what do you know about Japanese restaurants? For your information, there are some restaurants that actually come with *karaoke* machines!" Pei had said, an unmistaken tone of contempt in her voice. "Besides, what do you care about what I do or not do? You were perfectly fine with me being left behind in Dalian for three long decades. I could have died and you wouldn't know it. Why fake the dutiful mom now? It's a bit too late!"

Yan was speechless. Old debts! Since Pei's arrival to Tokyo, the woman wouldn't stop jabbing at her mother every chance she got. Yan recognized the jabs were Pei's way at getting back at her, an outlet in venting years of frustration and anger at being left behind in China alone. Oh how very alone.

Yan could imagine how Pei must feel. Yes, she'd wronged Pei. But it wasn't the original plan. No, far from it. Yan and Yiwen had every intention of bringing all three children out with them. But how did you fight a law set up to curtail the huge floods of Chinese refugees pouring into Hong Kong, which had already absorbed millions of Chinese immigrants in 1960? The Chinese were desperately hungry from the famines and droughts created in the aftermath of Chairman Mao's failed Great Leap Forward campaign. In 1962, when they set sail to Hong Kong, she knew in her heart that she and Yiwen never meant to leave their precious first-born behind in China for long. It was only supposed to be for a year or two. But what use was it to bring it up with Pei now? Would it make any difference?

Since Pei's arrival in Japan, Yan had spent many a sleepless night tossing and turning, wondering what she might have done differently for Pei if she had to do it all over again. How she wished she could turn back the clock.

Yan unplugged the stopper to drain the dirty water from the sink. Without thinking, she turned on the faucet to start the water running again. She dumped the laundry into the water and mechanically rinsed it with both hands. When all the washing was done she meticulously wrung dry every single piece and went to hang them on the clotheslines on her tiny balcony. Pei's blue jeans, heavy from the absorption of water, pulled the entire line's weight down in the middle, the dripping legs almost touching the floor. Yan let out a long sigh.

In normal circumstances, Yan knew Pei would have been the pride of the family because she had been the brightest of the three children. But life was unpredictable, and history had a funny way of playing tricks on people.

The sudden ring of the phone stirred Yan from her troubled thoughts. She rushed back inside to pick up the receiver.

"*Wei,* hello?"

"How's Pei?" It was Yiwen. During the past nine months, he'd only called about once a month, and mostly to inquire about Pei.

Yan sat down by the *kotatsu,* her brow tightly knitted. She couldn't help it. Every time she heard her estranged husband's voice she cringed a little.

"Not great."

"Why not?"

"She's always complaining about everything. There's no pleasing that woman."

"Why? I pay her tuition, and she has a roof over her head. What else does she want?"

Yan clicked her tongue. "It's so like you to be talking like that. Don't you see? She's still furious that we left her in China for so long."

There was a brief silence on the other end. "Tell her I've already wired the rest of the tuition money. She really ought to be thankful. Not every Chinese student out there is as lucky as she is, having all of her food and bills paid for—"

"Ai-ya," Yan let out an aggravated grunt. "I feel like I'm speaking to a wall when I'm talking to you sometimes. Never mind! And you still owe me some money for this month." Yan had stopped calling Yiwen by his name long ago. She no longer saw the point of being cordial.

"What?" Yiwen raised his voice. "I just wired thirty thousand yen to you last week."

"I spent the money already to buy Pei some extra bedding and school supplies. Thirty thousand yen is nothing these days— her quilt alone cost twenty thousand yen. Besides, I need more for her school expenses, and I still have to pay rent on top of all this."

"What school expenses?"

"The two annual field trips, for starters. She's going to Hokkaido next week, for five full days. Expenses for these trips are not included in the tuition. Everyone knows that."

The phone went silent again. Then Yiwen hissed, "Sons of bitches! Always trying to squeeze more money from the parents!"

"Spare me. I don't have time for your commentaries. Just wire me another one hundred thousand yen, will you?"

"A hundred thousand yen? You've got to be joking!"

"I hate to break it to you, old head, but having an extra family member here is going to cost you a little. Pei isn't a stone statue that can dine on the northwest wind."

"Look, I can only afford fifty thousand yen. You can cover the rest with your wages, can't you?"

"I swear, every time I mention a sum you always try to bargain me down. We're not negotiating the price of a watermelon here."

"Fine. Sixty thousand yen! That's my last offer. I'll wire it into your account tomorrow. I've got to go." The phone went dead.

Yan slammed the phone down. Yiwen always had to have the last word. He had made it a habit to hang up on Yan without ever saying goodbye. She suddenly felt her face flush, followed by a splitting headache. She strained to breathe, and her limbs had gone weak. She knew her blood pressure must be surging. She had to lie down for a while, at least until she could catch her breath again.

You were perfectly fine leaving me behind in China for three long decades. Why fake the dutiful mom now?

In the dark, she heard Pei's voice again. Pei was right. She hadn't been a mother to Pei in the true sense of the word. Yes, she had let down her daughter. And yes, she should have tried harder to retrieve her in 1964. Now, because she hadn't been decisive all those years, Pei had to learn a new way of life as she neared the ripe age of forty.

In 1978, China officially opened to the rest of the world, one year after Pei married, and three years before Da Shan and Da Hai were born. That would have been a perfect year for Pei and her husband to leave China. The transition would have been seamless. And Pei would have been much younger too, only twenty-four. In theory, Yan could have gone back to China and taken her out then. In theory.

But the letter. Yiwen's expressionless face! The dark tunnel! Nineteen seventy-six, the year the family was turned upside down. Nothing was ever the same again after that. Even now as she closed her eyes, Yan could still vividly see the long, neat handwriting on the wrinkled letter she'd discovered in Yiwen's coat pocket.

My dearest Yiwen, I've been waiting for you all these years. I can't believe we are finally to meet again in Kyushu. My heart is soaring. I can't wait for your warm embrace. Yours always, Manyong

Yan could still feel the convulsions in her body as she read and reread the letter, overpowered by waves of shock and pain. Yan and Yiwen had lived apart for many years on several occasions during their marriage. She had heard from friends that there was once a young woman who was quite enamored with Yiwen, an assistant who used to work with him at a news agency in Beijing. Still, Yan never dreamt of the possibility that another woman could come between her and Yiwen. Could this Manyong be that young woman?

She thought of all the years she had spent waiting for Yiwen. First in Dalian, then in Beijing, and eventually in Tokyo, going through life counting days. How could he betray her like that?

No! They were supposed to build a better future together, and for the kids. It wasn't supposed to end like this! She could still remember how she'd torn the letter into tiny pieces, her body screaming from the inside out.

The handwriting told Yan that the sender was a cultivated Chinese woman and the tone that she'd known Yiwen a long time. She felt madly jealous, imagining that the writer of the letter had every fine quality she lacked. Was that why Yiwen was drawn to this woman?

Yan stewed for several days over what she should do. When she finally summoned enough courage to confront Yiwen, his reaction had been surprisingly calm. "So what if I've kept another woman? She's an intelligent woman and at least I can talk to her. But you—you can't even pick up a newspaper to read! I don't remember when we last had a real conversation."

"You—how dare you humiliate me like that? I—I may not have finished high school, but I'm the mother of your three children, you bastard ... heartless beast ..."

Yan remembered how she had stammered, her words flooding like an alphabet out of sequence. But before she could finish her sentence, Yiwen was already out the door. Yan stayed in bed all day and the day after, feeling weak and dizzy as though all her blood had been drained dry. It was around that time that she'd developed a heart condition.

Yiwen didn't come home until nearly a week later. From then on, he was a different person—cold and aloof, speaking only when necessary, and when he did speak, his eyes never met hers. It was as though he wanted to punish her for daring to challenge him with his secret. His home visits became increasingly erratic. He would come home unannounced, stay for a day or two, then disappear again for another week or so. When Yan complained, he would snap: "Look, you've got a roof over your head and three warm meals a day. What else do you want from me?"

By the time Vivian and Da Wei were in high school, Yan and Yiwen had practically become strangers. Although friends suggested that she divorce Yiwen and make a fresh start, she couldn't bare the thought of it. The children were still too young and needed to finish school. She also depended on her spouse visa to stay in Japan. She had been a housewife all these years. Could she make a living and raise two children on her own?

Was she taking the easy way out by staying with the status quo? Over the years, Yiwen had whittled away Yan's allowance. By the time Da Wei and Vivian were ready for university she barely had enough to cover her rent and was forced to start cleaning offices to make ends meet. Taking Pei out of China to share the family's 'wealth' was the last thought on her mind. There wasn't much to go around; she had tried to explain all this to Pei when she took the first trip back to see her in Dalian in 1980; then again in 84, and finally, at the most recent trip she'd taken with Vivian in 1990. And yet, how do you make an impatient young woman listen to what she had no intention of hearing?

Yes, she had wronged her daughter. But she was weak and powerless in the face of the cruel history, like a lone tree beaten and battered by the relentless desert storm. What gave her some hope was that times were different now, and that China was a different place. Perhaps Pei, her own daughter, would be able to do something about the future, and about her own children, and to, like Pei had said, "right a wrong" so the vicious cycle of a mother leaving behind her children in search of a false promise would finally come to an end. That was her wish, her only wish now.

Fifteen

Ten days later, Pei found herself pacing back and forth in the living room of Cousin Jian's Dalian apartment. Tiantian, her darling niece, was on a marathon phone call, her giggles getting steadily louder. She was sprawled face up across the couch in the living room, her feet propped up on the armrest. She'd been on the phone for the past thirty minutes, and there was no sign of her quitting anytime soon.

Pei, sitting in a chair next to Tiantian, drummed her fingers on the coffee table in irritation. She really needed to get of ahold of Jian, but with Tiantian tying up the phone, there wasn't much she could do. When she couldn't bear the wait anymore, she got up to open a window to try to cool off. She'd love to yank the phone away from the teenager and tell her that she was behaving like a spoiled brat. But she also knew better than to act on her impulse. Offending her niece was not something Pei could afford to do, not when she was a guest at the girl's house. Sure, she used to change Tiantian's diapers and take her shopping. But that was long time ago. Now, she was merely a distant relative passing through.

When Pei arrived in Dalian a week earlier, she'd initially thought of staying at a guesthouse. But when Cousin Jian offered her to stay with his family, she did not object. Pei had grown up with Jian. He was the second child of her maternal uncle, and the one who'd spent the most time with her during their middle school years. Although they had fought like cats and dogs as children, they became better friends as young adults, especially after both of them were married. Before Pei left China, Jian used to be very warm and chatty with her, often inviting her, Guomin, and the boys to his house for dinner. But now that she was back, this time as a houseguest, he seemed cooler and quieter toward her, as if something fundamental had changed between them.

Jian didn't even thank her when Pei handed him the two cartons of Marlboros and the duty-free Shiseido lipstick packs meant for his wife, Weiling. "Just leave them on the table," was all he said. Did he think the gifts had been too light?

Jian, being Da Shan and Da Hai's first cousin once-removed, had arranged for the boys to come directly to his house that day so they could have supper with Pei that evening. At first, Guomin wouldn't agree to let the boys see their mother, but he relented after Jian's active negotiation. He and Jian had been good friends, and he had to give him some face.

To help make matters easier, Jian even volunteered to meet the boys at a nearby bus station, allowing Pei to concentrate on the cooking instead. Pei was grateful for the arrangement. That way, she and Guomin could both save the embarrassment of having to meet in person. But the arrangement did come with a small price—she was not to take the boys out on the actual day of their birthday. Guomin wanted to save the big day for a home celebration with the boys and his new girlfriend. So as a compromise, Pei agreed to see the boys a couple of days earlier. The night before, with the help of Jian, Pei managed to have a brief phone conversation with the twins, which left her listless all night.

The first thing Pei did that morning was shop with Weiling at the Central Fish and Produce Market. They returned with bags upon bags of seafood and vegetables. Once back, she immediately began to prepare seafood dumplings—the boys' favorite. Weiling also helped, and together the two cooked up eight dishes in addition to the dumplings. Considering only three adults and three children were having dinner, the meal was practically a feast.

Still, Pei couldn't relax. She worried she didn't have enough snacks for the boys. So while waiting, she hurriedly went to the local stores to buy some nuts and candy. After that, she searched her suitcases to double-check the presents she had brought for the twins. Would they like the Power Ranger guns she'd so painstakingly picked for them? If not, at least the digital watches would be a sure hit. They were the latest model of a name brand. When all was done, she'd asked Weiling for ribbons and dressed the wrapped packages up with more bows. Only then did she return satisfied to the sofa with her cup of lukewarm jasmine tea.

By five o'clock in the evening, Pei could no longer sit still. She paced to the window, looking down at the front entrance of the apartment building three flights below. Jian and the boys should have arrived half an hour ago. What was keeping them? Pei so wanted to call Jian on his beeper, but Tiantian still wasn't quite done with her phone call. Shaking her head, Pei went back into the kitchen to reheat some of the dishes.

Finally, by the time the last rays of the sun had all but faded, and the lights had begun to come on one after another in the nearby buildings, Jian arrived with the boys. The boys seemed taller, their hair longer, almost covering their eyes now. That Guomin! Why couldn't he spare a few minutes to take the boys for a haircut?

"Oh, look at you! You have both grown so tall! Let me take a good look at you!" Pei squealed, rushing to hug her sons. But the boys didn't return her hug. They merely studied her with puzzled eyes.

"Ma, what happened to your hair?" Da Shan said, pointing at Pei's shoulder-length hair.

Of course, Pei realized, the boys had never seen her with dyed hair. Since working at Club Asia, she highlighted her hair a reddish brown at the suggestion of Hana in order to give herself a more modern look. To adults, the change would have been negligible. But to Da Shan's sharp, innocent eyes, the red color must have been glaring. Pei had forgotten how observant Da Shan was.

"Oh, it was a new color I tried out at a beauty salon the other day. It's very fashionable to wear your hair like this in Tokyo," Pei said, quickly brushing her hair back with her fingers. "Come here, you two. Come see what I have gotten you for your birthday!"

Pei handed the boys the packages she'd been fretting over only an hour ago. Just when Da Hai was about to tear into the larger package, Da Shan stopped him. "Don't! Remember, Baba said that whatever presents we receive today we should wait until day after tomorrow to open."

"What? Nonsense! Your father didn't say that, did he, Da Hai?"

Da Hai nodded sheepishly.

"That's very silly. This isn't his house. You boys can do whatever you want here," Pei said, her hands propped on her waist. "Come, boys, go ahead and open them. I want you to."

But neither boy moved. They looked at each other, confusion and apprehension written all over their faces.

"Come, don't be afraid. Today's our special day. I have flown a long way to see you two, so you can do whatever you want for a day. I promise your Baba won't get angry."

"But he will, and so will Auntie. She would get very mad at us if we didn't listen to Baba," Da Shan peeped.

This was the first time Pei had heard the boys make a direct reference to Guomin's girlfriend. She clearly played a much more prominent role in the boys' lives than Pei had expected.. "What would she do if she were angry?" Pei asked.

Da Hai shrugged. "She would smack us, and—"

"She what? Has she smacked you before?"

Both boys nodded.

"When?"

"Last Chinese New Year, after we went home from Grandma's," Da Shan said, referring to Guomin's mother.

"But why?"

"Because . . . because we . . ." Da Hai struggled for words. He always stammered a little when he was excited.

"We opened the red envelopes before we arrived home," Da Shan said, jumping to the punch line before Da Hai was able to finish his sentence.

"How dare the witch! I insist that you open the gifts now and see what she's going to do. You're *my* children, and—"

"*Suanleba*! Just let it be," Jian interrupted. "Why not just let the boys open the gifts later, like they agreed? Why ruffle things up and make life difficult for them? You will be gone in a few days, but they will have to live with the consequences."

Shocked by the sudden intrusion, Pei was speechless. She was already very upset at the unreasonable demands of her ex-husband and at the knowledge that her boys had been abused at his girlfriend's hands. Jian's words were like a hidden stick smacking her where she least expected. Why would he deal her a blow like that, further undermining her authority in front of her sons? Couldn't he see what the witch was trying to do to her and the boys? With clenched fists, Pei rushed to the kitchen, tears pouring down her cheeks.

"Look, you're really upsetting her."

In the kitchen, Pei could hear Weiling chiding Jian. A moment later Weiling came into the kitchen. "Pei, don't let what Jian just said upset you. He didn't mean any harm. He has a habit of speaking without thinking. Besides, you've come all this way to see the boys. Don't spoil it like this. This is a very precious opportunity. Don't you at least want to spend some quality time with the twins and have a hearty meal? Come. Let's go back to the dining table." Weiling gently tugged at Pei's sleeve toward the living room.

Pei nodded, wiping her tears away with the back of her hand. Da Shan and Da Hai looked confused at their mother's moistened eyes when she came out, but happily accepted some peanuts and candy from Weiling. After a while, they both followed Tiantian to her room to play video games.

They didn't come out to eat until almost eight o'clock. When they ate, they insisted on watching television at the table. Pei was sure half of the time they had no idea what they were eating. The meticulously planned night had turned into a total disaster. What was the point of her flying all this way? Her sons didn't seem to know what to say to her, and she didn't even get the satisfaction of watching them tear open their gifts. She longed to explain to them why she had left China, how their father had prevented her from seeing them, and how much she was saving for their education. But, as so often happened, she found herself tongue-tied. Plus, this was not a discussion she wanted to pursue in front of Jian, Weiling, and their snippy teenage daughter.

Pei saw the boys once more before leaving, and she had to beg for that visit too. She took them shopping for clothes at the Friendship Store in downtown Dalian. The boys were well behaved, but the busy shopping area offered no opportunity for a heart-to-heart talk. When it was time for her to say goodbye, she stuffed a one-hundred *yuan* bill in each boy's pocket. "Here's some spending money for you. You don't need to mention it to your father if you don't want to. Save it for the times when you want a special treat or a small toy, okay?" The twins looked at each other, then nodded with a smile. And that was that.

After seeing her sons off, Pei hailed a taxi for Shanshan's house. Pei hadn't seen her childhood friend for nearly a year. Shanshan, her old neighbor who was one year Pei's senior, had been working as a clerk at a municipal office. Pei wondered how her old friend was getting along. When Shanshan came to the door to greet her, Pei burst into tears, finally giving way to the deep sadness she had been feeling for the past few days. Over a plastic, green thermal pot of buckwheat tea, Pei recounted to Shanshan the story of her visit, adding how helpless and heartbroken she felt now that she was no longer the all-important figure in her boys' lives.

"Pei, don't take it too hard. It's a natural progression," Shanshan said, gently patting Pei's shoulder. "When boys are young, they tend to cling to their mothers. But once they turn ten or older, it's inevitable that they look to their father as a model. Besides, you mustn't forget that you haven't seen them in almost a year. They probably didn't know what to expect, given how you left them without saying goodbye and all. Of course, that doesn't mean you can't make amends. Why don't you tell them you will stay in closer touch with them from now on? Tell them you will come to see them next year and the year after . . ."

"But I can't. Not next year," Pei said, shaking her head.

"Why not?" asked Shanshan, slurping a gulp of tea from her jam-jar glass.

"How can I? My life in Japan is still so shaky. I don't want to make empty promises like my mother did. Who knows? I may not be able to come back for quite a while. I'm always broke. I had to borrow money to make this trip, you know."

"Broke? You?" Shanshan shook with laughter. "Come on, my friend, you don't need to hide the truth from me. Ah, I get it. You're afraid I might ask to borrow money from you? Don't worry, I haven't thought of that yet—at least not right away."

"No, Shanshan, I'm serious. You must have heard how bad the Japanese economy is getting. Many businesses have already folded. The restaurant I work at has just cut my work hours," Pei said, referring to Club Asia. "You do know that most Chinese who go to Japan start out by going to a Japanese language school in order to keep their visas? Well, it costs a lot of money to go to a school like that, and if I don't have enough work, I don't even know if I can pay my tuition, let alone buy plane tickets to come home," Pei added. She deliberately chose to blemish the fact that it had been her father paying her tuition all along. She didn't know exactly why she lied. Perhaps she wanted to sound like a hero in front of her childhood friend. Besides, she really didn't want Shanshan to think the family was swimming in money, lest her friend might get the wrong idea and start pushing to come stay with Pei in Japan. Then it occurred to her that she was trying to dissuade her best friend from leaving China in the very same way Meiyin had done to her ten months ago. But what to do? She was in no position to host anyone in Japan. Life was an odd thing, and the table could turn quickly on a dime.

Shanshan frowned. "Look, Pei, I don't care how bad you say the economy is. The truth is, you're still in a capitalist country, a free world. Surely you can make a lot more money than we can ever imagine back here. So what if Japan's economy is bad? You'll find a way sooner or later. Geez, what's happened to you, Pei? You used to be so full of hope. Really, don't underestimate your ability. I'm counting on you now."

"Counting on me? What for?"

Shanshan's eyes widened with excitement. "I've been doing a lot of thinking since you left China. I think I want to leave China too. I don't want to waste my life here without ever venturing out to see the world, especially now that my daughter is in college. You're my dearest friend and my inspiration. Do you think you can find a way to get me out of here?"

Pei knew it was coming, but she was still taken aback by her friend's forwardness. The Shanshan she remembered from before she left Dalian wasn't this insistent and pushy, bombarding her with all these questions and demands. Couldn't Shanshan tell that she was distressed? Or could it be that the lure of money and opportunities outside of China had changed her friend overnight?

"Shanshan, haven't you been listening? I *don't* have money."

Shanshan clicked her tongue, her head shaking. "See, I knew you were afraid of lending me money. Look, I'm not asking for money. What I need is for you to become my sponsor in Japan. I want to go there; I want to be just like you."

Pei sighed, her shoulders slumping. "You're asking the wrong person. To qualify as a sponsor in Japan you need to be a Japanese national or someone who has a stable job with a large Japanese company. I'm neither."

"Well then, who is *your* sponsor?"

"My brother."

"Good. You can ask him to sponsor me then!"

"I don't know, Shanshan. This is a big favor. He doesn't even know you."

"But *you* do. Come on, Pei, you and I have been the best of friends since childhood. Can't you vouch for me?"

"What about your husband?" Pei asked.

"Oh, we haven't been getting along too well since he lost his job. Besides, I'm not young any more—I'm about to turn forty. I need to get out. Really! I feel that it's now or never."

That sounded familiar. It was the same excuse Pei had used with her mother and Meiyin. How could she argue? "I suppose I can give it a try. But I can't guarantee that my brother will say yes," she replied, even though she knew very well she would never mention any of this to Da Wei.

"Of course, of course. I just want to at least give it a try. Pei, I'll be forever grateful if you do this for me," Shanshan said, reaching out to give Pei's hands a little squeeze.

The following day, before Pei was to leave for the airport, Jian insisted on taking her out to lunch at a glitzy seafood restaurant. He ordered several dishes, including razor clams, shrimps, and abalone, and appeared to be particularly attentive to her. He made sure her glass was always filled with beer.

After most of the dishes were served, Jian turned to Pei with beer-reddened cheeks. "By the way, Pei, how's Cousin Da Wei's business?"

"It's not his business. He's only an employee."

"But he does work for a big trading firm, no?"

"Yes." Pei nodded.

"And he's in a managerial position, right?"

"That's right."

"Do you think he might be able to persuade his boss to invest in our business? A very good friend of mine and I are thinking of starting up a car parts company here, and we need some capital. It's a good time to be investing in China now."

Pei scratched the back of her neck. "That, I'm afraid, is something you should ask him directly."

"Don't you see him?"

"Not often enough. Besides, this concerns money. It's best that you speak to him directly."

"Very well then. You have his phone number?"

"My mother does. I can ask her for you if you want."

"Good. Perhaps I can convince Da Wei to come here for a visit with Auntie first. When you see Auntie, do send my best regards. Tell her to come visit us and to invest in the motherland. Tell her that she's most welcome to stay with us here in Dalian."

"I will try," Pei said, resigned. *So that's what this meal was all about.* She wondered what her mother would say to Jian's idea.

"Here, let's drink to Auntie's good health," Jian said, filling Pei's glass with more beer.

"Enough, enough!" was all Pei could manage. She was very relieved when it finally came time for her to go to the airport.

Sixteen

In Tokyo, Vivian had turned her cozy loft apartment into a battle zone, with half of her living room floor covered with her dirty laundry. It was a beautiful fall day. After a week of rainy days, the sun had finally come out, and Vivian thought it was an excellent day to do her laundry, which had piled up into a small mountain.

After finishing the rinse cycle on her washing machine, she took the clean wash in a basket and opened the sliding door to her veranda. That was when she saw the creature—a huge black crow with mean eyes. The bird had been prancing along the edge of the veranda looking for food. The sudden squeak of the sliding door startled it. Instantly the crow took flight, letting out a couple of piercing caws before swooping down and disappearing into a nearby bush.

Crows. The nightmare of Japan's metropolis! It wouldn't be that far off to call them rats with wings because you could always find them among Tokyo's garbage dumps and trashcans. And they didn't always wait for the trash either. They sometimes stole and plundered in broad daylight. One time, a crow made away with her bag of sandwiches when she was picnicking at Yoyogi Park. The sight of the bird made her blood curdle.

Vivian leaned against the edge of the veranda and let out a loud hiss, as if the feathered scavenger could still hear her. The afternoon sun shone brightly. She looked out to the landlord's meticulously pruned garden below. In the middle of the lawn stood a lone persimmon tree. Although almost entirely stripped of leaves, the ripening, red persimmons were weighing down its boughs. The plump, succulent fruits reminded her that the moon festival was not far off. The thought of double egg-yolk moon cakes made her mouth water. She must call her mother to plan a family get-together soon.

She bent down and drew a wrinkled blouse from the basket, shaking it once with force. *Crash!* When Vivian looked down, she saw that she'd accidentally knocked down a bell-shaped porcelain wind chime that had been hanging from the frame of the sliding door, its broken remains now scattered on the tile floor at her feet.

Damn! Vivian squatted and picked up a single shard. The ceramic chime—a delicate ware done in the exquisite Kiyomizu-yaki style—had been a gift from her mother. It was a souvenir from a trip to Kyoto her mother had taken with a colleague many years ago. It was one of Vivian's favorite things around the house. Now the chime had been silenced forever; she would no longer hear its clear ringing against the wind. She shook her head, angry with herself.

After she was done sweeping up the broken pieces, Vivian picked up her Chinese textbooks and left to meet with Shizuka, her new Chinese language student. A couple of weeks earlier she had met the woman at a work-related party and became immediately intrigued by her background as a Japanese-born Chinese. When Shizuka, who spoke almost no Chinese, asked Vivian to become her private Chinese tutor, Vivian readily agreed. She was happy to help the young woman to become more fluent in her mother tongue, knowing how devastating it could be for a rootless Chinese to be living in a foreign country not having a solid grip of her own identity. It didn't occur to her that her own identity wasn't that much more solid than her friend's, even if she did speak more Chinese.

It was after 9:00 when Vivian finally came home. She and Shizuka had had such a good time chatting over their lesson they'd decided to go out for dinner. She'd barely set foot in her apartment when the phone rang. Who could be calling her at this hour?

"*Moshi, moshi,*" she said, picking up the phone.

"*Sumimasen.* Is Vivian-san there? My name is Hashimoto, a neighbor of Wu Yan's."

"This is she. Hi, Hashimoto-san, how are you?"

"Ah, am I glad to finally reach you, Vivian-san. Listen, this is about your mother—"

"My mother? What happened?"

"She collapsed this afternoon." Hashimoto went on to say her mother had had a stroke and had been taken to a hospital. She said it was a good thing she'd been on her balcony that morning too. She'd heard a big thump next door, so she peeked through the crack and discovered Yan laying on the tile floor. "If I hadn't called the ambulance, who knows what would have happened to her? You know, you really should check on your mother more often. She's getting old and needs better care from you."

"I had no idea! Wait, where is she now?"

Mrs. Hashimoto said her mother was at a hospital in Shinjuku. "Look, if I were you I'd go see her right now. She has been waiting for you all afternoon."

"Of course. I'll go right this minute. Thank you so much for your help, Hashimoto-san. I don't know what I would have done. . . ."

Her mother was wide awake when Vivian arrived at her hospital bed. She was talking to a nurse, who'd come in to refill her intravenous drip.

"Mom, how are you feeling?" Vivian rushed over to grab her mother's hand.

"Ah, you're finally here," her mother snapped, turning to face the wall. "I'm still alive, thanks for asking."

"Mom, sorry it took me so long, but I came just as soon as I could."

"You know how long it's been since I was checked in here?" her mother said, craning her neck to look at Vivian. She looked tired, her eyes bloodshot, and one side of her face sagged in a peculiar way.

"Mom, I didn't know about your stroke until Hashimoto-san called me, which was thirty minutes ago. I dropped everything to come here."

"And if it weren't for her, God knows where I would be now."

"I'm sorry."

"When Hashimoto-san brought me in, she helped take care of the paperwork and paid the initial thirty thousand yen for the hospital bed. You must thank her properly for me when you see her again."

"Of course I will. I'll pay her first thing tomorrow. I'll even take a present."

"I want you to go to my apartment and retrieve my pajamas and radio," her mother said.

Vivian nodded. "No problem."

Her mother let out a long sigh. "So where have you been all night? Hashimoto-san probably called you ten times."

"I was teaching Chinese to a friend. I went out with her to dinner after that."

Her mother sighed again. "I wish you'd settle down and find yourself a real job so I wouldn't have to play detective to find you," she said, struggling to sit up.

Vivian, still standing, was quick to give her a hand.

"I felt ... so totally helpless today. It was as though I didn't have any family or friends this afternoon. I'm not young anymore. I'm sixty-four, an old lady now. The least you could do is to call and check on me from time to time. What if I dropped dead tomorrow? Would any of you find me?"

"Mom, don't be like that. I'll try to call you every day from now on, okay? What else do you want me to say?" Vivian said, raising her voice.

Vivian took a deep breath, then settled down in a chair by her mother's bed. "You know, you could have called Pei at work too," she said in a softer tone. "Does she know you are here?"

"No. Didn't I tell you? She went to China a week ago."

"To China? To see her boys?" Vivian was a bit surprised that her sister had left for China so suddenly. She didn't hear about any of this from either her sister or her mother. Then it occurred to her it had been almost two weeks since she last spoke to her mom. She'd been a horrible daughter.

Her mother nodded. "She won't be back until next Monday."

"Hmm. She's never around when you need her. But Mom, how did it all happen? What did the doctor say?"

Her mother said the doctor told her she'd had a stroke, a mild one. At first she couldn't understand him completely. Luckily, he wrote down the words in Chinese. Now her entire body felt numb on her left side. At times it felt as though she was lying on a thousand needles.

"The doctor warned that if I wasn't careful, my entire left side could become paralyzed. He said he could help correct the problem, but I must stay in the hospital for a while to undergo intensive rehabilitation."

"How long is a while?"

"He didn't say, but the nurse told Hashimoto-san that it could be as long as three months."

"Three months? That's a long time."

"The doctor said I was one of the luckier few because the stroke was mild, which was why I woke up fairly quickly." Her mother said she'd been feeling rather tired that morning after work. She had taken an early nap and went to do the laundry, only to find the clothesline was broken. She bent down to mend the clothesline, but when she tried to get up, she felt an acute pain in her head and collapsed.

"Hashimoto-san told me she had to make her daughter climb over to my side of the balcony in order to get to me."

"That's incredible! We're so lucky that she was around."

"Shhhh! Can you two please keep it down? The other patients are trying to sleep." A nurse, who had come to pull the bed curtains for Yan, frowned at Vivian. "You really should be going now. Your mother needs her rest, not getting excited at this hour." She gave Yan some pills and handed her a glass of water. Vivian noticed her mother could only hold them with her right hand. She had to put the pills into her mouth first, then take the water glass with the same hand.

Vivian nodded to the nurse. "Sorry. I won't be long now." After the nurse left, Vivian poked her head back into the curtains. "I'll be back first thing in the morning. You sleep tight, Mom."

Her mother nodded. And within minutes, Vivian could see her body rising and falling gently with the rhythm of her soft breathing.

Seventeen

At the Yoneda Language Institute, Mrs. Ohashi pointed at two unfamiliar words she'd written on the whiteboard. "What's the difference between *saseru* and *saserareru*? Anyone?" she asked, looking at the class.

"No one? Well, they're both imperatives. While one's active, the other one is passive ..."

Pei frowned. She found it difficult to concentrate on what Mrs. Ohashi was saying, her memory pulled back to the conversation they had had in the teacher's small office just a few minutes ago. Pei had gone into Mrs. Ohashi's office asking for a letter of recommendation, which she had heard was an important accompaniment to a job interview in Japan. A week earlier, the principal had issued a note reminding everyone at the language institute that the recruitment season for both company employees and college students was upon them, and that those looking to join a Japanese company or pursue a higher degree at a Japanese university must take care to make the necessary inquiries well in advance.

"Frankly, at thirty-nine you're too old to be employed as a junior employee at any Japanese firm," Mrs. Ohashi had said. "I can't imagine any company would want to hassle with a work visa for an unskilled worker like you. A letter of recommendation wouldn't do you much good anyway, so why waste time with that?"

Pei felt restless, her entire body itchy with rashes. She was near the end of her journey as a Japanese language student. In another five months, she'd have to leave Yoneda. She must do something now.

The obvious thing to do was to apply for a job, as many of her schoolmates were doing. The thought of going to college didn't even cross her mind because she knew she wouldn't be able to afford the expensive tuition. But Pei soon discovered she wasn't up to the task of a job search either.

With the list of companies suggested by the school principal in hand, she started out by buying several packets of resume forms at a stationary store. The writing part wasn't easy; she'd never had to put together a resume in her life, since her jobs in China had either been secured through an introduction or assigned to her by the local government.

After soliciting help from some more knowledgeable friends, Pei finally managed to put together a sample resume. She sent out more than twenty copies to various companies, but quickly realized her chance of finding a white-collar job was next to zero. In her research, Pei discovered she had a few fatal handicaps. The first strike against her was that she wasn't Japanese, which meant her application would immediately be put in the "junk" pile of dubious jobseekers. Any company looking to employ a foreigner must apply for a work visa for the would-be employee, a process that could take months, so unless the foreign applicant had some really marketable skills, no company would bother.

And while a small number of Japanese companies were happy to hire some Chinese to help them break into China's huge market, Pei knew her chances would still be extremely slim because there were simply too many Chinese students like her swarming Tokyo's streets, most of them ten or even twenty years younger. In a market economy, younger means cheaper to hire. This was something Pei didn't fully appreciate until she began her job search. Her age meant she was virtually unemployable. Now the task of finding a job seemed daunting.

She thought of approaching Da Wei. Even though her brother had moved to Taiwan, she reasoned he could probably still use his *guanxi* to get her an interview at his Tokyo office. Da Wei was eager to help on the phone, and promptly directed her to the right person. But Mr. Tanaka, the human resource manager at his company, was less than enthusiastic. "I'm afraid we will only be interviewing for junior employees up to the age of twenty-nine in the next couple of months," he said politely on the phone. "Perhaps we can invite you for an interview in the future when we're ready to hire those in their mid-careers," he offered.

"When might that happen?" Pei asked, her voice sounding a little desperate.

"I'm afraid I don't know yet."

Worried about her future, Pei felt sick for two days, unable to sleep or eat. It was only as a last resort that she decided to visit Mrs. Ohashi's office. She reckoned at least Mrs. Ohashi could vouch that she had been an A student at Yoneda Language Institute, complete with a near-perfect attendance record. With no experience interviewing for a white-collar job in Japan, Pei also thought a letter of recommendation might boost her confidence at job interviews.

But the meeting had been a disaster. Not only did the teacher refuse to write Pei a letter, she had further undermined her confidence by cutting her down. She told Pei that her English degree received from the night school of Dalian University of Foreign Languages, which Pei had initially hoped would separate her from other Chinese like her, meant very little to Japanese companies. "Only an advance Japanese degree can help you if you wanted to get a job here," Mrs. Ohashi had said coldly. The last suggestion she gave Pei was to seriously consider going back to college to learn more skills.

By the time Pei left Mrs. Ohashi's office, she was trembling so badly with anger and humiliation she came very close to just turning around and going home. It was only after the first break that Pei finally calmed down slightly. Although she hated Mrs. Ohashi for refusing to write her the recommendation, her teacher's suggestion finally began to sink in. Perhaps furthering her education wouldn't be such a bad idea.

Her nights working at Club Asia had also made one thing very clear: money could only take you so far unless you had the right kind of credentials. Tired of dealing with what she now saw as the lower life forms of society at the club and yearning for something better, Pei was convinced that education would be her only answer to moving forward.

Having made up her mind about continuing school, she spent the next few hours thinking about nothing but college options. She had always been a top student and had kept good grades even when she was attending night college in Dalian. But what should she study now?

She thought of the different choices of schools, fantasizing about the many possibilities. If she went for a liberal arts degree at a graduate school, she could become a professor at a university. Then again, studying business might be even more practical; she could then become a high-ranking manager at a multinational firm. She let her mind race through different options, until she started thinking about how she might raise funds for the hefty tuition required by most colleges.

Then the thought of majoring in fashion suddenly came to her. That was it! Pei had developed a passionate interest in fashion once she'd experienced how different a flattering, up-to-date outfit could make her feel. During slow times at the club, she and the other hostesses pored over the latest fashion magazines, discussing each designer and hairdo.

In China, she grew up wearing the same baggy, drab colors and fabrics as everyone else. One good thing about living in the sophisticated, fast-paced culture of Tokyo was that it had shown her how one's confidence and self-image could be expressed through clothes. China was still very much behind the rest of the world as far as fashion went. She could study fashion and start her fashion house someday in China. Many fashionable young Chinese women were following the trends of Japan. With a degree from a Japanese fashion school to back her up, she could be a great success. Then she remembered Zhou Jing talking about starting her own boutique in her hometown in Sichuan. Perhaps the two of them should go into business together. Zhou Jing would be a great partner.

There was another up side if she went to a fashion school: the relatively cheaper tuition. She remembered someone at school mentioning that tuition at a fashion academy could be half the tuition than at a regular university because the program usually took two years instead of four. Learning a new professional skill in two years would not only save money, but precious time too.

Still, tuition could go for at least one million yen a year, or roughly twice the amount she was paying at her language school. Where was she going to get the money? She had about half of that saved from working at the club and from pocket money given to her by her mother and siblings. But she couldn't imagine spending any of it. It was all she had, and she needed to save it for her boys and for other emergencies.

She thought of her father. Didn't he say he would pay her tuition for two full years as long as his company was still standing? If she left Yoneda in March, she would only have been in school for eighteen months—six months short of two years, which technically meant that her father would still be obliged to help her out. Perhaps her mother might also be willing to help a bit. Her recovery was coming along well. And after all, Pei was also doing this as a way to ensure a visa to stay in Japan.

If her parents agreed to help her halfway, she would only need to raise half a million yen. She thought of Mito, realizing she hadn't seen him for a little over three weeks since she got back from Dalian. She must call to see how he was getting on.

During lunch break, Pei found a public phone and dialed Mito's work number.

"*Moshi, moshi!*" A man sounding just like Mito answered the phone.

"Hello, Mito-san, is that you?"

"You're looking for Mito? Sorry, he's just stepped out of the office for his lunch break. Can I take a message?"

"Ah ... that's strange. Well, I'll call later. Thank you." Pei hung up the phone. She swore the man she'd just spoken to was Mito. But why did he refuse to speak to her?

Before leaving for Dalian, Pei had told Mito she would be back in twelve days. That was mid-October. It was the beginning of November, and he hadn't bothered to call or visit her at the club. Even at Murasaki Inn, which Pei continued to use as her dressing room, she hadn't detected any signs of a recent visit by the man. Before her trip to Dalian, Mito did mention he'd be away on a business trip. Still, he should be back by now. Was there something wrong?

They had last seen each other at the inn. In the bathtub, she had gently massaged his back, pouring warm water over him as she tenderly worked her hands down his spine. She had causally mentioned the prospects of them sharing an apartment together someday.

When Mito made no attempts to answer her, she slapped him playfully on the shoulder. "Look, I'm not asking you to marry me. That can wait until your divorce is finalized. All I'm asking is that we try to live together like a couple should."

Still he'd said nothing. That was when she snapped. "You men! What's wrong with you?" She rose abruptly from the tub and stomped out of the bathroom wearing a towel.

A few minutes later, Mito had followed her to the bed, his naked torso dripping with water. He put his wet palms on her shoulders, rubbing her bare nape with his rough hands. "Listen, Pei-chan, why don't you give me some time to think it over? It's not as though we need to make a decision right now. The matter can wait until you come back from your trip. Why don't we just focus on having a good time tonight?"

That was twenty-four days ago. Did Mito have a change of heart? Feelings were tenuous. A lot could happen in the course of a month. Pei paced the marble floor of the school hallway, her spirits low. She wished she could go check on Mito right that minute, but she couldn't. She had to go to the hospital after school because she hadn't seen her mother in two days.

Eighteen

In the hospital hallway, Yan had been struggling to walk with the help of a walking stick. The doctor said she must try to walk around the hospital twice a day for thirty minutes, adding that the exercise would be crucial to her full recovery.

When she came to an open window, she stopped for a break, poking her head out to watch the comings and goings of visitors from the hospital entrance down below. It had become a daily ritual: after she finished with her nap, she would take her walk, waiting for one of her daughters to show. For six weeks, Pei and Vivian had taken turns coming to see her in the afternoons. At first Pei, having just returned from her trip to Dalian, was good about showing up on time at around 3:30. Then her visits would become tardier and tardier. One time, she didn't show until well after 4:30. Two days ago, she failed to show at all, but merely called to say she'd been asked to take an earlier shift at the "restaurant" that afternoon, and that she had a lot of homework to do.

Later, when Yan mentioned this to Vivian, she seemed annoyed. "What's wrong with her? Can't she spare one hour of her day to be with her mother, instead of only thinking about what's convenient for her?" Vivian had said.

Yan, however, saw it differently. "Your sister didn't grow up with me. Perhaps she doesn't feel as strong a bond with me as you and Da Wei. Perhaps she already feels that she's fulfilling her duties by coming to see me at the hospital at all."

Yan sometimes wondered if Pei saw her more as an aunt than a mother. On a good day, Pei would be cordial, if distant to her.

But on a bad day, she was sullen and stoic. Yan almost never got the feelings of love and warmth from her the way a mother would normally receive from a daughter. And yet she couldn't, in good conscience, blame Pei. The child had gone through so much in her life she probably could not feel much of anything anymore. Poor child. She was made to shoulder so much of the history—the history of a nation, the history of a family. It wasn't fair. No, not at all. But Yan had no idea at the time that her ploy of making Pei play a losing game would cement her daughter's destiny for life. She was essentially choosing a loser's fate for her first-born. What had she done? If only she knew.

Below the hallway window appeared a frail man with a distinguished head of silver hair. He hobbled out of the hospital entrance with the aid of two crutches. A middle-aged woman, probably the old man's daughter, helped him into a cab. Yan found it agonizing to watch him lying still in the car seat while his daughter tucked his lifeless legs into the taxi. She frowned. Old age could be so ugly!

A young cleaning lady in a light blue uniform passed by Yan, a mop in her rubber-gloved hands. She politely excused herself to clean the area near the window. Yan staggered to a nearby bench and watched the young janitor do her work. There was a magic quality to the young woman's movements, her mop zigzagging on the tiled floor as if she were working on some gigantic piece of brushwork. Without realizing why, Yan felt droplets of hot tears rolling down her cheek. She used to be able to do this kind of work with similar ease and grace.

Her boss, Morita-san, had told her on many occasions that she was one of his best employees. The other day he had surprised her by coming to visit at the hospital. Morita-san was cordial and sweet, but expressed a strong interest in her returning to work once she had recovered. To this, she merely nodded. She knew better than anyone that her days as a janitor were over. She couldn't see herself bending down to scrub the grime off the toilets of office buildings anymore. The doctor had told her that exerting herself in any vigorous way would be flirting with death. But what good were you if you couldn't work?

The worst part about not being able to work was that she would lose her autonomy, as well as her only source of income. She had limited savings, and the thought of a long future without money frightened her. Yes, she could always ask the children to help. But a life of dependency and constant pleading for money was not in her character. If Yiwen hadn't had a change of heart, it wouldn't have come to this. It had been a month and a half since Vivian last called Yiwen, informing him about the news of Yan being in the hospital. Vivian said her father had given the usual excuse about being busy, although he had promised he would come for a visit later. But would he? Would he care enough to see how she was doing?

Tong! Tong! The chime of the grandfather clock in the hallway told Yan it was already three o'clock. Pei probably wouldn't show for another thirty minutes. Yan stood up with the help of her stick and was just about to walk back toward her room when she heard someone calling to her from behind.

"Mother, where were you? I was looking all over for you."

Yan turned around and saw Pei. How did she get past the hospital entrance without her noticing?

"How're you feeling today?" Pei asked, helping Yan walk back to her bed.

"Not much different from yesterday. Being confined to bed all day has got to be the most agonizing way to live, I must say. So, how's school?"

"Okay." Pei pulled up a chair and sat down.

"You seem unhappy. Something's bothering you?" Yan leaned against the pillows to make herself more comfortable.

"I was thinking about tuition," Pei said.

"Tuition? But your father already paid your tuition in full for the year!"

"I'm not talking about the language school. I'll be done with it in three months. The question is: Where do I go next? I have to secure a new school before my visa expires."

"Ah, that same old question again! So what're your thoughts?"

Pei gave a small smile. "Fashion school."

Yan nodded slowly, her brows knitted. "Fashion school? But why?"

"Mother, I'd love to get into a university or graduate school program, but I know we don't have that kind of money. Fashion schools, on the other hand, are more affordable. I just called a fashion academy near Ryogoku today, and they told me their tuition is only about one million yen a year."

Yan stifled a gasp. "I don't know about spending so much money just so you can learn how to sew."

"It's not about sewing, Mother," Pei said, rolling her eyes as if Yan were a stupid child. "Japanese fashion is well known. If I can't go to graduate school, at least let me learn something useful. I'm not asking you and father to pay for the whole thing this time. I only need you to help with some of it, maybe half—"

"I knew it, it's always about money with you," Yan said, shaking her head. *Why does it always have to come to this?* "Does your father know about your plans?"

"No, but I'm sure he won't object because this is crucial to my securing a visa."

"If your father is willing, I won't object either. But I'm afraid I can't help you with the money this time. You can see I'm ill; I probably won't ever work again. Your brother and sister are already helping with the hospital bills, so I can't very well ask them for too much more. I'll need all the money I have saved for my own keep."

Pei was quiet. She turned away and let out a long sigh.

"Pei?"

But Pei was motionless. "All my life, I'm always the last person anyone would think of," she finally said in a soft voice. "The truth is, nobody in the world really cares if I live or die."

Pei's words tumbled down like a rock on Yan's back, making it difficult for her to breathe. How could a mother say no to her child when she was begging for another chance in life? She thought of all the years she had spent away from Pei. She thought of how she'd left without saying a proper goodbye to Pei and instead, let her younger brother hold her daughter back at the train station. She was a cruel mother!

Yan covered her face with both hands, unable to think of anything to say. There was a stifling silence in the room, a poison threatening to pull mother and daughter further and further apart.

Pei rose to pick up her bag from a hook on the door. "I'd better go now."

"Wait." Yan looked up. "Why don't I help you with two hundred thousand yen, if this is really what you've set your mind to do? But you will have to come up with the rest somehow. That's about all I can afford to offer you. I hope you understand."

"Yes, of course," Pei said, her face brightening. "Mother, you can't imagine what this means to me! I won't forget this." She gently held Yan's hands.

Nineteen

Another month went by. On a Friday evening in mid-December, Pei found herself handing out packets of tissues on a street corner of Kabukicho. Tucked inside the back of the tissue packs was a small ad for Club Asia, which Pei tried to bring to the attention of passersby's. Already, she'd stopped several salary men walking by, giving them the five-second prepped talk about Club Asia: "We're all super-nice ladies from Asia. You ought to come by and see us," she said, pointing them to a black building just a little way down from where she was standing.

She wasn't very good at this game. Most men just waved her away and moved on without taking the tissues. One middle-aged man had stopped briefly to read the ad on the tissues, but as soon as he realized Club Asia was a hostess bar he laughed and walked off.

Pei was getting more and more uncomfortable in her tight-squeezing shoes; she had been on her feet for about two hours now. After five months of working at the club, she had learned to dress more provocatively in short skirts and high heels. The price, of course, was that her feet were forever killing her. She was only too glad to be able to finally sit down when she returned to the club around 10:30.

No sooner had she settled on a couch than she saw Hana coming toward her with two tall glasses of oolong tea.

"There you are, Zhang Peiyin. I've been meaning to have a chat with you," Hana said, pulling out a chair to sit across from Pei. "How did it go tonight?"

"Not so good, Mama-san," Pei said, straightening up a bit. She had kicked off her heels, baring her sore feet under the table. "I was able to convince one guy to come, except the old fart changed his mind at the last minute and ran off." Pei laughed apologetically.

"Well, you win some, you lose some. What can you do?" Hana said in a sweet voice.

"I'm getting the hang of it, though. Come Wednesday I'll wear my new outfit: a red mini dress with a bit of cleavage. I think the dress will help attract more attention, and hopefully more customers."

Hana pulled a Virginia Slim from her purse. Pei hurriedly lit it with a lighter. Hana inhaled deeply, then slowly puffed out a column of smoke. "Actually, Ms. Zhang, I was thinking you ought to take a break on Wednesday."

Pei drew back, startled. "Why?"

"Take a look at this club. How many customers do you see?"

Pei didn't have to look. She knew that apart from the lone customer sitting with Zhou Jing in a corner, there was nobody else in the club.

Hana flicked her cigarette ashes into an ashtray. "You see, we simply don't have enough business to justify keeping everyone here."

"But Mama, didn't you say yourself that this economic slump may just be a temporary thing? That business is bound to pick up again soon?"

"I may have said something like that a month ago. At that time, I was still hopeful. But now, it's becoming very clear that we *are* in the middle of a recession. Do you know how many customers we had in the last two days? I can count them on one hand!" Hana stared at Pei, as if waiting for a response.

Then she smiled tightly. "Look, I'm not saying I'm letting you go. All I'm saying is that you should take some time off and relax a bit. As soon as business picks up again, I'll call you. Okay?"

"But Mama, you can't just fire me like that. I really need the job," Pei said, feeling deeply hurt.

"Look, you're not the only one. Zhou Jing and two other girls have been notified already. If I don't do something now, I will have no choice but to close shop. And then we'll all be out of a job."

"And Xiao Hong? Is she leaving too?" Pei asked.

"Well, she's an exception. In fact, she's the only one I'm keeping for the time being. You know why? Because for the past month she's the only one who has been able to bring in customers. She's got a business knack, something she obviously picked up from her past experience as a sales clerk."

"Sales clerk? Is that what she told you? Ha! The only *sales experience* she ever had was hawking cheap underwear and lingerie in Yancheng! You know, I'm not boasting, but I have a lot more sales experience than she does. I worked at Dalian's Number One Department Store for more than ten years. I was about to be promoted as assistant manager before I left for Japan. Mind you, that's the biggest store in the city. I don't see why you shouldn't give me another chance to prove myself."

Hana's eyes flashed, but her voice was perfectly controlled. "Zhang Peiyin, you must be kidding, trying to sell me your sales experience now. I've been to China enough times to know the department store you worked at was nothing more than a quasi-state-run business. Your so-called sales clerks are people who don't have the faintest idea about customer needs. You hang around with each other all day long, gossiping about others while cracking watermelon seeds, the whole time pretending your customers don't exist. I would be lucky to get someone to notice me if I went in a store like that. Socialism has done wonders for the work ethics of the Chinese people, especially those who work at state-owned enterprises. Let's face it: you people don't live in the real world—you're too used to eating from the communal rice-pot. Only those who have worked for themselves, the self-starters, have some idea about making it in the real world. And that's precisely the difference between you and Xiao Hong. You two are really very different breeds altogether, even though you've both come from the Mainland.

"So, do me a favor, Miss Zhang, spare me your talk of sales experience. Here in the capitalist world, what really counts is the bottom line. If you haven't got what it takes, then move over and make room for those who do. It's as simple as that." Hana took a deep drag of her cigarette and slowly exhaled.

Pei was stunned. Until Hana pointed it out, it had never occurred to her that her job experience at a large establishment back home would get in the way of her adapting to the outside world.

"Thank you, Mama-san," she mumbled, and walked stiffly to the door after picking up her coat. She left Club Asia with a heavy heart, knowing that she might never set foot in the bar again.

Back on the street, her feet still aching, her first thought was to call Mito. She found a public phone and dialed his private number at home, but he hung up as soon as he heard her voice. When she tried ringing him again, she kept getting a busy signal.

The following morning, Pei tried calling Mito's office, determined to reach him somehow. Thinking Mito might dodge her calls again, she decided to assume a fake identity, pretending to be a customer interested in buying some real estate. The trick worked, and Mito took the call.

"Listen, Mito-san, don't you hang up this time, or I'll come to your office and make trouble," she said calmly but firmly.

Mito hesitated for a second. "Very well then, I won't hang up. What is it you want?"

"I want to talk to you, in person. Can we meet somewhere today?"

Mito sighed. "I'm quite busy today. But if you must, you can come by my office around eight-thirty tonight."

"Okay, I'll see you there."

Pei arrived at Mito's office an hour earlier than the said time; she didn't want to tempt fate this time. When she arrived, Mito was the only person working at the small office. He was busy talking on the phone, a couple of files spread out in front of him. He gestured for her to wait, pointing to the couch near the door. Pei sat down. She noticed Mito kept a very clean desk.

When Mito got up, keeping the customer on hold to look for something in the back room, Pei took the opportunity to go to his desk. She picked up a family portrait of him, his two children, and his wife. The children, a boy and a girl both in their teens, bore a striking resemblance to Mito. His wife, although looking close to her fifties, was quite pretty. She was dressed in an elegant silver suit with a ruffle-neck blouse underneath, a subtle smile on her face. It suddenly dawned on Pei that Mito had never entertained the thought of leaving his family.

When Pei noticed Mito was wrapping up the phone call in the backroom, she dashed back to the couch.

Mito returned with an apologetic smile. "Sorry. That was an important call that I couldn't cut short," he said, pulling out a chair to sit across from Pei. "So, what can I do for you?"

Pei cleared her throat. "I wanted to know what's happened to you lately. You don't ring anymore, and you have been avoiding all of my calls. What's happening?"

Mito put on a business face. "I've been very busy, and I just don't have time for anything else."

"So busy you couldn't answer one single call? I don't understand. How is it that your business is doing so well when everybody else is moaning they don't have enough customers?"

"I do a lot of businesses with foreign companies. It's a totally different market."

"Still, it shouldn't have prevented you from calling for weeks, or from accepting my calls. Unless, of course, you're hiding something," Pei stared at him, waiting for a response. But Mito just sat there toying with his ballpoint pen.

"Minoru, I'm asking you a question," Pei said, surprising even herself that she'd addressed Mito by his first name. It was the first time she had done that.

"Shhh, please calm down. You know what's wrong with you? You're always angry," Mito said, stroking his thinning hair.

"Well, you would get angry too if someone was deliberately rude to you."

"Pei-san, I don't know," Mito said, calling her by the respectful address of *san* now. "You and I—sometimes I really think that we shouldn't see each other anymore."

Pei took in a sharp breath. "Why?"

"I . . . just can't deal with your temper and your many problems. My life is stressful enough right now. I don't need any more com—"

"Complications? What do you mean by *complications*? Oh, I see, you're talking about the two hundred thousand yen I'd borrowed from you for my China trip. Fine! If you want, I'll return the money to you next week," Pei said, knowing darn well that Mito's male pride would never allow him to take back the money.

"No, no. I don't mean that at all."

"Then what *do* you mean?"

"It's . . . it's just that I feel we're not good for each other. We're just too *different*." Mito scratched his head.

"What're you trying to say?"

"I'm saying, well, I don't think my personality goes very well with yours or with any women from China for that matter. You're much too strong for me. You say whatever is on your mind whenever it pleases you. I'm afraid I'm far too delicate for that. Sometimes I feel overwhelmed by your bluntness and your single-minded ambition. As much as I hate to admit it, I think I much prefer the softer, more deferential approach of Japanese women."

"Wait, don't forget: *you're* the one who seduced me."

"Yes, that's true. But I didn't know anything about Chinese women until I met you. I had to go out with you in order to find out what it's like to be with a Chinese woman. Now that I know, I've decided I'm not as strong as I thought I was, as much as I wanted to be different."

"That's a damn lie. I know I'm not your first Chinese girl-friend. I heard you and Xiao Hong were lovers before—"

"So you've heard. Well, we did date briefly."

"And? How did you find her?"

"She was a lot of fun."

"That's not what I'm asking. Did you find her strong like me?"

"Perhaps. She certainly seems like a very ambitious person. But she didn't pressure me to move in with her."

"Aha, so *that's* the reason you want to break up with me. But you know what? Xiao Hong would have made you live with her too, had she thought you worth her while. She didn't because she found a better sugar daddy than you—a company executive who's richer and more generous than you, someone who's willing to spend more money on her than you could ever afford."

"That may be so, but as least she was always cheerful. She never got angry with me the way you do. When we were together, we had a good time and laughed a lot. She was nothing like you. When we dated she knew we were in it just for a good time. But you're different. You just want to grab the first man who lays eyes on you, and all you care about is whether the man can provide for you or not."

Pei felt her fury growing. "You know what? You're a coward. You want to drop me because you can't face the pressure of getting serious with me. You men are all alike. When you wanted sex, you said you cared about me and wanted to take care of me. But the truth is you never remotely considered the possibility of divorcing your wife."

"Look, I got to know you at a club. Any guy who goes into the club can have you for the night if he wants," Mito said with a sneer. "How can you expect any man to get serious with a woman who's not that far off from a prostitute?"

"Who're you calling a prostitute? I'm not a prostitute, you scumbag!" Pei sprang up and started pummeling him with her fists. "Now that you're done with me, you think you can just throw me away like some disposable chopsticks. It's not that easy—"

"Calm down, calm down," Mito said, forcing Pei back onto the couch. He kept his strong hands on her shoulders until she started easing up.

"You're a bastard!" Pei said between pants, her face deep red. "When I first came to you, I did it because I thought I could trust you. I found you during my loneliest months in Japan, and I thought you were a trusted friend, the only hope I had left in Japan. I confided in you, let you take away my body and heart. I can't believe you would turn around and bite me . . ." Pei suddenly lost her voice. A sob escaped.

"Hey, what's the matter?" Mito went over to sit with Pei. "Come on, don't be like that," he said as he gently rocked her, her face pressed against his shoulder.

They sat like that for a while, neither saying a word. After Pei had calmed down, she told Mito about being fired at the club and the tuition she must pay for the fashion school, adding that if she couldn't come up with the money soon, she would have no choice but to leave Japan.

Mito got up from the sofa and began pacing the small office. He was silent for some time, his facial muscles twisting as if in pain. Finally, he stopped and turned to face Pei. "Listen," he started, "what do you say if I let you borrow another two hundred thousand yen? Call it gift money, call it whatever you want. You can take it and not worry about paying me back. But there's one condition: after tonight, you are not to call me again—not at my office, not at my home, not anywhere. We'll make tonight our last meeting. Agree?"

Pei glared up at him in disbelief, unable to find words. After a while, she looked down at the hardwood floor and said slowly, "This is the buy-out money, isn't it?"

"I wouldn't put it that way. It demeans our friendship and my sincerity."

"Fine, I'll accept," Pei said, her face hardened. "When will I get the money?"

"Just give me your bank account number, and I'll wire the money to you in a few days."

"No, I want it in two days, by Wednesday, at five p.m."

"Fine, consider it done."

Pei and Mito didn't speak as they walked out of the office. When they turned the corner toward the main street, they saw a stall selling hot noodles. The wooden stall had a red lantern hanging from its roof, bringing some warmth to the chilly winter night. It looked very inviting.

"Want to have a bowl of noodles with me?" Mito chirped. But Pei shook her head. He shrugged. "You're right, that was a bad idea. It's late, we should both go home."

They crossed the street and continued walking toward the station. Then Mito stuck out a hand, just in time to stop an oncoming taxi. "Here, get in," he said, opening the door for Pei. Before closing the door, he got out his wallet, pulled out several bills, and pressed them into Pei's hand. "This is for the cab. Go home and take a good rest."

She took the money and looked away.

"Miss, where're we going?" the taxi-driver asked, craning his neck to look at Pei.

"Oh, to Higashi-Kitazawa, please."

The taxi started. Despite herself, Pei peered out from the rear window to see if Mito was still standing on the sidewalk. But the street was dark and empty, except for the lonely shadows of streetlights.

Twenty

A couple of days later in Shibuya, Vivian arrived at Amano Enterprises a few minutes late. She turned the doorknob, half expecting to see the disapproving face of Noriko. But the office was quiet as a church. Where was everybody? Once at her cubicle, Vivian's eyes were drawn to a long, pink envelope sitting on her desk. On it, in bright red, was marked the English word "Invitation." Vivian was intrigued. For the thirteen months she'd been with Amano Enterprises, she had never been invited to a work-related function. What could this be?

The invitation card said it was for the opening of Amano's new art gallery, set for the evening of December 27. Finally, she was wanted for something. Just as Vivian was congratulating herself, she found taped to the back of the card a small message: "Attendance is required, and please come in your Chinese dress." The note was signed by Noriko Wada.

Vivian read the note again to make sure she hadn't misunderstood the message. But there was no mistake. Chinese dress was the Japanese reference to *qipao*, the traditional Chinese silk gown with a high collar and long slits on the sides. Yet you wouldn't call an invitation an invitation if your presence was demanded, especially with a strict dress code. Besides, had it not occurred to Noriko that she might not even own a Chinese dress? The idea of her wearing a *qipao* to a gallery opening also seemed absurd. It wasn't as though they were attending some Chinese function. Then a question flashed in her head: Were Becky and Patricia also "required" to wearing something formal to the occasion?

"Becky, did you get an invitation to the gallery opening?" Vivian threw the question at her colleague the minute she walked in.

"Yeah. I did get something like that this morning. You going?" Becky asked.

"I don't have a choice. Noriko attached a note saying I must go. Did you get a note like that?"

"No, although Noriko told me this morning that it's an important event and that my attendance would be *greatly* appreciated."

"She didn't mention anything about a dress code, did she?"

"No. Why?"

Vivian told her about the Chinese dress.

"Uh-uh, she didn't say anything. Why don't you ask Noriko? Maybe it's just a misunderstanding."

"Maybe. You see her around?"

"Nope. Teruko said she had some errands to run for Rijicho today."

Vivian found Teruko among boxes of stationery in the back-room. "What're you working on, Teru-chan?" she asked. She felt vaguely guilty every time she saw Teruko, because her suggestion that Teruko sent the Valentine card to Brian Watts never produced any results.

"Oh, some company brochures. Rijicho wants to update them," Teruko said, smiling in her usual good nature. "And how's your mother?" she asked, looking up at Vivian.

"Doing much better, though the healing takes time. The doctor says she can leave the hospital in another month or six weeks."

"That's good news."

"Teru-chan, can I ask you something?" Vivian told her about the invitation. "Did anyone in the past have to wear a traditional dress for these sorts of functions?"

"I haven't been here long enough to say. But two years ago, when the graphic art school first opened, Rijicho made a big deal about the launching party and made Mamba, who was from Nairobi, wear his traditional costume too."

"Is that so?"

Teruko nodded. "So are you going to wear your Chinese dress?"

"I haven't decided yet. I have to speak to Wada-san first. My feeling is, if Becky and Patricia don't have to wear anything special, why should I?"

Teruko nodded. "I can see your point."

"How about you? You coming to the ceremony?"

Teruko nodded again.

Vivian waited all afternoon for Noriko. Ten minutes before the clock struck five, she finally heard Noriko's high-heeled shoes clacking into the office.

"Teruko, give me a hand!" Noriko hollered, waving several shopping bags. "Oh, what a day!" she said, before dumping the bags into Teruko's opened arms.

"What're all these, Wada-san?" Teruko asked.

"Christmas decorations for the office. Rijicho has another advertorial photo shoot with a magazine tomorrow."

Vivian waited until Noriko had settled down at her desk. "Wada-san, I want to talk to you."

"Yes, what about?" Noriko said, turning to look at Vivian.

"It's about your note. I want to know why I need to wear a Chinese dress to the gallery opening. Can't I go in a business suit instead?"

"No, Vivian-san. All members of the foreign staff will be on stage with Rijicho that day, so we want you to dress up nicely. This is very important for the company's image. Surely you can understand that."

Vivian nodded. "But why am I the only one asked to wear something different? I know Becky is not expected to wear anything special. She's coming in a business suit."

Noriko pressed her lips. "Just think. You're all going to be on stage. Now, with Becky, people can tell right away that she's a foreigner. But you, unless you emphasize the fact to them, how in the world would the guests know that you're not one of them?"

Vivian's nostrils flared. "Oh, so you want me to go to the party packaged like a fruit basket. Is that the idea?"

"Vivian-san, please don't make a joke about it. I can't stress enough how important this is for the image of Amano Enterprises and for Rijicho. We're an international company! If you're so strongly against wearing a Chinese dress, then I suggest that you not come to the ceremony at all. But I warn you: it may count against you, with serious consequences."

"But that's absurd!"

"No, it's *not*. You're paid plenty to perform a simple task. If you can't even do that, you should consider getting another job. Now if you will excuse me." Noriko turned away to make a phone call.

Vivian left Noriko's desk in a huff. How unfair! Not only was she asked to degrade herself at a work function by masquerading as some exotic club hostess, she was essentially told she'd be fired if she dared to ignore the order. She was tempted to call Amano directly about this whole thing; if only she knew his home number.

On the train ride home, Vivian struggled to reach a decision about the gallery opening. She did own a red *qipao*, a piece of memorabilia she had acquired in New York's Chinatown. But should she wear it? If not for Noriko's sake, should she at least do it to save her job? The ceremony was only a week away—not much time to find another job. An employment ad with a conspicuous line saying, "Only native speakers need apply" flashed across her mind.

Still, the thought that she would be the only one among the company staff wearing a loud, red gown on stage bothered her. It made her feel cheap. Yes, they paid her good money. But how far should she put up with this rubbish before she should say enough was enough?

If you don't emphasize to them, how else will the guests know that you are not one of them? Noriko's words rang in her ears. It was as though Noriko had deliberately wanted to remind Vivian that she wasn't one of *them*. She had spent more than twenty years in

Japan. In the end, she was still not treated like a normal person. She may as well spend her whole life in Japan and still remain as an "other."

The train felt crowded and stuffy. Vivian looked around her at the packed train. She noticed a young woman standing nearby, deeply absorbed in a magazine article she was reading. Curious, Vivian peeked over her shoulder to catch a glimpse of the headline: "How to Find Passion and Respect in Your Job." The title stirred something in Vivian. What was the one thing she felt passionate about doing for a living? She asked herself that question as she strolled back home. She thought about how much happier she was when she worked in New York as a translator of art brochures at a small gallery. Even her brief stint teaching at NYU as a Chinese language teacher's aid and the occasional translation of Chinese literature pieces for a comparative literature professor at the university gave her a lot more satisfaction.

It suddenly dawned on her that her passion didn't include dressing up as a Suzy Wong on stage so some guy could further his false image of "globalization."

Twenty-one

"Stop it now. People are looking at us."

Nine days after her break up with Mito, Pei was doing some late afternoon shopping at a fancy supermarket near her mother's when she heard a shrill voice giggling from the next aisle. The woman was speaking in Japanese mixed with a distinctive Chinese accent, her voice vaguely familiar. Curious, Pei turned the corner to see who it was.

Near the end of the aisle, a man and woman were locked in a passionate kiss. Tall, with long, dark hair, the woman was wearing a rabbit-fur jacket, a super-mini leather skirt, and a pair of high suede boots that accentuated the lily-whiteness of her exposed thighs. The woman had her back to Pei, but judging by her voice, Pei thought she must be in her twenties.

The man seemed a lot older. Dressed in a business suit, he was also a bit shorter than the girlfriend, though he was well built. He had his face buried in the woman's hair, his large hands holding onto her head. The couple clearly had money to spend. Their shopping cart was filled with fine wines and exotic fruit juices, along with trays of vegetables and red sirloin steaks.

Pei could tell the man was very strong by the way he was holding the woman. It must hurt being held like that, she thought. Just then, the man raised his head and his eyes met Pei's. Pei froze—the man was none other than Mito.

"What's the matter, Minoru?" The young woman turned, sensing that something was wrong, but she quickly looked away when she saw Pei.

"Xiao Hong?" Pei cried, a hand over her mouth. She couldn't believe her eyes. What was Mito doing with Hong at the supermarket? They were the last two people on earth she could imagine being together. Hadn't Xiao Hong called Mito a "cheap ass?" And Mito! Only a week and a half earlier he'd told her he couldn't handle going out with a Chinese woman.

Hong turned around to face Pei reluctantly. "Hi, Cho-san. Haven't seen you in months! You well?" She spoke in her phony Japanese, a fake smile on her face. She was trying her best to sound composed. She looked as though she'd lost a few pounds, although she seemed to have become even more coquettish in her heavy makeup.

Pei felt as if a bolt of lightning had ripped through her body. She ignored Hong, turning to Mito instead. "So, what are you two doing here? Playing house? Oh, let me guess—she's going to cook you a luscious meal, is that it? And where are you having dinner?" she asked despite herself. "At her place, or is it going to be at Murasaki Inn?"

Mito turned away from Pei, pretending that her questions had nothing to do with him. Hong also became tongue-tied. She bent over to arrange the trays of steaks and the beautifully wrapped yellow and red bell peppers, as if she had also become deaf suddenly.

"Minoru, what is this about? I thought you said you didn't like Chinese women?" Pei said, switching to Chinese. In a heated argument, Pei found speaking in her mother tongue always gave her a greater edge and control, even though her Japanese was quite fluent by now. She reasoned Mito knew enough Chinese to understand her anger.

Mito was still playing mute. He scratched his thinning hair, as if there was an itch he just couldn't stand.

"Wait! So this is what our break up was all about, wasn't it? It really had nothing to do with me, but everything to do with this prostitute, this back-biting snake who would stop at nothing to get what she wants, right?"

"Watch your mouth, old bag! Who are you calling a prostitute?" Hong shrieked in Chinese, a furious finger pointing straight
at Pei's nose.

"You, of course, you shameless *tattered shoe*," Pei barked
back. She felt a sudden deep hatred for the woman standing in
front of her, remembering how Hong had called her pathetic
and pushed her out of her door with a loud bang. Now this. The
woman was full of lies. All those months she'd thought Hong was
her best friend. How could she had been so blind? But the worst
part was the realization that she was no match for this younger
woman, who was far better than her in both her sales skills and
her entertainment skills. Now, she was reminded, once again, that
Hong had not only stolen her man, she had also stolen her job
because Hong was the only one who was kept on at the club by
Hana. "Mind you, this is a supermarket, not a whorehouse. Can't
you save your tricks for somewhere more discreet?"

"Mind your own damn business." Hong charged forward to
face Pei, her arms akimbo, her whiskey-scented breath assaulting
Pei's nostrils. "This is not your fucking country, so I can do whatever
I want, wherever I want. You're just jealous. You were dumped by
Minoru, so you can't stand seeing him having a good time with me."

"Can you two keep it down? We don't need trouble!" Mito
whined, his eyes swiveling fearfully up and down the aisle.

"Shut your mouth, you louse!" Pei charged another step closer
to Hong. "I can never get a word of truth from you. You said you
couldn't stand Mito, so what the hell are you doing kissing him?"

Hong snickered. "That was then, and this is now. Besides,
I don't have to answer to you for what I do. Who are you to tell
me whom I can date and whom I can't? You can't stop other people just because you yourself can't keep a man. You should have
known better than to try to get into the water trade. You have no
talent for it, and you're too old, you ugly bag!"

Pei felt like her blood vessels were bursting. How dare Hong
suggest that she was trying to muscle her way into Japan's sex
industry? She picked up a carton of tomato juice from Hong's

shopping cart and bashed it against her opponent's face. "You shameless hussy! You cheated me of my hourly wage at the club, and now you're stealing my boyfriend? I'm going to finish you off today, once and for all!"

Hong managed to fend off the attack with a hand, forcing the carton back onto Pei. Pei felt something cold spilling on her face and chest. The juice box had burst. Pei let out a cry and grabbed Hong's long hair. Thick red tomato juice ran down her arm. She was just about to scratch her rival in the face when she felt a pair of strong arms pulling her away from behind.

"Stop, right now," demanded a man's voice.

Twisting and struggling, Pei saw it was a guard. Evidently, someone at the supermarket had alerted the security office. From the corner of her eye, she saw that Hong had been overpowered by another guard.

Things happened very quickly after that. Before Pei could fully comprehend what was going on, she found that she and Hong had been forcibly removed from the aisle and taken into a small room in the back of the supermarket. They were ordered to sit down at opposite ends of a table. Pei couldn't remember seeing Mito when the two of them were taken away. He must have fled when the guards arrived. The coward!

A few minutes later, a fortyish man who looked like a store supervisor entered the small room. "I want to know what happened back there. What were you two fighting about?" he asked in a stern voice.

Pei clamped her lips shut, still smoldering. Hong turned her back, crossed her arms over her chest, and tapped an impatient foot on the floor.

"Look, you two were getting violent out there, disturbing other shoppers and destroying our merchandise. We're running a business here; we can't afford to have you do that. I'm afraid I'm going to have to report you to the police," the man said.

The word *police* made Pei flinch. How stupid she was! She had allowed her emotions to get the better of her. She'd once been told that as a foreign student in Japan, the police were the last people she would ever want to see.

Hong suddenly spoke up, as though she also felt the need to avoid the police. "Sir, what happened back there wasn't my fault. I was peacefully shopping with my boyfriend until this crazy woman barged in on us and started to hit me with a box of tomato juice. You know, she could have picked up a bottle of wine and really hurt me."

"That's not true. This woman cheated me of my money first. Then she stole my boyfriend," Pei yelled, jabbing a finger at Hong.

"Stop, both of you," the manager ordered. "This is what you will do: you will each write down your name, address, and alien registration card number on this form, and then write a detailed report about what happened. You do have your alien registration card on you, do you not?"

Hong nodded, producing her alien registration card from her purse. "See sir, I'm a good citizen here in Japan, with a proper visa and a good job," she said, flashing her card in front of the supervisor.

Pei fumbled through her purse in search of hers and panicked when she realized she didn't have it. "Sir, I'm afraid I don't have mine with me. You see, I changed handbags this morning—"

"That's it. I'm going to have to call the police now. I was really hoping I could make a report of this incident quickly, give you each a warning, and let you both be on your way. But if you don't have your alien registration card, then I can't let you go."

Pei's heart skipped a beat. "But sir, I can't stay. I must go home, *now*."

The man shook his head. "Not after what happened. I'm afraid you both will have to stay until the police arrive. I have no choice." He left the room to make the call.

Twenty-two

A week after her conversation with Teruko in her office, Vivian dragged herself home from the evening company party. When she got home, it was already half past nine. She felt tired and humiliated, her feet aching from standing for hours without a break. She kicked off her black pumps, gently rubbing her swollen feet, realizing she would have plenty time to rest them now that her services were no longer needed at Amano Enterprises.

She peeled off her black wool suit jacket, sprawled out flat on her sofa, her feet propped up on her small coffee table. She closed her eyes, revisiting the scene at the gallery's opening party near Tokyo Tower.

At the spacious new gallery, guests were swarming in and out, drinking French wine and snacking on salmon bits and cheese crackers while admiring the watercolor paintings of the five featured Chinese artists. Vivian arrived at the gallery slightly after six that evening, and didn't immediately see Noriko. She mingled with the guests, taking care to explain to them the subtle stylistic differences between artists, with which she had become very familiar after spending days translating the background material.

She found Becky, Patricia, and Teruko at the reception desk and stole a moment to sip a glass of Sauvignon Blanc with them. Then she returned to greet the arriving guests, who steadily swarmed into the gallery. All went well for the next hour, until Noriko, dressed in a fiery red cocktail dress, strode over to the reception desk.

"How are you all doing here, ladies?" she had asked with a smile. She seemed to be in a good mood.

"Great," Becky offered. "We must have over a hundred guests in here already."

"That's right. And everyone seems impressed with the art catalog," Vivian added, speaking with the confidence of a great hostess.

Noriko's face darkened. "What's this you're wearing?" she asked, looking Vivian up and down.

"I decided that I'd be more comfortable in a business suit, just like everyone else here," Vivian answered without blinking an eye.

"Is that so? I'm afraid you will feel a lot less comfortable after this party," Noriko snapped, before turning to the rest of the staff. "Listen, Sampson-san, Seibert-san, and Teruko, you need to be ready to step on stage in five minutes. Please, can you follow me right now to the side of the stage, where Watts-san is waiting already? When I give you the cue, you will all come up with me and stand behind me. Is that clear?"

The women nodded.

"What about me?" Vivian demanded. "Even if you don't agree with me wearing a business suit, I'm still one of the staff here!"

Noriko said nothing, but merely swept past her, leading the other women away.

Before Vivian had time to wonder about her fate, she heard Amano's voice coming through a microphone.

"Ladies and gentlemen, it is my great pleasure to welcome you to the opening of Gallery Kaze, the latest addition to the chain of Amano Enterprises—"

Vivian walked toward the front of the stage to get a closer look. The speech barely lasted three minutes before Vivian saw her colleagues filing on to the stage, with Noriko leading. As they all took their positions, they formed a hierarchical triangle on stage, with Amano at the forefront, Noriko and Teruko at his sides and half a step behind, and Patricia, Brian, and Becky in a line behind him. *It's time for Rijicho to show off his foreign staff now,* Vivian thought.

From the front of the stage, Vivian could see Becky beckoning to her to come up stage. She hesitated, then, to her own surprise, she stepped up to the stage and joined her colleagues. She barely had time to squeeze between Becky and Brian before Amano turned around to begin his introduction. In passing, she saw the surprised look on Noriko's face. But it was too late—there was nothing she could do now.

By the time everyone had stepped offstage, Vivian could see Noriko was fuming. She almost immediately pulled Vivian aside to a corner. "That was most ungracious of you, pulling a stunt like that," she said in a controlled, but very agitated voice.

"I thought it was only fair that I should be up there with everyone else. I work for Amano Enterprises too." Vivian was unapologetic.

"Vivian-san, you have *really* blown it. You ignored my warnings again and again, challenging my authority. And for that, you shall have to face the consequences," Noriko said with narrowed eyes.

A few minutes later, Teruko came over and said Noriko had just gotten permission from Rijicho to fire her. "She said your services would not be needed after tonight and that you can come to the office to pick up your paycheck any time after tomorrow."

Shocked, Vivian couldn't bring herself to stay at the party. She knew that Noriko had warned her, but she truly hadn't believed her little protest would come to this. Near the exit, she ran into Becky, who didn't seem to have a clue about the misfortune that had just befallen Vivian. When Becky asked her why she was leaving so early, Vivian merely shook her head and ran out the door.

Now, listless and angry, she rubbed her feet. She was just about to head into the shower when the phone rang.

"Miss, this is Shinjuku Police Office. We have a lady here by the name of Cho Baion, or Zhang Peiyin in Chinese. We're looking for her sister."

"This is she. What's wrong?"

"We need you to bring your sister's alien registration card here. Evidently, she has forgotten it at your mother's house. Do you think you can bring it over for her?" The police officer then described the incident at the supermarket and explained that they needed Pei's registration card for the report.

"But sir, it's already half past ten. It would be midnight by the time I pick up her card and bring it to you. Can't this wait until tomorrow morning?"

"Miss, you don't seem to understand: We won't let her out until we see her card. We will keep her for the night here if you don't show."

Vivian covered her face with a hand. She had just been fired, and now she had to deal with her sister's stupidity and irresponsibility, just what she needed. "Okay, I'll come right away," she said with resignation.

It was near midnight when Vivian finally managed to find the police office. She was appalled to find her sister sitting in a corner in a dim room with a police officer, her medium-length hair half wet, her white shirt soiled with large, dark red stains.

"What happened to you? Is that blood?" she asked in alarm.

Pei wouldn't answer, except to look meekly at Vivian with apologetic eyes.

The police officer explained at greater length what had transpired at the supermarket and showed her the reports Hong and Pei had written.

"Are you saying that my sister was fighting with a Chinese hostess over a Japanese man?"

"Precisely! Evidently, it was a love triangle! Did you know that until only two weeks ago, your sister had been working at a hostess joint called Club Asia?" the officer asked.

"Is that true?" Vivian said, her brows shot up. She had her suspicion all along, but she needed to hear this directly from her sister's mouth.

Pei nodded with downcast eyes.

"So where's the other woman?" Vivian asked, looking at the officer.

"We let her go after she showed us her alien registration card," he said. "Do you have your sister's card?"

When all the paperwork was done, Pei was told to write an apology letter promising that she would never repeat what she'd done that night. She was also made to swear that from now on she would carry her alien registration card with her at all times, or she would be detained.

By the time the sisters got out of the police station, it was two in the morning. The trains were not running by then, and they had to share an expensive taxi home. Inside the taxi, the sisters were quiet at first, until Pei broke the silence.

"Meiyin, I'm sorry to have troubled you," she said, her voice barely audible.

"Really, what were you thinking?" Vivian snapped, finally letting out her frustration and anger. "Fighting with a young prostitute over a sleaze-ball Japanese salary man? Are you out of your mind?"

When she saw that Pei was silent, she pressed on. "And how long did you work at the club? Why did you lie to me and Mom?"

"I only did what any woman in my position would do. I wanted to make money, lots of money, and as fast as I could."

Vivian shook her head. "But why? What do you need all that money for? I thought Mom and Dad are doing a fine job providing for you."

"So Da Shan and Da Hai can go to a decent university in America someday," Pei said softly. "I have already done the math; in order to send both of them to a good American college I'll need at least 160,000 dollars. I know I may never reach that goal, but I must try." Then Pei looked down, as if talking to herself. "It may be too late for me, but I want them to have a better future, a much better future than what I had."

Vivian gazed at her sister in the darkness of the taxi, surprised by her answer. It had never occurred to her that Pei could have a motive nobler than just satisfying her immediate wants and vanity. "But surely you don't expect your sons to want the money, knowing you had to earn it by working as a bar girl?" Vivian said despite herself.

Pei was quiet again. Vivian had obviously touched a raw nerve.

"Are you going to tell Mother about tonight?" Pei said after some time, looking up at Vivian.

"I haven't thought about what I'm going to do yet."

"Please, can you not tell Mother?" Pei asked with pleading eyes.

Vivian wasn't used to her sister begging. She thought about it for a moment, then nodded. "Fine, I can keep a secret, but on two conditions. First, you mustn't burden Mom again about your tuition. Mom is getting old, you know. Besides, you should be able to take care of yourself, now that you have been in Japan more than a year."

Pei nodded. "Okay."

"Second, you must never go back to working as a hostess again, or I will tell. Agree?"

"Agree."

The taxi arrived in front of their mother's house first. When Pei got out of the cab, she turned around to wave at Vivian. "Thanks again for all your trouble," she said with a deferential smile.

Vivian nodded, offering a kind smile in return. She'd been furious at Pei just a few minutes before. But now she found her anger slowly dissipating. Her sister had made some bad choices in life. Still, she was trying her best to survive, Vivian decided, like so many other immigrants who were new arrivals in their adopted homelands. And it couldn't have been easy for her proud sister to take work as a bargirl, she reflected. As badly as Vivian had been treated by Noriko, she could only imagine how Pei must have suffered while serving all those drunken Japanese men. And she did it for her boys. She must really love them, Vivian thought. She must really miss them.

Twenty-three

In early April, a few months after her humiliating experience with the police, Pei filed through the gate of Toyo Bunka Fashion Academy in Ryogoku. It was one of the better fashion schools in Tokyo, and Pei was so glad that her father had finally come through with the rest of the tuition money, enabling her to further her education at this modern-looking school. At the hallway of the main building, Pei stopped to ask two young Japanese women for directions to her classroom for "An Anatomical Study of the Human Body"—one of the first courses she had to take for her major in the General Fashion Department.

"Room 216. It's right at the end of the hallway on the second floor," answered a young woman with long, bleached-orange hair and black-and-white knee-high socks. She was with another girl donning a very short, asymmetrical haircut but large hoop earrings. "Are you a new instructor here?" the orange-hair girl asked after eyeing Pei up and down. When Pei told her she was a new student, the young woman put a hand to her mouth to stifle a giggle before scurrying away with her friend.

It soon became evident that the young women's reaction was far from the exceptional: every time Pei settled at a desk in a new classroom, she immediately drew stares from fellow students. Her classmates, mostly teenage girls fresh out of high school, looked at her with cold receptions, as if saying, "You don't belong here." By the end of the first day, Pei became convinced that the entire student body knew she was not only the oldest student there, but also the only Chinese.

Another three weeks passed. One day, in between her classes, Pei had the misfortune of overhearing a conversation about her in the bathroom.

"Have you ever wondered what that Chinese woman is doing here?" a young woman asked from behind the closed door of a bathroom stall. "She's practically my mother's age."

Pei recognized the voice to be that of Agemi's, one of her classmates in dressmaking.

"No kidding. Who would want to hire an old lady like her? Even Hanae Mori would think she's too ancient to work in her fashion house!" said another woman from the next stall, her piercing laugh echoing in the background.

The vicious remarks caught Pei by surprise. Bewildered and deeply hurt, she rushed out of the bathroom and ran several flights upstairs to the rooftop of the school building, where she knew she could find some peace and quiet.

That was when she made a promise to herself—she only had one mission in life, and that was to finish her studies as fast as she could. And once she had a diploma in hand, she would get out of Tokyo and find a way back to China. If Japan wasn't welcoming of her for who she was, maybe she could go back to China. She had no desire of going back to Dalian and become a laughing stock of her relatives and friends who would surely see her as a failure, but Shanghai or Guangzhou would be a great city for her to start a new life in. She could start fresh and make some good money, and continued her dream of sending her boys to a foreign college.

A couple of months ago, Pei had mentioned to Zhou Jing about her plans of starting a boutique together, and Zhou Jing seemed pleased with the idea. "Well, if one of us were a fashion expert backed with a proper degree from a Tokyo college, it would make our business that much more credible," her dear friend had said. Zhou Jing's encouragement was what had given Pei the will she needed to keep going back to school, despite the jeers and cold shoulders.

But school wasn't the only thing that was tough going for Pei. Now that she had broken off with Mito and stopped working at Club Asia, Pei felt she was becoming a bore. Except on the occasional afternoons when she needed to go to the local library to do research for her homework, she had grown accustomed to going straight home from school. The only thing that gave her something to look forward to in her otherwise mundane daily life was going to work three nights a week at a friendly health-food restaurant called Ninjinya—the Carrot House.

Mr. Takahashi, the restaurant owner, was an unusual guy in that he was both kind and open-minded. At thirty-six, he was the youngest boss Pei had ever worked for. He was a dropout from college, but had a real knack for business. His organic food restaurant was always packed with college students and young office ladies. Pei had heard that Mr. Takahashi had traveled extensively outside of Japan during his twenties, especially in Asia and Southeast Asia, which helped explain why he didn't make a big fuss about hiring non-Japanese like her. In fact, he seemed to genuinely enjoy working with Pei and Min, a young student from Vietnam, asking them both a lot of questions about their cultures and history whenever he had a chance.

Pei wouldn't have found her way to Ninjinya had it not been for Bill, Zhou Jing's new Canadian boyfriend, who happened to be a close friend of Takahashi's. Having promised Vivian that she would never go back to hostessing, Pei looked for work as a waitress for weeks, but never got anywhere. Zhou Jing, who was already working as a supermarket cashier in Matsudo near where she lived, had tried to find Pei a job there too, but the near-two-hour commute each way proved far too strenuous and impractical for Pei. So naturally, she was overjoyed when Mr. Takahashi offered her the job at the restaurant, which was conveniently located a few subway stops away from her mother's house.

This was not to say Mr. Takahashi wasn't demanding. On the contrary, Pei had to work very hard, running nonstop for the five hours she was at Ninjinya, including mopping the floor and scrubbing the kitchen after the restaurant closed at midnight. Pei soon realized why Mr. Takahashi kept her on after letting go of many others before her—she was the only person willing to do menial chores in addition to waiting tables. Most Japanese helpers before her had refused to do the heavy-duty cleaning, saying it was either too tough or too dirty a job for them.

Pei knew she too would have turned down the job only half a year before. But times had changed, and the shortage of available jobs had forced her to learn to accept menial work with more grace. She was beginning to understand what her mother had to face, lacking even the education that she herself had. And because Mr. Takahashi was helpful and straightforward about all the rules and expectations, Pei knew she didn't have to tiptoe around him or worry about missing a cultural taboo that might get her into trouble. For the first time she realized such kindness was worth more than just having an easy job. And for that, she was willing to work a little harder.

Twenty-four

Another week had gone by. In Shinjuku, Yan was waiting in her hospital room for Vivian to come visit. Under the doctor's strong recommendation, Yan agreed earlier in February to undergo an additional two month treatment to ensure the full use of her limbs. She calculated that by the time she was done with the whole treatment, she would have been in the hospital for a total of six months. Luckily, the rehabilitation treatments in Tokyo were affordable, and the insurance was paid by Da Wei's company.

Yan was watching television from her bed when she noticed a Japanese man about Yiwen's age pop his head into her room. The man smiled in recognition to her new roommate, a frail Japanese woman in her mid-fifties. The man's visit reminded Yan that Yiwen hadn't come to see her once during her entire stay at the hospital for the past five and a half months.

The thought of Yiwen left a scowl on her face. She didn't know how she really felt about the man anymore. She used to loathe it whenever they had to talk on the phone. But ever since she'd had the stroke, she felt differently—she had developed a tender nostalgia for him. No, not for him, but for the times when they were happier as a couple, when there was still love between them.

Of course, all that changed after Kyushu, when he left Tokyo for the southern island to start a new office for the company. It was upon his return, in 1976, that the love letter from his mistress surfaced, which ruined everything for them and for the family.

The long walks along Yokohama Bay, the toasty hotpot dinners in the neighborhood of Meguro, where they used to live . . .

Even now, as Yan thought of those five years, it brought a smile to her face. Those were the best years of her life, though they seemed so far away. Now that she thought about it, she realized they hadn't been a true couple since 1975, the year Yiwen was taken away to Kyushu for work. They had been strangers for nearly sixteen years. So why was she still holding on to those moments, the loving, tender thoughts of their past?

Since she'd been hospitalized, Yan had asked Vivian many times if Yiwen was coming to see her. But every time the answer had been the same: he was too busy to make the trip. If today she were lying on her deathbed, waiting desperately for him to come see her for the last time, would he come? She felt a deep sadness in her heart when she realized that she had ceased to mean anything to Yiwen. She might as well be a fly on a wall.

"Hi, Mom." Vivian's cheery greeting jarred Yan from her wandering thoughts. Her daughter was carrying a bouquet of fresh yellow roses.

"Oh, you're early today!" Yan perked up a little.

"But I always come around 10:30 on Saturday mornings. You must be in a good mood today." Vivian smiled, arranging the roses in a vase.

"I don't know about being in a good mood, but I do feel stronger, like I haven't felt in a long time."

"Maybe you're getting ready to come home finally."

"The doctor said I'm recovering well, and that in another week or two I should be able to go home."

"About time too!" Vivian said, opening the window to let in some fresh air.

"Vivian, I was thinking—" Yan said, gesturing for Vivian to sit by her bed.

She breathed deeply of the outdoor air, now scented by the perfume of the roses. "I was thinking I should go home to Dalian. I don't know why, but I've really begun to miss home. The doctor also thought it would be a good idea for me to receive some acupuncture treatments in China, given that the quality of such treatments is better and much less expensive. It would hasten the recovery process. Only thing is, I'm still rather weak, and I don't want to go by myself."

"Are you asking me to go with you? If you are, then you're in luck. I'm a *freeter* now, and I can go on vacation whenever I want to."

"A freeter? What's that?"

"I work for a temp agency, and I only work on weekly contracts. I can pick and choose my employers and the hours I want to work."

"What about that other job you had in Shibuya?"

Vivian frowned, and then told her the story about the Chinese dress.

Yan sighed. Even if she hadn't approved of Vivian's job, at least it was steady money. "You can't go on forever working as a freeter," she said. "Do they even offer you a work visa?"

"No, but I still have over half a year left from my previous job. Don't worry, Mom. I'll find a real job soon enough," Vivian said dismissively. "Besides, I'm also considering the possibility of going back to school in the US—I'm applying for the Ph.D. program in Literature at the University of Washington in Seattle. If I get a scholarship, I'd definitely go for it."

Yan shook her head and smiled. "I don't know how you do it, but you've always been very resourceful. I only wish your sister was more like you."

"Big Sister? Uh-oh, what did she do now?"

"Last week she asked me for money again to help pay for her school supplies. You know, your father and I have already poured over half a million yen into her fashion school. She has become a bottomless pit, and there's just no end to filling that hole."

"She did? But she promised—" Vivian stopped mid-sentence. "Mom, you really need to learn to say *no* to her sometimes." She paused. "Maybe we should ask her to come with us to Dalian."

"I can ask her, but I seriously doubt that she would come. She was just there last fall. Besides, it costs a lot of money to live up to the image of a successful overseas Chinese returning home. And she knows so many people."

"Too bad. It'd be fun to see her with her boys. I know she misses them."

Yan gave a bittersweet smile. "I'm sure she does." Then she brightened, and said, "You know, if there's one thing I've done right in my life, it was raising you and Da Wei. You're both good children, and that's something I can take great pride in!"

Vivian went over to give Yan a hug. "That's because you're a great mom. Now, let's plan our trip."

Twenty-five

Three weeks later in Shinjuku, Pei was finding her way to the municipal library shortly after lunch. The production planning assignment from school was harder than she'd expected, and she needed to find some reference books to help her complete her homework. She would have to make the visit brief though, having promised her mother she'd be back in a couple of hours to help her cook a few dishes.

Her mother, having spent the entire winter and spring at the hospital, had finally come home four days ago. Upon hearing that Da Wei was in Tokyo on a short business trip from Taiwan, she decided on a whim to call a family dinner.

Once inside the library, Pei fumbled her way to the fashion and design section of the library shelves, her head preoccupied with the assignment. She wasn't paying attention to where she was going, and suddenly found herself falling flat on the floor—she had tripped on a guard rail, her books and notes sprawling outward.

"Are you all right?" A man reading at a nearby table rushed over to help her, bending down.

Pei regarded the man, who looked to be in his late-thirties, with dark, bushy brows and a broad jaw, his lips thick and well defined. He reminded her of the famous Japanese musician Ryuichi Sakamoto.

She felt her face flush. "Yes, I'm okay." She quickly got up on her feet and started collecting her notes.

"Please, allow me," Bushy Brows said. He drew a little closer to pick up several scattered pens. Pei noticed he kept his left hand tucked lifelessly in his coat pocket. Was he hurt?

"It's all right. Really—" Pei accepted the pens from the man, accidentally brushing his extended hand. Was that a spark? Startled, she immediately withdrew her own hand. "Oh, sorry!"

Bushy Brows smiled. "Are you a designer?" he asked.

Pei clutched her drawing pad, her cheeks a rosy red. "I'm a student at a fashion academy. I was hoping to find some reference books on fashion design. You wouldn't happen to know where I might look."

"Yes. This way please." The man gestured for Pei to follow him to the next aisle. "Are you looking for a particular book?"

"Yes, *The Basics of Fashion Design.*"

Bushy Brows and Pei searched all over the shelves, but couldn't find anything by that title.

"How strange! A friend of mine swore she'd seen the book here a couple of weeks ago," Pei said, a little flustered.

"Wait. Let me check with the librarian."

A moment later, Bushy Brows came back, shaking his head. "I'm afraid the book has gone missing. The librarian said they have already started a search for it, but it will take some time."

"Missing? No! How am I going to finish my homework now?"

"What's your assignment? Perhaps I can help. I teach computer graphics at a junior college, and I know a thing or two about fashion techniques."

"You do? That's wonderful!" Pei couldn't believe her luck. She eagerly agreed to the suggestion, and the two soon settled down at a library table. Bushy Brows obviously knew his subject. With his explanation and help, Pei was able to finish her homework in less than an hour. In the process of working on her homework, she learned that his name was Ryo Hayashi.

"I don't know how to thank you, Hayashi-san. And you've been so patient with me too," Pei said as they walked out of the library.

"It was nothing, really."

"I have to run home now. But can I take you to coffee some-time soon? You have been very generous with your time, and I want to thank you properly for this."

Ryo nodded and grinned. "I'd like that very much," he said, his left hand still in his pocket.

After the two exchanged phone numbers, Pei quickly left for the train station. They agreed to meet for lunch at a noodle shop near the library a week later.

When Pei arrived at her mother's it was already 4:30. She felt vaguely uneasy when she noticed Meiyin was already at the house helping their mother cook. She hurriedly put on an apron and squeezed into the tiny kitchen, looking for chopsticks and soupspoons. But she couldn't find them anywhere.

"The chopsticks are already on the table, if that's what you're looking for," her sister said behind her back.

"You sure are efficient!" Pei said sheepishly.

"And you're late," her mother snapped. "You're never around when we need you."

Pei said nothing. She wasn't in the mood to argue with any-one. She focused her attention on the table and realized her sister had forgotten the water glasses. She went back to the cupboard, bringing out four glasses, then to the fridge to retrieve two cans of beer, the whole time avoiding eye contact as best as she could with Meiyin. She couldn't say why, but she found it difficult to look at her sister since the incident at the police station. She felt rather like Cinderella tiptoeing around her stepsisters.

That evening, her mother had decided against making dumplings. Instead, she'd opted for a few routine, everyday dishes. Despite having been at the hospital for so long, her mother hadn't lost her touch and managed to cook up quite a feast. There were fried shrimps with eggs, moshu pork, cucumber salad with sea-weed, spicy chicken with peanuts, and home-style braised tofu. Although Pei was never a huge fan of her mother's cooking, she was impressed with her enthusiasm and ability to entertain on such short notice. Just when her mother was about to bring out the sizzling rice soup, the very last dish, Da Wei appeared at the door.

"Ah, just in time," their mother said with a hearty smile. "Come, Da Wei. Wash your hands and join us at the table,"

"Mom, I haven't seen you since last December. How are you getting along?" Da Wei stepped up from the entrance to give his mother a hug.

"Oh better, much better now that you're here." His mother lovingly patted the growing bulge around Da Wei's waist. "Looks like you've expanded a little!"

"Ah, that's for sure. I've been eating like a swine lately—a hazard of entertaining one too many clients," Da Wei said with a grin.

"It's good to be a bit round—a sign that you have attained certain success in life. Now, let's sit down and eat!"

The sisters joined in, and the four huddled together around the *kotatsu* table. Soon chopsticks were waving and glasses were clinking. It had been almost a year since the four had had dinner as a family, and they had much to catch up on. Pei was pleased that everyone seemed to be in good spirits for a change.

Again, Da Wei took the lead to amuse the family, talking nonstop about his Taiwanese colleagues, the muggy weather, and the latest politics in Taipei. The mood was very cheerful until Da Wei mentioned a Shanghainese man who had built a brisk business in Japan by selling a special hair-growth product originally made in China.

"Big Sister, you heard of the *101 Formula*, you know, a hair product that treats severe hair loss?"

"That's right, wasn't that the product you tried to sell a year ago, with the help of a friend?" her mother said.

Pei nodded her head. "Except she never got back to me, even though she'd promised she would do whatever it took to help me. People are so strange. They change so quickly once they're out of their country."

"Well, the product is a huge hit, and the thirty-something Shanghainese man who brought the formula to the Japanese market is now making a huge profit. He has inflated the price by at least twenty-fold. Imagine the money he's been making! You should look into it."

"Very clever of him! How did he know what would sell and what wouldn't?" Meiyin asked.

"There's a bit of trial and error, of course. But all it took was for him to have one hit product, and bingo, he's got it made!" Da Wei said, waving his chopsticks in the air. "Big Sister, I really think you should get into the act too, you being the Chinese expert in the family. All you need to do is to match your knowledge of Chinese products with your understanding of the Japanese market. I know there's a Chinese seaweed soap that's becoming quite popular in Hong Kong. You really should look into it."

"I don't know about that," Pei said a little defensively. She thought of mentioning her idea of starting a fashion house in China someday to Da Wei and Meiyin, but thought better of it. It was a bit premature to mention anything now, she reasoned. Her siblings certainly didn't seem to have much confidence in her abilities. And given how Hana had belittled her sales skills on her last day at Club Asia, she wasn't entirely sure herself if things would go well with this boutique thing. Better wait until she was more sure of what she was doing, she decided. "Doing business in Japan is not as easy as you think," she said vaguely to Da Wei.

"Wait, Sis, don't dismiss it so readily. It's a great idea," Meiyin said. "Besides, I thought you always wanted to make something of yourself. Didn't you say that yourself? Now, here's your big chance."

Pei lowered her gaze to the half-emptied tofu dish in front of her, trying to think of a comeback.

"That's right. You really ought to give it some serious thought," Da Wei joined in. "It's a lot easier than you think. All you need to do is pay closer attention to what the Japanese customers want, especially those cash-rich, young, single women obsessed with beauty and hygiene. How difficult can that be?"

"I'm sure many local Chinese are thinking of doing the same thing," Pei said finally, her eyes still fixed on the tofu. "But in reality, how many of them really make it big? For every success story, there will be hundreds of failures we will never hear about."

"But how would you know? You haven't even tried!" Da Wei raised his voice, his brows knitted.

"Listen, I happen to have spent thirty-eight years in China, and there are a few things I'll always know better than you two!" Pei shot back, her face now a crimson red. She couldn't stand being with her siblings. They were always trying to tell her what to do.

"Even if one product didn't work, there must be a million others that might. There's always a way, as long as you're willing to try." Da Wei was unrelenting.

"It's not that simple," Pei snapped. She suddenly felt sick to her stomach. She had had enough. Without warning, she rose from the *kotatsu* and rushed to the toilet, slamming the door loudly behind her. Once inside she started sobbing, her tears surging like floodwaters. They were so mean, her brother and sister. They understood nothing about her, nothing about the odds she had to overcome in life, despite her best effort.

"Right, just run away. Why not!"

"Shhh."

In the narrow toilet, Pei could still hear Da Wei's loathing remarks and her mother's attempts to silence him. She couldn't understand why her brother had become so critical of her. She used to think he was the most understanding and supportive of her family members. Had his time spent in Taiwan turned him against the Mainlanders? What rubbish were his Taiwanese colleagues feeding him now about the Mainlanders? Thinking about this, she cried even more bitterly. She didn't know how long this lasted, except that after some time the living room had grown absolutely still. Da Wei and Meiyin had left.

"You okay?" her mother asked from the other side of the toilet door.

"Mmm," she mumbled under her breath.

"Then come out. You can't stay in there all night."

But she didn't move until she heard the dishes clinking in the kitchen sink. When she finally emerged, her mother came to her, her hands dripping with soapy water.

"Look at you, your eyes all puffy. You okay now?" her mother said, peering at her face.

Pei shook her head.

"Tell me, what's wrong, my child? Why are you so upset?" her mother asked, pulling her close.

"Da Wei and Meiyin, they are so insensitive. They have no idea what life is really like for me. Yet they criticize me from their high horses. Has it ever occurred to them that I have so many more handicaps, not having gone to Japanese colleges and being an older woman starting from the bottom in a foreign country?" Pei said.

"Child, I know it must be hard, but I think Da Wei was only trying to help."

After wiping her nose with a tissue, Pei calmed down a little. It was then and there that she was hit by an epiphany: her siblings' aggression toward her was probably because she'd appeared weak and spineless in their eyes. After all, had she not taken money time and again from Da Wei, Meiyin and her mother like some pathetic panhandler? How then could she stand up like a proud woman in front of them? .

"Mother, Meiyin and Da Wei may not think much of my abilities and my character, but that's okay," Pei said, looking at her mother. "However way they choose to see me, I'm not going to let them or anyone else dictate how I will live my life from now on. Whether I might do business in Japan or elsewhere would be my decision and my decision alone because from now on, I've decided I won't beg or borrow money from them or for that matter, from you any more." Pei's words came out in a rush, surprising even herself. Yet strangely, she felt very relieved and dignified when she was done.

"Good for you Daughter, for having the courage to find your own way," her mother said patting on Pei's shoulders. "I welcome this new outlook of yours."

After a while her mother brought over some chilled Japanese buckwheat tea and placed it in front of Pei. "Child, I'm thinking of going back to Dalian for an extended visit. Would you like to come with me?" she asked.

"No, never! I'm not about to go back and be mocked and laughed at by Shanshan and Guomin," Pei said, biting her lips. "Shanshan wanted me to find her a sponsor in Japan, and I have ignored her. I'll have no peace from her if I went back."

"But she's your best friend!"

"Was—she *was* my best friend. I don't think I know who she is anymore. She seemed so greedy, so impatient to get what she wanted when I last saw her in Dalian."

"What about all those disadvantages you said you have here?" her mother said.

Pei shrugged. "It's true I have a lot of handicaps living here. But if I must struggle, then I'd much rather struggle here anonymously. At least no one will bother me no matter what happens to me here. But not in China! Not when everyone knows everyone else's business. It would be too humiliating to become a laughing-stock among friends and relatives."

Her mother nodded thoughtfully, as though this contrast between the two societies had never occurred to her before. Then Pei and her mother took the rest of the dirty dishes to the kitchen sink and began washing together.

Twenty-six

When Pei got home from work at Ninjinya on an early June evening some four weeks later, she was startled by the sight of her mother sitting on her futon with all the lights on.

"Mother, why are you up so late?" she asked, taking off her shoes.

"Sit down. We need to talk," her mother ordered.

"But it's almost midnight."

"Pei, I'm leaving for Dalian in five days," her mother said. "Your sister just booked me a flight this afternoon."

Pei went to her room and took off her jacket. "I thought you said you weren't leaving until next month. What made you change your mind?" She retrieved her pajamas from the closet and began unbuttoning her shirt.

"Pei, are you listening?"

"Mother, I've got an exam early tomorrow morning. I need to go to bed right away. Can't we talk about this tomorrow night?"

"I'm not coming back!"

"What?" Pei paused. "What did you say?"

"I said I'm going back to China for good."

"Where did this idea come from? I thought you were only going back for a visit."

"I was, but I've changed my mind," her mother said, stopping briefly to clear her throat. "I've been thinking about this a lot lately. They say fallen leaves must return to their roots someday. Well, I've been away for half of my life. I think it's time for me to go home to *laojia*. Now that you have become adjusted to life in Japan, there's really nothing to hold me back here."

Pei came out of her room, frowning with annoyance. "Mother, you make it sound as though you have been making a sacrifice for me by staying in Japan this past year and a half. But you and I both know that's not true. If you were worried about me, then why run away now, knowing darn well that I still have so many hurdles ahead of me here?"

Her mother shook her head. "I wish I could do more for you, child, but your mother is getting old. If I were still in good health, I could imagine staying on for another few years. But now that I can't work anymore, I can no longer afford the high prices of Tokyo. With the money I have saved over the years, I imagine I can live fairly comfortably in China for another ten to fifteen years. But in Japan, I probably wouldn't last more than one year. The rent for this apartment alone, as you know, is seventy thousand yen!"

Pei nodded, at a loss about what to say.

"I know your father won't help me," her mother continued dryly. "He didn't bother to come visit me once at the hospital. And I swear I won't beg from any of you just so I can stay in Japan. I'm too old for that. So this is really the best solution—for everyone concerned."

"What did father have to say about this?"

"I didn't ask him; the decision was entirely mine. I don't see why I should bother getting his permission now that I'm not counting on him anymore."

"But you *will* let him know that you're leaving, won't you?"

Her mother thought for a moment. "Perhaps I'll phone him before I leave."

"What about Da Wei and Meiyin? Do they know about this?"

"Vivian does, and Da Wei will soon enough. Really, my going to China will help ease their financial burdens too. I'll tell them I will only need them to wire me some money from time to time, China being so much more affordable and all. From you, though, I don't expect anything."

"So this is it?" Pei said, looking up at her mother.

"Yes, everything is more or less ready. Your sister will be accompanying me to Dalian. She will stay for two weeks, perhaps longer, depending on how she feels. She said she has always wanted to see what it's like to live in China. If her experience suits her, she might even try to find a job and live there for a few months. We will have to wait and see."

"What about this apartment?" Pei said, her panic slowly settling in. "Didn't you say the rent contract expires sometime this summer?"

"Indeed. That's what I must talk to you about. The apartment lease is in my name, so when the contract expires, you must leave. I know you never really liked living here. Perhaps this will give you an opportunity to find something better."

"But how, Mother? You know I can't afford to pay for the key money and the standard four-month deposit."

"I know, which is why I'm telling you I'd still welcome you to come back home with me when the contract runs out. Really, you ought to give this a serious thought: Do you want to stay on in Japan and be haunted forever by visa problems, or do you want to come back with me? I know you and I can live quite comfortably together in a nice rental apartment somewhere in Dalian. You'll be close to your boys. I can go first and set things up for us. You can take your time and look for a job once you're back in China. Honestly, I don't think it would be hard for you to find a job in Dalian now that you speak very good Japanese, and—"

"Forget it, Mother," Pei interrupted, recalling Guomin's stiff face and Shanshan's fawning smile as she begged for help with an entry visa to Japan. "I won't go back to China. I'd rather die than go back to Dalian."

Her mother nodded slowly. "Well, I'm not leaving until Saturday afternoon. So you have until Saturday to decide what you want to do. If you end up deciding to stay, I'll tell your father to help set you up in a new apartment. It'd be a much smaller place though, I imagine. You know how stingy—"

"Mother, how much time do you have left on your rent contract exactly?" Pei cut her mother short. She was tired of hearing her mother's criticism of her father.

"Forty days. I'll notify my landlord about my decision to leave. I can ask your sister to come give you a hand with the move if that helps. You can do whatever you want with the furniture."

"Enough, Mother," Pei said, pressing her hands over her ears. "I really need to go to bed now. All this talk about you leaving is giving me a headache."

That night, Pei slept very badly. The announcement of her mother's imminent and final departure came too much like a thunderstorm on a quiet spring night, leaving her breathless and feverish. She would be very much on her own once her mother left. How would she cope with life in Japan? She rolled back and forth on her mattress like an ant on a burning wok, desperate for some relief. It was a long while before she finally drifted to sleep.

There was the little girl again. Pei couldn't see her face clearly, but knew the girl couldn't have been more than eight years old. *No, this is not fair!* The girl was shaking her head. She let slip from her hand the strip of paper that had the Chinese character "stay" written on it. *I'm not staying, I'm not staying!* the little girl whimpered, her head still shaking.

But you have to. The slip you chose said you have to stay, so you must honor your words and let Mei go. This is your destiny! the woman said firmly, a stern look on her face.

Mama, let me go with you. Please don't leave me behind, please, the girl wailed, clutching at the woman's coattail. But the woman brushed her aside and left, slamming the door shut behind her. The young girl screamed, *Mama, Mama!*

Pei woke with a start, her body drenched in sweat.

"Pei, what's the matter?" Pei could vaguely hear her mother's voice through the *fusuma* door.

"Huh? Where am I?" Pei heard herself saying in a dreamy voice.

"Did you have a bad dream? Go back to sleep now, it's only two in the morning!"

But she couldn't. She lay wide awake on her futon, her eyes focusing on the ceiling in the dark. Her mother was right; she had never liked the apartment. Still, the idea of having to move was making her stomach turn. She hated that her mother never once let her in on any of the important decisions. She was always on the receiving end, the last one to know. A tear quivered, before rolling down her face, then another. She did nothing to stop their flow. She covered her head with the bed sheets, stifling her cries. She didn't stop until a large patch of her pillow was soaking wet. She finally drifted back to sleep as the first rays of the sun touched the sky.

Pei was fifteen minutes late to class the following morning. She did terribly on her exam. Not only was she pressed for time, she also had a splitting headache. Getting an "A" was out of the question. In fact, she would be lucky to get a passing grade.

During lunch break she noticed her hands wouldn't stop shaking. She had another class in the afternoon, but she really didn't have the heart to stay at school. She couldn't wait to talk to Ryo Hayashi. When she was depressed and overwhelmed, he was the only one she felt could offer her some solace. She found a public phone and dialed his number. Ryo readily agreed to meet her at a nearby park. He was always like that, always on hand to help when she needed him, even though he was the one with a bad arm.

Since their initial meeting at the library two months earlier, Pei and Ryo had been meeting often, at least twice a week. It was on their third date that Ryo spoke openly about his arm. He said he used to work as an in-house art director at an ad agency, but lost the use of his left arm after a car accident, which led to the loss of his job. The accident devastated him, and he wasn't able to find work for almost a year. It was only six months ago that he'd finally climbed out of his depression and found a job teaching part-time at a vocational college while moonlighting as a freelance graphic designer.

Despite his handicap, Pei found herself more and more drawn to the man with each passing day. At first they would meet at a coffee shop or a restaurant near his apartment on the pretext of him helping with her homework. Then things quickly escalated into his tiny apartment, then onto his bed.

Even before Pei became intimate with Ryo, she sensed that he was a man very different from the type of guys she was used to meeting at Club Asia. Though shy and somewhat reserved, there was a pure, almost childlike quality about him that made her heart melt.

And while Pei was used to being in the role of a "man-pleaser" from her job at the club, with Ryo she found she was on the receiving end of this cycle, as he often tried hard to make sure she felt welcome at his place and took care to ask for her opinions with respect. This attitude was also evident in their physical relationship, as Ryo was a caring and earnest lover. When they came together, he always found a way to make her feel as though she was the most important person in his life. In his eyes, Pei saw hunger, even a touch of desperation in his need for her. This touched something very deep and fundamental in her, and soon she was head over heels in love with Ryo.

If she hadn't seen him for two days her body would start aching with desire for him. This was the first time she had felt that way about a man, any man. Her feelings for him surprised her, even awed her; they were beyond explanation. All she knew was that when she was with him, she felt completely free from the need to appear more than what she was, unlike the way she'd felt when she was with Guomin or Mito.

Yet there were also times when she got the distinct feeling that she couldn't reach him, that somehow, he was holding back from her. In the beginning, Ryo said very little about himself, other than that he was forty-two years old, a father of one daughter, and had been divorced for two years. He deliberately avoided talking about his failed marriage or his former wife. Then one day by chance, Pei found an old family portrait of him, his wife, and his daughter hidden inside a book. When she confronted him with his past, he finally confessed that he had not been entirely truthful about his broken arm. Eventually he admitted he didn't lose the use of his arm in a car accident. Rather, it was caused by an injury inflicted on him by a gang member.

"My wife became romantically involved with a gangster while working as a waitress at a coffee shop," he said. "When I tried to pressure her for a divorce, she was quickly instructed by her boyfriend to turn things around by serving me with a threat: either I grant her a divorce with custody of our child and a generous alimony, or she would charge me with domestic violence and molestation of their daughter." He said this with great pain in his face.

When he refused his ex-wife's blackmailing, her boyfriend ambushed him and beat him up in a car park with two other gang members.

In the end, he lost the use of one arm, custody of their child, ownership of his house, and all of his savings. He was in such bad shape he was almost driven to commit suicide.

Ryo lost his voice when he finished his story. Covering his face with his good hand, he told Pei that he did not want to tell her about his past because he was so afraid she would not find him attractive anymore. He said he felt like such a failure in life that he had wondered if he would ever find love again.

That was when Pei pulled him close to her and told him softly that she loved him and that she wanted to help him build up his life and confidence again. And as long as he didn't mind that she was a foreigner with an uncertain future, she would always be there for him. Never before had she felt so strongly the power of helping someone else. Being with Ryo made her feel that she was the one holding the helm of the ship. That night, Pei saw the first sparks in his eyes, and the distance she had felt between them slowly fizzled away.

When Pei arrived at the park, Ryo was already sitting on a bench waiting for her. He had prepared rice balls for her, knowing that she would be hungry. Pei broke down in tears the minute she saw him. She told him about her mother's decision to leave Japan and her pending living situation, as well as the nagging issue about her visa and what she might do for the following year's tuition.

The school was already pressuring her about her plans. "Maybe I'm destined to become an illegal immigrant, which, I suppose, wouldn't be so bad," she concluded with a sigh.

Ryo took a fleeting glance at Pei, then lowered his gaze. He tightened his fist and said, "Your living situation is not really a problem, because there's plenty of cheap housing if you're not fussy about needing a private bath. Besides, you can always move in with me if you want. The real problem is your visa. I'd offer to help with the tuition, but I have very little savings. I suppose I can ask around to see if my friends might be able to help. Why don't you wait a few days and let me see what I can do?"

Pei's heart skipped a beat. Had he really suggested they live together? She nodded with a grateful smile. By Chinese standards, Ryo was not a prize catch by any stretch of the imagination. But the sheer fact that he was so earnest and sincere was enough to move her. It wasn't every day you would meet people like that anywhere, whether in your home country or a foreign land. She felt a warm current going through her, despite her seemingly impossible situation. At last, someone truly cared. Someone she loved.

Twenty-seven

"Look, Mom, the Korean Peninsula! We must be really close now." Vivian peeked out the airplane window in childlike excitement as a landmass came into sight several miles below. After a week of scrambling for tickets and helping her mother pack, they were finally on their way to Dalian.

It wasn't Vivian's first trip to China, but it was her *first* to her ancestral home. After thirty-five years, she was at last on her way to see Dalian and some of her extended family—people she had heard about, but never had the opportunity to meet. She would learn about her roots and see with her own eyes the very city where she'd spent her first couple of years as a baby with her Grandma. *Home, I'm finally home!* she thought with excitement.

Between beverages on their flight, Vivian peppered her mother with questions about Cousin Jian, knowing they would be spending a lot of time with him during their stay. What was he like as a child? Did he get along with Pei? What was he doing now, and whom did he marry? Then out of the blue, she turned to her mother and asked, "Mom, is Big Sister going to be okay without you?"

"Hard to say," she said with resignation. "I've tried everything to convince her to come back with me, but she wouldn't listen. Honestly, I think my leaving will be good for her in the end. I was too much like a crutch for her. Every time she had some difficulties, no matter how trivial, she immediately came to me for help. She's still a child really; never learned to solve problems on her own. Now that I'm gone, she will finally have to rely on herself. If she can do it, fine; if not, she knows where to find me."

Vivian said nothing. She wasn't convinced her sister would be as independent or understanding as her mother made her out to be. Really, what would Pei be like now that their mother had left Japan?

The flight was shorter than Vivian had expected. As they rode in a taxi past Changjiang Lu toward Zhongshan Square—the heart of Dalian—she was surprised to see the city dominated by cloudy smokestacks and dusty construction sites. Except for the grimy shipyards and a grayish landscape that stretched as far as the eye could see, she detected little in the way of real culture.

She had secretly hoped the city might have something significant to offer in terms of historical relics. Even if it weren't famous as a site for ancient tombs of past emperors or empresses like Xi'an or Beijing, she hoped that it might at least be a home to some thousand-year-old temples or ornate, pagoda-style gardens like the ones she had seen in Suzhou and Hangzhou. She was quite disappointed when the taxi driver told her there was nothing of the sort in the city.

She soon learned that Dalian was part of the rustbelt of the northeast and had an urban history of only about one hundred years. For the longest time, Dalian was nothing but an obscure fishing port. It rose in prominence only at the turn of the twentieth century, when it became a target of bitter rivalry between Russia and Japan. Somehow its association with the neighboring Port Arthur, a naval base, and its access to northeastern China as the only ice-free port in the zone made it a much-coveted prize for the Japanese and Russians alike.

Although Dalian was eventually won by the Japanese and was developed as part of Manchuria into a major industrial hub and an international port, the city seemed barren in every other way.

For days, Vivian could not rid herself of the sense that she had been cheated and let down somehow. Why didn't her ancestral home have a longer history? A hundred years was like a tiny drop of water in a vast ocean, given that Chinese history stretched back five thousand years! Even if Dalian wasn't historically important, why couldn't it at least be more charming and cosmopolitan, like Shanghai or Guangzhou? Even Ji'nan, where her aunt lived, sounded like it had a lot more going for it, being over four thousand years old and the capital of Shandong Province. But what was Dalian's claim to fame? She'd waited a lifetime to come back to her ancestral home. And *this* was it?

Her mother had tried to cheer her up. "Don't underestimate Dalian. There's more to it than meets the eye. Did you know that Dalian was the first rat-free city in China? It's also rated one of the cleanest and most livable cities in the country!"

Vivian knew her mother wanted her approval. She was her tour guide and took a certain pride in the city where she had spent a good twenty years of her life. But nothing her mother said could ease Vivian's disappointment. Finally, when her mother began her acupuncture treatments at a Chinese medical center, she passed on the job of tour-guiding to Cousin Jian.

Jian seemed more than happy to assume the task. He took it upon himself to chauffeur Vivian around town in his white Jinbei van, taking care to explain to her every twist and turn of the seacoast.

While Vivian wasn't enthusiastic about the tour initially, offended by Jian's atrocious habit of chain-smoking, she went along because she felt an obligation to be polite. She also wanted to give Dalian another chance. Maybe, just maybe, like her mother had suggested, there was more to the city than what she saw.

Jian had taken her to every possible beach and mountain he could think of, dragging her from Tiger Beach to the Imperial Jade Peak and from Fu's Village to the Wooden Club Island. Every time they arrived at a new spot, Jian would invariably turn to ask Vivian, "So, what do you think, Cousin Mei? Beautiful, huh?" To which she would merely mumble in vague agreement.

Vivian had to admit, the scenery at some of the spots was spectacular. But her improved mood was short-lived, for their sight-seeing excursion came to an abrupt end after just two days, when it became clear that there was nothing else left for Jian to show her.

"Cousin Mei, it's been decades since Auntie Yan last lived here. But I was born and raised here. I've never left Dalian—never wanted to either. It's paradise here, don't you think?" Jian said as they stopped for a break at the edge of a mountain road.

"Yes, there're some beautiful resources here," Vivian said, smiling politely.

"Huh, what did you say?"

"I said there sure are some beautiful resources here," Vivian said, raising her voice a bit.

"Oh, *resources*! How interesting that you know difficult words like that. You know, for someone who has spent most of her life outside of China, you do pretty well with your Chinese," Jian said with a sly smile.

"You really think so?"

"Yes, I do," Jian said, taking the cigarette briefly out of his mouth. "I understand your Chinese most of the time, although once in a while your vocabulary comes out a bit funny. It seems antiquated, like something people would say long before the liberation. And a couple of times, I noticed your tones were off. But you sound pretty good—most definitely better than folks from Hong Kong or Taiwan, whose Chinese I can never understand. You, though, if you spent a year or two in Dalian, I'm sure you would sound just like one of us, speaking with the perfect local Dalian twang."

Vivian cringed at the thought. Could she handle all the smoking in Dalian? Could she handle the bad manners of the locals? "I don't know about that, Cousin! A year is a long time. I think I'll be long gone before I can acquire that special twang."

Jian blinked. "But aren't you going to stay with Auntie Yan? She told me she's here to stay, like a leaf coming home!"

"Yes, *she's* staying, but I'm not sure about myself yet. I'm a bit ... well, a bit of a stubborn leaf. I was uprooted from China quite early, so I'm not sure how I really feel about this so-called *home*. At first I was considering finding short-term work and possibly staying for a few months to see what it's like to live in China. But now I'm not so sure."

"Why not? Dalian is a great city. It's been voted one of the most livable cities in China."

"I know. Heck, for all I know, Dalian could be the very best city in all of China. But to me, the problem is with the people," Vivian said. "The other day I went to buy our plane tickets for Ji'nan, and I was pushed this way and that because no one wanted to line up for anything. People never say sorry if they bump into you. When I insisted that there should be some order at the ticketing office, people just stared at me with this incredulous look. I ended up waiting for over thirty minutes for my turn, even though I was the third in line. It seems to take a lot of energy to get anything done. I just don't know if I have the patience to take on the task of working and living here."

Jian seemed a little hurt by Vivian's critical view of the local people. "But you *were* born here, and technically you're one of us," he said.

Vivian shrugged. "I only spent the first four, five years of my life in China, and only two in Dalian. I don't think I could ever be one of *you* even if I wanted to try."

"So it is a foreign country to you altogether," Jian said after a pause. "Well, then at least bring your boyfriend here for a visit and show him your birthplace."

"You may have to wait for quite a while I'm afraid. I don't have a boyfriend."

Jian's eyebrows shot upward. "No? Why not? Ah, I know: you must be very picky." He blew out a stream of smoke. "But you're thirty-six years old. You really should hurry and get married soon."

"I haven't met anyone I'd want to spend the rest of my life with. I much rather be alone than be stuck with someone I don't love," Vivian said, her eyes focused on the distant mountains beyond the horizon. She was getting bored with the small talk.

"That's true." A long silence followed. Jian seemed to be struggling with the conversation too. "So, when do you leave for Ji'nan?"

"In about five days, when Mom is finished with the initial acupuncture treatments. We're planning a tour of Shandong with Auntie Zhen. We'll meet up first in Ji'nan, then take the train to see Qufu and then onto Qingdao."

Jian thought for a moment. "Is Auntie Yan still going to settle down in Dalian?"

"Don't know. She was leaning toward settling in Dalian until Auntie Zhen invited her to stay with her in Ji'nan a couple of days ago. Mom liked the idea. She said it would make her transition back to China that much easier if she had other family members around."

"What if Auntie Yan doesn't like Ji'nan?"

"I imagine she'd want to come back to Dalian then."

"I see," Jian said, staring at the windshield. "Cousin Mei, you must tell Auntie Yan that she's most welcome to count on me and Weiling to help her should she decide to make Dalian her new home. Just remember, we're her family too."

Vivian nodded. "I'm sure she'd be very pleased to hear that."

The next morning, Jian called the hotel before Vivian and her mother even got around to eating their breakfast. "Cousin Mei, you must come see my company. I'll give you a grand tour." He sounded very proud on the phone.

An hour and a half later, Jian hauled Vivian all the way to his auto repair shop some forty kilometers away from the city center.

"I started this repair shop about a year ago with Weiling, after I left the *danwei* I was working for. See, here's the showroom, and the garage is on the other side."

Jian pointed here and there in the wide-open space of the shop. But all Vivian saw were half-empty shelves, dusty parts that looked like they had been left in the showcases for months, and dirty tools strewn everywhere.

"You make money with these parts?" Vivian asked.

"We're still sort of new here, and business is done mostly by word of mouth. It might take another year or two for us to turn a profit, but word travels fast, and I'm very hopeful," Jian said with a huge grin.

Jian looked somewhat disappointed when Vivian didn't offer any praise. But he instructed his wife to put on a large teakettle to brew some tea. "Not that many people are entrepreneurs in this part of China, you know. I'm not boasting, but I must say I'm quite proud to be a business owner," he said as he dusted his showcase with a rag.

"That's wonderful, Cousin Jian. May your business prosper," Vivian said, finally catching on that Jian was fishing for a compliment.

"Thank you, thank you."

Vivian didn't fully appreciate the meaning of the tour until that evening, when Jian and Weiling insisted on taking her and her mother to a banquet-style dinner at Furama's—one of the most expensive hotels in Dalian.

At the dinner table, a dizzying parade of dishes was brought to them shortly after Vivian and her mother settled in their seats: sea urchin sashimi, sea snail salad, steamed sea bass, fried crabs with ginger, sweet and sour shrimp, and other local delicacies, not to mention the noodles, pot-stickers, and Chinese pancakes. The plates piled on top of each other, making even a large table look small. Vivian felt stunned to realize the sheer waste of food. Although Tiantian, Jian and Weiling's pampered daughter, eventually joined in the dinner, the volume of food could easily have fed twelve people.

"This is our treat, an official welcome to you two, our special guests," Jian said, raising a glass of a fine grade of sorghum wine to propose a toast. After some time, he stood up to pour more of the amber liquor into Vivian's glass. "This is Wuliangye, one of the best wines in China," he said with an erected thumb.

Vivian knew the Sichuan wine was very strong. Not wanting to disappoint her hosts, she accepted another glass. Soon Vivian's vision began to blur, her balance growing unsteady. She knew she must stop accepting any more wine.

"Cousin Mei, come, have some more sea snails. It's a Dalian specialty." Weiling doubled up on Jian's effort by piling food onto Vivian's plate, building a small mound in front of her. The husband and wife showed equal attention to Yan, although they were easy on her with the sorghum wine, knowing she couldn't handle alcohol at all.

Vivian tried as best as she could to finish the food on her plate, until her tummy was so full she began to feel a little sick. When she looked across the table at her mother, she saw a satisfied smile. She was glad that her mother felt happy. And why shouldn't she? She'd waited decades to return home to her extended family, and now her dreams had finally come true!

When most of the food had been consumed and Jian's face and neck had turned a bright red, he leaned over to Vivian and said loudly, "Say, Cousin Mei, you know I have this nice auto repair business, right?"

"Umm, very nice indeed." Vivian nodded.

"Do you think, uh, you or any of your friends in Japan might be interested in investing in it? I know many Japanese companies are interested in doing business with China."

"Ah, you're talking to the wrong person, Cousin Jian. I'm only a bookworm. I know nothing about business or investments. You should talk to Da Wei instead." Vivian didn't believe that her brother would be interested in doing business with Jian, but it was the best excuse she could think of to end the conversation. She figured Jian wouldn't be able to get to her brother easily anyway, because he was so far away.

"Da Wei? How ... f–funny! Your sister s–said ... said the very same thing." Jian was beginning to slur his words. "Maybe I'll do that later. But wh–what ... about you? Don't you have ... savings?" Jian stared at Vivian, his body unsteady. "Whether you understand business or not, Cousin Mei, y–you should know that investing in the mother country is ... a glorious cause!"

"Please, Cousin Jian, I told you: I'm not a businesswoman. Besides, I've made a promise to myself that I'd never do business with relatives."

Jian's face darkened. "But ... what's wrong with doing business with relatives? We ... all have to make money in order to eat. The entire nation is now mobilized to the very ... very cause of making it ri–rich! Besides, you always stick with your clan during thick and thin. It's called ... sharing your wealth. There's nothing dirty ... dirty about that!" Jian pounded on the table for emphasis, inadvertently tipping over his glass of sorghum wine. The costly contents poured outward. The women around the table all jumped.

Weiling stood to try to clean up the soggy mess with some paper napkins.

"More wine! Wh–where's the wine?" Jian yelled, lifting the empty glass. He got up to try and find the waiter, wobbling on his rubbery legs.

"Sit down! You're drunk!" Weiling said, trying to pull him back into his seat.

"I'm not drunk!" Jian shouted, pushing Weiling away. "Who ... are you calling a drunk, you ... stupid ..." But before he could finish his sentence he collapsed onto the floor.

"Come on, you fool." Weiling quickly pulled him up and gripped his arm to steady him. Her face had turned a scarlet red.

"Is he okay?" her mother asked, stretching out a hand to help support Jian.

"He's fine," Weiling said with a wave. "This is not the first time. He's always like this when he has a few glasses too many. He'll be okay after he sleeps it off." She dragged Jian toward the exit door. "Come, Jian, let's go home. Tiantian, come give me a hand with your father!"

"But I'm not finished—" At her mother's stony glare, the teenager rolled her eyes and flounced up from the table.

Vivian, flustered at having caused all the hoopla, chased after Weiling to offer to hail a taxi for them, but Weiling pretended not to hear and stomped out of the restaurant.

As her relatives vanished, Vivian stood speechless by the door; how could her simple refusal to do business with Jian have triggered such an explosive reaction?

"Big Sister, your bill!" A waitress came running after Vivian, waving a piece of paper in her hand. In the rush, Weiling had forgotten to settle the check. Or had she done so on purpose?

Before Vivian could find her wallet, her mother appeared and swiftly took the check from the waitress. She took a quick look and stuffed eight 100-*yuan* notes into the young woman's hands.

"Mom, did I misjudge the situation tonight?" she asked after they had gotten into a taxi.

"I suppose you could have been more skillful when you said no to Jian," Mom said dryly. "Your cousin is a very proud man. He's not used to being rejected."

The two spent the rest of their taxi ride in silence. The incident had simply been too upsetting and strange for words, and clearly her mother felt the same. One hundred and forty dollars! So much for being the honored guests!

Twenty-eight

It was well after ten when Pei finally decided to get out of bed. She moped around in her room, fiddling with her clothes and organizing her shelves. Since her mother's departure ten days earlier, she had already missed two days of school by feigning sickness, and she knew by skipping yet another day she was edging that much closer to failing the immigration requirements of an eighty percent attendance record for a visa renewal.

She was reaching the point of not caring anymore, especially after she realized she'd failed the mid-term exam for her fashion technology class. She would have a hard time convincing the immigration officer to let her stay on come next year. Besides, with all her money resources dried up and her allies gone, she had no idea if she could summon enough will to continue on with the new school term anyway. She was feeling miserable, and she so wished that she could just quit now.

At eleven o'clock, driven by hunger, Pei finally wandered across the living room looking for some food. There wasn't much in the refrigerator: just one egg and two shriveled-up cucumbers. A week after her mother's departure, she had pretty much devoured everything around the house. The thought of walking to the supermarket ten minutes down the road seemed daunting. It dawned on her she hadn't shopped for food for four days now. She dug around the kitchen and found some ramen packs in a box below the kitchen sink. Cucumber and egg ramen for lunch? Not very appetizing, but it would have to do.

While slicing up the cucumbers, Pei was overcome by a wave of loneliness tinged with bitterness. Hadn't she always wanted a place of her own? Now that she had the entire apartment to herself, why did she feel this overwhelming emptiness inside?

Ryo hadn't called her for five days now, which was not like him at all. She longed to pick up the phone and call him. But something told her she should wait for him to call first this time. Maybe he was avoiding her. Maybe he had decided he couldn't help her after all, and he just didn't know how to tell her.

That would be okay, she thought. She was a liability, she knew. Mito had told her as much. She had too many problems, none of which was easy to solve. It would be one thing if Ryo called to tell her he couldn't do anything to help. But what if he never called again? What if he'd decided he didn't want to see her anymore? Could she stand losing yet another boyfriend because of her tenuous visa status and uncertain future?

Suddenly, Pei realized she was far more afraid of losing Ryo than of his not being able to help her. She wanted so much for him to be there to hold her, to comfort her. But with each passing day in the absence of any news from him, the threat of losing him forever was becoming more and more real.

The noodles came out a gluey mess; she had forgotten to stir them, and there wasn't enough soup in the pot. Didn't matter. She emptied the contents from the pot into a large bowl—the food all ended up in the same place anyway. She slurped down the noodles, a teardrop quietly inching down her cheek. She felt like a gypsy, forever wandering and not welcomed anywhere. Everything about her life was temporary.

She picked up the phone to try to reach her father, thinking he might be able to help her, or at least offer her a few words of consolation. He wasn't in, she was told.

While washing the dirty dishes, she thought of Zhou Jing. She wondered how her friend was getting along, realizing she hadn't called her in almost a month. It was almost noon. Zhou

Jing usually worked the early afternoon shift. If she hurried, she might still be able to catch her at home.

When she got through, a man's voice greeted her at the other end.

"Hello, is Zhou Jing there please?"

"No, she's back in China now," the man said in accented Japanese. He sounded like Zhou Jing's boyfriend.

"Is it you, Bill?" Pei asked. "It's Zhang Peiyin, Zhou Jing's friend."

"Yeah, I remember you. How are you, Ms. Zhang?" Bill said, pausing briefly. Then he broke the news: Zhou Jing had been deported from Tokyo two weeks earlier. The immigration department had carried out a sudden crackdown on illegal immigrants in the Matsudo neighborhood, and the supermarket where she was working was one of their targets, it being a holdout for many Chinese. Bill said she'd been taken to the airport and put on an airplane almost immediately, after a night at the detention center.

"I had to loan her some money so she could pay for her ticket to Chengdu," Bill said, adding that he just happened to be cleaning up Zhou Jing's apartment at the moment.

"This is so sudden," Pei said, trying to absorb the news. "We didn't even have a chance to say goodbye!"

"Zhou Jing had been an illegal immigrant for some time, and we both knew this could happen. Still, it came as a shock when it finally did," Bill said with a sigh.

"Where is she now?" Pei asked.

"At a friend's in Sichuan. Maybe she'll find a job and work for a while."

"Will she be able to come back to Tokyo?" Pei said, wondering what she would do now for a business partner.

"I don't know if she ever can. It will depend on the Japanese immigration."

"How can I get in touch with her?"

Pei hung up the phone after jotting down Zhou Jing's address. She sat down heavily on the *tatami*, still trying to come to terms with her latest loss. Her closest friend in Japan was gone, whisked away by the wind. By calling Zhou Jing, she'd hoped to alleviate her anxiety and dampened spirits. But now, she was thrust deeper into the dark hole. The thought of Zhou Jing spending the night at the detention center frightened her. It reminded her of her own night at the police station in Shinjuku.

Pei had been entertaining the thought of becoming an illegal immigrant, but the news about Zhou Jing was too shocking. The humiliation of being kicked out of the country as a criminal would be too much to bear. She must find a way to remain in Japan legally somehow. She lay down on the *tatami* floor, covering her face with both hands.

Pei was awakened by the piercing sound of the ringing phone. It was her father.

"Your mother left word for me to help you move. Have you decided where you want to go next?" he asked, before telling her that her mother had already paid the last month's rent, knowing the seventy thousand yen would have been too heavy a burden on Pei.

"Father, I don't want to go to school anymore. Can you help me find a job instead? Can't you find a spot for me at your company?" Pei pleaded.

"But you were so adamant about fashion school! Why the sudden change of mind?"

Pei explained how she had been feeling like a fish out of water at the academy, and that she wasn't sure she could fund her tuition for the second term. What she didn't say was how the departure of both her mother and Zhou Jing from Japan had been a tremendous psychological blow to her confidence. She wasn't sure she had what it took to keep the fight of staying in Japan alone.

A long silence. "Give me some time; I need to think about this," her father said eventually.

"How much time do you need, Father? Would it help if I come to talk to you in Osaka?" Pei asked, clutching the phone.

"No. I'll be going on a business trip to Fukuoka tomorrow. I have a lot to do today. I simply won't have time to see you."

"When can we talk?"

"Next week, after I come back. Why don't you call me next Friday?"

"Father . . ."

"I must go now." *Click.*

Pei slowly put down the phone. Next week! That was practically a lifetime! She couldn't put her life on hold another minute while waiting for her father. She needed to have an answer right away.

It was Thursday. If she didn't want to wait for another week, she must do something now. Perhaps she should pay her father a surprise visit in Osaka that very afternoon and finish her talk with him in person. She had always wanted to see her father's office anyway. This would be the perfect opportunity. Osaka was only a little over two hours from Tokyo on the bullet train. If she hurried, she could be there around three. With a bit of luck, she could be back the same night. If not, she could always spend the night at a motel. She took some money from inside her pillow, where she had hidden a wad of bills, packed a light day-bag, and headed for the train station.

By the time she arrived at Shin-Osaka Station, it was already 3:30. Fighting the blistering June sun, Pei got lost quite a few times trying to find her father's firm. Only when she boarded the local subway train did she realize her father's office was in Ikeda, another forty minutes from the heart of the city. Once in Ikeda, she asked around with her father's name card in hand, finally stumbling into a five-story building in the back of a shopping street, where the Grand Source Co. Ltd. was supposed to be located. She looked at her watch—it was close to five.

Pei spotted the name of her father's company among the fifteen mailboxes near the building's entrance and rode the elevator to the third floor. *Finally,* she thought to herself, a little relieved. The door to the small office was open. Inside were four metal desks, arranged in blocks of two at the center of the room. In the far corner near the window was a bigger desk. This one, Pei thought, must be her father's. Except for the desk closest to the door, which was occupied by a woman dressed in a Hello Kitty T-shirt, no one else was present.

The woman looked up. "Can I help you?"

"Yes, I'm looking for Zhang Yiwen . . . I mean, Cho Keibun," Pei said, handing the name card to her.

The woman, who looked to be in her late twenties, sized Pei up and down. "Cho-san is not in the office. And you are?"

"I'm a relative. Can you tell me when he'll be back?"

"Not sure. Maybe another thirty minutes, maybe longer," she said dismissively. "He's very busy today. You might want to come another time—"

"No, I'll just wait here," Pei said, taking a sofa chair by the door.

The woman shrugged, then turned away to pick up the phone. "Grand Source Co. Ltd. May I help you?" she said in a high-pitched voice. "Oh, Yoshida-san, how are you? Thank you for calling back. Yes, I wanted to confirm my boss's itinerary one more time. That's right; it's party of three, to Hawaii, leaving tomorrow at twelve noon. The spelling? Let me get the passports."

The woman walked to the window desk, returning to the phone with three passports in hand. "Yes, his passport name is Zhang Yiwen. Yes, yes, that's the spelling, just the way he had last time. And her name is Chen Manyong; M-a-n-y-o-n-g. Their daughter? Yes, she's seventeen . . . her name is Emi. The spelling is E-m-i. The reservation is at the Sheraton, for five nights."

Pei had turned cold. Her father was traveling with a woman to Hawaii? And they had a daughter together? There must be a mistake!

She waited until the woman put down the phone. "Excuse me, Miss, but are you sure Cho-san is going to Hawaii tomorrow? I thought he was going to Fukuoka."

"There's no mistake. His tickets will be delivered to us in about half an hour," the woman said sharply. She walked the passports back to the window desk.

A few minutes later, a man came to the door with a parcel. The receptionist went to answer the door, and the two seemed to be engaged in a very involved conversation about a special delivery for the following day. Pei took the opportunity to tiptoe to the window desk. She had to confirm the matter with her own eyes.

Sitting near a pile of papers on the desk was a striped blue silk tie. Pei recognized it as her father's; it was the same one he'd worn to the Golden Phoenix when the family had its first reunion. Scattered on the desk were the three passports. Pei picked up one of them and opened the pages. The man in the picture looked younger than her father, but he had the same narrow eyes and wispy eyebrows. There was no mistake—the man was her father.

The second passport showed a woman with long hair who looked to be in her late forties. She wore a bright smile, and though a little plump, she exuded an air of confidence that was missing in Pei's mother. This, Pei realized, was the woman who had stolen her father away. The birthday listed was June 24, 1945. The woman was only nine years older than Pei.

Before Pei was able to reach the third passport, she felt someone tapping on her shoulder.

"Just what do you think you're doing?" the receptionist yelled.

Pei jumped, quickly putting down the passports. "I just wanted to ... never mind," she said, before scurrying out of the office and frantically running down the stairs. At the bottom of the staircase, she slowed to catch her breath; the shock of her chance discovery had simply been too great for her.

Her father had another family! How was this possible? All these years her father had led a double life. She had always assumed it was her mother who had driven him away, having turned into such a sourpuss. But now Pei wasn't so sure. If her father had another daughter who was already seventeen, then the affair must have been going on for at least eighteen years.

It suddenly dawned on her that her mother had tolerated this betrayal for almost two decades. Instead of choosing a divorce, her mother had accepted her lot by taking whatever she could from her father, eking out a miserable life in Tokyo. The cold bed at night! His long absences from home! How had she endured the pain and insult all these years? When Pei was little she'd always thought her mother was the most beautiful and elegant lady on earth. It pained her to think her mother had been trampled on by her father like that.

Chen Manyong, the home wrecker! Pei felt a sudden anger toward this woman, the third party who had come between her parents. Her mother had once told her that had it not been for her father's change of heart, the family would have been in a much better financial position to bail her out of China. Who knows, they might even have been able to take her out as early as 1978, when China first opened its doors to the world. She would have been able to come out fourteen years earlier!

Then the face of Mito's wife came to her. At least in her photo, she still had a hint of a smile on her face, the ruffled neck of her blouse cradling her jaw. Until now, Pei had never once thought of how Mito's wife might have felt about her affair with him, not to mention his many other infidelities. Even though Pei had been unsuccessful in her attempt to lure Mito away, she could now see how, in a way, she was no better than Chen Manyong.

But her father—why? He was worse than Mito. At least Mito would never leave his wife impoverished, scrubbing floors. Pei wasn't sure if she was angrier with her father for having lied about the business trip or for betraying her mother and family for nearly twenty years. The worst part about the discovery was the knowledge that she wasn't the only one vying for her father's love and attention over the past nineteen months.

The thought of her father taking his other family to Hawaii was particularly difficult to swallow. No doubt he was planning to spend a luxurious vacation with his mistress and this other daughter, while his firstborn had to struggle in order to stay in Japan.

Pei felt her stomach turn. All this time she'd thought it was Meiyin who was stealing from her what was rightfully hers, be it her parents' love, money, or attention. She'd never dreamed that she had been competing in the dark with a half-sister only a fraction of her age!

Pei was about to step out of the building when she saw her father walking toward the entrance. He must have just gotten out of a taxi.

"Pei? What're you doing here?" her father said as he came through the entrance, adjusting his glasses as though he had trouble believing his daughter was indeed there.

"Father, why did you lie to me?" Pei demanded. "Why did you say you were going to Fukuoka when in fact you're going to Hawaii with your other family?"

"Who told you this?"

"I saw her picture, the woman named Chen Manyong. You never mentioned you have a seventeen-year-old daughter!" Pei yelled. She was near tears.

Her father looked away to avoid Pei's unrelenting gaze. "Life is complicated," he said evasively.

"Who is she, an overseas Chinese? Why did you do this?"

Her father did not immediately reply. "We were very different people from the start, your mother and I," he said after some thought, his eyes still focused on the floor. "I didn't realize how different we were until we started living in Hong Kong. I should never have agreed to the arranged marriage. I should never have let things go as far as they did."

"If you didn't love Mother, why didn't you divorce her?"

Pei's father met her angry questions with sad eyes. "It wasn't so easy to get a divorce then. We were in the middle of a war, then one political campaign after another. And you were all so young then ..."

Pei lowered her gaze, trying to absorb what her father was saying.

"Why have you come?" he asked.

"I was hoping I could convince you to find me a job," Pei said after a sigh. "I just can't see myself going on with that school anymore."

"I can't help you, I'm afraid," her father said shortly. "Business has been so bad I had to let go of one employee recently. I can help you move to a new apartment if you want. But beyond that, I'm afraid I can't do more. Your half-sister is about to go to college, and I have a big financial burden ahead of me."

"Oh please, don't say any more. You've helped me enough," Pei said, turning abruptly to leave.

"Pei . . ." her father called behind her, but she had already left the building and started running in the direction of the train station. She didn't believe her father's excuses any more. All she knew was that she'd just lost a battle of love to a half-sister she didn't even know existed until ten minutes ago.

An image flashed in her mind. She was a little girl again, only about five years old. She was riding on her father's shoulders as they browsed through the toy section of a Beijing department store. She had rejected everything her father had shown her at the store until he handed her a long tube wrapped in red paper.

"Here, a kaleidoscope. Take a look inside, dear. See? It'll change whatever you look at into a million little stars," he said. It was the most magical thing she'd ever seen.

"Baba, I want it. Buy it for me! Please, please," she demanded excitedly. And he did. He seemed so much like a magician in those days, ready to do anything just to please her. Anything! But that was long, long ago.

Pei couldn't recall how she found her way back to Shin-Osaka Station that evening. By the time she finally got home to Tokyo it was already past midnight, and the sky had shattered into a million tiny stars.

Twenty-nine

After the disastrous dinner, Vivian and her mother did not hear from Jian and Weiling for several days. At first Vivian was glad, taking advantage of the time to catch up with her mother about her future plans in China. But by the end of the third evening the silence was beginning to consume them, and they both wondered if they might leave Dalian on a sour note with their relatives.

Finally, on the fourth morning, just one day before they were due to leave for Ji'nan, their hotel phone rang. It was Tiantian, Vivian's niece.

"Auntie Mei, can you and Grandma Zhang come to our house for dinner tonight?" she asked, adding that her parents were planning a feast for them and wished to send them off properly to Ji'nan.

It was so like Jian to use his daughter as the icebreaker, Vivian thought. "Hmm, let me check with Grandma first. Can I call you back?" she said. Vivian put down the phone and turned to her mother. "What do you think, Mom?"

"We really should go. It's a goodwill gesture and their way to make amends for the other night," her mother said.

"But what if the subject of 'family investment' comes up again?"

"I'm sure Jian got the message. Besides, if we say no, Jian will take it as an insult. Let's be gracious, even if it's only for the sake of saving his face."

Vivian nodded. Only in the past few days had she truly understood how important face was to the Chinese, particularly the northern Chinese.

Jian and Weiling's apartment was dark and smaller than Vivian had expected. But at least the two-bedroom unit came with a separate dining area, which was considered quite luxurious by Chinese standards. When she and her mother arrived, the table was already set with a few home-cooked dishes: Moshu pork, bitter melons and tofu, fried prawns with eggs, spicy chicken with cashew nuts, and a beautifully steamed sea bream.

"Come and have a seat!" Jian waved excitedly toward the couch, his happy-go-lucky self again. He offered Vivian and her mother peanuts and left to fetch some beer. He made no mention of the dinner fiasco four nights before. It was as though nothing had ever happened.

Vivian quietly surveyed the apartment. The dining room was dimly lit by fluorescent lights. A rectangular table, surrounded by six metal folding chairs, was squeezed tightly in one corner. Across from the table and near the window, a twenty-eight-inch TV dominated the entire room. A moment later, Tiantian came out to say hello. The young girl plopped herself down in the middle of the couch, clicked on the television with the remote, and raised the volume to its full capacity. A comedian came on the screen. He was teasing a woman in the audience about her name. Tiantian told Vivian's mother that it was the city's hottest entertainment show.

Jian soon reemerged from the kitchen with a beer bottle in hand, taking his seat next to Tiantian. Without offering the beer to anyone, he opened it, took a sip, and immediately lost himself to the television show. Yan took things in stride and soon joined in the laughter with Jian and Tiantian. She asked questions about the show between commercials—who was the comedian, why was he so popular, and which part of China was he originally from. She seemed to want to devour the local culture whole. Vivian was less enthusiastic. She couldn't understand half of the puns and thought the jokes were cheap. She also thought the couch had become a little too crowded now. Knowing Weiling was cooking by herself; she got up and slipped into the kitchen, thinking she might give her a hand.

Weiling, who was dipping an eggplant in a flour batter, scowled as soon as she saw Vivian coming in. "Don't come in. There's no room here," she said, an unmistakable chill in her voice. "Go join Jian in the dining room, will you? Dinner will be ready in just a few minutes."

Vivian tried her best smile. "Let me help you, Weiling. You shouldn't have to do so much cooking all alone."

"I can handle it. I do this all the time. Now go on," Weiling grumbled, waving Vivian away.

"Weiling, are you angry at me?" Vivian asked. A mistake; apparently the way to save face was to pretend there was nothing wrong. Weiling continued to dredge eggplants in the flour batter. "Look, I don't know what you're talking about. Go back! I can't cook with you being so noisy here."

Vivian left the kitchen. When she returned to the dining room, she found a newcomer sitting by Tiantian—a man with dark, greasy hair.

"Ah, Cousin Mei, come! Let me introduce you," Jian said. "This is my friend, Chen Xiaoli. Xiaoli and I have been friends for decades. We used to be neighbors."

"*Ni hao*, Mr. Chen," Vivian said, extending a hand.

"*Hao, nihao*." Mr. Chen rose from the couch and returned the greeting with a firm handshake.

Vivian couldn't help noticing how finely the man's fingers were manicured. When she settled down in a metal chair next to him, she stole another glance at his face. He looked to be in his mid-thirties, long-faced, with a square chin and long, narrow eyes. Not a bad-looking man, except for his greasy hair and strange taste in clothes. He had on a white shirt and a pair of black bell-bottoms, definitely not your everyday Dalian kind of guy.

"My cousin has lived all her life overseas and was educated in America. She has a master's degree in art." Jian described Vivian in the third person, as if she weren't there.

"Ah, a real scholar!" Mr. Chen nodded to Vivian with a smile.

Vivian forced out a smile, her legs shifting uncomfortably in her seat. She'd heard that in China, because of the disruption of the Cultural Revolution, all the schools and universities had to be closed. This meant between the years of 1966 and 1976, the nation did not produce a single college graduate. Vivian was almost certain Mr. Chen was among the batch robbed of a proper education.

"Not only that, she also had a full scholarship and graduated with honors," interrupted her mother, who had been listening to the conversation from the couch.

Weiling came out with two dishes in hand, including a bucket of bright pink crabs. "Ah, Xiaoli, you're here. Dinner is just about ready. Come and sit by Jian, would you?" she chirped, gesturing with her chin for Mr. Chen to sit at the head of the table. Mr. Chen stood up.

"No. Second Aunt is our guest of honor today. Come, Auntie, you sit here." Jian held out the chair at the head of the table and helped Yan take her seat. "Cousin Mei, you sit on the left side of your mother. And Xiaoli, can you sit on my aunt's right?"

Jian took the chair next to Vivian and settled Tiantian opposite him and next to Mr. Chen. Weiling took the seat nearest the kitchen, at the foot of the table. The conversation naturally revolved around traveling, partly because Vivian and her mom were leaving the following day for Ji'nan, and partly because Jian wanted Vivian to introduce to his friend her extensive knowledge about living and studying abroad.

"What's it like living in America?" Mr. Chen asked Vivian midway through dinner.

"Hmm, where do I begin?" Vivian hated questions like that.

"I mean, is it really easy to make a fortune there? You hear so many stories about how new immigrants have made it big there," Mr. Chen said, peering at Vivian with his long eyes, an eager smile on his face.

"It all depends. America is a land of opportunities if you're creative, hardworking, and good with your head. But for those too used to the socialist system of China, it may work against you. I've read in the Tokyo-based Chinese papers that quite a few Chinese who made the move from Japan to America had to work their way back to Japan. They said they found America's cutthroat capitalism intimidating and preferred to work under the more traditional approach of the Japanese system after all."

"Is that so?" Mr. Chen mused.

"But surely any Chinese would prefer the American way to the Japanese system," Jian said, intercepting the exchange. "Most Chinese are smart. Surely they'd find the Japanese way of doing things too inflexible and rigid. I've met a few Japanese businessmen here in Dalian, and I must say they all seem a little too cautious and unimaginative. They take forever to make up their minds about the most trivial things. You can't do serious business with them."

"That may be so, but don't underestimate what it takes to make it in America," Vivian answered. "To survive well in America you have to take risks. Sometimes that means gambling your entire life savings away. Of course, some do manage to weather the challenge and come out ahead, but often only after years of hard work, plus putting up with racism, exploitation, and abuse. Being a new immigrant means you are always a threat to other members of society. So once in a while, you hear about a new immigrant being beaten up, robbed, or even killed, either by jealous compatriots or disgruntled local Americans."

Now, both men had fallen silent. This wasn't what they had wanted to hear, which suited Vivian just fine. She was so tired of people dreaming they could make it in a foreign country without knowing the first thing about the place. All they wanted to hear were gimmicks and shortcuts to making it big, easy, and fast.

"Oh, what nice crabs these are!" her mother practically shouted as she helped herself to a large crab from the bucket. Clearly she wanted to warm the chilly mood at the table.

Weiling smiled proudly, revealing her not-so-white teeth. "There are more. We caught at least a couple dozen with our friends near the harbor yesterday afternoon. Don't they look delicious?"

"But why so many little ones? Like this one," Vivian said, holding up by two fingers a crab barely the size of a credit card. "I dare say a third of the bucket is filled with these little critters. Aren't you supposed to throw these smaller ones back?"

"Why would you do a thing like that?" Weiling snarled, a horrified look on her face. "I don't know where you're coming from, Mei, but here, nobody would throw anything edible back into the ocean. That's wasteful!"

"But you're eating into the future's resources." Vivian knew she should just hold her tongue, but couldn't help herself. "Just think, if everyone did this there would be no more crabs left in a decade. Have you ever thought about that?"

Weiling's eyes flashed with fury. "Look, I don't know what you're trying to get at, but if you're so damned concerned about the future of the crabs, then leave them in the bucket. It will only mean there's more for us." She slammed her chopsticks on the table. "Here I thought we'd show you a good time by treating you and your mother to something special. But what do we get in return? A lecture! It sure doesn't pay to be nice." Weiling grabbed a crab from the bucket and threw it onto her plate.

Jian seemed more amused about the whole thing than his wife. "I don't know what this resource talk is all about. But here, we've learned to take whatever we can while we can," he said, his mouth half full of food. "You've lived overseas all your life and there're things you don't know. China maybe open, but regulations can still change in a heartbeat. You assume things are going well during the day, but there's no telling what the government might bring you by night. One appeal from the party, and there goes whatever you might have in your hand."

"That's right," said Mr. Chen nonchalantly. "Being a Chinese means you have to be tough, sometimes even a little heartless. You always want to grab more than your share whenever there's a chance, whatever it happens to be. There's no room for playing

Mr. Nice Guy. For if you don't do it, there're plenty of people out there who will. That's just how it is when you're competing with 1.3 billion other Chinese!"

Mother nodded in agreement. "You're both right. Meiyin didn't grow up in China. She doesn't have the slightest idea of any of the practical difficulties of living here. Please excuse her ignorance."

Vivian looked down at her table. It was no use. Conserving resources was a foreign concept wasted on the Chinese. She might as well be talking to the moon. She suddenly lost her appetite. She got up and went into the kitchen with her plate. When she saw the mess in the sink, she hesitated. Should she stay to wash the pots and pans? She could use an excuse to stay away from the hostile table. Maybe she would gain points with Weiling for being helpful.

A few minutes later, Weiling came into the kitchen with a pile of dirty dishes. "What do you think you're doing in here?" she yelled. "You're a guest!"

Vivian knew better than to argue with Weiling. She hurriedly washed her soapy hands and left. When she returned to the dining room she found Mr. Chen sitting alone.

"Where has everyone gone?" she asked.

"Old Jian's in the bathroom. I don't know where everybody else is."

Not wanting to face Mr. Chen alone, Vivian made an excuse and went to look for her mother. She found her in Tiantian's room—the two were playing cards on Tiantian's bed. Vivian thought it funny that her mother should enjoy the company of a fourteen-year-old. She remembered a friend had once told her that older people, with their brain activities slowing down, sometimes could better relate to children and young teenagers than adults. It must be easier to deal with the honesty of children than the hypocrisy of grown-ups, Vivian thought, smiling to herself.

Back in the dining room, Vivian found Jian and Mr. Chen both smoking by the window, their backs turned as they gazed out. Just as she was about to ask if she could warm their tea, she was horrified to hear Jian saying in a low voice to Mr. Chen, "It's true, she's not the most agreeable person in the world—she's a bit spoiled, having lived overseas for too long." The two were clearly discussing her.

"She has this sense that she knows more than anybody else, probably because she's read a few more books than us. It's trendy for women brought up in the West to talk like they're really tough and smart. But it's all a cover. Once you get her to know you and like you, I'm sure she will quickly calm down. If I were you, I'd definitely give it a go. Tell her you want to correspond with her as a pen pal, or something like that."

Jian was coaching Mr. Chen on how to court her! Outraged, Vivian quickly headed for the bathroom before the men had a chance to notice her. Sitting on the toilet seat, Vivian ran Jian's remarks over in her head. How dare he suggest to his friend that she could be used as a handy bridge to America, a shortcut to the land of opportunity? She had read newspaper stories about gullible foreigners and unsuspecting overseas Chinese who had been duped into sham marriages by unscrupulous brokers. Their clients were inevitably calculating Chinese with a single motive: to escape from China. But she'd never thought her own cousin would plot against her like that, taking her for a pawn!

Vivian returned to Tiantian's room. She stayed there with her mother until Weiling called for everyone to return to the dining table for some mandarin oranges and sweets. For the rest of the evening, Vivian deliberately avoided talking to Jian and Mr. Chen. A couple of times Mr. Chen tried to offer her some tea, but she flatly refused. No way in a million years would this grease ball and her conniving cousin ever get anything out of her!

Vivian and her mother were very happy to see Auntie Zhen when they arrived at Ji'nan Airport the following day. They were so looking forward to a tour of the city with her over the next few days. But after the exchange of pleasantries, Auntie Zhen blurted out something they hadn't quite expected: Uncle Hua had had a relapse of stomach cancer and had been hospitalized just a couple of days ago. The news was a blow. Their elected tour guide now had a more urgent task at hand and must be excused from their planned trip together.

Out of politeness and concern, Vivian and her mother accompanied Auntie Zhen to the hospital to pay Uncle Hua a visit. But after two days, and at the insistence of Auntie Zhen, mother and daughter decided to push on with their original sight-seeing trip on their own.

For four days, Vivian and Yan played tourist and visited the many natural springs and parks that had made Ji'nan famous. Then they went on to visit Qufu, the birthplace of Confucius. They didn't mind that the temples and sights were less than spectacular. They were just happy to be finally left on their own, free to say whatever was on their minds, and released from observing the dozens of little obligatory gestures required when they were with their relatives.

Before she knew it, Vivian's sixteen-day vacation tumbled to an end. On the afternoon of their last day at the hotel, as Vivian laid out her clothes on the bed to pack, she asked her mother what she wanted to do about a more permanent place to live. Would she go back to Ji'nan to be with Auntie Zhen, or would she consider living in Dalian?

"I have been thinking about that for some time now," her mother said. "My sister is so busy taking care of her husband it probably doesn't make sense for me to stay in Ji'nan now. My being here would only add to her burden. Besides, I don't know Ji'nan at all. It may make more sense to stay in Dalian. After all, I spent many years in the city as a young woman and know it quite well."

"You know Jian and Weiling will be the first ones to knock on your door the minute they find out you're in town," Vivian warned. "I'm sure they will want to help you with this and that. But, Mom, don't trust them one hundred percent—you never know whose interests they're looking out for first."

"Don't worry. It's not as if they're the only people I know in Dalian. I have many old friends, and I intend to look them up once I've settled down. I should be fine," she said firmly. "By the way, are you still thinking of finding a job in Dalian?"

Vivian thought of the ocean of cars coming at her when she tried to cross Zhongshan Street, a sense of panic overcoming her. She thought of the loneliness she felt as she stood at train stations among the people who were supposedly hers. Then she shook her head. "You know, I really wanted to give Dalian a chance, but I've decided I would never feel welcome here. Not after what I've seen over the past two weeks. I hope you're not too disappointed."

"No, not at all! I totally understand." Her mother gave a feeble smile.

"I promise I'll come visit you often though. Have you any idea where you might settle in Dalian?"

"I have all my savings with the Bank of China now. I think I have enough money to buy a small flat if I wanted to. As long as you and Da Wei don't mind sending me a small allowance from time to time, I should be fine."

"Of course we will. That's the least we could do. But promise me that if things don't work out here, you'll come back to Japan. Okay?"

"Really, I should be all right. Besides, my mind is made up. Like it or not, China is my home. I'm very happy to be home finally." She smiled broadly.

Vivian nodded and resumed her packing. She felt relieved that her mother seemed so happy about finally being back in her *laojia*. But would things pan out the way her mom expected? It had been decades since she had last lived in the city. She was practically a stranger now.

Vivian suddenly realized her mother would very much be at the mercy of Jian and Weiling. She wished she had been more courteous with the two during her stay in Dalian. She never dreamed that her mother would come under their care. She wished she could take back all those critical things she'd said. Perhaps there was still time to make amends. Perhaps she could buy some gifts at the airport duty-free shops before departure. Maybe a yellow-gold necklace or a charm would please Weiling.

When Vivian looked up again from her suitcase, she saw her mother had dozed off in an armchair in front of the dresser. She had aged in the past few months, her once salt-and-pepper hair now a silvery white. The stroke had robbed years from her, making her look much older than her sixty-five years.

Vivian felt a pang of sadness as she stared at her mother's shriveled frame. She'd known her mother wouldn't be returning to Japan with her, but she had held out the slight hope that she might change her mind at the last minute. This didn't seem likely now. Vivian's family life in Japan as she'd known it since her teens had come to an end. The casual chats over dinner after a shopping trip together, the heart-to-heart talks over a shared weekend now were things of the past. She wondered how often she would see her mother after this journey. She went over to her mother and gently stroked her thinning hair. She already missed her.

Part Three
Seattle

Thirty

Ten days after her trip to Osaka, Pei received a phone call on a Saturday evening, after a long day's work at Ninjinya.

"Hello, Pei?" asked a familiar voice.

"Zhou Jing?" Pei said excitedly.

"Yes. And I'm so glad you're home," Zhou Jing chirped from the other end.

Pei let out a squeal. It had been almost two months since she'd heard her friend's voice. She hadn't realized how much she missed her.

After their excitement subsided, Zhou Jing told Pei what had happened to her. "I was helping customers at the checkout stand at Maruichi as usual, until my supervisor asked me to report to his office immediately," she said. There, she explained, two policemen were already talking to another checkout girl from Harbin. The girl looked flustered, and Zhou Jing knew immediately that something was wrong.

When her supervisor asked her to show her passport to the police officers, she made an excuse, mumbling something about having left it home. She knew once they saw her expired visa and that would be it. But the police officers didn't give up; they insisted on going with her to her apartment to get it. They pushed her into the police car and drove her home, where she had to show them her passport.

The worst part about the whole thing was that Mr. Kaneko, who had hired her when she swore she was legal, ended up with a hefty fine.

"A day later I boarded the late-night plane for Shanghai, thinking all was over for me. Only I refused to let that happen," Zhou Jing continued. "Instead of going home to Sichuan, I boarded a train for Shenzhen to look up a friend I knew would be able to help me find a job."

While working odd jobs at hotels, Zhou Jing said she asked friends and acquaintances to help invest in a business of her own. After a lot of pleading and begging, she finally found an overseas Chinese partner who lent her enough money to start a boutique on a small, busy street. She knew young working women in the bustling city had a lot of disposable income and the desire to become trendy just like the rest of the world, and she wanted to tap into this potential market before other people got the same idea. She was now frantically preparing for the opening of her shop, which was to happen in a week. She said many friends had already asked her about her shop and were all eagerly anticipating the big day of the opening.

"I can't believe I'm finally going to become a business owner! I only wish that you could come and help me run the shop, you being the fashion expert and all," Zhou Jing said. "Even if you can't come and run my shop, it would be wonderful if you could become my buyer and help me import things from Japan from time to time. Wasn't it your idea that we go in on a fashion business together someday? Now, by me being deported, I've jump started the business for us. "

Pei was stunned. It was so like Zhou Jing. She was always so resilient and full of confidence, never letting anything get in her way, despite her terrible setback. After telling her best friend she would seriously consider the offer, she put down the phone.

In her mother's small apartment, Pei paced back and forth on the *tatami* floor, struggling over this surprise proposition of Zhou Jing's. A business owner in the booming southern city of Shenzhen, how about that!

Zhou Jing's boutique idea was inspiring, her invitation tempting, even though it had come at least a year early. Now that

Pei had been to Osaka, it was amply clear that she could no longer count on her father for help. She truly was on her own now. Yet Zhou Jing's timely phone call made her see that there was always a way, even when everything seemed hopeless. If her life should fall apart in Tokyo, she could always fly to Shenzhen and start life anew alongside her best friend.

As long as she didn't overstay her visa in Japan, she could always fly back and forth between Tokyo and Shenzhen and play the buyer and fashion advisor for Zhou Jing's business—no, "their business". Tokyo department stores had steep bargain sales all the time, and even year-old fashion would be huge hits back home, she was sure, given how bleak things were still in China as far as trends went. And yes, she may not have finished the full two-year degree, but she'd learned enough to become the expert now. It'd be so nice to be near someone as energetic as Zhou Jing again! The idea of leaving Japan suddenly seemed welcoming. She could start fresh again in China, away from all the troubles with tuition and visas!

Pei was feeling very good about herself until she thought of Ryo. What should she do about the relationship? She was painfully reminded that Ryo hadn't called her in two weeks. The possibility that he might never call again left a stinging pain in her heart. Perhaps she should just pick up the phone and call him. She would have to face up to the inevitable sooner or later anyway.

She scanned her mother's apartment, her mind drifting back to the landlord's phone call just a day ago: *You must vacate the apartment by the thirty-first of August, and not a day late!* She had only two more weeks at the apartment. Suddenly, she had the urge to go to Ryo's apartment right there and then. It didn't matter that her father had already wired money for her to move to a different apartment. She must find out how Ryo really felt about her. If he'd had a change of heart, or was afraid of taking on the responsibility of helping someone worse off than him, she needed to know now so she could make a timely decision for herself. If that was the case, she could pack up her mother's apartment and leave Japan right away. Zhou Jing had left a phone number for her. She could call and be gone in a few days.

All her life she had been looking for a sense of belonging, a feeling that she was finally home. But Japan had offered her no such solace, even though she did manage to reunite with her family. Now that her mother had gone back to China, her dream of getting settled at a home here was lost forever.

She had hoped for another chance in love, but appeared to be failing miserably at that too. Perhaps it was not her time yet. Perhaps life had different plans for her, and she was meant to learn some other lessons. She decided the moment had come for her to let go. She'd had enough rejections in her life before—she would survive this one too. She also knew that she wouldn't loathe Ryo even if he couldn't love her anymore. He was, after all, one of very few people she had encountered in Japan who had truly cared about her. And that alone was enough.

She looked at the clock: 10:20. If she went to Ryo's apartment now she could be there a little shy of eleven, not too late considering Ryo was such a night owl. She rushed out the door and hopped on a train for Koenji. When she arrived at his apartment, she saw that his front door was ajar. He must have forgotten to lock it.

"Excuse me. Are you in there, Ryo?" she called, peeking in the metal door.

"Pei? What a surprise!" Ryo said, coming to the door. "I just came back from Fukushima this morning and I've been calling you since. Evidently, you've been out all day."

He was wearing his pajamas. After two weeks, Pei's heart beat fast when her eyes met his. He appeared to have been hard at work on a design project, his table filled with drafting papers, paintbrushes, and felt pens. He seemed to have lost some weight. He let her in, pulling out a chair and signaling for Pei to sit down.

"I'd been working at Ninjinya all day. My boss had a large group of private diners, and he asked me to help out. I was home an hour ago. You must have just missed me," Pei said, catching her breath. "So why did you call?"

Ryo brought out a jar of cold buckwheat tea from the fridge, putting it gingerly on the table. "Why don't you tell me what brought you here first?" he said.

Pei told him why she had come.

Ryo nodded, taking a seat next to Pei. "It wasn't what you think at all. After our conversation, I spent a lot of time calling friends, thinking maybe I could help you borrow some money. But I wasn't able to get anywhere because I still have a lot of debts to friends. This was such a blow to my pride that I became deeply depressed again, and to be honest, I was too ashamed to call you.

"A week ago I left for Fukushima to see my sister, hoping that she might have some ideas. She had her own problems and was in no shape to help. I did some soul searching and started thinking: this whole idea of going to school in order to secure a visa just made no sense to me. It's such a waste of money. It's a stopgap measure, definitely not worth getting into debt for."

"I know," Pei said slowly, feeling her heart sink.

"Then an idea came to me. Perhaps you and I should just get married. It'd solve the visa problem once and for all. Except, when I mentioned this to my sister she was adamantly against the idea of us getting married, saying I was making a big mistake. I was so confused. I didn't know what to do because she is my only family now."

Pei looked up, a hint of sadness on her face. "She didn't like the idea because I'm Chinese, is that it?"

"People have funny ideas about cross-marriages, and my sister turns out to be a lot more old fashioned than I'd thought. But the thing is, in the end I didn't care. All I knew was I couldn't let you go. My time away had made it clear to me that my life without you would be meaningless. I had to come back to tell you this in person," Ryo said, pulling Pei closer and holding her hand.

"Pei, I know we've only known each other a few months, but I really like you. You're one of so few people I know who believe in me; you give me so much encouragement. Knowing you is the best thing that has ever happened to me. If you're not against the idea, I would like to give marriage another try. I don't have much to offer, except for my humble lifestyle and my feelings for you. If the marriage works, it would make me very, very happy. If it doesn't, at least you could stay in Japan for a while, which I'd like to see happen more than anything else. It's the best solution as far as I can tell. What do you think?"

"Are you sure you want to do this?" Pei asked, holding her breath.

Ryo nodded emphatically. Pei looked up to meet his dark, brown eyes, a tear streaming down her cheek. At the ripe age of thirty-nine, she felt she had missed that narrow window for love and marriage. And then there he was, a perfect stranger in a foreign land, pledging to risk everything just to give her another chance.

"I shall never forget this," she said, gripping his hand. He pulled her closer to him and held her in a tight embrace. In the world of have-nots, they both knew she needed him as much as he needed her. The two held on to each other tightly for a long time, happy that they had finally found each other.

Thirty-one

Vivian had been trying to reach Pei for two days. It wasn't until the third evening that she finally got through to her sister.

"How was Dalian?" Pei asked in a cheerful voice.

"Okay. Mom was very happy about finally going home."

"How about Jian and Weiling? Did Jian try to make you invest in his auto parts business?"

Vivian didn't feel close enough to her sister to gossip about relatives yet. She still felt she needed her mother as a buffer when dealing with Pei. She paused, then said, a little irritated, "Look, Sis, I didn't call to chitchat. I called because Mom was worried about you. Do you need any help with the move? You *are* moving, right?"

"Uh ... there has been a slight change of plans," Pei said evenly. "I'll be moving in with my fiancé."

"Fiancé? When did you get engaged?" Vivian cried, unable to suppress the surprise in her voice. The thought of Pei keeping this a secret from her and her mother was unbearable. How rude!

"His name is Ryo Hayashi. He's a graphic designer. We met at a library and have been dating for about three months. A few days ago, while you and Mother were still in Dalian, he proposed to me."

A Japanese, and they have only known each other for three months! "Does Mom know about this?"

"Not yet. I thought I'd wait until you got back."

"When's the wedding?"

"There isn't going to be one. We will go to the ward office next Friday to sign the marriage registry, that's all. It's the second marriage for both of us. We thought we would keep it simple. Besides," Pei paused, "Mother's lease will run out in just ten days. There isn't time to plan a wedding."

"Wait, this isn't about his apartment, is it?"

"Of course not," Pei said sharply.

"Why the rush then?"

"Look, I really need to go to work now. I don't have time to go into it."

"Fine. Do you need help with the move or not?" Vivian snapped.

Silence. Pei seemed to be doing some thinking. "Well, I will need some help cleaning and hauling away bigger pieces of furniture over the final weekend, although I've already moved a few things to Ryo's."

So that was why she wasn't able to reach her sister for two days! "When shall I come?"

"How about next Saturday, around four in the afternoon?"

After her awkward conversation with her sister, Vivian immediately phoned Jian and Weiling's house looking for her mom. She couldn't stand the absurdity of her sister getting married so suddenly to a man who was practically a stranger. She had to share the news.

It took her a while to reach her mother. Vivian had no idea she had already moved out of Jian's house. Before Vivian left Dalian, she specifically remembered Jian had agreed to Mother staying with them. Vivian had even paid Jian several thousand dollars "investment money" for his business as a goodwill gesture, after he had hinted at it repeatedly to her again. The understanding was that Mother could stay there until she found her own apartment. But with the help of an old family friend, her mother was able to find an apartment a lot sooner than expected. The friend knew of a landlord in a quiet neighborhood who was looking for tenants, and her mother soon moved in.

When Vivian finally reached her, her mother told her things were coming together. She sounded cheerful on the phone. As soon as all the furniture was delivered, she would be able to invite Vivian over.

"Great," Vivian answered excitedly. "Maybe I can be your first houseguest."

"Why not?" Mother clearly liked the idea. "And you can stay as long as you want."

Then Vivian told her about Pei's marriage plans.

"You know, it's best that things turned out this way," her mother said evenly, adding she'd thought it would come to this sooner or later. "You know your sister. She wouldn't do well being alone."

"But Mom, she hardly knows the man. She's only marrying him for the visa!"

"Maybe," her mother said. "But then again, maybe she's deeply in love with him. Either way, at least this arrangement will allow her to stay in Japan, which is something we can all be happy about. No?"

"But will she be happy?"

"Well, happiness is a relative thing. One could be happy or unhappy anywhere. There's no guarantee she would be happy in China either. So why don't we all feel happy for her for a change?"

Vivian nodded to the receiver. Her mother was right: she should be happy for Pei. She suddenly felt ashamed over her own selfishness. All this time she had been so bent on driving Pei back to China she had never once thought of what might make Pei happy. Her sister had been working hard to stay in Japan for the past year and a half. Hadn't she earned the right to be wherever she wanted to be?

Thirty-two

On Saturday afternoon, just two days before the rent contract was to run out, Pei and Ryo arrived at her mother's to finish up the final cleaning of the apartment. While Ryo helped out by putting old books and notes into boxes, Pei concentrated on clearing the closet drawers and shelves, which remained half-filled with her mother's things.

On a lower shelf Pei discovered two plastic boxes chock full of her mother's stretched and discolored sweaters, frayed underwear, and old linens, once white but now yellowed from having been exposed to too much sun. She emptied all the used clothes into a black plastic garbage bag—no point in saving them because there wouldn't be any takers for such ratty stuff! Japan being such a well-off country, its people had a distaste for anything less than perfect.

Then, in a half-emptied photo album left on the bottom of another plastic box, Pei found an old photo of her parents standing in front of a Japanese temple. Looking to be in their early forties, they both wore a hint of a smile. It must have been taken during the happier days when her parents were still getting along. Pei flipped through the album to see what else was there, but quickly realized most of the remaining photos were of her mother, Da Wei, and Meiyin. The photo taken in front of the temple was the only one of her parents together. Her mother must have forgotten to take the album with her. Pei felt a sense of irony that she should be the keeper of her mother's old memories when she'd only been in her mother's life for the past nineteen months.

Pei's thoughts were interrupted when Ryo held up a heavy Chinese-Japanese dictionary, asking her what he should do with it. Should he throw it away with the trash, or should he save it?

"Oh, this one is worth some money; we should definitely save this one," she said.

Pei hadn't been entirely honest with Ryo about why they were at her mother's apartment in the first place. Not wanting to go into the details of her family history, she had made up a tale about how her aunt had suddenly decided to go back to China because of an ailing relative, leaving her to deal with the aftermath. With Ryo's help, Pei had divided the boxes of books into two groups: one going to the garbage dump, the other to be sold to a secondhand bookstore in Jinbocho. She then bundled up the black plastic bags and carefully lined them up by the front door. They would have to take them to the side of the building later for disposal.

After she'd cleaned out all the closets, Pei vacuumed, being meticulous about sweeping every corner clean. Later, she would wipe every window in the apartment spotless in order to earn her mother's first month deposit back from the landlord. The seventy thousand yen was something she could keep for herself, her mother had told her. The thought of making some extra money made her smile; it was cash she could use to buy a few clothes to take to Zhou Jing's boutique—no, their boutique—an idea Ryo was very supportive of. After the apartment was returned, it was her plan to start working for the new business venture with Zhou Jing. She had already told Zhou Jing she would be visiting her in the fall.

Pei didn't notice Meiyin coming in until she saw her waving at her—the noise of the vacuum cleaner had been too loud.

"Ah, you're early!" said Pei, still in her checkered apron and pink rubber gloves. She switched off the vacuum cleaner, wiping her perspiring forehead with an arm. "Oh, let me introduce you. This is Ryo Hayashi, my husband. And this is my sister Meiyin. She's a longtime resident of Japan."

"I've heard a lot about you. It's an honor to finally meet you," Ryo said with a polite bow.

"Likewise!" Meiyin returned the bow. "So sis, tell me what can I do to help?"

"Uh, let's see. Can you sweep the floor of the front room? Also, the kitchen windows need cleaning—they are filthy. I'd ask Ryo to do it, except he can't stay. He's got a private lesson. As soon as I'm done cleaning the glass doors here, I'll come give you a hand."

"Okay."

"Wait, Pei. Isn't that too much to ask of your sister? Why don't I do it after I'm finished with my student?" Ryo said.

"Don't worry, dear. She won't mind. She wouldn't be here otherwise, right?" Pei said, smiling at Meiyin. "It's nearly 4:30. Shouldn't you be going back home now? Your lesson will start in half an hour, remember?"

"Yes, indeed. I'd better go."

"So did you tell Ryo everything?" As soon as Ryo was gone, Meiyin asked Pei.

"You mean about why I was left behind China for so long? No, I didn't. I blemished it a bit by saying I'm your half sister, the product of a previous marriage of our father."

"What? Why did you do that?"

"Because it's too complicated," Pei said, trying to understand her own reasoning behind lying. Maybe she was ashamed of her broken family; maybe she was ashamed that she never had a home to call her own. "I mean, how else do I explain that we're sisters but were raised separately? That I grew up not with my parents but with an abusive uncle and an ailing grandmother—"

"Abusive uncle? What're you talking about?"

"That Uncle Feng would beat me up whenever he was angry and frustrated."

Meiyin shook her head. "Mom never said anything to us."

"You really don't know anything, do you?" Pei said. For the first time, Pei realized her sister had been kept ignorant of many of the family secrets. Her chance discovery of the existence of her half-sister also deflected a lot of her anger toward Meiyin.

Suddenly, she saw Meiyin less as a threat than someone who might have the potential of becoming a good friend.

Pei stopped wiping the glass door, peeled off her rubber gloves, and went to sit down on the *tatami* floor. She tapped on the floor next to her, signaling for her sister to sit down. Slowly, she began to tell Meiyin the tale of her lonely years spent under the roof of Uncle Feng and his family. She told of the cold winter nights when she had to cook for the entire family, and how she was only allowed to eat after everyone was finished. She told of the bleak Sunday afternoons she'd spent watching the ocean waves pounding against the rocks, fantasizing about the day she could leave China and join her own family. She was dry-eyed when she was done with the story. She had no more tears.

"How come Mom never mentioned any of this to us? We just assumed Grandma and Uncle Feng took very good care of you, since Mom and Dad always sent so much money and gifts to them," Meiyin said, her eyes wide with disbelief.

"I don't think Mother wanted to know or hear about my mistreatments. To her, whatever she didn't see simply didn't happen. Every time I mentioned Uncle Feng she immediately changed the subject. I think she didn't want to face up to the past. Confronting the issue would mean admitting that she'd made a mistake, which would require her to make amends and physically remove me from China, which she wasn't prepared to do. It was much easier to assume the best and forget about me."

"Or maybe Mom just felt too guilty to know what to do," Meiyin said, still sounding a little suspicious.

Pei bit her lip. "You know, Mother never talked to me about my feelings. When she came to see me in the early 80s, she kept saying how happy she was to see me 'happily married,' even though I was far from happy. Sometimes I wonder if Mother and Father ever really cared about me."

"Of course they did," Meiyin said, instinctively extending an arm to pat Pei's back. "In fact, Mom talked about you all the time, and she said you were the smartest in the family, and Dad's favorite child. It used to make me really jealous."

"Really? she said that? Then why was she always in such a hurry to leave me every time she came to see me? You know, Mother never said goodbye the day she left China with you and Da Wei."

"She didn't?"

Pei shook her head. "She told me you weren't leaving until four in the afternoon that day. But when I came home, it was Uncle Feng who told me Mother, you and Da Wei had already left for the train station. I begged to go to the train station, but the train had already started moving when we got there. I barely saw Mother waving at me from the window. That afternoon I cried and cried. I couldn't understand why Mother would do a thing like that."

To Pei's surprise, Meiyin reached out to hold her hand. "I'm so sorry. I had no idea Mom had left you like that," her sister said. "But then knowing Mom, I'm sure she did it because she didn't have the courage to face you. She probably thought it would be easier that way. Sometimes I wish Mom was a bit stronger, a bit more honest with all of us."

Pei sighed. "You know, I did the very same thing to Da Shan and Da Hai. The morning after I signed the divorce papers from Guomin, I snuck out the apartment without saying goodbye to the boys. I vowed I'd be a better mother, but in the end, I was no better. I was just as much of a coward." She covered her face with her hands.

"I'm sure you did it because you were so confused, Sis," Meiyin said, her voice full of empathy. "We all make mistakes in life. What matters though, I think, is how we deal with our mistakes. Da Shan and Da Hai are still young. Someday in the near future perhaps you can talk to them honestly about why you left, and how you didn't mean to hurt them." Meiyin's eyes were now filled with tenderness.

Pei nodded. When she looked up again, she felt tears in her eyes. For the first time Pei thought her younger sister understood a little better how she felt. This, after almost two years!

"Sis, sometimes I wondered how different life would have been for you if only Mom and Dad had gotten along a little better," her sister said, looking into the distance. "Mom just shriveled up after Dad left home. I don't understand why they just drifted apart like that."

Pei hesitated for a fleeting moment; then she told her sister about what she'd seen in Osaka. "I didn't want to believe Father had a mistress when Mother told me about him before. I couldn't believe he's kept this double life for almost two decades, lying to us all."

Still in shock over what she'd just heard, Meiyin then told Pei about the month their mother could do nothing but stay in bed all day and night after the discovery of the love letter addressed to their father. "Mom was like a different person, very depressed and emotional, unable to cope with anything. She didn't cook for months, and we had store-purchased bread most of the evenings when we came home from school."

"It sounded like you had it pretty rough too. But at least you never had to feel abandoned like me. You and Da Wei were able to enjoy some of the good times while Mother and Father were still together," Pei said. Then she thought of the photo albums. "Vivian, look what I found in the closet," she said, calling her younger sister by her English name for the first time. She pulled the album from a pile of books.

"A photo album? Mom must have forgotten it." Her sister took the album and flipped through the pages with eager hands. "Oh my, look at these pictures! They were taken in Meguro, when we first moved to Tokyo from Hong Kong. It was such a long time ago ..."

"And this one, where was this taken?" Pei asked, pointing at another picture of Da Wei and Meiyin standing in front of a giant Buddha. They were still in their late teens.

Before they knew it, the two were huddling side by side, going over the photos one by one. At one point Pei looked up and saw that the late afternoon sun had flooded the empty room, turning them both into gleaming images. She forgot why they were there, surprisingly happy to lose herself with her sister down memory lane. When they noticed how late it had become, they both agreed they should come back and finish the cleaning the following morning.

That evening, Pei invited Meiyin out to a favorite restaurant near Koenji, where she and Ryo now lived. After they ordered, Pei asked for Yin Hao Jasmine, a high-grade jasmine tea she had come to appreciate after coming to Japan. To Pei's surprise, Meiyin seemed to really enjoy it too, and said it was the best jasmine tea she had ever had.

While sipping tea, Meiyin slowly filled Pei in on how she and Da Wei had spent their childhood years in Japan. Sitting side by side, she told of their father's long business trips, the subsequent rumors of his affairs in Fukuoka, Kyushu, and how their mother slowly fell apart after that.

Then, bit by bit, feeling increasingly at ease, Pei told Meiyin about her first husband and how she'd been driven to the marriage without feeling any love for him. Finally, she told Meiyin how she'd met Ryo, what he'd told her about his past, and how he lost the use of one arm.

"You know, I was not in the least bothered by his handicap. In fact, I feel very fortunate to have Ryo because he genuinely cares about me. I don't know what came over me, thinking that I should try every possible way to make as much money as I could and go home a rich woman. When you think about it, to have a loving home and someone who loves you is worth more than any money I could ever make."

Meiyin nodded dreamily. "It takes time to learn what's really important to us in life, doesn't it?"

That night the two parted ways on a positive note. On her way home, it struck Pei that it was the first time she and Meiyin had ever gone out for a real dinner together. It had taken their mother's departure from Japan for the two to finally realize the need to open up to each other.

Thirty-three

The urge caught Vivian totally by surprise. When her train made a brief stop at Higashi-Kitazawa, she was driven by a sudden but very strong impulse to get off. Almost in a trance she hopped out, just moments before the train doors closed.

She was on her way to an interview a few stops further along the line to discuss a potential job as a translator. Her visa was about to expire, and she must look for a job quickly. But when the train came to the small station—the one she had used a million times to get to her mother's—she found herself landing on the platform before fully comprehending her actions. She had about fifteen minutes to spare; if she made her trip brief, she could still be on time to her interview, she reasoned.

She hurried out of the ticket booth and turned right on the small road leading to her mother's old neighborhood. It had been six months since her mother left Japan, and a little less since her sister made her final move away from the apartment. She had no business going there anymore. So what was she doing there?

Vivian wouldn't say she was very fond of the neighborhood. The area was much too quiet for her taste. But over the years, the windy path with sparsely scattered shops had grown on her. Walking slowly down the narrow path, she was relieved to find the small wine shop and mom-and-pop toy store still in business. She marveled that these seemingly insignificant establishments had come to mean so much to her over time. For years, she'd frequented the road, each time coming away with a deeper appreciation for how lucky she'd been to have her mother as a most loyal friend and dependable confidante. True, her mother's advice on life and work was old-fashioned and often out of sync with the real world. Still, on a rainy day, when she was stuck with nowhere else to go, she knew she could always come to her mom's, where a warm meal would be waiting on the stovetop.

When Vivian finally came face to face with the decrepit apartment building at the bend in the road, she was dismayed to find the modest second-floor apartment still vacant. The door and all the windows, now covered with a layer of dust, were tightly shut. The mailbox attached to the front door had not been replaced with a new nameplate. Half rusty and with most of its blue paint peeling, it was now stuffed with small ads and junk mail. She felt oddly comforted and saddened at the same time by the sight. She hadn't fully appreciated until that moment just how much her well-being and sanity had depended on this rundown apartment.

No, it wasn't just her own well-being, but her brother's and her sister's, too. Her mother had been the core of the Zhang family's extended life, the epicenter of their very existence in Tokyo. Vivian had lost count of how many family parties and birthday meals she and her siblings had shared there. The Chinese New Year was approaching, and the prospects of celebrating the occasion without her mother grieved her. Maybe she wouldn't bother doing anything this year. Without Mom here, Tokyo just didn't feel like home anymore.

Vivian stood outside the apartment door for some time. No steady job and no home! And her work visa was soon to expire. She wondered why she bothered to struggle in order to stay in Japan. Once an outsider, always an outsider. Perhaps it was time to look elsewhere. Perhaps it was time to move on. She took a deep breath and slowly turned to leave. She didn't look back.

At the job broker's office, Vivian felt distracted. She knew she wouldn't get the job just by the way the interviewer looked at her. He must have sensed that her heart wasn't in it. She told herself it was okay when she was back on the street. She wasn't sure about the extended commute and the long working hours anyway. She felt tired and sleepy, and all she wanted to do was to go home and rest.

When she arrived at her apartment, she was intrigued by a bulky, flat package left on her doorstep. The upper left corner of the package said University of Washington. Vivian's heart skipped a beat. She tore open the envelope to find a thick stack of photocopied Chinese prose and an invitation to a Chinese fiction translation contest co-sponsored by the university and a Chinese culture promotion foundation. She had sent for information about the contest after Becky had pointed it out to her in a literary magazine a month back, but Vivian had forgotten all about it. Prizes for the competition would include a scholarship to continue studying Chinese literature at the university. For some time she'd been looking for a way to reestablish her career back in the US. Already, she'd applied for the Ph.D. program in Chinese literature at the university. But if she won, it could provide her with a perfect reentry opportunity without her spending a dime.

The translation assignments included parts of a long novel and two short essays by Zhang Wei, a Chinese author she'd never heard of. Her heart sank when she started reading the text—it was laden with the Shangdong dialect, which she found nearly impossible to wade through. She had taken Chinese literature as a minor at New York University. Still, her training was of little use to her. With the help of a large dictionary, she was only able to muster the bare gist of the storyline. How was she to render this into palatable English?

"Sis, I need a favor, please." That evening, after tormenting herself for hours over a solution, Vivian picked up the phone and called Pei. She remembered Pei had worked for a literary magazine once, and was familiar with the Shandong dialect from years of living with Grandma and Uncle Feng. Her extended family had originally come from Shandong, before settling down in Dalian.

Vivian could hear Pei's stifled yawn on the other end. It was eleven o'clock. She'd called too late, and was robbing her sister of her precious sleeping time.

"Have you heard of a writer by the name of Zhang Wei?" Vivian asked.

"Isn't he the Shandong writer from a small town called Longkou? He won many prizes some time ago. Why do you ask?"

When Vivian explained to Pei about her predicament, and how important it was for her to do well on the contest, Pei immediately said yes, much to Vivian's relief.

"But I'm a bit busy over the next few days. I'm working almost every night at Ninjinya this week," Pei said.

"How about if we meet up over the weekend then?" She set up a time to meet with her sister that Saturday, on the eve of Chinese New Year. Perhaps the two of them could even have a little celebration for the New Year together, Vivian thought.

Vivian's plan was interrupted by an unexpected call from her cousin Jian two days later.

"*Wei*, Cousin Mei? Am I glad to finally catch you!" Jian was breathing heavily on the other end.

"What's the matter?" Vivian immediately sensed that something was wrong.

"I don't know how to tell you this . . ." Jian said with a long pause. Then in his stiff voice, he told Vivian her mother had collapsed while she was out with Tiantian on a stroll in a park earlier that day, obviously from another stroke. To make matters worse, she'd injured her head in the fall, leaving her in a coma.

"How could this be? Wasn't Tiantian watching Mom?" cried Vivian.

"Please, calm down. Look, Tiantian is still just a child, and this is no time to be assigning blame. Besides, Auntie wasn't entirely well from the first stroke, and accidents can happen anytime!"

"Where is she now?"

"At the Zhongshan Hospital. We're in a total panic here because the doctor said her condition is very grave. Not only do we need someone to be with her at all times, there're so many decisions that have to be made, not to mention the money. Can you and Pei come to Dalian tonight?"

"But that's impossible. It's already four in the afternoon. And there's no way for me to reach Pei now. She's on her way to work."

"Well, you need to do something. If not tonight, you'd better come first thing tomorrow morning."

The phone call threw Vivian into total panic. She had no idea what she should do. Finally, after she'd calmed down a little, she called Pei's workplace to leave a message for her to call back. Then she made numerous calls to travel agents to scrounge for tickets. Most agents told her the upcoming Chinese New Year had created a ticket shortage for Chinese destinations, and leaving that very evening for Dalian was impossible. Vivian had no choice but to settle for two business class tickets leaving the following day around noon.

Pei returned Vivian's call half an hour later. Although she was initially hesitant about leaving, wary about missing too much work at Ninjinya, she went along with Vivian's travel plans in the end.

After Vivian had made arrangements for Jian to meet them at the airport, it occurred to her that she should also call her father and Da Wei. She tried Da Wei first and was told by his Taiwanese colleague that he had left on a business trip to Shanghai. She eventually reached Da Wei at his hotel. Da Wei immediately agreed to fly to Dalian that evening. Vivian heaved a sigh of relief when she put the receiver down; at least someone from the Zhang family would soon be by their mother's side.

When she dialed her father's office number, it was already eight o'clock. She worried she might have called too late, but she got through to him on the third ring.

"Father, I have bad news about Mom," she said, asking him if he might consider going to China to see her mother.

"No, I can't. I just got back from a busy business trip, and I have lots of work to catch up on," he said, sounding quite distant. "Besides, isn't it enough that you and your sister are going?"

Did her father know that she already heard about his other family through Pei, Vivian wondered. "But Father, Mom's in serious condition. The doctor said she might not make it," Vivian pleaded.

"I can't. Sorry, I have to go now." *Click.*

Vivian gripped the receiver for a long time before finally putting it down. She couldn't believe her father had become so cold. Some people would travel miles home just to catch a last glimpse of a sick puppy. But her father wouldn't move an inch to bid farewell to his partner of forty years. Even a longtime colleague deserved better than this! She felt something dying deep down inside her when she remembered how sad her mother had been when her father failed to show up at the hospital. She gritted her teeth. She could bring herself to forgive her father for having a mistress and another family, she decided, but she would never forgive him for his refusal to see her mother in the final moments of her life.

The following morning, Vivian got up early to pack for the journey. She had to be out the door by 8:30 in order to make it to the airport in time. Not knowing how long she would be staying in China, she decided it was best that she travel light. She could always fly back to Dalian again if need be. Then she was overcome with guilt, realizing she'd never once intended to stay very long in Dalian. Not this trip, and certainly not the previous one.

Now that she thought about it, she wished she had stayed a little longer with her mother during the first trip. She had been very selfish and naïve to presume that her mother could fend for herself alone in an environment she no longer knew or understood. She also regretted her decision to let Jian be her mother's main caretaker. Her mother had already been hospitalized once, and she was sixty-six. She should be in a wheelchair for all practical purposes, or at least be under the care of a responsible adult at all times. If only she had stayed a little longer, or taken the time to set her mother up with a proper caretaker, perhaps none of this would have happened.

Vivian was just about to rush out of the door when the phone rang. She was sure it was her sister. Was she running late again? But it was Da Wei's cracked voice on the other end of the line.

"I have bad news," he started.

"What?"

"Mom doesn't look good. I don't know if she'll make it till this afternoon."

"How is she now?"

"When I arrived at the hospital in the wee hours of the morning, the doctor was giving her resuscitation. He revived her, but said we almost lost her. I thought her color was a little better early this morning, but her breathing grew uneven again a couple of hours ago. Now the doctor is saying he's not sure how much longer she can hang on."

"What should we do?"

"Just board the plane. But be prepared for the worst."

Thirty-four

When Vivian and Pei came out of customs, Da Wei and Jian were already waiting at the gate. Vivian searched their faces for clues, afraid at the same time to learn the answer. Da Wei's eyes were bloodshot.

"How's Mom?" Vivian asked.

Da Wei shook his head, the muscles of his face contorting painfully.

He had warned her. Still, Vivian wasn't prepared for this; she'd been hanging on to that last shred of hope that their mother might still be alive. She closed her eyes. They were too late. She felt Pei grip her hand.

"Where is she now?" Pei asked, her voice hoarse.

"In the mortuary behind the hospital," Jian said plainly. "We have to hurry, because they said they would wait for us only until five."

The sun had just made it below the horizon, leaving on the edge of the sky a tinge of silver the color of a fish belly. Shadows of darkness slowly crept in, weighing heavily on the hearts of the four as they made their way to Jian's van in the parking lot. They headed for the mortuary in stark silence. In her mind's eye, Vivian saw the pictures her mother had sent her shortly after her move to her new apartment. In one of them, she was all smiles, sitting on her new coffee-brown sofa. *Finally settling in at my own little haven*, she had scribbled in her uneven handwriting on the back. Vivian felt tears welling in her eyes.

The so-called mortuary was a run-down wooden shack hidden in the back of a nondescript garden. The doors of the building, which were peeling their white paint, were held shut by a heavy metal lock. Near the front of the building was a flowerbed, where several dirty urns were left sitting willy-nilly in the muck. Jian disappeared for a moment and came back from behind the shack with the mortuary keeper, an old man somewhere in his late sixties. Gingerly the keeper unlocked the door, still chewing noisily on his dinner. He turned on the light switch by the door and let the four in.

The room smelled heavily of mildew. It was lit by a single naked bulb covered with a thick layer of dust. In the dim light, Vivian could make out a couple of wooden trunks stored at the back of the room. Lined along one side of the wall, a few tables had been stacked on top of each other. It could have been a storage room for all Vivian knew. Their mother, laid out in the middle of the room in a propped-up coffin, was covered in a white shroud. The keeper drew back the shroud and slipped out of the room.

Their mother looked pale but composed. Caked in white makeup and red lipstick, she wore a turquoise blue *shouyi*, the Chinese traditional dress for the dead. But the silk gown made her look more like a Chinese opera singer than the mother she knew. Vivian frowned. She drew closer to the coffin, reaching out to touch her mother's hand. It felt cold, icy cold, and stiff like a bird's claw.

"When did you move her here?" she asked, fighting back tears.

"Two hours ago," Da Wei said.

"What did the doctor say? I mean, what was the exact cause of her death?"

"A stroke. He used the term *intracerebral hemorrhage*."

"That's right. Dr. Wang said it had nothing to do with the fall," Jian said. Clearly he'd been worried about being blamed for his aunt's death.

Vivian felt a sudden burst of anger. "But why the rush? Why was she moved over here so quickly?"

"It was the doctor's idea," Jian mumbled. "They needed the bed for the next patient. You know how short they are of beds at city hospitals."

"Couldn't you have made them wait a little, at least until we arrived? We were only a couple of hours late. We wanted to at least be given a chance to talk to the doctor and see Mom in her final, natural state without all this ugly makeup on her. Look at her, she looks ridiculous!"

"I know you're frustrated, Cousin Mei, but it's the custom here. Once you're pronounced dead, you have to vacate the bed," Jian said with a hurt look, as if he had been wronged.

"He's telling the truth," Pei said, coming to Jian's rescue. "There's always a long waiting list for beds here, and very little respect for the dead."

Vivian looked at Da Wei, as if seeking his confirmation. But he said nothing, his eyes vacant. He looked as if he hadn't slept at all the night before.

Vivian sighed. She walked to the far corner of the room and sat down on a wooden trunk with her hands on her face. Pei followed her, and caught Vivian by surprise when she leaned against her shoulder and began to sob. Vivian stroked Pei's disheveled hair gently, saying, "It's okay, it's okay."

"It's getting late. We should go. We have much to do," Jian said as he started for the door.

It was almost completely dark outside now. Walking ahead, Jian led the Zhang siblings to a shallow pit in the backyard. Sitting nearby on the ground was a large, black plastic bag that had been set aside for them.

"Come, let's burn some papers for Auntie," Jian said, blowing hot air into his hands to create some warmth against the chilly northeast wind. He opened the bag to reveal a pile of paper money, a paper house, and other articles for offerings. He looked up at Vivian. "You know what this is for? For Auntie's use in the other world."

Vivian nodded.

Jian squatted and built a fire in the pit with the help of a match and strips of day-old newspapers. In a second, the flames leapt up, licking the paper articles with long, greedy tongues.

Vivian joined Jian, helping to feed the fire with more torn-up papers. "You believe people still have the need for money and all that materialistic stuff once they're on the other side?" she asked. The silhouette of her cousin's face brightened to a reddish-gold in the reflection of the blazing fire.

"Sure. Why not?" Jian said, looking up at Vivian. "Even ghosts have to be bribed if you want anything done in the afterworld."

Under Jian's guidance, Da Wei, Vivian, and Pei each took turns pushing more of the paper articles into the flames with metal tongs, bowing as they bade farewell to their mother. They watched with resignation as a column of blackish smoke billowed up, rising higher and higher into the bitter cold air, until it became light gray, then a part of the starry sky.

The Zhang siblings spent a sleepless night at Jian and Weiling's. They took turns informing relatives of the funeral services scheduled for the following day. They also cooked sacrificial dishes for use at the cemetery, and folded heaps of rough straw papers into small triangles. Weiling said the folded triangles were symbols of money, to be burnt at the funeral. Normally they wouldn't have to rush so much, but with Chinese New Year pressing so closely, Jian and Weiling were afraid the funeral homes would all be closed for at least a week. The two insisted it would be best to finish with the funeral services by noon on the following day, which was Chinese New Year's Eve. That meant they had to finish all the necessary arrangements before dawn.

Early the following morning, with red eyes and disheveled hair, the Zhang siblings rode in a minivan to the funeral home with Jian, Weiling, Tiantian, and Pei's two sons. Everyone wore a black armband to indicate that they were in mourning. Pei had been overjoyed to see her boys, despite her grief at their mother's passing. At least Guomin couldn't stop them from spending this day with her, she told Vivian bitterly.

The dirt road to the funeral home was bumpy, tiring, and seemingly endless. The place turned out to be some one hundred kilometers away from the city center. An hour and a half later, when Vivian saw several hawkers selling plastic flowers and tokens on a dirt road, she knew they were near their destination.

The funeral parlor was huge: there were numerous halls and wings in the main building. Not far from the back of the building was a very large open area for burning sacrificial offerings and an entirely separate building just for the storage of cremated ashes. Since it was a day before the lunar New Year, Vivian thought the place might be relatively empty, as people would be home busy making preparations for the festivities. But no—the funeral parlor was swarming with people, who seemed to be filing into the main building from all directions, like ants drawn to a sugar bowl. Apparently death didn't care it was New Year's Eve. And in a country as large as China, it appeared there were mile-long queues even in death, and the wait was impossible.

It could have been due to lack of sleep, or perhaps it was the mere sight of the massive number of people closing in on her, because Vivian suddenly felt like she couldn't breathe. She grabbed onto the armrest of a nearby bench, afraid she might faint. She sat down to compose herself, letting some of the crowds behind her pass by. The sight of Pei, Da Wei, and her nephews coming to sit with her gave her some comfort, but she said nothing. When Jian emerged from a side hall, Pei and Da Wei both got up.

"I'll confirm the timing for Auntie's service at the crematorium," Jian said before disappearing again.

In Jian's absence, some distant relatives, none of whom Vivian had met before, started trickling in. They found their way to Pei one after another. Some of them pointed to Vivian and Da Wei after offering their condolences. *So these are your siblings,* they seemed to be saying. Pei nodded, turning to look at Da Wei and Vivian, as if telling them to come join in the conversation with the guests. From the corner of her eye, Vivian saw Da Wei walking over to the guests and shaking hands with some of them. But she could not find the strength to do the same, hard as she tried. She felt stuck solid to her seat by some unspeakable force.

Watching from a distance, she could make out very little of what was being said. It was as though she had been placed in a glass box with all the noises blocked out. *It's just as well,* Vivian thought. She wanted more than anything else just to be left alone. Later, she could recall none of the relatives' faces.

The side hall was very crowded. People kept coming in and out of it, their incessant wailing and cries filling an atmosphere that was already stuffy. Time seemed to have stopped, and Vivian was a teenage girl again. It was Christmas Eve, and she was putting on her best dress for a party at her favorite friend's house. Shufang, another overseas Chinese friend whom she'd befriended at her international school in Yokohama, had invited her to her home for a special Christmas dinner. Vivian was excited, humming to herself in her room as she tried to tame her wavy hair. From the hallway she could hear her mother banging around in the kitchen, making loud noises with pots and pans for no obvious reason.

"Mom, what're you doing?" she had asked, popping her head into the kitchen.

"Where do you think you're going?" her mother snapped.

"To Shufang's. She's having a party at her house tonight, remember?"

"Just because she has invited you doesn't mean you have to oblige, you know!"

"But I do, Mom. I've been waiting for this invitation for a long time. Shufang is a nice girl. She's my best friend at school— my only friend, in fact. I don't want to disappoint her. Besides, her mother's going to roast a duck for us. It's a big deal!"

"You and your father, you're both the same. Selfish! All you think about is yourself."

"How am I selfish, Mom? Why do you say that?" How Vivian wished her brother was around at that moment. But Da Wei was living in a dorm appended to a university in another town, which meant Vivian was her mother's only companion at the time.

"Have you ever thought about me, huh? Leaving me all alone at home while you're out partying, on Christmas Eve!"

"Mom, please don't do this to me. I thought you said it was fine for me to go ..."

"Never mind! If you want to leave, then leave!" Her mother slammed a pan onto the kitchen counter. "I'm a cursed woman," she said, knocking her head against the cupboard door, mumbling to herself.

"Mom ..."

"You all can't wait to leave me. You're all the same," she chanted in a trance, her head still banging against the cupboard.

"Mom, don't do this! Okay, what is it you want me to do? Not go?" Vivian pleaded, trying her best to stop her mother from hurting herself.

"I toil day in and day out for you and Da Wei, but for what? In the end I'm still alone," her mother said, her voice cracking.

"You want me to call Shufang and say I'm not coming?" Vivian said, tears welling in her eyes.

"Would you do that?" Her mother suddenly turned to her, her eyes lit up.

"If that makes you happy ..." Vivian bit her lips, trying her best not to let her tears run.

"Good. Then call her now."

It was one of the hardest things Vivian had had to do in her life, calling her best friend to say she wasn't coming after all. She was so looking forward to seeing Shufang. That night, she'd spent that entire evening with her mother, but mostly in silence, sulking.

"Vivian, don't hate me, please. I don't have anyone else but you," her mother said later. But Vivian only shook her head. She didn't hate her mother. She only felt sorry for herself. She also felt sorry for her mother. She remembered she had cried herself to sleep that night. That night also marked the beginning of Vivian taking on the role as her mother's confidante, protector, and spokesperson. From that day on, whenever her mother wanted something from her father, it was always Vivian who did the talking for her, often at the expense of her own relationship with her father. She did this until she left for New York. But by taking on these roles she had also turned herself into a hermit, forsaking many budding friendships and possible romances in favor of staying home with her emotionally unstable mother.

Vivian sometimes loathed her mother for turning her into a crutch, pushing her into a role far beyond her age. But deep down inside, she also knew her mother was desperate, alone, and had nowhere else to turn. Early on, long before Pei had told Vivian about her chance discovery of their father's other family, she'd known that her father was not living by himself in Osaka like he pretended. She had heard enough rumors from acquaintances to know that there must be another woman. That was enough to make her hate her father and to side even more with her mother. Da Wei, being a boy, couldn't relate to their mother's neediness, and by age twenty, chose to cope with the impossible family situation by moving out of the house altogether.

Thus it was Vivian who had stayed with their mother over the years. By default or by choice, Vivian couldn't be sure. It was only years later that Vivian recognized it to be the price she had to pay for being the "luckier daughter" who got out. Little by little, she'd also grown used to her role as her mother's sole emotional support and trusted confidante. She knew long ago she was never her mother's favorite child, and the only way she could change that was by showing her mother how far she was willing to go to win her love.

During the weeks following their mother's discovery of a love letter from her father's girlfriend, Vivian was the only one who was able to offer her some comfort. Her mother had no friends, being an immigrant in a foreign country, her Japanese ability almost nonexistent. The opportunity brought Vivian closer to her mother in a way she couldn't have imagined. Only now could Vivian fully appreciate how special and hard-won her bond with her mother had been—just as her mother was about to be cremated.

Jian's agitated calls woke Vivian from her wandering thoughts. She couldn't immediately make out what he was trying to say to her, except that he was very excited. When Da Wei, Pei, and her boys all rose from the bench, Vivian realized it was finally their turn to go to the crematorium.

There must have been dozens of these crematoriums at the gigantic funeral home. The one assigned to the Zhang family was in the east wing of the second floor. Led by Jian and Weiling, the lone brother, two sisters, Tiantian, and Pei's twins, along with several dozen relations and close friends, filed into the hall. The coffin had been placed in the middle, surrounded by gaudy imitation flowers. Standing in the corner of the hall nearest the coffin was a middle-aged master of ceremonies, dressed in a gray ceremonial gown.

"Line up, line up in one row and circle the coffin," he shouted to the mourners in a clear, monotonous tone. "Mourners may come closer in threes to pay respect to the deceased. You may now bow to the deceased: first bow; second bow; third bow."

The service ended more quickly than she'd expected. Before Vivian knew what was happening, four attendants appeared from nowhere and swiftly hauled the coffin away to a side door in preparation for cremation.

Suddenly, Pei dashed out from the crowd like a madwoman, screaming incoherently in a voice that was not recognizable to Vivian. "You think you can leave me just like that, huh? You can't do this to me again, Mother! Mother ..." She followed the attendants and shouted with rage, but before she reached the coffin she tripped and fell to the ground.

Jian and Da Wei moved to help Pei up, then ushered her to a bench outside the crematorium. Vivian quickly followed. Pei was lying on the bench, her sobs becoming more and more uncontrollable.

Vivian had never thought that hidden behind Pei's steely exterior could lay such a delicate, fragile soul. It dawned on her that her sister was a child again—the same child who was left behind at the Dalian train station some thirty years before. Deep down inside her sister was a scar that wouldn't heal.

Slowly, Vivian took Pei in her arms, softly massaging her back as if she were lulling a baby to sleep. She so much wanted to tell Pei that everything would be all right, and that she shared her deep pain at the loss of their mother. But something caught in her throat, and she could not make out what she was trying to say to her sister. "There, there," was all she could manage. "There, there."

Thirty-five

Two weeks after the funeral, Pei was sitting in Meiyin's sunny apartment in Gakuen Daigaku. Her sister had invited her over for a pasta dinner, and Pei, still misty-eyed from the loss of her mother and longing for some companionship, gladly accepted the invitation. As Meiyin cooked spaghetti sauce over the stove, Pei started making a salad. She was amazed when her sister instructed her to put chopped raw cabbages in a bowl and sprinkle pepper and salad dressing over it. "Why eat raw leaves when you could have them cooked?" she asked. "How's that different from eating like a cow?"

Meiyin clicked her tongue. "Mind you, this dish is an American's favorite called *coleslaw*. Besides, haven't you heard that raw greens are much better for you than cooked ones?"

Pei laughed. What was with the Japanese and Western penchants for raw foods? Wasn't cooking with fire evidence of a higher form of civilization? The Chinese would never touch anything that was uncooked, but her sister was too Americanized to even notice the difference.

Pei felt like saying something to Meiyin, but thought better of it. After all this time, she began to see that when people had lived overseas for some time, they often had to synthesize many different ways of doing things. So much so that there wasn't any one distinct culture anymore, but a hybrid, new culture. And that, she realized, was what most immigrants needed to do in order to sustain their existence overseas. She wondered if she was on her way to creating her own third culture. Would she make Chinese dumplings on *oshogatsu* from now on instead of on Chinese New Year?

Over dinner, Meiyin suddenly announced she would be leaving for the US in five days. A week earlier she had received an invitation to be the research assistant of a Chinese art history professor at the University of Washington in Seattle. The professor, a friend of Becky's, was urgently looking for help to complete a book project and had asked around for possible candidates. At Becky's suggestion Meiyin had sent him a letter and resume. Her knowledge of Chinese art history and research experience at the small New York art gallery evidently had made a big impression on him. He told her the job would require her to research the life of a twelfth-century scholar and painter for a book he was working on. The four-month-long research assistantship would pay quite well, with the possibility of renewal if she were accepted into the Ph.D. program in the Chinese literature department of the university. The only catch was that she needed to start the job right away, as the professor was on a tight deadline.

"You've already put in the application?" Pei asked. This was the first time she'd heard about her sister's plans of studying in the US.

Meiyin nodded. "I applied to their Ph.D. program in Chinese literature after Mom left for China. With Mom gone, Tokyo just doesn't feel like a home to me anymore. Besides, I want to seriously think about what to do with my career. I really think that I'd have a better chance of finding what I like in America, it being a country of misfits."

Pei eyed Meiyin thoughtfully, registering for the first time that after her sister had left, she would truly be on her own. She reflected on what her sister said about Japan not feeling like a home because of the absence of their mother, and wondered if she herself shared the same feeling. No, she quickly decided. After all, not having spent the same thirty years with their mother, she hadn't cultivated the kind of emotional bond that Meiyin had with their mother.

In fact, it struck her now that the mother she'd been dreaming of going back to all those years had largely lived in her memory only. The mother she'd finally reunited with felt like a different person, a stranger even.

And yet if their mother wasn't exactly the "emotional home away from home" to her, where then *was* her real home now? The question felt heavy on her chest. Until now, she hadn't thought of home in that way. For as long as she could remember, she had always been searching for a home of her own. If home was a safe haven where you were readily accepted and understood, a place where you never had to apologize for who you were, could she finally find that home in Ryo?

Her thoughts were interrupted when Meiyin brought dessert to the table: ice cream with cookies and strawberries. As her sister poured coffee into cups, she said even if she weren't accepted at the university in the end, the research position would provide her with a chance to look around for other opportunities in the US. And she could always return to Japan afterward and ponder her next move.

"So, Big Sister, do you have any regrets about leaving China?" Before putting the dishes away, Meiyin surprised Pei with a question she suspected her sister had always wanted to ask her, but never dared to until now.

"Absolutely not!" Pei said. She remembered her mother had once asked her the same question. "When I first arrived in Japan I'd felt so starved I wanted everything—love, hope, respect, success, and new possibilities. I was eager to grab the first things that came my way and hoped that I would somehow strike gold," she said thoughtfully.

"When I was still in China, I was terrified of being left behind. Although I'd failed miserably at achieving what I set out for myself, it was important that I'd tried my best. And for that alone, I have no regrets."

Pei continued to say that while she hadn't found fame and wealth, she'd found something else, something unintended but more valuable to her: a peace of mind and the liberty to do whatever she pleased, without having to worry about other people's judgments. In China, she never felt she had that option because all her life she'd been told to do this or that—she was forever following orders and other people's leads, so much so that she felt she was no longer her own separate entity, but part of a huge collectivity of buzzing bees. "Some people are comfortable with that, I suppose, but I'd always found it exhausting, suffocating, and relentless."

Now that she was out of China, Pei said she no longer heard that massive hum. Sure, she was poor, and by Chinese standards a miserable failure, but that was her own business. Here, once she closed her apartment door, she could sink into anonymity without anyone noticing. She was able to set her own agenda and priorities in life, which felt incredibly satisfying and liberating.

"Of course I'd paid a hefty price for it, being separated from Da Shan and Da Hai, and they are paying too," Pei said, looking away to avoid Meiyin's gaze. "The honest truth is that I don't know if I can ever provide them with a home secure enough to thrive in. There's still so much that's unknown in my life." Then she told her sister about her decision of going into business with Zhou Jing, and how she was contemplating a trip to Shenzhen in the fall. "So far, I have saved about 7,000 dollars from my jobs and gift money. It isn't a large sum, but I hope to use it as capital for the business."

"What about your boys? Weren't you going to save the money for their college?" Meiyin asked.

"I was, but I have to make an investment now with the business, or else, the little bit of my savings will always be just that. My dream is that the business will expand quickly, and hopefully, in a few years, I can turn a profit with Zhou Jing and be able to send the boys to college in time," she said, a glimmer of hope in her eyes.

Meiyin looked at Pei and nodded gently. "There's a lot that's uncertain in my life too. But I'll do everything to help you in whatever way you think is best for the boys. It's important that we do this together. We're a family after all."

Pei broke into a smile. She never once allowed herself to see her sister as a possible ally. Now that their mother had passed away, and Meiyin was about to leave Japan, she saw no reason to hold back. She returned Meiyin's kindness with a gentle pat on her hand, mouthing, just lightly, the words *xiexie* for her sister to see.

Thirty-six

O n a mid-July morning, Vivian looked up from her pile of research notes to witness the first hues of daybreak out of her open window. The chilly early-morning breeze coming from the Puget Sound needled her face, reminding her she'd been up since four-thirty in the morning.

Professor Howard's book project had kept her busy; she had been working almost fourteen hours a day, six days a week for the past four and a half months, and had seemingly permanent dark circles and puffy bags under her eyes. There had been a couple of deadline extensions. Luckily, the end was finally in sight. Just the other day Professor Howard told her his writing was coming along well, and he credited this to her efficient help. He said they should be able to wrap up the entire project in just three more weeks.

When Vivian got up to look at her calendar on a nearby wall, she suddenly realized Pei's birthday was only one week after her final deadline. Her sister would turn forty in thirty days—an important threshold. How could she help make it a memorable event for her? Should she fly her sister over to see her in Seattle? Wasn't coming to see the US one of her sister's cherished dreams? It would certainly make it an unforgettable birthday for her sister.

It dawned on her she and Pei hadn't spoken since a brief phone conversation two months ago. She quickly found a birthday greeting card in a drawer and began writing:

Dear Pei,

You must be wondering about my long silence, or why I haven't called or written since April.

The truth is, for the last ten weeks I have been extremely busy working on the book project with Professor Howard. It was just a couple days ago that we were finally able to take a small break. Professor Howard has been quite pleased with my work, and he extended my assistantship again in three weeks, meaning I won't finish work until mid–August.

I didn't win the translation competition, despite our best effort, but I have been officially accepted into the Ph.D. program at the university, and with Professor Howard's help, I have been granted a part–time assistantship (Hooray!). I'm scheduled to start school in late August, and the department head has kindly agreed to waive my out–of–state tuition, which is a huge relief.

I'm very much looking forward to starting something new here finally. Unfortunately, the extension of my assistantship means I might not have enough time to come back to bid everyone a final farewell, given how much I still have to do to find an apartment here. But I promise I will try my best to see if I can make a quick trip toward the end of August.

Sis, I have to say I'm very happy about being back in the US. In some strange way, I feel very comfortable here, like I'm back exactly where I left things four years ago, even though I'm now in a new city on the opposite side of the US. Seattle is a wonderful city—every day I look out to the majestic skyline and the stunningly beautiful waterfront, and I feel just so incredibly lucky to be here.

I think I feel life is easier here because I know how the system works—everything in this country is clearly defined and stated, be it rules or expectations. It's funny how I spent twenty–four years in Japan and never once felt I really belonged—I was forever someone looking from the outside in. The other night, as I was working late into the evening, it occurred to me that you and I have both spent the last thirty–odd years of our lives feeling like an outcast: you

*were sentenced to the life of an unwanted "orphan" after Mom
and Dad left you behind in China, while I was relegated to living
constantly on the edge of the crowd.*

*By the way, I'm thinking of going back to Dalian for another
visit next spring. I've been offered an opportunity to participate in a
two-week exchange program at the Shandong University next April.
Since Dalian is only a short flight away, I thought I might tack on
a weekend trip at the end of the program and pay the city another
visit. I haven't been able to put the place out of my mind after my
last disastrous trip with Mom.*

*I realized a lot of my disappointment came from my own
unrealistic expectations. My preconceptions were mostly based on
Mom's romanticism of her laojia. When you think about it, Mom
had been away from Dalian for so long—how could she possibly
have painted an accurate picture for me? So I'm thinking I should
go back there again, but this time look at it more realistically
without any tinged sentiments. It is my ancestral home, and I think
it deserves another chance. Besides, it would also provide me with a
great opportunity to visit Mom's grave with Da Shan and Da Hai.*

The thought of her nephews made Vivian feel guilty. She
should really do something for the boys, like setting up a college
fund for them and getting them out of China before too long.

On their last dinner together, she remembered how Pei had
beamed when she mentioned she'd help her get her two boys out
of China. In the past couple of years Pei had spent in Japan, getting the boys out and sending them to college was all she could
think of doing. And yet, it remained a distant dream to her. If that
was the case, shouldn't she help finance the boys' college fund in
her position as auntie?

Vivian got up from her desk and started pacing back and
forth on the carpeted floor of her boxy apartment room—her
temporary home for the duration of her research project. She
thought of all those years her sister had spent looking out of her

window as a little girl, dreaming about a life that could have been beyond the waters of the Yellow Sea, wishing for the day when she could finally be with her mother again. She wondered if Pei's deep wounds from the loss of her mother as a young child would ever heal.

But Da Shan and Da Hai were only just about to turn thirteen—it wasn't too late for them if she and Pei did something about it *now*. Vivian felt a certain responsibility to do this for her sister, not only because she felt a vague guilt that she had been the lucky one allowed out of China while her sister was made to stay behind, but also for the simple fact that she could not, in good conscience, let the vicious family history repeat itself again.

China had become more open now, and there were plenty of opportunities for people to come and go as they pleased. It would be a crime not to take advantage and bring the boys out now simply because her sister was strapped for money. Even if it weren't for the sake of making a better future for the boys, she felt she needed to do this so Da Shan and Da Hai would be one with their mother again soon. Who was to know, maybe it would also be her sister's first step back toward healing. Perhaps she could also persuade her brother in their next phone conversation to go in on it too. It was a family affair, after all. She and Da Wei spoke very regularly on the phone now thanks to his corporate job, which routinely covered such expenses.

With this thought, Vivian continued her note, which she realized was turning into a letter:

Speaking of the boys, how are they doing? Those rascals must be getting to be like little gentlemen now. I'm seriously thinking of setting up a college fund for them so you won't have to work toward the goal alone. I also want to make sure they can come out and join you as a family in a year or two, not after they are married and with children of their own, as was the case with you. It's time that we put this cycle of family separations to an end.

On another note, did I mention that Becky, my best friend from Japan, will be moving back to the US in three months? I'm thinking of inviting her and her Japanese boyfriend to Seattle this winter for Christmas. It would be great if you could come too. Becky is a wonderful soul, and I know you and Ryo would really enjoy meeting her. If you're willing, I'd be happy to help pay your tickets— it's time for you to finally come see America. So think about it!

Okay, I must stop now. I have a lot of work still ahead of me. Do let me know of your thoughts soon so we can make plans. Until then, please keep well.

Your sister,
Vivian

Vivian went over to her tiny kitchen to make herself some Yin Hao Jasmine Tea, a farewell present from Pei. She made a mental note to discuss ways to set up the college funds for their nephews when Da Wei would make his next weekly call. She would also ask him to help her buy the boys' plane tickets so they could visit their mother in Tokyo in a year or two.

In her most recent phone conversation with her sister, Pei had mentioned that Guomin just married in March. Perhaps he wouldn't be so adamant about not letting the boys see Pei now.

Vivian brought her tea mug back to the desk, her small room now filled with the fragrance of jasmine. She looked out the window and saw that it was turning out to be a glorious day, the skyline of the city gleaming magnificently against the sun. She thought how wonderful it would be if she could share what she saw with her nephews one day. Perhaps they could both come to study in Seattle in a few years, with her by their side as a guardian.

Yes, this was the right thing to do. If love between a husband and a wife could not survive the erosion of distance over time, then how much more would the love between a mother and child wear away? There was simply no replacement for those seemingly trivial but daily gestures of kindness and tenderness of a mother to a young son or daughter.

It might have been too late for Pei to change her tormented past, but Vivian would see to it that it wouldn't be the case for her young nephews. Vivian picked up her mug and took a sip of the amber-color tea, feeling a sweet tingling slowly expand inside her.

Glossary of Japanese Terms

fusuma	Japanese paper screen doors
gaijin	foreigners
gyoza	Japanese version of Chinese pot-stickers
katakana	one of the three writing systems of the Japanese
kanji	Chinese characters that have been adapted with Japanese readings
kotatsu	a heated Japanese table
obento	Japanese boxed lunches
omiai	a formal arranged meeting between a male and female with a view to marriage
onigiri	rice balls
oshibori	towels
Oshogatsu	The Japanese New Year, celebrated on January 1 on the Gregorian calendar. This is different from the Chinese, who continue to observe the New Year celebration according to the lunar calendar either in late January or mid-February. Dumplings are one of the favorite foods for Chinese New Year, while the Japanese cook a sticky rice soup called ozoni
pachinko	a pinball parlor
rijicho	CEO

Roppongi	a district in Tokyo famous for its nightlife and is very popular with foreigners
sake	Japanese rice wine
sensei	teacher
shakuhachi	flute
shinajin	a derogatory reference to the Chinese during World War II.
shosha	Japanese trading firm

Glossary of Chinese Terms

Beida   short for Beijing Daxue or Beijing University

danwei   work unit

guanxi   social or business connections

kang   traditional heated platform bed that is raised off the floor with heat source underneath. This kind of bed is common in northeastern part of China.

Laolao   maternal grandma

laojia   home province, ancestral home

motianlo   skyscrapers

Putonghua   Literally the common language. Refers to the standard Mandarin based on the Beijing dialect. It's the official spoken language throughout China

qipao   traditional Chinese silk gown with a high collar and long slits on the sides

tongxiang   fellow villagers, who invariably feel like relatives for those Chinese traveling far away home

waihui   foreign currency

xiexie   thank you

yuan   Also known as Renminbi, or RMB. It is the colloquial expression of the Chinese currency. In the early 90s, the yuan-dollar exchange rate was about 5.8 yuan to a dollar

Acknowledgements

This book has been a long and arduous journey for me, and could not have been possible without the help and support of many people.

I'd like to thank Benython Oldfield and Sharon Galant for seeing the potential in the novel. I've benefited greatly from their early encouragement and sound editorial and media advice.

I'm indebted to my dear friend Geling Yan, who not only offered excellent suggestions and advice throughout the years, but also continues to inspire me as a truly gifted and compassionate fiction writer.

My thanks also goes to Michael Dodson, Betsey Osborne, Liu Hong, Barbara Demick, Edward Gargan and Oliver August for generously taking the time to read my manuscript and making invaluable suggestions along the way. Similarly, I wish to thank Carol Gaskin, Roy Kesey and Sean Ennis for their help and expert advice at different stages of the novel's development.

I'm deeply grateful to Chris Robyn at China Books for taking me on board, and to Allison Itterly, whose insightful questions helped improve the book in numerous ways.

I feel fortunate to have Dianne Highbridge as a creative writing teacher at Tokyo's Temple University, whose steadfast belief in my work has helped keep me going over the years. I also feel blessed to have Helena Maria Viramontes and Viet Thanh Nguyen as my mentors at the Bread Loaf Writers' Conference, who gave me food for thought and taught me the value of editing and re-editing.

I also want to thank friends from the intimate writers' support groups during my Tokyo and Beijing days, including Sharon Moshavi, Helen Wing, Didi Tatlow and Lijia Zhang, for their words of encouragement over the many gallons of teas and coffees we shared. I've drawn great strength from their unwavering love and friendship.

My biggest thanks, however, goes to Mark Magnier, my long-suffering husband. Without his understanding and love, expert help with pitch letters and editing, and mediating fights between our children Tyler and Vita so I could write, this novel would not have been possible. This one's for you.

About the Author

KAREN MA was born in China, raised in Hong Kong and Japan, and educated in the U.S. She holds a M.A in Chinese Literature from the University of Washington (Seattle, U.S.) and is fluent in English, Mandarin Chinese and Japanese.

Formerly a news reporter for Kyodo News and NHK Radio Japan, she has also written for *The International Herald Tribune, New York News Day, The Japan Times, Kyoto Journal, South China Morning Post* and the Delhi-based *Mint*. She is also the author of the non-fiction book, *The Modern Madame Butterfly: Fantasy and Reality in Japanese Cross-cultural Relationships* (1996 Charles E. Tuttle)

After a stint of five years living in India and teaching as a middle school teacher of Mandarin, Karen has now relocated to Beijing, working as a freelance writer and researching for her next book.

Made in the USA
San Bernardino, CA
19 April 2014